THE WARRIORS

ALSO BY TOM YOUNG

FICTION

The Renegades

Silent Enemy

The Mullah's Storm

NONFICTION

The Speed of Heat:
An Airlift Wing at War in Iraq and Afghanistan

THE

WARRIORS

TOM YOUNG

G. P. PUTNAM'S SONS | NEW YORK

PUTNAM

G. P. PUTNAM'S SONS
Publishers Since 1838
Published by the Penguin Group
Penguin Group (USA) Inc., 375 Hudson Street,
New York, New York 10014, USA

USA · Canada · UK · Ireland · Australia
New Zealand · India · South Africa · China

Penguin Books Ltd, Registered Offices: 80 Strand, London WC2R 0RL, England
For more information about the Penguin Group visit penguin.com

Library of Congress Cataloging-in-Publication Data

Young, Thomas W., date.
   The warriors / Tom Young.
      p.   cm.
   ISBN 978-0-399-15847-6
   1. Parson, Michael (Fictitious character)—Fiction.   2. Gold, Sophia (Fictitious
character)—Fiction.   3. Soldiers—Fiction.   4. Afghan War, 2001—Fiction.
5. Afghanistan—Fiction.   I. Title.
      PS3625.O97335W37   2013   2013009343
      813'.6—dc23

Printed in the United States of America
10 9 8 7 6 5 4 3 2 1

Book design by Gretchen Achilles

FOR THE MEN AND WOMEN
OF THE 167TH AIRLIFT WING,
WEST VIRGINIA AIR NATIONAL GUARD

In the towns with funny names,
hit by bullets, caught in flames,
by and large not knowing why,
people die.
—JOSEPH BRODSKY,
"Bosnia Tune"

1

A COLD FRONT SWEPT ACROSS the steppes of Central Asia like an invading army. The wedge of dense, frigid air slid underneath warmer air, lifting the warm air higher until thunderheads spawned and stalked through Kyrgyzstan. The black clouds assaulted the terrain with lightning, and booms reverberated like the peals of distant air strikes.

At Manas Air Base—officially called Transit Center at Manas for political reasons—Lieutenant Colonel Michael Parson stood in the control tower with American and Kyrgyz air traffic controllers. The controllers fretted about the weather, and so did Parson. His new job had him watching weather conditions pretty closely. He'd arrived in Kyrgyzstan only yesterday to start a yearlong assignment as the base safety officer. Parson welcomed the noncombat position after seeing more than his share of action in Afghanistan and Iraq as a U.S. Air Force aviator.

Manas served as a major stopover for troops and cargo on the way into and out of Afghanistan, but at least the base wasn't in a hostile fire zone. Parson considered the place a relatively laid-back outpost: You could sip a beer in your off-hours. Even during the duty day, you could take a break and go to the coffee shop, get an espresso, and pet the big gray cat that always slept on one of the chairs. Parson thought he'd like Manas, except for the weather.

"Shall we call a ground stop?" a Kyrgyz controller asked in good English.

"Not yet," the American tower chief said.

Neither man looked at Parson, because Parson exercised no authority over the controllers. But he understood their dilemma. Cumulonimbus the color of wrought iron loomed to the north. The low-level wind shear alert system already indicated trouble near the approach end of Runway Two-Six. But a lot of traffic needed to come in today, and wind shear always presented a problem at Manas. Every chart for every approach carried the notation: *Heavy turbulence with downdrafts and wind shear may be expected on final.* You could eliminate the risk only by not flying at all.

The controllers had the tower's VHF frequency on the speakers. A pilot with an Afghan accent called.

"Manas Tower," the pilot said, "Golay One-Three is Afghan Air Force C-27 on VOR/DME approach to Runway Two-Six."

Parson recognized the call sign, though not the voice. He thought of his tour as an adviser to the Afghan Air Force, and he felt proud to hear an Afghan crew on an international flight. Parson wondered where they were going, what they were doing. During his year working with Afghan crews, he'd made a lot of good friends, but most of the pilots he knew flew helicopters. This C-27 Spartan was a twin-turboprop cargo plane.

"Golay One-Three, Manas Tower," a controller called. "You are cleared to land, Runway Two-Six. Use caution for low-level wind shear."

"Golay One-Three cleared to land," the pilot acknowledged.

Parson peered through the tower's windows, scanned for the Spartan. At first he saw only roiling clouds bearing down on the airfield. Large raindrops began to smack against the glass, and a gust of wind swirled dust outside on the tower catwalk. A controller raised his binoculars and pointed. Parson spotted the aircraft just under the cloud layer, in a right turn onto final approach.

The plane rolled out of the turn, leveled its wings. The landing gear doors opened as the aircraft descended, and the wheels came down and locked into place. The wings rocked a bit; Parson could almost feel the turbulence jolting the airplane. He'd made a few landings here himself in a C-5 Galaxy, riding down the glide slope with the jet crabbed sideways, dancing on the rudder pedals at the last moment, and always keeping his thumb on the GO AROUND button in case the wind shear got so evil he had to abort the approach.

The rain fell harder. Drops pounded the roof until the sound rose to a dull roar. Water streamed down the tower windows, and outside visibility dropped by half. Parson could still see the C-27, though, now on short final. The aircraft continued its descent—a little too steeply for Parson's comfort. The Spartan should have flown a nice, gentle approach angle of about three degrees, but this looked like six or eight. At this rate, Parson thought, the aircraft might even touch down short of the runway. Time to climb away for another try.

But the Spartan continued to descend. By standard procedure, the crew should have set up a stabilized approach by now: configured to land, on glide path, within a few knots of approach speed, and descending at no more than about seven hundred feet per minute.

These guys weren't even close to stable. Parson guesstimated their descent rate at around fifteen hundred. Harder to judge their airspeed, but the approach looked a good twenty knots hot. What the hell? All the Afghan pilots he knew could have done a better job. Their stick-and-rudder skills weren't usually the problem. Parson had preached the fine points like checklist discipline, not basic piloting skills. But whoever was flying that C-27 couldn't find his ass with both hands.

"Go around, you idiot," Parson muttered under his breath.

Most crashes happened on landing. Airplanes were especially vulnerable to wicked weather on final approach. The nearer the ground, the thinner the margin for error. That's why a good missed approach beat a bad landing any day of the week.

The pilot's voice came over the radio again, the resin of tension in his voice:

"Golay One-Three going around."

So the clue light finally came on. Parson thought he heard the aircraft's engines advance, though the rain noise made it hard to tell. As the C-27 flew closer, he saw the landing gear retract and the nose pitch higher. But the aircraft did not climb. The Spartan's descent continued, only at a slower rate.

Caught in a downdraft, Parson realized. Or maybe even a fully developed, honest-to-God microburst that could slam a plane into the ground. That's why you don't dick around in weather like this, he thought. Now cob those throttles and get the hell out of Dodge.

Lightning speared the ground. Veins of quicksilver spiderwebbed across the sky, so bright they hurt Parson's eyes. The Spartan roared along the runway, clawing for altitude, gaining none.

Parson could imagine the scene in the cockpit: the pilot pulling back on the yoke while watching the flight director's pitch steering bars. The ground prox warning system blaring, *DON'T SINK, DON'T SINK.* And the vertical speed indicator still showing a descent.

Then came the moment when Parson knew what would happen but could do nothing. The Spartan pitched up even higher, near the verge of a stall. The aircraft floated just a few feet above the pavement, seemingly in slow motion. Inevitably, the tail dragged the ground, and the C-27 pancaked to earth.

The propeller blades struck the pavement, bent backward into fishhooks. The left engine tore from its mount under the wing. Flames blossomed as fuel and hydraulic lines ripped open. The engine shed its cowl panels and prop as it cartwheeled forward, ahead of a spreading black-and-orange fireball. The grinding sound of metal across pavement joined with the boom and crackle of flames.

All four controllers rose to their feet, uttered epithets in English and Kyrgyz. As the aircraft continued to come apart, the tail section separated and skidded sideways out of the flames. The bulk of the wreckage slid forward along the concrete. Streamers of fire erupted from the exploding wings. Metal fragments shot clear of the smoke and bounced along the taxiway.

A Kyrgyz controller reached for a touch-screen computer and tapped a red icon marked PCAS. That button activated the primary crash alarm system, and in seconds Parson heard the sirens of crash trucks. Three yellow-and-red Oshkosh trucks charged down the taxiway, red lights flashing. The first truck braked to a stop just short of the flames and opened a blast from its foam cannon. The other trucks positioned themselves around the front of the wreckage, sprayed white chemical onto the burning fuselage.

Firefighters in silver proximity suits jumped down from their vehicles. One man took hold of the plane's crew door handle and pulled. The handle would not budge, so another firefighter lifted a crash ax from his truck and slammed the ax at the crew door. When the door finally dropped, smoke rolled from the opening.

One of the foam cannons sprayed through the doorway, and two firefighters climbed inside, breathing from air bottles mounted on their backs.

Parson leaned on the back of a chair, closed his eyes. Felt his skin grow flush. He'd lost too many friends and crewmates in accidents and shootdowns. He didn't know this crew, but he knew plenty of people like them. And he knew they all had family—spouses, parents, children. When one of the controllers made the next radio call, the words barely registered in Parson's mind.

"Attention all aircraft," the controller said. "Manas is closed for emergency operations."

Parson then heard the controller talking to a KC-135 tanker jet, giving the crew instructions to enter holding over the Bishkek VOR.

Two ambulances converged on the crash site. Parson appreciated the quick response. He especially admired the courage of the firefighters, but he doubted they'd find anyone alive inside the Spartan.

The two firemen who'd entered the C-27 came back out carrying a limp body. They took the crewman well away from the smoke and flames and laid him down. The medics went to work, but in a few moments Parson could tell from their gestures that the man was dead.

The same thing happened when the firefighters brought out the other two victims. Though Parson watched from a distance, the appearance of their clothing suggested that at least the crew had not burned to death. Their Nomex flight suits still held the original desert beige coloring. When exposed to fire, flameproof Nomex would not burn, but it would discolor to nearly black. Apparently all three—pilot, copilot, and loadmaster—had died of some combination of crash force trauma and smoke inhalation.

Part of Parson's mind was already investigating, analyzing. Though powerless to prevent the crash, now he would lead in determining causes. He had hoped he would pass his time as safety officer without handling anything more serious than a maintenance guy falling off a stand. But sadly, his new assignment had begun with a Class A mishap, defined as an accident causing loss of life, loss of an aircraft, or more than two million dollars in damage. This crash covered all three.

Parson sighed hard, looked at the floor. Ignored the chatter on the control frequencies. When he looked up again, he saw three arcing streams of foam attacking the tallest flames—those rising from the tangled metal of the wings. No one remained alive to save, but the crash team kept working, making sure fire and cinders spread no farther to threaten aircraft on the ramp. The three parabolas of foam seemed a grotesque tribute to the lives just lost.

Life seemed so fragile now to Parson. He used to consider himself master of his own fate, someone who steered events instead of merely reacting to them. But time and time again, he'd seen events overcome even the strongest and the most skilled aviators—not to mention boneheads like the crew who'd just flown that Spartan into the ground. The Air Force talked about risk management as if a hazard were something you could get your hands around. Choke it and drown it in a bathtub. But a hazard needed little opening to cause harm. Just a miscommunication or a failure of equipment. A moment's inattention, an ounce of bad judgment.

Parson struggled to turn off his emotions the way he might use an isolation switch in an airplane to de-energize a bad electrical circuit. He had a lot to do, and his feelings would only get in the way. First, he needed to identify witnesses and make sure the crash site didn't get disturbed any more than firefighting required. Even though he'd seen the disaster himself, he wanted to record the statements of other onlookers. Then Parson would turn to the big picture: examine the size and shape of the debris field, take photos, establish a grid to pinpoint where all the parts had come to rest. As a safety officer he was not an expert. But he would gather evidence and information, call in experts as needed.

He thought he already knew the cause of this accident: a wind shear event with an unsuccessful recovery. Tragically straightforward. A major contributing factor: stupidity.

However, he couldn't help thinking maybe the crash was a little *too* straightforward. Avoiding the accident would have been so easy. For now, he would just let the evidence tell its story. And he felt that story might lead to places where he didn't want to go. Parson had expected this assignment to turn out easier and safer than some of his previous deployments. But this part of the world had long served as a crossroads of continents. Down through the centuries, East invaded West; West attacked East. All sorts of trouble had ebbed and flowed across these steppes that led the way to Europe.

2

FOR THE FIRST TIME in years, Viktor Dušić felt fulfilled. Not because of his money, though he had plenty. But because of his new sense of purpose. After more than a decade in the arms business—building connections, making deals, showing he could deliver the goods anywhere needed—Dušić controlled a network of suppliers, buyers, and discreet middlemen that spanned a third of the globe. And now his wealth and the breadth of his network had reached a tipping point: Perhaps he could not only profit from events but control them.

Luxury had its place: He enjoyed his Lamborghini Aventador, his Patek Philippe watch, his cognac, his women. But a warrior didn't let those things distract him. Not with a mission yet to accomplish. Dušić felt he possessed the talents, the audacity, and, at last, the resources to bring his people the justice, the land, and the glory that rightfully belonged to them. He had so much to do.

By now, Dušić thought, Greater Serbia should have become a powerful nation, free of Muslims—or Turks, as he called them. However, meddling from the UN, NATO, and especially the Americans had denied Dušić and his people a richly deserved victory. So he had bided his time, formulated plans, maintained hope.

In his Belgrade office, on the right bank of the Sava River, Dušić picked up the phone and punched a number. Normally a man of his stature would have his secretary initiate his calls, but Milica, faithful though she was, did not need to know of this conversation. The number rang at a flat in Sarajevo, and the call went unanswered for so long that Dušić nearly hung up. But on the ninth ring, a gruff voice answered.

"Yes?" the voice said.

"Stefan, this is Viktor."

"Ah, good morning, Lieutenant." Stefan coughed, cleared his throat, and asked, "What time is it?"

"Nearly noon, you drunk. And I am not a lieutenant anymore. Have you considered my proposal?" The conversation's start troubled Dušić. His friend Stefan had once been a good soldier. But now Dušić wondered if drink and age had dulled the man's reflexes and clouded his judgment.

"Viktor," Stefan said, "I admire your vision. But I do not know if you'll find enough people. A lot of the former officers feel lucky not to have been arrested and sent to The Hague. They don't want to take chances now."

Weaklings, Dušić thought. They had once sworn an oath to Republika Srpska. But now they just wanted to lie low, work their meaningless jobs, and bang their wives. Dušić knew why they'd lost their nerve. Their commander, the great General Ratko Mladić, had faced a war crimes trial after eluding capture for fifteen years. Their president, the poet politician Radovan Karadžić, had suffered a similar fate. And the head of the Yugoslav

Republic, Slobodan Milošević, had died in prison. The meddling nations did not pursue those of lower rank, at least not yet. But warriors should not live in fear. Warriors should make their enemies live in fear.

"The brothers' hesitation disappoints me," Dušić said.

"Perhaps we will find more willing hands among veterans of the Volunteer Guard."

Dušić thought for a moment. "You may be right," he said. He preferred professionals—trained officers, disciplined sergeants. Some of those Serb Volunteer Guard men, Arkan's Tigers and other militias, had been little more than criminals in uniform. But what they'd lacked in smarts, they'd made up for in zeal. Dušić would consider his friend's suggestion. A commander must make do with the tools available.

"Then there is the question of funding," Stefan said. "I imagine you could bankroll the initial mission with what you have in your pocket right now. But the remainder of the campaign could exhaust even your deep accounts."

Dušić chuckled. "Don't worry about that, my friend," he said. "I have arranged a stream of income that will cover our needs."

"Ah, yes, Viktor. You always excelled at logistics. May I ask how you did it?"

Dušić wanted to tell him all the details. But Stefan had no operational need to know. And this was not a secure phone connection. In Dušić's line of work, one did not profit by making sloppy mistakes. So he said only, "Let me worry about that."

"So I shall, Viktor. I will rest easily with that matter in your hands. You are a fighter with the heart of a comptroller."

No, Dušić thought, I am a fighter with the heart of a poet. But he took his friend's compliment in the intended spirit.

"So will you talk to some of the old Volunteer Guards?" Dušić asked.

"Of course. If I find some who are willing, how many do you want?"

"Three or four," Dušić said. Though he planned on arming and leading many more men later, he needed only a few for the initial mission. They had to be absolutely trustworthy. Men who would carry a secret to their graves.

At least he could trust his old friend Stefan, as long as the man remained sober. Their association went back to the early days of the Bosnian War.

Dušić remembered one day in 1995 when Stefan had demonstrated his worth. Dušić's platoon patrolled around the region of Mount Javor to make sure all the UN observers had retreated. His thirty men climbed a wooded hill and emerged at the edge of an open but unplanted field. Grass and wild clover sprouted where Dušić would have expected wheat or corn. That fallow field could mean that the farmer had become a good Muslim in the only way possible—by becoming a dead Muslim. Or it could mean the field was mined. Dušić elected to take his men around the field.

He motioned to one of his sergeants, ordered the man to walk point along the tree line. The rest of the platoon followed until they came to a narrow garden planted in peas and lettuce. Beyond the garden lay a bombed-out home, its tiled roof blown open by a mortar round or tank shell.

The cultivated garden seemed a safe avenue, so the Serb soldiers walked along its rows. The men scanned left and right, held their weapons at the ready. Dušić walked a few paces behind the sergeant on point, the rich, loamy soil sticking to his boots. When they came within two hundred meters of the house, Dušić heard the supersonic crack of a high-velocity bullet. The sergeant dropped to his knees as if to rest. Then he fell forward, flat on his face, rifle still clutched underneath him. Blood gushed from the exit wound in his back, spattered the black loam and the green leaves of lettuce.

"Sniper!" Dušić shouted.

His men rushed to cover. Dušić dived for the scant protection of furrows. Some of his men took positions in the woods to the side of the garden.

The sniper's weapon boomed again, and a soldier behind Dušić screamed. The sniper, that Muslim piece of excrement, had set a trap. The Turk had known the minefield would channel any patrol right into his sights.

Some of Dušić's men—the ones among the trees—opened up on full automatic. Under the shield of that covering fire, Dušić and the rest of the soldiers still in the garden rose to their feet and sprinted for the forest. They left the two wounded troops where they'd been shot: to treat them now would amount to suicide.

Dušić slid onto the carpet of pine needles inside the woods. Beside him, one of his soldiers fired burst after burst into the house.

"Did you get him?" Dušić asked.

"No, sir," the soldier said. "I can see his head and part of his weapon, but the distance is too great, and he ducks when I fire."

"Listen, everyone," Dušić said. "Cease fire." Dušić thought for a moment. His men had handled this ambush well, thanks to his quick-thinking NCOs. Otherwise, his youngest troops, mere fuzz-faced *razvodniks*, would have died where they stood, pissing their pants. He called on his best NCO. "Stefan," he whispered, "get up here."

Dušić's own sniper came forward in a crouch. Stefan carried an M48 Mauser equipped with a ZRAK scope. Dušić had offered to get the man a more modern weapon than that bolt-action relic, but Stefan said he needed no higher rate of fire; one bullet at a time would suffice.

"Viktor," Stefan said as he kneeled beside Dušić. First names between officers and sergeants did not accord with Yugoslav military tradition, but Stefan had earned enough respect that Dušić permitted it. Dušić would have slapped any other enlisted man who dared call him Viktor.

"You know what to do, my friend," Dušić whispered. Then he hissed, "Five of you, retreat farther into the woods, and make some noise doing it. Let that Muslim think we're leaving." As the men began to move, Dušić shouted, "Fall back!"

A few of the soldiers crawled several meters away, cracking twigs and kicking their boots against the trunks of trees. "Good," Dušić whispered, "good."

"You are one crafty bastard," Stefan said.

"Flatter me later," Dušić muttered. "Now kill that son of a whore."

Stefan adjusted the windage knob on his scope, regarded the house, settled into a prone position. Old M48s like Stefan's weapon were common as dirt. Dušić's mind strayed for just an instant—maybe after the war he could sell those things to sportsmen. Then he chided himself: Pay attention. An officer must command at every moment.

But at this moment, Stefan needed little by way of command. He watched through his scope with what seemed to Dušić a preternatural patience, like a cat waiting to strike, motionless but for the flick of its tail—waiting, waiting for the rat.

And the rat took the bait. The Turk sniper peered from the broken lumber of a shattered upper floor. A splintered plank hid the Turk's left shoulder and part of his head. The rat exposed only part of his face. Enough for Stefan. He pressed the trigger.

The M48 slammed, rocked Stefan's upper body with recoil. Dušić saw the briefest spray of red as the eight-millimeter bullet found its target. The Turkish rat dropped.

"Bravo," Dušić said.

"Wait," Stefan said, almost as if he were giving the orders. But Dušić knew he was right. No way to know how many enemy were in the house. Stefan opened the bolt on the M48, ejected the empty brass, and loaded another round.

No sound came from the house for several minutes. Dušić considered what to do next. He needed to know if more enemy remained inside. Normally, officers did not make targets of themselves, but enough of Dušić's men had suffered wounds already. And his men would trust him more if they saw him display courage. Dušić rose to his feet.

"Viktor," Stefan whispered, "do not—"

"I know you will cover me," Dušić said. He stepped into the open, walked toward the house. Held his breath, watched the home for movement. Listened for a shot. Nothing happened.

When Dušić made it halfway across the garden, he knew the threat had passed. "Medics," he called, "take care of those men."

"Yes, sir!" came shouts from the woods. Two soldiers ran from the trees to their fallen comrades. The medics reported that both of the wounded had died. Dušić felt fury rise within him. Two Serb lives taken by this Turk.

Inside the house, upstairs, Dušić and Stefan found the Turk. He lay on his back, most of his face blown away. Blood spatter ran from the wall, and a pool of red crept across the wooden floor. The Muslim's eyes stared at the ceiling. Dušić wondered why the bullet hadn't simply taken off the rat's head. But then he realized the Turk must have turned his face at the instant Stefan fired. The bullet had ripped away his cheeks and jaws, left the brain intact. A gurgling sound came from what remained of the palate and throat. Breathing.

"Damn your Ottoman mother," Dušić said. "You are still alive."

Dušić drew his CZ 99, aimed the handgun. Started to pull the trigger, but decided to enjoy the moment for just another few seconds. Savor the vengeance.

"Your friends at the United Nations have declared this a safe area," Dušić said. "Did that scrap of paper in New York protect you, Turk? Do you feel safe now?"

The bloody mess at Dušić's feet gurgled again. Dušić fired. Brains spattered his boots.

ALL THAT HAD TAKEN PLACE nearly twenty years ago, but Dušić remembered the events as if they had just happened. He saw the glory of his youth as a promise unfulfilled. He and his people had been traveling a brilliant path to the future, but outside intervention had denied them their destiny.

After Dušić hung up the phone, he told Milica he would be out for a while. He took the elevator down to street level, found his blue Aventador in the garage. Dušić raised the driver's-side door, lowered himself into the leather seat, pulled the door closed. In his forties now, he remained agile, able to climb into the low-slung vehicle comfortably. During his war years he had escaped injury, fortunately, and he knew the tasks ahead of him might require personal strength and endurance.

He placed the key fob in the ignition, raised the cover for the start button on the center console. Dušić pressed the button, and the V12 behind him rumbled to life. He pulled out of the garage, drove through the city, and headed west to Nikola Tesla Airport. When he arrived, he saw the tail fin of the Antonov An-124 looming above the cargo terminal, just as expected. Originally designed to project Soviet military power, now many of the huge Antonov cargo jets flew for civilian operators. Dušić maintained a contract with this particular company, with deals to fly his AK-47s, RPG-7s, and crates of land mines wherever needed. All transactions completely aboveboard and known to the authorities. The people who ran these freight carriers always complained about fuel prices, and those Cossacks used that as an excuse to charge exorbitant fees. But they paid their aircrews like peasants, and that gave Dušić the leverage he needed to ship certain products off the books. A little supplemental pay got him a little supplemental cargo.

Dušić found the Antonov's captain, Dmitri, smoking an American cigarette, watching the ground crew unload his aircraft. An overhead crane built into the An-124's cargo compartment lifted the pallets.

"Did your trip go as planned, my friend?" Dušić asked.

Dmitri took a drag on his Pall Mall, nodded, exhaled through his nostrils. The captain looked tired. His face bristled with black and gray stubble, and the skin sagged under his eyes. An oversize flight suit hung from his thin frame, the fabric rumpled and marred with coffee stains.

"It did," Dmitri said. "We began our day in Dubai, and we made a stop in Kuwait. Then we picked up your cargo at Manas. We got into Kyrgyzstan just ahead of a storm. The packing material is as you described."

"Excellent." Dušić reached into the inside pocket of his H. Huntsman coat, extracted an envelope, handed it to Dmitri. The pay did not cover flying; the Antonov had been scheduled to land in Manas anyway. The money paid for the ongoing operation: offloading some of the cargo and swapping out the packing material. Dušić watched the crane lower a pallet onto a flatbed truck. A crewman started the truck and drove it into a warehouse. Dmitri took a final drag on his smoke, then flicked away the butt as if something disgusted him.

"You don't approve of this business, Dmitri," Dušić said, "yet you profit from it."

"If fools inhale that poison or inject it into their veins," the captain said, "I care not."

"I do not mean to chide you, Captain. I dislike this product as well. I have never traded it before. But it provides a means to an end."

Inside the warehouse, the ground crew repackaged the opium, bundled it into plastic wrap, and bound it with tape. Then they boxed the contraband in pasteboard cartons and loaded it onto another truck. Finally, the men used foam pellets and newspaper to pad the cargo of electronic gear. The electronics would fly on to Frankfurt, and the opium would wind up on the streets of Paris and London, Brussels and Berlin. Maybe even New York and Los Angeles. Dušić hoped so, anyway, but where dealers sold to final customers was not his problem. He did not dirty his hands with such matters.

"Take care that you get it all," Dušić ordered. He could not tolerate stupid mistakes.

"Yes, sir," a crewman answered.

Rumor had it, Dušić knew, that he'd eliminated employees and contractors who displeased him. The tales exaggerated the numbers, but he did nothing to discourage the stories. They helped motivate the lazy, speed up the tardy. His clients respected ruthlessness and efficiency, so Dušić made those qualities part of his brand.

As he watched the ground crew finish their work, one of his cell phones chimed. It was the throwaway phone that he'd purchased on a pay-per-call contract under a false name. He glanced at the number; the call came from a contact in Kyrgyzstan. This annoyed him; he had told that moron to ring him only for emergencies. Dušić wanted to keep his digital footprint as small as possible. He flipped open the phone.

"What?" he asked.

"Lieutenant Dušić, we have a problem," the caller said. "One of our planes has crashed." The caller described how the Afghan C-27 had burst into flames when it tried to land at Manas.

Dušić said nothing, simply let the information sink in. Burned with silent rage. He wanted to kill the fools who'd failed him, but they were already dead. Temper would not serve him well now, anyway. He needed a clear mind. The accident could have ripple effects, unpredictable consequences. It might threaten the operational security of his mission.

"Lieutenant," the caller said, "are you there?"

"I heard you, idiot." Dušić clapped the phone closed. He needed to think. And he wished his helpers wouldn't call him by his old rank. He was making decisions far above that grade now.

Less than a half hour later, Dušić accelerated down Kralja Milana, using the paddle shifters behind his steering wheel. When he turned onto Kralja Petra, he found what he had come to see—the Patriarchate of the Serbian Orthodox Church. Constructed in the 1930s, the Patriarchate building hardly ranked as the most ancient site in the history of Dušić's religion. But the structure had become one of the most important. Soon the Patriarchate would host the Holy Assembly of Bishops. Dušić often came here to reflect. As he drove by, he regarded the portico and the columns, and he considered the treasures in the library and museum. The church had never played a big role in his life, but now it played a big role in his plans.

He drummed his fingers on the wheel, let those plans sink into his subconscious. Brilliant ideas needed time to distill. Sometimes he woke in the night as he thought of a detail he had overlooked, and he would pen a note, printing neat figures in Serbian Cyrillic.

With much on his mind, Dušić turned the corner, weaved through central Belgrade, and once again drove down Kralja Milana. He stopped at Pionirski Park and shut down the Aventador, though he did not get out. He only stared at the trees, thinking. Though he never doubted the rightness of his cause, sometimes he had second thoughts about his opening tactic. If all the details came to light, some people would never understand. The mission must take place under strict and permanent secrecy.

Genius, he considered, was a curse. How much more simply he

could have lived as a common farmer, or perhaps a gunsmith. Better yet, a poet, concerned only with advancing the literature of his nation. But those given rare vision, the ability to take the long view, must not waste it. He found no time to write poetry now, but he could take inspiration from poems. In his briefcase on the passenger seat, he carried one of his favorite works, *The Mountain Wreath*. A play written in epic verse, penned in the nineteenth century by the Montenegrin prince-bishop Petar II Petrović-Njegoš, who dreamed of liberating all his people from the Turks. Dušić turned to one of his favorite verses, in which the character Bishop Danilo speaks of Muslims:

> *Besides Asia, where their nest is hidden,*
> *the devil's tribe gobbled up the nations—*
> *one every day, as an owl gulps a bird . . .*

But the devil's tribe would soon choke on this nation, if Dušić had any say in the matter. The plane crash at Manas could complicate things, but he would not turn back now.

BY THE TIME PARSON REACHED the crash site, the rain had stopped and the fires had gone out. Blankets covered the dead. Medics lifted the bodies onto litters and loaded them into the ambulances. Parson's investigation would include the condition of the bodies—which bones were broken, the nature of internal injuries. That kind of information—coupled with clues from the cockpit voice recorder and flight data recorder—could tell you what had happened at the moment of impact. Two broken forearms, for example, suggested a pilot with both hands on the yoke.

However, Parson felt grateful that the medics and their blankets spared him the sight of corpses. He'd seen enough dead bodies in his career already. The ambulances drove away, and Parson made a mental note to get autopsy reports.

A strong odor of fuel and ash permeated the debris field. Mist rose from the wet pavement. A combination of firefighting chemicals, hydraulic fluid, and oil formed a coffee-colored slurry that stained Parson's suede desert boots. He picked his way through the mess, snapping photographs and inspecting parts. The base commander, a full-bird colonel on loan from the Tennessee Air National Guard, accompanied Parson.

"Sad business," the commander said.

"Yes, sir," Parson said. Raised the camera, pressed the button halfway to focus on a charred turbine, then pressed harder to take the digital shot. He usually had little patience for people who stated the obvious, but this colonel seemed all right. Sounded genuinely saddened for the Afghan crew. And who knew? Maybe this scene reminded the guy of things he'd like to forget. Sure as hell had that effect on Parson.

"Sorry you have to deal with this in your first week, Michael," the commander added.

Parson looked at him. Gray hair, almost too long for regulation. An Air Guard patch on his leather A-2 jacket, which, in this theater, made him technically out of uniform. The wings of a command pilot on his name tag, which read *Terrence C. Webster, Colonel, USAF.*

"It is what it is, sir," Parson said. "We'll just deal with it."

"Call me Terry."

A good sign, Parson thought. He despised salute-hungry jack-asses taking a command assignment just to get a ticket punched for promotion. But Webster apparently cared little for spit-and-polish protocol. Maybe Parson could work with this guy.

Parson stepped away from the tangle of charred aluminum, considered what else he should note. Oh, yeah, point of initial impact. He walked away from the main body of wreckage and counted paces as he strode toward the approach end of Two-Six. Stopped when he found the propeller scars. Took photos of the gray gouges in black pavement—lens-shaped cuts slashed at evenly spaced intervals until they ended at a more general scraping and burning. A flock of sparrows trilled past, exploring a part of the base usually forbidden to them by the constant roar of jet engines.

And that roar needed to start again soon. Webster, to his credit, had not told Parson to hurry. But Parson knew this base had to reopen as quickly as possible. Pakistan had closed its land routes into Afghanistan again, which made Manas all the more important as part of the lifeline for American troops.

Back at the debris area, Parson found Webster directing two maintenance men to find the cockpit voice recorder and flight data recorder. The mechanics went to work inside the tail section. The empennage had broken away early in the crash sequence, so it had suffered little fire damage.

"What do you do back home, Terry?" Parson asked. He didn't usually care for small talk, but maybe now it would keep his mind from wandering into dark places.

"I'm a lawyer."

Well, that was different. So many Guard pilots flew for airlines. Some seemed pretty cool, but others stayed mad at the world because they weren't 777 captains making three hundred grand. Normally, Parson had little use for lawyers. But at least he wouldn't have to spend a year listening to Webster whine about airline work rules.

"What kind of lawyer?" Parson asked.

"Prosecutor."

"You a district attorney?"

"At one time."

Short answers, Parson noted. That usually meant modesty, secrecy, or plain old rudeness. Parson thought he could rule out the third option. No point pondering it now, though. He walked over to the open crew door, tested the boarding steps with his boot. Parson really didn't want to climb into what remained of the cockpit, but he knew he must. In the Aircraft Mishap Investigation course at Kirtland Air Force Base, New Mexico, his instructors had emphasized thoroughness. He reached into a leg pocket of his flight suit, pulled out his Nomex gloves, and put them on.

Parson placed his hands on either side of the entrance. He pulled himself inside, taking care not to slip on the foam that slickened the charred steps. Daylight streamed from the open fuselage, metal broken and burned away. An angle of light he'd never seen on a flight deck.

In the cockpit, he found little blood. Typical for blunt force trauma. The crew's personal effects remained in place as if waiting to be used again: A flight jacket draped over the back of a seat. A checklist open to the Before Landing page, its plastic binder partially melted by heat. Headsets on the floor, still plugged into interphone cords. A loose shoulder harness, unspooled from its broken inertial reel.

The instrument panel appeared pretty much intact. Parson made another mental note: He'd ask maintenance to remove the entire panel, then send the panel to a stateside lab. In some instruments, phosphorus paint coated the needles. On impact, the needles might smack against the glass faces of the gauges. The paint residue, seen easily under a black light, could tell you the position of the needles at the moment of the crash. Parson wondered especially about the airspeed indicator. He knew these guys had come in too fast. He could write a better report if he could say exactly *how* fast.

Parson focused his camera on a wide shot of the panel and snapped a photo. Zoomed in, took a closer shot. Then he took an image of the throttles, still shoved up to the stops. The pilots had probably overtorqued the engines, he thought, and they still didn't get enough power to save themselves. Few airplanes could blast out enough thrust to escape a fully developed microburst. Parson turned off the camera and stuffed it into the pocket of his flight jacket.

Back outside, he heard the ratcheting of a socket wrench from inside the empennage. Next came metallic bangs, curses, and more ratcheting. The mechanics emerged with two bright orange electronic boxes.

"Found 'em," one of the mechanics said.

The voice and data recorders usually answered most questions about a mishap. Their orange color made them easy to find amid wreckage. Nobody in aviation ever called them "black boxes" because they were never black.

So what story would those recorders tell? Parson had already heard the pilots' radio calls, but he didn't know what they'd said among themselves. The CVR would have recorded at least the last thirty minutes of conversation. The Afghan pilots had probably spoken Pashto to each other, though some Afghan fliers spoke Dari as well.

Parson took the orange boxes from the maintenance men, set the recorders down in a patch of grass well away from oil and foam. He eased himself down on one knee, thought for a moment. Looked over the wreckage, creaking as it cooled. Gazed to the southwest. In that direction, beyond the horizon, lay Afghanistan.

No, he told himself. Don't even ask her.

His old friend Sophia Gold was the best Pashto interpreter in the business. She possessed a wealth of knowledge about Afghan culture and history. She had shared his greatest trials and deepest pain. In some ways he loved her more than any of the girlfriends he'd had in a long string of short relationships, though he'd never been intimate with Sophia. Parson had once saved her life. And then later he'd damn near gotten her killed.

But not even a bullet through her chest could keep her from Afghanistan. She worked there now, in some civilian capacity with the United Nations. After an honorable discharge from the active-duty Army, she remained a sergeant major in the Individual Ready Reserve. Silver Star, Legion of Merit, Purple Heart.

The last time he'd seen her, she'd looked good. Sitting across from Parson in a German pub, just released from Landstuhl Regional Medical Center, Sophia appeared nothing like the wounded troop who had practically been pulled from the grave. Her blond hair spilled across her shoulders. She usually wore it a little shorter, but during her months of recovery, she hadn't cut it. Parson liked the effect, and he enjoyed just looking at her in civilian clothes. Her sweater and slacks revealed little but could not hide her attractiveness, which seemed only to increase as she approached forty. A career as an airborne-qualified soldier had kept her in better shape than most women half her age.

Parson liked looking back on that dinner of pepper steak and Rhine Valley wine. The image of Sophia relaxed and happy—and pretty—countered a more vivid memory: that of a woman with a catheter punched into her rib cage so she could breathe, clinging to life in a rescue helicopter, blood smeared across her breasts and pale skin. He had wondered if that dinner would mark the start of a different sort of relationship with her, but it didn't seem proper to ask for a date right when she'd gotten out of the hospital. And maybe it wouldn't be proper, ever. That might just ruin a unique friendship and partnership.

So, instead of talking about a date, they'd chatted about so many things they might have talked about earlier if their circumstances had allowed. She recommended books. He told her about places to hike in national forests. She described what it felt like to jump from an airplane. He told her she should try his venison barbecue sometime, but he doubted he'd sold her on that idea.

It would be great to work with her again. And he *did* need someone who understood Pashto. Even if the pilots had spoken Dari instead, Sophia might have at least a passing knowledge of that language.

And this time, he wouldn't be summoning her to a combat

zone; he'd be getting her out of one. Parson decided he'd talk to Webster about it. For Sophia, Manas would almost amount to a vacation. Just translate a half hour of conversation, then kick back in a place where she didn't need to carry a rifle. Good coffee and hot chow. Maybe even get one of those Antonov crews to pick up a case of Georgian wine for her. Parson would find excuses to stretch out her visit for a couple weeks if she wanted. For a change, he could do her a favor.

Parson rose to his feet, went back to the wreckage. Webster was looking through what remained of the fuselage.

"What were these guys hauling, anyway?" Webster asked.

"Let's find out," Parson said. The C-27 had carried three pallets of assorted cargo: metal boxes and Pelican cases covered with charred netting. Some of the Pelican cases had melted, and Parson didn't even try to open those. But he popped the fasteners on one of the metal boxes.

The burned metal left black gunk on Parson's gloves. The box didn't want to come open all the way, so he unclipped his boot knife and pried the lid with the blade. He hated to use his prized Damascus steel knife for such a purpose, but at the moment he had no other tool. Inside the box he found an electronic device protected by padding covered in plastic that had partially melted. He lifted the object.

"What you got there?" Webster asked.

"Looks like an IFF transponder for an airplane," Parson said. "Maybe they were shipping stuff out to get it refurbished or recalibrated. I always used to preach to them never to skimp on maintenance."

He put the IFF back in the box. Then he kicked at the pile of scorched cargo, dislodged another container. This one opened more easily. Inside, Parson found another electronic component: an inertial navigation unit. A delicate piece of gear that included a ring laser gyro. The box contained even thicker padding. Parson hefted the navigation unit, showed it to Webster, replaced it in the box.

"I'll need some help on this investigation," Parson said. He told Webster about Gold, why he wanted to ask her to come to Manas.

"Sure, I'll approve that," Webster said. "I remember seeing her name somewhere. I'd love to meet her."

"We can't order her here," Parson said. "She's a civilian now. She'd have to agree, with the permission of her bosses."

"Who does she work for?"

"The United Nations."

"Hmm," Webster said. "Maybe I can help with that."

"How?" Parson asked.

"I know some people."

"At the UN? I thought you were a lawyer from Tennessee."

"I did a little work in international law."

Sounded like this guy kept his fingers in all kinds of pies. Parson knew a few people like that: interested in everything, keeping two or three careers going at once. Just listening to them could make you tired. Sometimes they had good stories, if they could tell them.

Parson moved to another charred pallet. On top lay a metal box similar to the others. He released the fasteners and pushed on the lid, but the warped hinges allowed little movement. Once more Parson used his knife as a lever. Damned shame, he thought, to ruin a good edge this way.

When he pulled up on the knife handle, the lid squeaked open. But the blade slipped and the tip dug into the padding that protected more electronic components. The padding consisted of some kind of soft material covered by partially melted plastic. As Parson pulled out the knife, he noticed a brown sticky substance along the blade. He took off his gloves, touched the stuff with his index finger. Tacky consistency. He sniffed it, and it gave off a slightly sour smell, almost like pickles.

Parson lifted an INU out of the box, and he stabbed again into the padding. More of the brown substance spilled out.

"What the hell is this?" Parson asked.

Webster leaned toward the metal container, inhaled through his nose.

"Opium," he said.

4

AS THE KYRGYZSTAN AIRLINES Yak-40 descended toward Manas, Sophia Gold felt a little airsick. Rough air rocked the commuter jet, and in the tight confines of her seat, she could not find a comfortable position. A jolt of turbulence sloshed hot coffee out of her paper cup and onto her khaki trousers. The liquid dripped from her fingers and, lacking a napkin, she wiped her hand on her Barbour field jacket. Gold had not yet grown used to working in civilian clothes, and her attire still tended toward military.

She wasn't used to flying like this, either. She'd spent her professional life as a translator/interpreter with the U.S. Army, mostly with the 82nd Airborne Division. Gold would have felt more at home in the cargo compartment of a C-130 with a parachute strapped to her back. Or in an Afghan helicopter, on headset with the crew.

Two things had led her to leave the Army she loved: One, the

United States was winding down its presence in Afghanistan; inevitably the Americans would withdraw altogether, and the Pentagon would need fewer Pashto speakers. If she wanted to continue working with the Afghan people—whom she'd also grown to love—she'd have to find another way. And two, on her final military mission, while working as an interpreter for Lieutenant Colonel Parson, she'd suffered a bullet wound that nearly killed her. Gold had healed well enough to continue to pass the Army physical. But after seeing more than her share of combat, she felt she could best continue to serve as a civilian. When she contacted the office of the United Nations High Commissioner for Refugees, the UNHCR, they hired her over the phone without asking for a résumé. As a reservist, she kept a current military ID card.

The Yak touched down hard enough to send a stab of pain through her torso. Those pains still happened from time to time. The enemy bullet about a year ago had done a lot of tissue damage, and the soreness never completely left her. Gold had experienced other kinds of wounds as well. She'd suffered the night sweats and intrusive memories of post-traumatic stress disorder even before she was shot. Ironically, the PTSD symptoms eased after the nearly fatal bullet wound.

As the aircraft decelerated, it rolled past a blackened spot on the pavement. The crash site, Gold assumed.

Inside the passenger terminal, she found Parson waiting, along with a gray-haired man who looked older than Parson. Gold could not tell the man's rank; he wore a Bass Pro Shops baseball cap and a Vanderbilt University sweatshirt. Parson also wore civilian clothes—jeans and a wrinkled shooting shirt with a pad on the right shoulder. It was nearly six p.m. local time. Evidently, new base regs permitted civvies after duty hours.

Parson had aged little in the months since she'd last seen him.

And his old limp seemed less pronounced, old scars on his arms and fingers less noticeable. Eyes still alert, but without that hint of hypervigilance. The years might have eroded his youth, but maybe they'd given something back in healing. Gold hoped so, anyway.

She embraced him. Parson held her tightly enough that it hurt her chest. She uttered a little inadvertent cry of discomfort. He let go.

"Sorry, Sophia," he said. "Stupid of me." She took a step back from him but held on to his arm long enough to let him know it was all right. "This is Colonel Webster," Parson added.

"Terry," the colonel said. He shook Gold's hand.

"Good to meet you, sir," Gold said. "Thank you for your e-mails. How did you know people at the UN?"

"Let's talk about it over a beer," Webster said.

"We'll take you to Pete's Place," Parson added.

Whose place? Gold wondered, until she saw that the bar in the Manas rec center was named for Peter Ganci, the New York City fire chief who died on 9/11. A sign read THIS BAR DEDICATED TO COALITION MEMBERS WHO GAVE THEIR LIVES IN THE WAR ON TERROR.

Gold and Webster sat in metal folding chairs at a wooden table. Parson went to the bar. She smiled when he brought her a glass of red wine; he hadn't even had to ask. He handed a Guinness to Webster and opened a Bud for himself.

She tried to gauge Parson's manner, as well as the colonel's. Gold had made a life of communicating, of reading people. Something worried these guys. The crash, of course, provided reason enough to feel down. To witness untimely deaths, she knew far too well, unhinged you a little, even if you didn't know the deceased. But Gold sensed Parson and the colonel had something else on their minds. She didn't know how to approach the topic, so she stayed on safe territory by asking Webster about his background.

"I'm playing hooky from my day job," Webster said. "My law firm back in Knoxville does some international work. UN, ICC, that sort of thing."

"Interstate Commerce Commission?" Parson asked.

"International Criminal Court," Gold said.

"Oh."

"So when Michael said he needed you," Webster explained, "I called in some favors. But I told everybody not to lean on you."

"They didn't," Gold said. That was true. Her superiors had said only that she could go if she wanted. And of course she wanted to help Parson.

"Thanks again for coming," Parson said. "I hoped this would amount to a little break for you, but it's getting more complicated."

"How's that?" Gold asked.

"We found opium in the wreckage," Webster said. He took a sip from his Guinness.

The news saddened Gold, but it did not surprise her. About ninety percent of the world's opium came from Afghanistan. And the Afghan military had a long way to go toward rooting out corruption.

"How were they hiding it?" Gold asked. "Or could you tell?"

"We could," Parson said. He explained how the smugglers disguised the opium as packing material. Drug-sniffing dogs would have found it in an instant, but if the Afghans had brought dogs to this cargo at all, the animals would have been bomb-sniffing dogs. Somebody in the narcotics operation knew something about military air cargo.

Gold wondered if the crew's last words on the cockpit voice recorder would reveal any hints about the contraband. She doubted it, but she intended to translate anything she heard on that recording, no matter how trivial it might seem.

"When do you think we'll have the recording back?" Gold asked.

"We've shipped some evidence, including the CVR, back to the States," Parson said. "They'll send us the audio file over the SIPRNet."

Parson's reference to the classified computer net made Gold doubly glad she'd maintained her top secret clearance. She hadn't expected to need it with her new job, but both the government and civilian employers valued anyone with a TS, so you didn't let such a clearance expire if you could help it. Gold considered for a moment whether she and the two men should even be discussing this in the rec center if any part of the matter was classified. No one else was listening, and a Toby Keith tune blasted over the speakers. But just to be safe, she decided to steer the conversation to more routine aspects of the problem.

"So how do you piece together what happens in a crash?" Gold asked. She took a sip of the wine Parson had brought her. She'd expected cheap stuff, but the red tasted rich and smoky. Not what she thought she'd find in a prefab building with country music on the CD player.

"You try not to make any assumptions," Parson said, "and you listen to what the evidence tells you."

"Sounds like prosecuting a case," Webster said.

"I saw the crash," Parson said, "so that helps, and a wind shear event is pretty simple. But you still have to look at stuff like why they didn't go missed-approach early enough to make it."

He's in his element, Gold thought. She admired competence, and though Parson certainly had his rough edges, he spoke the language of aviation as if he'd invented it himself. She'd watched him fly a crippled C-5 Galaxy while badly hurt and in terrible pain. Gold remembered how he'd marshaled the combined skills of his crew to save his passengers—some of them, at least. This time, however, Parson could not save anyone; he could only try to keep other crews from making the mistakes that had killed the three fliers.

"You look at all the links in the chain," Webster said.

"Yeah," Parson said. "When something bad happens, it's almost never because of just one thing. You get a chain of errors and missed opportunities and bad attitudes, and they link up to cause a damned disaster like we just had out there." Parson gestured toward the runway with his beer hand, sloshing a little over his fingers. "Shit," he said.

"We teach aviators to look for accident chains as they form," Webster said. "If you remove one link, then there's no disaster."

"How do you do that?" Gold asked.

"You change what's happening," Webster said.

"Like if you just heard the tower give a wind shear warning," Parson said, "and you see you're coming down at about eight thousand feet per minute, you don't just sit on your ass and ride it in. You push up the throttles and go the fuck around."

Gold could feel Parson's anger over the accident. He had not trained this crew himself, but he'd helped train many other Afghan fliers; and he'd put a lot of sweat and even some blood into helping them create a professional air force. To see an Afghan crew die in what he appeared to regard as a preventable crash—while smuggling drugs, no less—must come as an awful disappointment.

She couldn't do much for Parson until the CVR recording came back, so she decided to change the subject. Maybe get everyone's mind off the destruction that had happened only steps away.

"Colonel," she said, "it sounds like you have an interesting job."

"Sometimes," Webster said, "but at other times it's boring as hell. At least the Guard lets me get out from behind that desk and do something different."

"Like trying to keep Michael Parson out of trouble?"

"Exactly," Webster laughed.

"Good luck," Gold said.

Parson smiled thinly and took a pull from his beer. He started to say something—probably to give her a good-natured retort—but jet noise drowned him out. The streak-scream of a jet fighter taking off rumbled in waves across the base, followed by the identical sound of a second aircraft. Lead and wingman, Gold supposed, heading out to hit a target in Afghanistan. Nice to be out of there for a little while, she had to admit.

"So what about you, Sophia?" Parson asked. "I thought you'd be working on a doctorate in philosophy or religion by now. Just can't stay away from the garden spots?"

"Something like that," Gold said. She took a sip of wine while she thought about the rest of her answer. "It's hard to let go when there's so much need."

"You've earned a break. I thought you wanted to go back to school."

"More than you know. And I did get accepted at Duke and Maryland."

"Congrats. Use that new GI Bill. Nobody deserves it more than you."

"Someday," Gold said. Someday.

IN THE TWO DAYS that went by while she waited for the cockpit recording, Gold had no official duties. Parson got away from his own duties as often as he could to spend time with her. They began both days with a run around the base, Parson wearing his blue-and-silver Air Force PT uniform, and Gold still using her old workout clothes with ARMY embroidered on the gray jacket. For most of her life, she'd nearly always led the pack on platoon runs. However, the insurgent's bullet had cost her some lung capacity, and Parson ran ahead. But in their five-mile runs, neither of them ever slowed to a walk. They shared every meal together in the dining hall, each going through the ritual of signing the roster and rubbing a dollop of hand sanitizer across their fingers. Gold had spent so much time in deployed locations that she associated the antiseptic smell of hand sanitizer with food.

Between meals, Gold passed the hours in the Green Beans coffee shop, delving into the wisdom of John Locke's *An Essay Concerning Human Understanding*. She was sipping an espresso, enjoying the company of the cat lounging on her table, when Parson came in and told her he had the CVR file.

"Let's listen to it in the intel vault," he said.

The intel vault amounted to a room in the command building with some extra soundproofing. In her career, Gold had seen intel facilities ranging from a tent with an armed guard to a high-tech SCIF, or sensitive compartmented information facility, with alarms and coded locks.

Following the usual protocol, Gold left her cell phone outside the room in a designated wooden box. Parson steered her to a computer reserved for her. She slid her ID card into the reader and signed on. An intel officer showed her how to pull up the audio file. Before she played it, she also opened a word processing program and donned a set of earphones.

"Are you ready for this?" Parson asked.

Gold thought for a moment, then nodded. But no, she wasn't ready for this, nor would she ever be. How did one prepare to listen to people die? Still, she appreciated Parson's question. He had the decency to realize how jarring it was to pull her away from a moment of leisure and sit her down to something like this. She took a deep breath and clicked PLAY.

In the first several seconds, she heard only noise: the hum of electronics, the rush of the slipstream over the hull of the aircraft. Parson had explained how she'd be listening to various inputs, including the radios, ambient sounds from an area microphone mounted in the cockpit, and chatter over the interphone from the pilot, copilot, and loadmaster. The area mike picked up a lot of extraneous sounds that mixed with everything else.

Gold listened for fifteen minutes, tapping into the keyboard everything she heard. She wrote the words in English, whether they were spoken in that language or in Pashto. Soon she realized the crew used English on the radios and Pashto over the interphone. So far, it all seemed routine. The pilots discussed the weather.

"That front is approaching Manas," one pilot said in Pashto.

"I can see that," the other pilot said. Tone a little condescending. So maybe this was the aircraft commander, Gold thought. But how could he see the front? Were the clouds that distinct? Oh, yes, she remembered. Airborne radar. Gold had learned a few things from Parson, seemingly by osmosis.

"Perhaps we should consider a divert," the copilot said.

"No," the aircraft commander said.

For several minutes, the crew said no more about the weather. They began some sort of checklist; Gold transcribed it all and trusted Parson to make sense of the technical parts. The sound of rain increased, and Gold heard grunts and curses. She took down all that, too.

"Bishkek VOR tuned and identified, sir," the copilot said.

"I will carry a few extra knots down final," the aircraft commander said.

"Sir, it is getting bad. We have plenty of fuel. Let us go to the alternate."

"Kochkor is no better. Can you not see the radar?"

"Then Almaty."

"That is in Kazakhstan, you fool. We have no diplomatic clearance for that country. If we declare an emergency and land in Almaty, we could get stuck there for days."

So the aircraft commander had a strong motivation to reach Manas, Gold realized. He apparently knew about his extra cargo and needed to get it there on time regardless of risks. Well, he got it there, all right. As for the copilot, maybe he knew; maybe he didn't.

A voice in accented English came over the radio: a Kyrgyz air traffic controller, Gold assumed.

"Golay One-Three," the controller said, "descend and maintain 4,400 feet. You are cleared for the VOR/DME approach to Runway Two-Six. Contact tower on one-one-eight point one."

"One-one-eight point one," the copilot said. "Cleared for approach." Resignation in his voice.

Silence for a few moments. Gold supposed the copilot was changing frequencies. Then he called the tower, and the tower cleared Golay One-Three to land. The tower also warned about wind shear, just as Parson had said. None of the crew members said anything else about diverting to an alternate airport.

The aircraft commander called for the landing checklist, and the copilot began reading the items. Gold continued taking down each word.

"Gear down," the aircraft commander said.

"Gear down," the copilot responded. Gold heard the landing gear lever seat into position as the copilot moved it. Then the copilot said, "Down and locked."

"I have the approach lights," the aircraft commander said. "Going visual."

Gold clicked on PAUSE to catch up with her typing. Absurdly, in some odd corner of her mind she wanted an interphone switch that would let her speak back in time, so she could tell the crew what was about to happen to them. Warn them off. Tell the aircraft commander he'd made a bad decision: So what if you're late? Whoever you're carrying those drugs for won't kill you any deader than you're about to kill yourself—*and* your crew members, jackass. She realized she was channeling a little of Parson's attitude now. She also knew there was no changing the outcome. Though Gold listened to events in real time, that real time had passed. What was done was done, and not even the angels could change it. She clicked PLAY.

The copilot swore, and Gold heard a jostling sound. Items in the cockpit, Gold imagined, helmet bags and checklists thrown by another jolt of turbulence.

"*Paam kawa,*" the copilot said. Gold typed: WATCH OUT.

"*Baad dai,*" the aircraft commander replied. Gold wrote: IT IS WINDY. Then the commander added, "We have all seen wind before."

"*Zmaa neh khwakhigee,*" a new voice said. Gold typed: I DON'T LIKE THIS. The enlisted loadmaster, apparently, now frightened enough to speak up to the officers.

"Quiet," the aircraft commander ordered.

A synthesized voice came over the recording, blaring in English: SINK RATE, SINK RATE.

"Correcting," the aircraft commander said.

"Descent rate, sir," the copilot said. "We have entered a downdraft." Evidently, the commander's correction wasn't working.

"Adding power," the commander said.

The engine noise rose, and the synthesized warning repeated: SINK RATE. The voice hushed for a moment, then screeched: PULL UP, PULL UP.

"Power!" the copilot shouted. Then he yelled, "I have the aircraft!"

"No, you do not!" the commander shouted.

Curses and rattles. Then the aircraft commander said, "Golay One-Three going around." So he had relented. But now it was too late to do the right thing.

"Gear up," the commander ordered.

"Gear up," the copilot acknowledged. Gold heard a *whack*, presumably an angry and fearful copilot slamming the gear handle.

The turboprops howled. The artificial voice again called: PULL UP, PULL UP.

The pilots stopped speaking. Parson had said that happens in so many crashes: right before impact, people lock up and shut up. Until the screams begin.

And the screams began. Underneath the screams, Gold heard a grinding or crunching sound. Only one voice spoke intelligible words. It sounded like the loadmaster, who ended his life in mid-sentence: "There is no God but God and—"

Unidentifiable noise rose in volume—then stopped.

Gold let out a long breath. She typed: END OF TAPE.

5

PARSON HAD MORE THAN just a plane crash on his hands, and he knew law enforcement would get involved one way or another. But to make things even more complicated, the United States didn't really have jurisdiction. The Manas Transit Center wasn't an American-owned base; the government of Kyrgyzstan simply allowed Americans to use ramp space at the airport that served the city of Bishkek. U.S. officials had to coordinate with Kyrgyzstan—not exactly the world's most stable government. And in Afghanistan, where the drug flight originated, some units of the National Police were practically criminal enterprises themselves. So when the Air Force Office of Special Investigations sent an agent to follow the opium trail, Parson did not envy the man.

Special Agent Carl Cunningham showed up in Webster's office, and Webster called in Parson and Gold to meet him. In his late twenties, Cunningham carried himself with the watchfulness of a cop in a bad neighborhood. Parson guessed that he'd come out of

Air Force Security Forces, though Parson knew OSI agents could also be recruited from other fields. Some were officers, some were enlisted, some were civilian, and some were reservists. But you seldom knew their true rank. To the outside world, they were all just "Special Agent."

Cunningham wore gray tactical pants with large cargo pockets. White cotton shirt. A canvas vest extended below his waistband, but the slight bulge gave away the presence of his sidearm. The agent's black beard looked newly trimmed. Parson wondered if Cunningham had worn his beard longer in the recent past to blend in with troublemakers in Afghanistan or Pakistan.

"Colonel Webster tells me you've already transcribed the cockpit voice recording," Cunningham said. Parson puzzled over the man's accent. It sounded almost British. "Transcribed" sounded like "transcroibed."

"We have," Gold said. "I made a copy for you." Gold handed him a manila envelope.

"Thanks very much," Cunningham said. "Did you find anything of interest on the recording?" Now, where had Parson heard people talk like that? Oh, yeah: while stationed at Pope Air Force Base in North Carolina. You occasionally heard that accent in coastal areas of the state. A few island communities had existed in enough isolation to keep some of the voice of their Elizabethan forebears. This guy wasn't a Brit; he was an Outer Banks redneck with an education. You're a long damned way from Cape Hatteras, Parson thought.

"The aircraft commander wanted to land here no matter what," Gold said. "You'll see what I mean when you read the transcript."

"If he'd landed safely, where would he have gone next?" Cunningham asked.

"Back home," Webster said. "We checked with the Afghan Air Force. He had orders to fly back to Bagram."

"What about his cargo?" Cunningham said.

"We haven't looked into that yet," Webster said. "It would have been offloaded here and then picked up by another flight. Probably a civilian cargo line." Webster explained that American and Kyrgyz authorities had not publicly announced the discovery of opium on the plane. No sense alerting the traffickers—they'd just suspend shipments until they found another route. "We figured we'd better let the professionals take it from here," Webster added.

"I appreciate that," Cunningham said. "If you'd snooped around without knowing what you were doing, the bad guys would have just disappeared."

Good thing Webster brought a background as a country prosecutor, Parson thought. At least he knows what *not* to do. Sometimes these Guard guys brought civilian skills that came in handy.

"So what do you need us to do?" Gold asked.

"Just maintain," Cunningham said. "Don't bring in drug dogs to check flights from Afghanistan. Don't change anything you're doing. Let 'em think we don't know anything."

"That's easy enough," Parson said.

The meeting broke up, and Parson headed for the door. He needed to write a report for the Air Force Safety Center—leaving out the drug connection, of course—and he dreaded it. The task brought back memories of papers he'd done for university professors and War College instructors. The papers usually came back with red marks all over them. Maybe Gold could help him with her plain old English skills. Cunningham held back, still standing by his chair. He looked down at the carpet; apparently he was thinking about something.

"Ms. Gold," he said, "how long will you stay here at Manas?"

"Well, I'd like to get back to my work in Afghanistan, but I could probably make arrangements," she said. "Why?"

"It would help if you can stay and find out if the Afghans have any ground support people here," the agent said. "If they do, talk to them—purely about safety. Tell me if anybody acts nervous."

"They'll all act nervous," Parson said. "They'll think they're in trouble because of the crash itself."

"Yeah," Cunningham said, "but that's a different kind of nervous. Anyway, it couldn't hurt as long as you're careful not to tip them off."

"Do you want to come with us if we talk to them?" Parson asked.

"Not now," Cunningham said. "They don't need to see me just yet."

Later in the day, Parson walked along the ramp area to watch the activity. In his flight suit, he could look around all he wanted without arousing suspicion. At any moment, a dozen other men dressed just like him worked on the ramp: pilots and flight engineers conducting preflight inspections, crew chiefs fueling their planes, loadmasters pushing pallets.

The morning looked pretty typical. Three KC-135 Stratotankers waited side by side, electrical cables snaking from generator carts to receptacles along the sides of the aircraft. Parson knew the tanker crews would take turns flying over Afghanistan in case any wayward fighter pilots needed an emergency refueling. The Stratotankers might fly planned refuelings, too. As American forces drew down, C-5 Galaxies and C-17 Globemasters hauled trucks, Humvees, and helicopters out of Bagram and Kandahar. Sometimes the big jets departed so heavy with cargo that they could not put on enough fuel to reach Europe and still get off the runway. So they'd take off with a light fuel load, then rendezvous with a tanker and get all the gas they needed. Parson remembered the pride he took in the deft control needed to fly one big aircraft within feet of another, the satisfying *whack* as the refueling boom seated in the receptacle.

Civilian aircraft came and went, as well. An Air Astana 757

from Kazakhstan taxied for takeoff. At the passenger terminal, an Airbus pushed back from the gate. The plane bore the green, gold, and white livery of Pakistan International Airlines. And a Russian Antonov lumbered toward a hangar.

In front of the hangar, a ramp worker beckoned the Antonov to a parking spot. The cargo jet rolled into its space, engines whining near idle. The ramp guy crossed his fists over his head, and the Antonov shuddered to a stop. After several minutes—a cool-down for the engines, Parson supposed—the turbines finally quieted. Crew members climbed from the aircraft as a forklift approached. The forklift carried a single pallet.

As Parson strolled nearer, he saw that the forklift driver wore a military uniform. The forklift stopped under the tail of the aircraft, and Parson walked over to talk to the driver. The man's uniform bore the insignia of an Afghan Air Force sergeant.

"Good morning," Parson said.

The bearded Afghan Air Force man looked at him and smiled. Then the man shook his head and said, "No English, sir. No English."

Parson held up one hand and said, "That's okay. No problem." He knew the sergeant probably hadn't lied. Few Afghan military personnel spoke good English. But now he knew the Afghans had a ground detachment at Manas. Nothing sinister about that; it made perfect sense for them to keep maintenance and cargo-handling capability here. But that also created an infrastructure that traffickers could exploit. So, Parson thought, Agent Cunningham had come to the right place to start his investigation.

In the afternoon, once ground crews had loaded the Antonov and sent it on its way, Parson returned to the Afghans' cargo facility with Gold. The two sat with the Afghan sergeant in a break room just off the hangar. The place smelled of cigarette smoke and grease. Parson slouched on a tattered sofa so worn that its stuffing spilled from rips and tears. Gold and the sergeant chose metal folding chairs, rusted and bent. Cases of Fanta lined the walls. The sergeant eyed Parson, then looked through the door to where the other Afghans folded cargo netting and swept the floor. Maybe the sergeant wondered why he was being interviewed alone, but that was normal procedure for a safety probe.

Parson opened a notepad, clicked a ballpoint pen, and said, "Tell him we're very sorry about the crash, and we're trying to learn its cause."

Gold spoke a long sentence in Pashto. Probably adding more courtesy to his opening statement, Parson imagined. Whatever she said must have worked; the man seemed to relax a little.

"Did he see the accident?" Parson asked.

Gold translated the question, and the sergeant said, *"Ho."* Parson had picked up that much of the language. The word meant yes.

"Tell him to describe what he saw," Parson said. Didn't really matter what the man had seen. Parson knew why the C-27 had pranged into the ground. But this question would get the sergeant talking—and, Parson hoped, thinking this was still just a safety investigation.

The man began a stream of words Parson could not understand. Parson tried to listen for pauses, to determine when one sentence ended and another began, but he could not even tell that much. Like every accident witness, this guy had a story to tell, and he told it in excited tones. He raised his hand with thumb and little finger outstretched to represent wings. The hand traced a slanting descent path, then crashed onto his knee. The sergeant said, *"Bhoom."* No interpreting needed there.

Gold told Parson what the man had described. The English translation included nothing Parson hadn't seen for himself during the event.

"Ask him what the plane was carrying," Parson said. Now I'm

acting like a lawyer, he thought, asking only questions to which I already know the answer.

Gold spoke, and the man responded. Shorter answers this time.

"Equipment in boxes," Gold said. "That's all he seems to know."

"All right," Parson said, "ask him where the plane would have gone if it hadn't crashed here." Another question to which he knew the answer.

After Gold asked the question in Pashto—which sounded like all vowels, to Parson's ears—the man answered quickly, rubbing the palms of his hands along his thighs.

"He says the plane would have gone back to Afghanistan," Gold said. "Civilian airplanes carry the cargo to Europe."

Careful now, Parson told himself. Don't get too close to the wrong topic.

"Tell him we're wondering how well the pilot knew the approaches to Manas," Parson said. "Does he know if that crew had flown here before?"

More chatter in Pashto. Parson envied Gold's language ability. He wished he could know what she knew, but achieving that would take more than a few hours of Rosetta Stone. Gold had studied hard for years. Making a good interpreter took as long as making a pilot. And she'd done all that work and training for enlisted pay.

"He says C-27s come here at least twice a week," Gold said.

"Interesting," Parson said. "Let me think for a minute." So they could have shipped a hell of a lot of opium through here, he considered. Maybe this guy knows about it; maybe he doesn't. Parson decided to quit while he was ahead and just ask some fluff questions to cover his tracks.

"Ask him if this aircraft commander had a good reputation, if his men respected him," Parson said.

Parson hardly listened as Gold translated and then came back with " 'Oh, yes.' "

Whatever. Jackass didn't deserve respect now; that was for damned sure. Parson remembered an old saw he'd heard from one of his instructors years ago: *A superior aviator uses his superior judgment to avoid situations that would require his superior skill.* Well, that bonehead who'd bought the farm out there hadn't possessed skill *or* judgment.

Gold and Parson spoke with the three other Afghans who made up the ground detachment. They all gave similar answers. Parson thanked them for their time, apologized for making them recount a traumatic event.

At the end of the day, Parson and Gold walked down the flight line and out of the ramp area. As they walked across the apron, sunset bled across distant mountains. The dying light lent a shade of rose to the snow on the peaks, and Parson thought of all the things he and Gold had endured among mountains like that. Their working relationship had begun when a terrorist's shoulder-fired missile had blown his C-130 Hercules out of the sky. Parson and Gold survived the crash landing, but the ordeal of surviving a winter storm and evading insurgents had left them with scars both visible and unseen.

Parson brought his thoughts back to the current problem. So we have regular Afghan flights into Kyrgyzstan, he noted, and a permanent ground crew here. Nothing necessarily incriminating there. But regular flights? How much cargo would Afghanistan really need to send out of the country?

"So what do you think?" Parson asked.

Gold stopped and looked down at the concrete for a moment. She opened her mouth to speak, but the roar of a KC-135's takeoff drowned her out. As the tanker jet retracted its landing gear and banked to the south, she said, "You touched a nerve somewhere."

"How's that?" Parson said.

"You made his palms sweat."

"How do you know?"

"Did you see the way he was rubbing his hands along his legs?"

Parson tried to recall the interview. Yeah, he remembered that. But so what? "Does that mean anything?" he asked.

"Nothing you could prove in court," Gold said. "But it's a classic sign of somebody getting skittish."

"How do you know this?" Parson said. "You're not a cop." He didn't doubt her; he just wondered how she could have picked up this particular tidbit. Gold knew so many things, and she never stopped surprising him.

"Interpreting for interrogations," Gold said. She looked off into the mountains, paused for a moment. Then she said, "I've heard things you wouldn't believe. I've heard things I wish I hadn't heard. And I've seen things I wish I hadn't seen. But I know when people are hiding something."

A SETBACK, NOTHING MORE. Dušić told his contacts in Central Asia, along with the European customers for his new product, not to panic. We lost some inventory, he conceded, but Afghanistan had no shortage of poppies. Yes, the risk of detection existed now, but according to all reports, the C-27 had burned on impact. Perhaps the flames had consumed all of the product. Neither the Americans nor the Kyrgyz government had said anything about finding contraband. It would look suspicious if Dušić and his contacts changed the schedules of their flights. Better to let operations continue as normal.

Dušić wanted to focus on the real mission; the dirty business of the drug trade only funded that mission, and drugs already took up too much of his time. At least he'd received some good news from his old army friend Stefan: Three veterans of the Volunteer Guard had pledged their support. And those three might help recruit more.

Stefan had also reported progress on technical issues. Dušić wanted to see for himself—and meet the new volunteers—so he took his Aventador over the border into Bosnia. At the checkpoint, his false passport received barely a glance from the idiot border guard. That border never should have been there, in Dušić's estimation. Greater Serbia should encompass the current Bosnia, and ultimately that was the purpose of his mission. He tried not to let his thoughts about the border ruin his day. For the moment, he enjoyed driving his Lamborghini down the winding rural roads. The sports car was designed for such motoring, not the stop-and-go congestion of Belgrade. He crossed bridges over streams running clear except where the water tumbled fast enough to turn white. The trip brought back memories as he sped past rolling green hills.

Dušić's unit served in this region, near Tuzla, early in the war. He remembered one day with particular vividness. As his men cleared a village of Turks, they found four women attractive enough to keep. The platoon gathered them in a house blown open by shelling, and the men waited for Dušić to come in from the field.

That was the protocol: Officers got first pick, and they each got a woman to themselves. The enlisted had to share. Dušić knew the one he wanted immediately—second from the right in the lineup, hands bound in front of her. Shoulder-length black hair and a cotton peasant blouse over large breasts. She kept staring at the floor, so he placed his hand on her chin and forced her to look at him. Very pretty—fair skin, but eyes filled with Turkish hate.

"It is your lucky day, my little whore," he said.

The girl spat in his face. His men hooted.

Dušić slapped her. Then he pulled his sidearm. With one hand, he grabbed her by the hair. With the other, he jammed the pistol barrel against her cheek.

"I bet you like it rough," he said. Dušić pulled her hair harder. He heard his men behind him laughing. "You're going to bear a Serb child," he said, "if I let you live that long."

Then he dragged her into a back room. How that bitch screamed and cried. In the end, Dušić chose not to shoot her. He figured she was worth leaving for the next patrol that came along. One of the other three women did not survive the night with his men. When they left her untied after all the fun was over, the crazy Turk hanged herself. Dušić could still see that purple, bloated face, the tangled hair. He told his platoon not to worry. Just showed how little value these Muslims placed on life.

Scenes like that raid repeated themselves many times for Dušić, but he remembered that one now because it had taken place not far from here. Younger days, better times, when victory seemed so near. He checked his GPS receiver—the handheld kind carried by soldiers, not the road-based type known to motorists. The place he was going had no street address; Stefan had chosen the location for its remoteness. Dušić was getting close. The GPS screen showed the destination at three-point-six kilometers ahead.

He steered the Lamborghini around a tight, tree-lined curve. When the road straightened, the pines gave way to an open field. The far end of the field bordered a small abandoned village. Five houses, roofs long since torn away by mortar fire, rotted under the advance of vines and weeds. The Turks, unfortunately, had managed to repair and reoccupy most of their damaged homes in this area. But for whatever reason, this village, once cleansed, had stayed that way. Maybe no children or heirs had survived to move back in and reclaim the property.

Dušić slowed as he passed the dead village. Stefan should be somewhere near, he noted. The GPS receiver indicated DESTINATION REACHED.

There. Two black SUVs sat idling on a dirt path that led deeper into more fields. Green stalks of corn grew in some of the fields, but part of the land lay fallow, producing nothing but brush and sapling trees.

Mines, Dušić supposed, were the reason these fields remained untended. Farmers wouldn't dare drive a tractor over land where mines might remain. Do-gooders had worked on demining here for years, but they hadn't cleared every field.

Dušić braked, turned off the blacktop and onto the dirt path. Just as Stefan had promised, the path was dry and level—suitable for parking the Aventador. Dušić would take his car no farther; he would ride in Stefan's vehicle from here.

The driver's door on one of the SUVs opened. Stefan stepped out of a Toyota, looked at Dušić, grinned, and stretched his arms wide. Dušić's friend appeared a little older now, the inevitable toll of time and too much slivovitz. More white in that shock of black hair, deeper lines across his forehead. But the green eyes still seemed alert, and Stefan wore no glasses. Maybe he still possessed the keen eyesight of the sniper he had once been. Dušić emerged from the Lamborghini, embraced his war comrade.

"Wealth will ruin you, yet," Stefan said. "Who drives a car like that to a meeting in the woods?"

"Risk has rewards," Dušić said.

"So you can pay our recruits well," Stefan said. "Let me introduce you."

Stefan motioned to the other SUV, and three men got out. Dušić looked them over with the eye of an officer sizing up new personnel. All seemed fit; that was good. No middle-age paunches among them, though he knew they had to be middle-aged if they were old enough to have served in the war. The bald-headed one carried the stocky build of a weight lifter. The scar across his cheek looked more like the result of a knife fight in a bar than a combat wound. The second man wore his hair cropped close. Black leather jacket over a black T-shirt. Maybe trying a little too hard to look tough. Thinner than his bald colleague. The third stranger was dressed much like Dušić: conservative blazer with a starched shirt open at the collar. Long gray hair tied at the back of his head.

"Gentlemen," Stefan said, "this is our paymaster."

Dušić shook hands with the men, noted their names: Andrei, Nikolas, Yvgeny. "I have not met troops in the field for a long time," he said. "I feel like a young man again."

"We will conduct the demonstration farther down the path, away from the road," Stefan said, "for obvious reasons." He told the three men to follow him in their vehicle. "Do not drive past the point where I stop," he added.

Stefan climbed back into his own SUV, and Dušić joined him on the passenger side. A leather rifle case rested on the back seat.

"How well do you know the landowner here?" Dušić asked.

"He is a loyal Serb," Stefan said. "He gave permission for the demonstration, and he asked no questions. I told him nothing he doesn't need to know—only to expect a loud noise. He will not allow the local Turks on his property, so we have privacy for this test." Stefan started the engine and drove down the path. The SUVs rolled by the overgrown, abandoned field on the left, the cornfield on the right. Both fields ended at a line of trees, and the path narrowed as it twisted into the woods. Brambles slapped at Stefan's windshield. The dense shade darkened the afternoon to near twilight.

"What about these three ruffians?" Dušić asked. "How much do they know?"

"Only that they will join a special operation on behalf of their people. One with a difficult but necessary opening shot."

Dušić considered that for a moment. Wise of Stefan to hold his tongue for now. He made an excellent aide. But sooner or later these men would need to know the true nature of their mission. Dušić asked himself whether he should tell them today. Perhaps, but only after a little more observation.

"So did you have difficulty putting the device together?" Dušić asked.

"No, it is actually very simple. I want a live demonstration to make sure my procedures were correct. But this is the same system the towel heads have used for years."

"Very good. We can afford no mistakes when we go operational."

The woods opened up to more fields, these planted in wheat. The land sloped downward for several hundred meters until the woods began again. Stefan stopped his vehicle, and the other SUV parked behind him.

"You will find field glasses in the glove box," Stefan said. Dušić opened the compartment and found a fine set of Leupold binoculars. Stefan always valued good optics, Dušić recalled. Dušić had seen his friend use rifle optics to deadly effect. "Look to the left of the path," Stefan said, "and you will see a metal barrel in the woods."

Dušić raised the binoculars. He rolled a focus knob, and the blurred image clarified into a crisp vision of bark and leaves. He searched for a moment and found the barrel—the common two-hundred-liter drum used by farmers for their pesticides.

"I see it," Dušić said.

Stefan rolled down his window, turned his head back toward the other SUV. "Gentlemen," he called, "I direct your attention to the tree line." He turned forward again, reached into his coat pocket, and withdrew a cell phone. With his thumb, he entered a number. Then he held his thumb poised over the CALL button. "I don't have a strong signal out here, but I think it will work. Are you ready, Viktor?"

"Fire," Dušić said.

Stefan pressed the button. A moment passed in silence as the call went through, bounced through whatever cell towers the signal needed to transit.

The explosion assaulted Dušić's ears as if the boom came from inside his head. He'd almost forgotten the intensity of an ordnance blast up close. Flame and smoke billowed from where the barrel had rested. The shock wave bounced the soil, made dust erupt from the ground. Branches twisted through the air and fell into the fields.

A few meters from the main explosion, another blast threw rocks and clods into the air. A secondary explosion? Oh, yes, Dušić realized. Not part of Stefan's device. The first explosion had triggered an old mine.

Dirt and bits of wood rained down on the SUVs. Something hard clanged off the hood, left a small dent. A fragment of shrapnel, perhaps.

"Damn it," Stefan said.

"Excellent," Dušić said. "And you gave your farmer friend a bit more ground to cultivate safely."

"That was one artillery round," Stefan said. "For the operation, I will wire several rounds in parallel. This will make the explosion much more powerful."

"Very good," Dušić said. He opened his door and stepped out. The air smelled of explosives and freshly turned soil. The three recruits emerged from their vehicle. They seemed properly impressed, but one of them, the blazer-clad man named Yvgeny, looked worried.

"You wish us to set off a bomb like this?" he asked.

"Yes, but do not concern yourself," Dušić said. "I will not ask you to die like some wild-eyed Muslim fanatic. Your task is dangerous, to be sure. But not a suicide mission."

Yvgeny nodded, looked toward the blackened and torn trees. Stefan pulled his rifle case from the back seat.

"I do not get to practice much anymore," Stefan said. "There is no sense wasting a trip out to the country." He uncased a scoped, bolt-action Sako and placed it across the hood. Stefan ducked back into the vehicle and retrieved an empty slivovitz bottle. The sight disappointed Dušić a little. Stefan had too much of a taste for that plum brandy.

The old sniper trotted down the hill toward the blast site, keeping to the field free of mines. He hunted around for something on the ground, picked up three fist-size stones. These he arranged to form a crude base, and on the stones he placed the bottle.

When he returned to his truck, he wiped away some of the dirt that had fallen onto the hood. Stefan hoisted his rifle and racked the bolt to chamber a round.

"What caliber is that?" Dušić asked.

"It is a .308," Stefan said. He leaned on the hood, using the vehicle as a rest. Sighted through the scope, clicked off the safety. Sighted again, exhaled, held his breath. Pressed the trigger.

The crack of the Sako sounded puny after the earlier explosion. But the .308 made a formidable weapon, especially in Stefan's hands. The bottle disintegrated in a spray of shards. So years and drink had not yet robbed him of his skill. Dušić had seen Stefan's rifles and ruthlessness in action many times.

"Very good, my friend," Dušić said.

Stefan opened the bolt, and the empty brass flipped to the ground. He closed the bolt on a fresh cartridge.

All these things made Dušić feel invigorated. To rejoin his war comrade. To see men under his command, testing military skills and equipment. To breathe fresh air in the field. And to look ahead to the greatest mission of his life. He decided to go ahead and brief the recruits.

"We will finish what we began years ago," Dušić said. "We will take this land—all of it—for our people."

The recruits looked puzzled, as Dušić knew they would. One of them, Nikolas, said, "How can we do this with so few?"

"A fine question," Dušić said. "We entice others to join us. Not just the most ardent patriots like yourselves, but all Serbs, even the armed forces of the Belgrade government. After your mission, Greater Serbia will rise up. And this time we will win. The wars in Iraq and Afghanistan have weakened the Americans. The British have made drastic cuts in their military. NATO will not stop us again."

Dušić discussed how NATO and the Americans had imposed the Dayton Accords, which set up a tripartite Bosnian presidency: one Muslim, one Croat, one Serb. A mongrel state with a mongrel government. Hardly better than foreign occupation.

"So what is our mission?" Nikolas asked.

"You will light the spark," Dušić said. "Bear with me as I explain. At first, you may find your task disagreeable. But you will begin a chain of events that will rid us of the Turks forever."

Dušić outlined his plan for a false-flag operation: a bombing that would appear the work of Muslim terrorists. The Serbian Orthodox Church's Holy Assembly of Bishops met twice a year. The next meeting would take place just weeks from now in Belgrade, at the Patriarchate. If a car bomb killed some of the bishops and destroyed the Patriarchate, the attack would ignite a new war in the Balkans. Correct an error of history. Complete the job these men had started as young soldiers.

Stefan would handle the bombing itself. The recruits would rake survivors with automatic-weapons fire while shouting *"Allah-hu akbar!"* Do not worry so much about accuracy, Dušić advised. The shouts carried more importance than the bullets.

The recruits stared at him. None spoke.

"You may love the church," Dušić said. "I understand. But you must understand that though God is eternal, religion is a human institution. A frail, finite construction of man's own making. And the symbols of that religion can serve our ultimate goals."

The recruit named Yvgeny stood trembling. He advanced toward Dušić, shook his finger in Dušić's face.

"This is madness!" Yvgeny shouted. "I thought you wanted us to kill Turks. But you tell us to murder our own clergy?"

Dušić felt a flash of anger rise within him. Who did this impudent ruffian think he was? In the old days, no *razvodnik* would have dared speak to him this way.

"You mind your tongue," Dušić said. "You may take a few days to get your mind around your task. But from here on, there is no turning back. You are now under my command."

"I take no commands from a psychopath," Yvgeny said. "This meeting is over."

Dušić gazed into the distance, stared at the trees. He had known this could happen—to enlist some poor fool unable to see the big picture. Someone whose sentimentality dulled his wits. And someone who, by his lack of vision, posed a security risk. But good officers planned for such contingencies. And so Dušić had.

"You are right," Dušić said.

"What?" Yvgeny asked.

"This meeting is over," Dušić said. "For you."

Dušić drew his CZ 99 from under his coat. Leveled the handgun at Yvgeny's torso. Pulled the trigger.

The blast, the recoil, felt good in Dušić's hand. A hollow-point slug tore into Yvgeny's shoulder, spun him to his left and to the ground. Dušić's pistol skills had grown rusty; his bullet had failed to inflict a fatal wound. Yvgeny lay on his stomach, moaning. Blood pumped from the exit wound, flowed scarlet across the man's torn blazer, and darkened to burgundy when it dripped into the soil. Chips of bone floated in the blood, fragments of the shoulder blade.

Dušić held the sidearm pointed downward at his victim, inhaled the aroma of pistol smoke. Considered whether to administer a coup de grâce to the head. No, he thought, drag this out a little. Create the most vivid impression possible for the remaining *razvodnik*s.

Yvgeny turned over. Smaller entrance wound, Dušić noted, but still messy. The wounded recruit pleaded to his comrades.

"Do not let this man kill me!" he said. "Stop him."

"None of you move," Dušić said, waving his sidearm. "Let this simpleton's fate serve as a lesson to you. I will tolerate no insubordination, no breaches of security."

Yvgeny struggled to his knees, then scrambled to his feet and ran. Dušić fired again. The round hit the man in the arm. Yvgeny screamed and kept running.

"Damn my poor aim," Dušić said. And now the simpleton was getting out of pistol range. Dušić turned to his friend. "Stefan," he said, "if you please."

Stefan shouldered his rifle. Aimed in the offhand position for just a moment. Fired.

Yvgeny's head flew apart in a spray of pink. The corpse dropped into the field. Like Stefan's best work of old, Dušić thought. The target utterly motionless now, dead before the shot's echo ever registered. The two other recruits gaped. Sweat beaded on Andrei's face, though the air felt cool. Nikolas inhaled and exhaled as if each breath required thought and effort. Message received, evidently.

"Find shovels," Dušić ordered. "Bury him."

7

IN THE BASE COMMANDER'S OFFICE, Parson and Gold briefed Webster and the OSI agent on the interviews with the Afghan ground crew. As Parson recounted the discussions, he felt he'd fallen short. The interviews seemed to raise more questions than they answered. But, to Parson's surprise, Cunningham appeared pleased.

"So we want to keep a closer eye on those boys," the OSI agent said.

"Sorry we can't tell you more," Parson said.

"No," Cunningham said, "you guys did good. You might have spooked them if you'd pushed any harder."

Even though Parson had no experience in law enforcement, he understood that concept because he'd hunted all his life. And it occurred to him this was a little like stalking game. You didn't blindly tear through the woods after a deer; the prey would just disappear. Sometimes you had to wait and watch. And that's what Cunningham wanted to do.

"I'd like to think of a way to conduct a little surveillance on that hangar for a while," Cunningham said.

Parson waited to hear the agent's plan, but Cunningham said nothing else. So he was open to suggestions, then.

"Anybody got any ideas?" Webster asked. Parson looked over at Gold. She usually did the creative thinking for him, but she seemed to draw a blank this time.

What they needed, Parson figured, was a deer stand. A way to sit still and observe without being observed. Or at least without being observed with suspicion. Parson turned a few thoughts over in his mind, ways to use the resources at hand. Would Webster and Cunningham just think he was crazy? Well, he'd heard of prosecutors and cops doing some pretty offbeat things to catch bad guys. Couldn't hurt to let them hear what he was thinking. Parson told them his idea.

"Sneaky," Webster said.

"You should have joined OSI," Cunningham said.

Gold just half smiled and shook her head.

First, they needed to borrow one of the KC-135s out there on the flight line, along with a crew. Webster called the 618th Tanker Airlift Control Center at Scott Air Force Base in Illinois. He asked for the director of operations, a full-bird colonel like himself.

"I have an unusual request," Webster said. After a few minutes of explaining, he added, "No, I'm not kidding." Then he said, "Let me let you talk to OSI."

The tone of the conversation seemed to change when Cunningham got on the phone, even though Parson could hear only half the discussion. "No, sir," Cunningham said, "we don't need to actually damage the aircraft." A few seconds later he added, "Thank you, sir." Then he put Webster back on the line.

The base commander worked out the details with the air refueling control team command post. The tankers at Manas had missions scheduled for today. After the crews returned, they would need proper rest. Parson, Webster, Cunningham, and Gold could have a tanker and crew for one day only, first thing tomorrow.

Better than nothing, Parson figured. When one of the Stratotankers landed just after dusk, he and Gold met the crew at their aircraft. Parson introduced himself to the pilot, copilot, and boom operator. The KC-135 also carried a flying crew chief—a mechanic assigned to the aircraft, chief of the ground crew that maintained the jet. To Parson, the Air Force's fliers kept getting younger and younger; all these guys looked about twelve. He remembered the days when he was just like them: fresh out of training, bulletproof, and ready to save the world. All wore slick wings on their name tags. None had enough flying hours to earn the star and wreath that adorned the wings of more experienced aviators. But these kids seemed sharp enough. Their aircraft commander, Hodges, was a captain in his twenties. Hodges chuckled as Parson explained his plan.

"Sounds like an easy day for us," Hodges said. The tanker pilot's flight suit bore the patch of the 171st Air Refueling Wing, Pennsylvania Air National Guard. On his left sleeve, over the pen pockets, he wore an unofficial emblem that read NKAWTG. Parson knew that acronym: *Nobody Kicks Ass Without Tanker Gas*. True enough. He and Gold would not be here now if tankers hadn't come to their rescue once upon a time.

"Should be pretty simple," Parson said. "Nothing you haven't done before."

"Only in the sim," Hodges said.

Parson laughed. "Believe me, my boy," he said. "If you haven't rejected a takeoff yet, you will."

"Just don't burn up my brakes," the crew chief said.

"Don't worry, chief," Hodges said.

"All you guys need to do is make it look good," Parson said.

He understood the crew chief's concern. Back when Parson had first begun flying the C-5 Galaxy, he lined up for takeoff one day at Charleston Air Force Base in South Carolina. Loaded heavily with fuel and with armored vehicles bound for Iraq, the Galaxy needed a lot of runway to take off and a lot of runway to stop. When the tower cleared him for takeoff, Parson advanced the throttles until the N1 tapes met the power-setting marker, and the turbines screamed. At first the big jet hardly moved. Then the tons of thrust began to take effect, and the aircraft rolled at walking speed. The C-5 accelerated, and the airspeed indicators came alive. As the jet neared refusal speed, Parson felt the wings start to pick up some of the weight. Almost ready to fly.

That's when a goose—a great big black-and-white *What the fuck are you doing this far south?* Canada goose—flapped across the runway. And right through the compressor blades of the number two engine. Parson felt the thump, heard the bang.

"Reject," the flight engineer called. "Flameout on two."

Parson ripped the throttles back to idle. "Spoilers," he called.

The copilot yanked the spoiler handle, and Parson pulled the outboard throttles into reverse thrust, stood on the brakes. The jet shuddered as the antiskid system cycled the brake pressure to help prevent blowing tires.

Parson got the Galaxy stopped before the end of the runway, and he'd managed to avoid taking a heavy plane into the air with a dead engine. But safety came at a cost. Objects in motion want to stay in motion, especially objects that big. When the brake rotors met the stators, all that speed, power, and weight got translated into friction. And heat.

"Reach Six-Two-Four," the tower called, "your wheel wells are smoking."

"Roll the trucks," the copilot said.

By the time Parson taxied off the runway, flames billowed from the brakes and tires. He shut down the aircraft, and he and his crew evacuated. Standing on the taxiway near the yellow hold-short lines, Parson watched the fire department hose down the wheel wells. The investigation that followed found no fault with Parson's procedures, but the incident reminded him how quickly an aircraft could get into trouble.

PARSON, GOLD, AND CUNNINGHAM met the KC-135 crew just as sunrise pinked the eastern horizon over Manas. The morning glow lit the scattered cumulus, giving the clouds the appearance of burning islands drifting overhead. When the blue Air Force van stopped in front of the Stratotanker, the crew chief emerged first. A generator cart sat beside the aircraft, its electrical cord still plugged into a receptacle near the 135's nose. The crew chief pressed a start button on the generator, and the diesel engine belched black smoke, clattered to life. After the generator accelerated and settled into a steady hum, the crew chief flipped a toggle switch, and a green contactor light came on. Good ground power available for the airplane.

Parson enjoyed watching these guys conduct the familiar ritual of waking up a cold jet. He'd performed the same tasks thousands of times, but not lately. Command responsibilities, most recently his assignment as a safety officer, had kept him out of the cockpit more than he preferred. He'd always known that would happen. If a pilot stayed in the Air Force long enough, there came a time to put away childish flying and focus on management. Part of him wanted to gather these young men around him and say, *Enjoy this time. Watch one another's back, serve your country well, and savor this part of your lives. It will pass far too quickly.*

Instead, he simply watched them unlock the crew entry door, extend the ladder, and climb aboard their aircraft. Parson followed them inside, and Gold and Cunningham came up behind him. Cunningham wore ABUs today, the standard Air Force camo, with the stripes of a tech sergeant.

The cockpit looked a little unfamiliar. Parson had never flown a Boeing product, and the panels were laid out differently from the Lockheed birds he knew so well. This aircraft dated from the Kennedy administration, old enough that all the crew stations had built-in ashtrays. Parson tried to stay out of the crew's way as they examined maintenance forms, powered up electrical systems, and ran through their preflight checklists. When they finished the preflight inspection, they let Parson take the cockpit jump seat. Gold and Cunningham sat in the back. Parson plugged in his headset just as the copilot made a radio call for a flight clearance.

"Cleared to destination as filed," the Kyrgyz controller said. "Climb and maintain ten thousand feet. Expect flight level two-niner-zero ten minutes after departure."

On the interphone, Hodges said, "Something tells me we ain't gonna make it."

The copilot smiled, took a sip of coffee from a foam cup.

"You guys *are* making it look good," Parson said. "Where are we going?"

"Istanbul," Hodges said.

"Always wanted to see Istanbul," Parson said.

"Engine start checklist," Hodges called.

The copilot put his coffee in a cup holder and picked up his checklist binder. Parson listened to the challenge-and-response rhythm of the checklist procedures, watched Hodges place switches on the panel in front of him to the GROUND START position. One by one, the pilot moved start levers on the center control stand, and four CFM56 turbofans roared to life. A tailwind pushed exhaust fumes in front of the intakes, and the odor remained in the bleed air that flowed through the air-conditioning system. The smell of a day's work beginning.

The boom operator locked down the crew entrance door, and the Stratotanker lumbered off Juliet Ramp and down Taxiway Alpha. Near the end of the runway, the copilot called for takeoff clearance.

"Clear for takeoff, Runway Zero-Eight," the controller answered.

Hodges steered onto the runway, advanced the throttles. The CFMs spooled up from a whine to a howl, and the aircraft began to accelerate. Parson peered around the copilot's shoulder to watch the airspeed indicator. As the instrument scrolled past eighty knots, the copilot said, "Reject."

With one smooth motion, Hodges pulled the power back to idle. Then he took hold of the speed brake lever beside the throttles. Hodges deployed the speed brakes to sixty degrees, and Parson felt himself pushed against his shoulder straps as the jet slowed down.

"Oh, my goodness," Parson said. "You boys got an emergency. Ain't that awful?"

"I'm terrified," Hodges said.

"Me, too," the copilot said. "Don't spill my coffee." Then the copilot pressed his transmit switch and said, "Sunoco Two-Eight aborting takeoff."

The tower controller gave the tanker crew a few seconds to stop their jet. When the aircraft turned off the runway, the controller said, "Sunoco Two-Eight, state the nature of your emergency."

"Ah, we have a hydraulic leak," the copilot transmitted.

"Lying sack of shit," Parson said on interphone.

"You should hear him on the satphone to his girlfriends," Hodges said.

"Do you require assistance?" the tower asked.

"Let's have the trucks stand by for us on the taxiway," the co-pilot transmitted.

Parson smiled, pressed his interphone switch, and said, "And the Academy Award goes to the crew of Sunoco Two-Eight."

"I'd like to thank my agent," the copilot said.

"And I told myself I wasn't gonna cry," Hodges said. Then the pilot turned serious, twisted in his seat to face Parson. "All right, sir," he said, "where do you want us to stop?"

Parson unbuckled and rose to look out the flight deck windows. "Shut it down close to that aerial port hangar, but don't block access," he said. "Make sure your tail clears the taxiway intersection. I want those guys in there to conduct business as usual."

Two crash trucks rolled out of the fire department garage. The vehicles drove more slowly than when they'd responded to the C-27 accident; this time they appeared only as a precaution. The trucks stopped near the Stratotanker's nose. Parson considered his next moves; the trickiest part of his charade would happen now.

"Tell ground control you're doing an emergency egress," Parson said. "When you get outside, tell the fire chief you had a hydraulic leak on the takeoff roll, but you didn't overheat the brakes." It helped that the trucks had come out, but now Parson wanted them to go away.

Hodges made the radio call as Parson ordered, and the crew shut down the engines. When Hodges reached for the battery switch, Parson said, "Hold on." Then, while he still had electrical power, Parson asked, "Crew chief, are you on headset?"

"Yes, sir," came the answer from the back.

"Cool," Parson said. "When you get out there, as soon as nobody's looking, I want you to dump hydraulic fluid all over one of the landing gear struts."

"Uh, yes, sir."

"See you outside."

Hodges flipped the switch, and the jet went dark. After the pilot, copilot, and boom operator climbed down the ladder, Parson followed them, headset around his neck, cord dangling at his waist. He looked up to see Gold and Cunningham coming behind him. The crew chief picked up two quarts of hydraulic fluid and a tool bag.

Once on the ground, the crew chief opened his tool bag and took out a sharp-pointed can opener, the kind mechanics called a church key. With the church key, the crew chief punched holes in the fluid cans, looked around. Hodges was talking to the firefighters, gesturing with his arms. The firefighters stood around their vehicles, the tops of their silver suits unzipped. One spoke into a handheld radio, and they remounted the trucks and drove back to the fire station.

Parson nodded to the crew chief, who walked over to the wheel well and poured both cans of hydraulic fluid over a strut assembly. The red liquid oozed across the concrete from underneath the aircraft. The scene put Parson in mind of a harpooned whale.

"What a mess," Parson said. "Might just take all day to fix this."

"Might," the crew chief said.

"Can't even tow the aircraft."

"Oh, no, sir. That might damage something."

Cunningham walked around the Stratotanker as if he were inspecting it. As he stepped past Parson, he smiled faintly and shook his head. The OSI agent reached into the crew chief's tool bag and took out a wrench. Found a dry spot between the landing gear struts. Then he put his hand into a cargo pocket and withdrew a camera.

8

GOLD SAT WITH PARSON on the ramp underneath the wing of the KC-135. Cunningham watched from the landing gear. Every now and then the OSI agent would pick up his wrench, pretend to work on something, wipe his hands with a rag. Just to make things look right, the crew chief opened a laptop computer and made a show of checking maintenance manuals. He also scattered tools around his computer: a Phillips screwdriver, a speed wrench, and a set of socket wrenches. The rest of the Stratotanker crew went to the chow hall.

"What if the Afghans recognize us?" Gold asked.

"Doesn't matter," Parson said. "They know I'm the safety officer. I'm supposed to be out here if somebody has an emergency and rejects a takeoff."

"What about me?"

"They know you work with the safety officer."

"Fair enough," Gold said. "So we're hiding in plain sight."

"That's kind of how a deer stand works."

Sounded like the Parson she had always known. A hunter at heart. An alpha wolf, ready to inflict violence when called for, but only to feed or protect his pack. And if Parson considered you part of his pack, he'd do anything for you. Gold had seen him prove that more than once. But he probably wouldn't like the wolf analogy, Gold thought. She and Parson had fought off starving wolves while downed in Afghanistan during a winter storm. Not one of her better memories.

For two hours, nothing of note took place on the ramp or in the Afghans' open hangar. Inside the hangar, a man swept the floor, then smoked a cigarette. As Gold watched, she felt a stitch of pain in her ribs. The bullet wound from her last mission. Afghanistan had left its mark on her. But the mission that had nearly killed her worked to heal her in some ways. She and Parson had helped rescue kids from a Taliban splinter group that used child soldiers. A mission worth her life. And one that made her feel her efforts had not been in vain. In a way, her physical agony eased some of her mental torments. More than a fair trade, in her view.

While they waited for something to happen, they used the time to continue catching up. Gold appreciated that Parson asked about Fatima, an Afghan girl they'd found orphaned. After Gold was shot, Parson had picked up where she'd left off and used information she'd gathered to find a good orphanage for Fatima and her brother, Mohammed. Though Gold and Parson had never been intimate, she thought of Fatima almost as their daughter.

"When's the last time you saw her?" Parson asked.

"About a month ago. She's reading so well now. She even tutors her brother." As part of Gold's work with the UN, she had toured schools and orphanages throughout Afghanistan. Fatima and Mohammed lived in one of the better facilities.

"I'm glad she's learning," Parson said, "but there are people in Afghanistan who won't like that."

Gold knew all too well what Parson meant. The Taliban opposed any education for girls. Terrorists blew up schools, threw acid in girls' faces, murdered teachers. In Pakistan, the Taliban had shot a teenage girl who had campaigned for girls' education. Gold offered a silent prayer for Malala Yousafzai, who survived the bullet wounds to her head and neck.

The growl of turboprops interrupted Gold's thoughts. She looked up, shielded her eyes with her hand. Parson had told her the distinct sound of a turboprop came not from its turbine engines but from the propellers spun by the turbines. A pure jet made more of a whistling noise.

And there came the plane, a C-27 Spartan approaching through a clear sky. The aircraft banked to the left.

"Hey, Cunningham," Parson whispered. "We're gonna have company in a minute. A C-27 just turned downwind."

"I see it," Cunningham said.

Gold took a pair of foam earplugs from her pocket; she knew the noise of the Spartan's engines would grow painfully loud when the aircraft taxied into parking. She twisted the earplugs, inserted them into her ears, and she watched Parson do the same thing. As the foam untwisted and expanded, her world grew quieter.

After a few minutes, the Spartan's wheels barked onto the runway. Puffs of blue tire smoke erupted where the C-27 touched down. The aircraft rolled toward the far end of the runway, and three Afghan ground crewmen strolled from the hangar and onto the ramp. One carried a pair of yellow wooden chocks, each with a three-foot length of rope attached. The men looked at the Stratotanker, gestured and spoke among themselves. Gold removed one of her earplugs for a moment so she could hear better. The Afghans pointed at the tanker jet, and one of them said in Pashto, "He will have room to get by the wings."

"Are they worried about us?" Parson asked.

"No," Gold said. "They're talking about wingtip clearance."

Parson nodded, apparently satisfied his plan was working. The C-27 rolled along the taxiway now, growing larger and louder. Gold replaced the earplug, and she smelled the exhaust whipped by propeller blast. The aircraft lumbered past the Stratotanker, and Gold noted the green, black, and red roundel of the Afghan Air Force. Through the cockpit windows she saw the pilots—one clean-shaven and one bearded—both wearing headsets and brown flight suits.

The C-27 made a right turn into the parking apron, and the move placed the exhaust and prop wash directly over Gold and Parson. The hot wind burned her eyes and tousled her hair, and the fumes of burning jet fuel stung her nostrils. She and Parson retreated to the other side of the tanker. After a minute or two, the Spartan's engines finally hushed, and the acrid gale subsided. Parson walked under the tanker's tail, feigned interest in the KC-135's boom assembly. From there, he gained a better vantage point to watch the ramp. Still hidden by the wheels, Cunningham began snapping photos.

The ground crew unloaded three pallets. Gold noticed nothing unusual, and Parson and Cunningham didn't seem to, either. She saw that Parson stayed away from the KC-135's gear struts to avoid drawing attention to Cunningham's hiding spot.

Gold joined Parson in the shade of the tail. She faced the runway, her back to the C-27, and whispered, "See anything suspicious?"

"Not really," Parson said, "other than that they're here at all. Can't think of any legitimate reason for them to ship out this much stuff."

"So what do we do now?"

"That's really up to Cunningham and the OSI. But I imagine they'll be more interested in who takes that stuff out than who brought it in."

"Where's Colonel Webster today?" Gold asked. "He might have enjoyed our little jaunt down the runway."

"He would have," Parson said. "But I think he's doing the lawyer thing. Checking manifests or something."

The Afghans left the C-27 unattended for more than an hour. Gold supposed the fliers and ground crewmen had gone to lunch. When they returned, one of the pilots walked around his airplane. He examined the underside of the wings, opened panels along the fuselage and then closed them, checked tires.

"What's he doing?" Gold asked.

"Through-flight inspection," Parson whispered. "We advisers and instructors all used to harp on good procedures. Maybe he listened."

The pilot climbed aboard, followed by the other two crew members. A few minutes later the auxiliary power unit howled up to speed, and one of the propellers began to turn. As the second engine started, Parson retreated to the far side of the Stratotanker. Gold followed him, sat beside him near the crew chief, who continued reading manuals on his computer. Probably not just acting, Gold guessed, but using the time to study. Warm wind from the C-27's props flowed around and under the KC-135, and Gold felt the smoky breeze on her cheek.

The engine noise made conversation difficult, so Gold and Parson did not speak. But Parson met her eyes, nodded, patted her back. She took his hand, closed her fist around two of his fingers shortened by frostbite years ago. Funny how we can communicate, Gold thought, even when we can't talk.

She released his hand, and he looked away from her. Parson unzipped a pocket, pulled out a datebook, and opened it. Back to business as usual. As he worked, Gold noticed his scars. When he pushed up his flight suit sleeve, the effort revealed a mark left by a terrorist's sword, of all things.

The Spartan taxied out of the parking apron. Its wings rocked with each dip in the pavement. The aircraft rolled down the taxiway, turned onto the runway, took off. Banked to the south and eventually vanished.

"The Poppy Express rides again," Parson muttered.

"Maybe," Gold said. "Hey—you're going to have a long day out here. Why don't I go get some food for you guys?"

"Thanks," Parson said. "That's a good idea. When you come back, just call my cell, and I'll escort you back onto the flight line."

Gold crossed the parking apron, hoped the Afghans would not see her. No big deal if they did, she imagined. They'd just think she was running an errand for the boss. But she preferred not to call attention to Parson's aeronautical deer stand. She made it to the flight line's entry and exit control point, waved to the security police as she walked through the opening in a chain-link fence topped with coils of razor wire.

In the chow hall, she found Webster finishing a late lunch. Across the table from him, she put down her bowl of potato soup, cracked open a can of Diet Coke. Ripped a cellophane packet that contained a napkin and a plastic knife, fork, and spoon.

"So how's the deer hunt going?" Webster asked.

"Good, sir," Gold said. "Or at least I think so."

"I saw we had a C-27 come in from Afghanistan."

"Yes, sir. They just left."

Gold took a spoonful of the soup. A little too salty, but better than eating MREs in the field. A group of soldiers, about twenty, entered the chow hall. Gold watched them as they signed in and took their plastic trays. Junior enlisted, mainly. Their camo bore a striped patch on the sleeves—the insignia of the Third Infantry

Division out of Fort Stewart, Georgia. Each soldier carried an M4 carbine with the magazine removed. As they shuffled along the serving line, they slid open glass refrigerator doors to pick up apples, prepackaged salads, boxes of Parmalat milk.

From their faded and worn fatigues, from their tired smiles, Gold surmised they were on the way home from Afghanistan and not the other way around. She knew well what they might have seen and done. These troops would return to their communities aged beyond their years. No one, not even their spouses or parents, would ever truly understand what they had gone through. Most of their old high school classmates experienced war merely as reality TV, an interruption to computer games and online shopping, with no personal stakes, no hard decisions, no consequences, no responsibilities.

Webster's voice brought Gold back to more immediate problems. "I checked some shipping records," he said, voice low. "Most of what those C-27s bring here goes on to Belgrade. I just called Cunningham to let him know."

"Belgrade?" Gold said. "Not what I would have expected."

She didn't know what she would have expected, but she hadn't thought the capital of Serbia served as a big transshipment point for opium. Dealers, she supposed, would ship anywhere and any way that made them money.

"Belgrade surprised me, too," Webster said. "They have some organized crime, but the State Department rates Serbia as only a medium-crime-threat country."

"Have you ever been there?" Gold asked.

Webster sipped his Mountain Dew, gave a wry smile. "Kinda," he said. He explained how he'd flown a tanker back in 1999 during the Kosovo air campaign. When ethnic Albanians in Kosovo tried to gain independence from what remained of Yugoslavia, a war ignited between Kosovo rebels and the Serbian military. NATO feared a genocidal campaign similar to what had happened in Bosnia, and the alliance launched air strikes. Webster refueled stealth fighters and other attack aircraft that hit targets all over Kosovo and Serbia, including Belgrade.

"I've heard Lieutenant Colonel Parson talk about that," Gold said. "He flew in Bosnia and Kosovo, too."

"We thought we were salty old veterans after that thing ended," Webster said. "Of course, we had no idea what was coming."

Gold made no comment, just looked around her at the veterans of the post-9/11 world. Most of these troops would have been children when Webster and Parson flew over the Balkans. She finished her soup, thanked Webster for letting her join him. Then she made her way down the chow line again, built roast beef sandwiches for Parson, Cunningham, and the crew chief. As she gathered packets of mustard, a jet landed outside. Sounded like a big one.

Carrying a paper bag of sandwiches, chips, and soft drinks, Gold pushed open the chow hall door, squinted against the sunlight. She called Parson from her cell phone when she arrived at the flight line's entry control point. He asked her to wait a few minutes. An Antonov had just taxied into parking. Parson shouted over the scream of its engines. In the distance, Gold could see the wings of the Russian aircraft looming across the tarmac, dwarfing everything else on the ramp.

PARSON HOPED THAT HE and Cunningham looked like maintenance guys taking a break as they ate their sandwiches underneath the KC-135. They saw Afghan ground crewmen load several pallets into the Antonov's cargo bay. As the ground crew worked, a man in civilian clothing stood outside the aircraft.

"Can you just roll those guys up right now?" Parson asked.

"I'm not sure we have enough to make an arrest," Cunningham. "They could claim they had no idea about the smuggling. We might not have the authority to arrest, either."

"How's that?"

Cunningham explained how Kyrgyz officials had the final say. If an American airman got caught trafficking drugs, the USAF security police or OSI could arrest him, no problem. But it got sticky with third-country nationals. What was America's status of forces agreement with Kyrgyzstan and Afghanistan? Who had jurisdiction? You could clap the cuffs on somebody at the wrong time, blow the whole operation, and watch the suspects walk.

"I'm not even sure this is our case anymore," Cunningham added.

"Why's that?"

"OSI's mission is to deal with threats to the Air Force and the U.S. government," Cunningham said. "Anything else is off my radar." Cunningham's brogue twisted "radar" into "rador." He explained that sticking to the main mission fit right in with what his elders had taught him as he grew up on North Carolina's Outer Banks. You defended your island, and you protected your town and your family. But the world beyond the breakers could tend to itself.

As he spoke, the OSI agent kept eyeing the man by the Antonov.

"Your boss feels differently, though," Cunningham added.

"Why's he so interested?"

"I don't know, exactly. But when he learned this thing had a Belgrade connection, his ears perked up."

The man in civvies hovered over the ground crew like a supervisor. Parson could think of no legitimate reason for a civilian to keep such close watch on Afghan military cargo. The guy pulled out his cell phone, dialed a number, and spoke for several minutes. Parson strained to listen amid the noise of aircraft coming and going. Sometimes the man's words got drowned out, and Parson could hear nothing. What little he did hear sounded like Russian at first. He understood none of it. But then he heard one word that he recognized: *poručnik.*

Many years ago, in a very different world with very different threats, he'd attended intel briefings on the Serbian military. Among other things, he'd learned the ranks. In Serbo-Croatian, a *poručnik* was a lieutenant. He told Cunningham what he'd heard.

"Oh, boy," Cunningham said. "If this is Serbian military

running drugs—or maybe some gang of ex-military types—that's damned dangerous."

Cell Phone Guy finally ended his call. The man looked European, and Parson guessed Serbo-Croatian was his native language. He certainly wasn't an Afghan.

Near the end of the day, the Afghans closed the doors to their hangar. Parson called the KC-135 crew to tell them they could move their jet. He felt he was climbing down from a deer stand, having bagged important information. When Parson and Cunningham left the flight line, Cunningham headed in the direction of Webster's office. The OSI agent disappeared for the rest of the afternoon.

Parson found Gold in the coffee shop, and he quietly told her about the out-of-place civilian he and Cunningham had seen. Gold sipped an espresso, and she'd clearly made friends with the resident cat. The Green Beans mascot lay in her lap, purred as she stroked its back. On the wall behind Gold's chair, Parson noticed the coffee shop's main decor feature: propaganda posters from the Soviet era. One showed a cosmonaut staring into the future, chiseled face shielded by a helmet visor. Red star on the side of the helmet. Another depicted a Young Pioneer wearing the red neck scarf of the Soviet youth group. In one hand the boy held a Mosin-Nagant bolt-action rifle. In the other he displayed a paper target with five holes punched in and around the bull's-eye. If I had grown up here, Parson admitted to himself, I would have wanted to be that boy, and later that man.

"Webster will want to know about those phone calls, especially if there's some kind of military connection," Gold said, "I suspect he'll be talking to the NSA."

"What about?"

"Well, the National Security Agency handles signals intelligence," Gold said.

"Ah," Parson said, "like cell phone signals." He raised his eyebrows, turned the thought over in his mind for a moment. "So they can listen to our boy out there."

"If they get approval."

Parson didn't know much about cryptology. As an airlifter, his contact with the intelligence world consisted mainly of background data like the ranks he'd just recalled, and pre-mission briefings before going out to fly:

Bad guys have mortared airfields here, shot at airplanes there. Foreign agents like to hang out in bars where you're going, so watch what you say. These guys in this village have given up their weapons. These guys in that other village have said, "No, I like my AK-47, and I like to shoot it. At you."

Good luck. Please file a report when you get back.

He had once taken a War College course that mentioned NSA capabilities. He couldn't remember all the details, but he did recall the NSA seal: an eagle clutching a key in its talons. For unlocking secrets.

Until Webster and those above him decided how to proceed from here, Parson found nothing to do except wrap up his safety investigation. The lab reports had come back; Parson had printed them out and stuck them in a lower leg pocket of his flight suit. The reports were unclassified, so he didn't need to study them in a secure facility. Parson unfolded his papers and perused them while Gold petted the cat to sleep.

Nothing unexpected in the autopsies. The crewmen had died of blunt force trauma and smoke inhalation. The C-27's flight data recorder offered no surprises, either. At the moment of impact, both engines showed max fuel flow and redline torque. Oil pressures and temperatures, hydraulic quantities and pressures, all within limits. Flight control surfaces and trim settings where they should have been. When the glass faces of gauges smacked against instrument needles, the positions of those needles reflected the expected values. In other words, not a damned thing wrong with the airplane. Just lousy airmanship, as Parson had suspected all along. He folded the lab reports and, in disgust, jammed them back into his zippered pocket. The open zipper scraped his hand, and that pissed him off.

Gold looked up from her book. "What's wrong?" she asked.

"Nothing," Parson said. "Just the data analysis on that stupid-ass crash." He rubbed at the scratch across his knuckles. The zipper had cut deep enough to make the capillaries bleed.

Parson needed something to change his mood, so he got up and ordered a cup of coffee. The barista, a dark-eyed Kyrgyz woman who spoke fluent but accented English, brought him his usual: dark roast, black, no shot of anything. He also bought a slice of carrot cake.

When he returned to his seat, the cat had moved from Gold's lap to the table and appeared to have gone back to sleep. Parson broke the cake slice in two, handed half to Gold. A dollop of icing stuck to his frostbite-shortened middle finger. He wiped the icing onto a napkin, slid the napkin under the cat's nose. The animal woke up and licked away the icing. Gold laughed, rare for her.

"I bet that's how he got so big," she said.

Two aviators from the United Kingdom entered the coffee shop. Parson knew their nationality from the style of their flight suits and the design of their wings. Both wore the chevrons of RAF flight sergeants. The cat leaped from the table and ran to the Brits.

"There goes our protocol officer," Parson said.

One of the flight sergeants picked up the animal and said, "Hello, mate."

Behind the RAF crewmen, Webster and Cunningham came through the door. Parson waved, and the two pulled up chairs and joined him and Gold.

"Anything new?" Webster asked.

"I was about to ask you that," Parson said.

"You first."

"Well, the lab reports confirmed what we already knew. Dumb son of a bitch flew a perfectly good aircraft into a microburst and didn't have the power to get out of the downdraft."

"A jet fighter might not have had enough power to recover from that downdraft."

"I know it. And our Captain Careless should have known it, too."

"Damned shame."

"So what have you two been so Secret Squirrel about today?" Parson asked.

"Can't talk about it here," Webster said, "but I think they're sending me some help."

"Really?" Parson said. He started to ask what kind of help. But before he could even begin the sentence, Webster shook his head. The commander apparently would not discuss it in public, even in the vaguest terms. Cunningham changed the subject.

"How long have you been flying?" he asked.

Parson explained how he'd begun his career as a C-130 navigator back in the '90s, then cross-trained to pilot and flown C-5s. He left out a lot of what came in between. Gold said nothing, only met his eyes and gave that half smile of hers.

"My grandfather was a pilot," Cunningham said.

"Air Force?" Parson asked.

"Civil Air Patrol."

The Air Force's civilian auxiliary. They wore Air Force–style uniforms and flew light airplanes for stateside emergency services such as search and rescue. The CAP also ran cadet programs to educate kids about aerospace.

"Good program," Parson said. "Did your granddad work with young folks?"

"Actually, no."

Then Cunningham described a corner of military history Parson never knew. Most people believe World War II combat never touched American shores, the OSI agent explained. But it did, quite literally. During the long-running Battle of the Atlantic, German U-boats targeted Allied shipping. Partly due to the course of the Gulf Stream, shipping lanes ran close to the Outer Banks of North Carolina. Perfect hunting grounds for the Kriegsmarine, where sub commanders could silhouette freighters and tankers against the lights of shore. Punch off torpedoes and vanish into the depths.

Cunningham said his grandfather recalled seeing fires burning offshore at night. Not just a distant glow but towering flames fed by diesel or crude, flickering as the stricken vessel flooded, heeled over, hissed and groaned through its descent to the continental shelf. By day, oil, life jackets, even corpses, would wash up onto the sand. CAP pilots patrolled from the air, reporting any sightings of the German wolf pack. In a move unimaginable today, the military even gave live ordnance to a civilian auxiliary, and the CAP destroyed or damaged at least two subs by itself. All for defending home turf, as his granddad had put it.

"After the war," Cunningham said, "my grandfather joined the North Carolina Highway Patrol, and he flew helicopters for them. That sort of led me into law enforcement."

Webster raised his eyebrows, apparently impressed. So was Parson. A lot of people told a story about how family history brought them into their careers, but few told a story like that. Family had also influenced Parson's career. His father had flown as an Air Force navigator, too. Not on big transports, but as a backseater in

fighter jets. The elder Parson died in the first Gulf War, in the crash
of his F-4G Wild Weasel. Never got to see his boy wearing wings.

Parson spent the next two days writing his report on the C-27
accident. He interviewed three more witnesses, just for the sake of
completeness. But their statements presented nothing new. He
typed the report into his computer and showed it to Gold. She
moved around a few paragraphs, took out some unnecessary com-
mas, and shortened some of his sentences. After Parson handed the
report to Webster, the colonel complimented him on his writing.
They sent the document to the Air Force Safety Center, to U.S.
Central Command, and to the Afghan Air Force.

That afternoon, Parson got to see what Webster meant by extra
help. Reinforcements came in a form Parson never expected: an
RC-135 Rivet Joint bird landed at Manas. Parson had heard of
Rivet Joints, but he'd never seen one of the Air Force signals intelligence planes up close. A four-engine jet that looked a lot like the
old Boeing 707, the aircraft flew as part of the 55th Wing, based at
Offutt Air Force Base, Nebraska. Antennas studded the underbelly
and the top of the fuselage. When the crew climbed down from the
aircraft, they needed a bus to get them off the flight line: two pilots,
a navigator, and twenty-five other crew members. Parson knew
some of them were electronic warfare officers and intel types, but
he had no idea what the rest of them did.

Webster and Cunningham briefed the crew in the air operations center. Parson didn't understand all the details of this unfamiliar mission, but he got the gist: Fly around in circles and find
out what all this has to do with a Serbian lieutenant.

After the meeting, Parson and Gold struck up a conversation
with one of the crew members. The young woman looked about
twenty. Her name tag bore the wings of an enlisted flier. Beneath
the wings, lettering read AIC IRENA MARKOVICH. An airman first
class, one of the lowest ranks in the Air Force. Airman Markovich

had just begun her career. Trim and in good condition, with a cold-cream complexion and deep-black eyes. Hair so black it shone, even tied up in a bun. Parson found her so attractive, he had to force himself not to stare.

"So what's your crew position?" Gold asked Irena.

"I'm an airborne cryptologic linguist," Irena said.

"What language?" Parson asked.

"Serbo-Croatian, sir."

"So you must have just graduated from the Defense Language Institute," Gold said.

"Actually, ma'am," Irena said, "I didn't have to take the course. My folks speak Serbo-Croatian at home, and I placed out when I took the proficiency tests."

"Wow," Gold said. "So you must have grown up completely bilingual."

"Yes, ma'am."

"Call me Sophia."

Seldom had Parson seen Gold so impressed. Apparently, it was a big deal to place out of DLI.

"Where are you from?" Parson asked.

"I was born in Sarajevo, but I grew up in Seattle." Irena spoke English with no accent that Parson could detect.

"What brought your parents to Seattle?" Parson asked.

"The war," Irena said. "I don't remember it, but the fighting destroyed our house. Our whole Serb neighborhood got wiped out."

Parson feared he'd put his foot in his mouth, but the young woman did not seem offended. Still, her answer left him puzzled. She might not remember the Bosnian War, but he sure as hell did. He'd flown his first combat missions in that bloodbath, mainly taking relief supplies to Muslims under attack from Serbs. The Bosnian Serb Army had carried out a genocidal campaign, and he'd always felt frustrated that the international community hadn't done more to stop those bastards sooner. But evidently there were innocent Serb victims, too. The proof stood right here in front of him.

The Bosnian War had never completely ended for Parson. Other conflicts, the events of 9/11, the wars in Afghanistan and Iraq, had consumed him for more than a decade. But the impact of his first battle experiences, in a war now obscure to many people, left permanent marks.

He never forgot the way his youthful belief in an ever-advancing humanity crashed and burned in the Balkan hills. For the second time in the twentieth century, concentration camps appeared in Europe—and politicians split hairs about how the numbers didn't compare. As long as six million hadn't died, it wasn't genocide. So killing a hundred thousand was okay. Well, maybe not okay, but stopping it would be . . . complicated.

Nowadays, he knew, a shaky peace held in Bosnia and other breakaway Yugoslav regions such as Kosovo. Intelligence agencies, peacekeeping forces, and Interpol still hunted war criminals from the 1990s. International observers kept an eye on things and hoped to prevent the match strike that would reignite the war. Parson guessed that was why Rivet Joints still carried Serbo-Croatian speakers like Irena.

But how had Webster talked someone into sending the jet to Manas? Parson harbored no sympathy for drug traffickers; he'd just as soon shoot every one. However, to employ this kind of hardware against a run-of-the-mill opium ring made him wonder. Used needles in the gutters of Stockholm or Chicago told of wasted lives, but they did not threaten anybody's national security. Maybe somebody suspected this thing could get far worse than a few more dead addicts.

STRATEGIC COMMUNICATION. Information operations.
Getting the message across.

Throughout history, Dušić knew, the best military minds
understood these concepts. Sun Tzu, Clausewitz, and Napoleon
may not have used those terms, but they certainly grasped the
ideas. So did Dušić. In a better world, he believed, his intellect
might have propelled him to the office of defense minister by now.
But the meddling and interference of lesser cultures had steered his
nation, and thus his own life, in directions unintended.

No matter. He had the brilliance, and now the means, to correct all that. So he turned his thoughts toward ways to maximize
the effectiveness of his opening mission. An apparent Muslim
attack on the Patriarchate would ignite public opinion, most certainly. But Dušić would get only one shot at this. When his car
bomb ripped apart the holy site, he wanted all Serbs as ready for
war with the Turks as he was. A leader must communicate, and a

communicator must prepare his audience. By the time Stefan and the rest of Dušić's team destroyed the Patriarchate, Serbs would view it as the latest and most extreme outrage in a series of provocations.

Sun Tzu, Dušić recalled, said all war is deception.

On a mission of deception, Dušić rode in the passenger side of Stefan's SUV. Darkness had settled on the countryside, and the Toyota's headlights pierced an empty road and dense forest outside Tuzla. Andrei and Nikolas rode in the back.

Stefan slowed and turned right onto a path of crushed macadam barely wide enough for his vehicle. The path snaked through the trees, led uphill into an open field atop a knoll. A cemetery appeared out of the gloom, crumbling crucifixes of stone. Some of the monuments had stood for so long that rain and snow had worn the Serbian Cyrillic lettering down to indecipherable grooves and scallops.

Beyond the graveyard, an Orthodox church appeared. From the looks of it, the church was a one- or two-room affair that might have served a rural community for centuries. Nothing like the cathedrals of Belgrade. On this evening, no one attended but the nighthawks. And Dušić's team.

"We shall burn for this," Nikolas whispered.

"Quiet!" Andrei hissed.

Dušić smiled to himself. Andrei, at least, had gotten the message about who was in charge. He elected not to threaten Nikolas now, not even to upbraid him. If Nikolas felt that way about the church, perhaps he could eventually understand the larger plan.

Faith had never played much of a role in Dušić's life. As a Yugoslav cadet, the state became his religion. Communism fell, but the state remained, infested by traitors who had converted to the creed of the invaders centuries ago. Dušić despised the Turks more from his gut than from his soul. But he knew most Serbs loved their

Orthodox traditions. For Dušić, then, religion existed as part of the battle space, a factor in the combat environment. A commander must know and utilize the human terrain.

Stefan stopped the Toyota, turned off its engine and lights. With no particular effort to stay quiet, Dušić opened his door and stepped out. The nearest houses lay three miles away, a tiny farming village. Even if someone heard noise, they'd probably think the priest had come to meditate or study.

Clouds scudded overhead, briefly revealing a thin, glowing crescent, the moon a cold shaving of itself. The symbol of the Muslims. The sight filled him with hate, strengthened his resolve like reloading a weapon.

Andrei and Nikolas emerged from the SUV, opened the back. Each man lifted a jerry can. Stefan took a can of spray paint from his glove box. The ball bearing rattled inside the can as Stefan shook the paint.

Dušić would not normally oversee a task so menial. Right now, the job felt more like a prank than a strategic move. A chore for *razvodnik*s, led by a junior NCO. But he wanted to observe Andrei and Nikolas before trusting them with greater responsibilities. If they failed to carry out this simple mission—well, Dušić wore his CZ 99 under his coat. But he did not expect to fire the pistol again. Dušić employed violence the way a painter worked with a brush: just the right strokes, made more powerful by judicious use. He had already established his point well enough.

At least he harbored no worries about Stefan. Dušić's old friend had proved his worth many times, and Stefan was something of an artist himself. One of his kills—a pair of kills, actually—became the stuff of legend during the Bosnian War.

Back in '93, with the siege of Sarajevo well under way, Dušić's unit occupied a position overlooking the Vrbanja Bridge. Stefan and other marksmen performed such fine work trapping the Turks within the city that the route the shooters guarded became known as Sniper Alley.

But on the afternoon of May 19, word came down that a cease-fire would take place, just for a few minutes. Some foolishness about a Serb and Muslim couple, Sarajevo's Romeo and Juliet, who wanted to escape the terrible fighting and cross the bridge to a life of wedded bliss. Perhaps they expected to float through Sniper Alley on a blanket of love, accompanied by flocks of doves and butterflies. Raise their mongrel children in Paris or Los Angeles.

The very idea made Dušić want to vomit. He had received no order to check fire, not from Mladić or anyone on the general's staff. Maybe another lieutenant, someone with no more authority than Dušić, yielding to sentimentality, had issued a command beyond his rank. To Dušić, then, not an order at all. More like a request. A stupid one, at that.

Some of the soldiers, however, apparently intended to play along with this maudlin drama. The firefight raging around the remains of the Union Invest building seemed to simmer down. The cackle of automatic weapons faded to sporadic bursts, then stopped altogether. Dušić kneeled beside Stefan in a hide site screened by dead tendrils of English ivy.

A young man appeared on the street near the foot of the bridge. He carried a knapsack. The man stopped, turned, spoke words to someone Dušić could not see. A woman caught up with him, and she also carried a knapsack.

"Shall I let them pass?" Stefan asked.

Dušić rolled his eyes, gave no order one way or the other. But he smiled when Stefan placed his cheek to his Mauser.

On the street below, Romeo took Juliet's hand for a moment, released it. Then he walked onto the bridge. Strode with his knapsack like some worthless tourist hiker who has spotted a youth hostel in the distance.

Stefan let him take only a few steps.

In the next moment, Dušić saw everything: The minute tilt of the barrel as Stefan aimed. The pigeon that glided over the bridge. The glint of sunlight off Romeo's watch. The flex of tendons in the back of Stefan's hand as he pressed the trigger.

The Mauser's report rolled across the ruined city in waves. Smoke curled from the muzzle, and more smoke wisped from the breech when Stefan racked the bolt and chambered another round. Romeo lay in a motionless heap.

The woman screamed and ran toward him. *The stupid bitch actually ran toward him.* What did she think would happen? Stefan fired again, dropped Juliet just a few meters from her dead lover.

Stefan raised his head from the rifle and scope, surveyed his handiwork. Reached for his bottle, unscrewed the cap, took a drink. Offered the bottle to Dušić.

Dušić raised the bottle to his lips, tasted the burn of slivovitz. Much like cognac, but with a sharper edge. He didn't normally drink with the enlisted, not even Stefan, but he made an exception this time. As he handed the bottle back to his sniper, he looked down to the bridge. Juliet was not dead.

Stefan had aimed lower, hit her somewhere in the torso. Lying on her back, the Muslim whore bled like a pig at slaughter. Forearms slicked with blood, she took her hands from her abdomen, rolled onto her side, then onto her stomach. Juliet pushed herself up with the heels of her hands, crawled. By centimeters, she dragged herself to Romeo. Embraced him there on the bridge.

She clung to life for perhaps fifteen minutes. It took that long for the spasms to stop, and when they did, Dušić knew she was dead. She clung to her lover for days. Sniper Alley remained impassable for the better part of a week. Eventually the command staff called Dušić's unit elsewhere, and someone cleared away the bodies.

Pure genius on Stefan's part, Dušić thought. The rifle barrel spoke as a poet's pen, an impressionist's brush. With two strokes, two words, Stefan had transformed a cheap romance story into an epic of nations. A message to Serbs: *Do not consort with the enemy.* A message to Turks: *Die.*

As Dušić recalled the event, he thought of an untitled poem by Radovan Karadžić. The poem ended with these lines:

> *And two lovers*
> *Shall stand by the first casket on hand*
> *And kiss each other as I command*

What a damnable travesty that the author of such words languished now in a cell in The Hague.

Dušić could not change the past. But he could alter the future by his command, and so he set his team to tonight's task.

"Keep your kerosene off the church steps," Dušić ordered. He wanted the steps untouched, for there Stefan would leave a message.

Andrei and Nikolas crept to the stone walls of the church, the dark outline of its bell tower backdropped by moonlit clouds. They worked by the green glow of penlights compatible with night-vision goggles. The men did not need NVGs for this mission, but Dušić supposed the green light would draw less notice from a distance than white light. As an arms dealer, he kept apprised of technology, and his troops, even the *razvodnik*s, would have the best.

Nikolas wrapped a cloth around the head of a ball-peen hammer. He swung the hammer against a windowpane. The warped glass shattered, though the cloth muffled the impact. Andrei lifted his jerry can and poured the liquid through the hole in the window.

The church's structure consisted mainly of stone, probably dug from the surrounding hillsides when kings ruled Europe, and men traveled by sail. But the roof, and of course the pews, chairs, and icons, were made of lumber and fabric. Fire could bring this building to the holiest purpose it had ever served.

The *razvodnik*s made their way around the church, breaking each window, pouring in kerosene. At the front steps, Stefan sprayed a few words, simple as a phrase of poetry. The verse would serve its purpose, but Dušić knew Stefan could never top his 1993 masterpiece.

At the last window, Nikolas dumped all that remained in his jerry can. He went to the Toyota and came back with a bucket of oily rags. Nikolas and Andrei picked up rags, shook them out. But then they hesitated, stood as if unsure what to do next.

Dušić knew when to use violence or threats. He decided now was not one of those times. Understanding, or at least the appearance of understanding, could serve as a tool as well. He had seen this kind of reluctance before, and he'd dealt with it swiftly and firmly. And since then, he had honed his leadership skills even further.

"Go ahead, men," he said. "I share your mixed feelings. But you are about to make history."

"Sir," Andrei said, "are you sure?"

Good. "Sir" was very good. A trainable recruit.

"Torch it," Dušić said.

Andrei stepped over to a broken window, took a cigarette lighter from his pocket. Flicked the lighter once. Sparks spat from the roller, vanished. Andrei tried again, and a yellow flame guttered and danced in his fist. He touched the fire to the rag, and flames spread along the wrinkles of the cloth. Just before the fire reached his fingers, he tossed the rag through a shattered pane.

For a second or two, Dušić thought the flame had gone out. But yellow and orange light began to dance and refract from inside the church, mirrored in cracked glass. Nikolas lit a rag, tossed it through another window.

Dušić recalled an American expression from the Vietnam era: *Destroy the village to save it.* Poetic, for Americans. A concise statement of a regrettable military necessity.

The *razvodnik*s lit more rags, pitched them through the windows. The flames inside the church began to join, spreading along the run of spilled kerosene and leaping up walls to drapes and icons. Smoke rolled through some of the windows.

"Fine work," Dušić said. "Time to go."

The team headed for the Toyota. Their commander held back for a just a moment. By the light of rising flames, Dušić read Stefan's words painted on the church steps:

Death to infidels.

11

GOLD HAD NEVER SEEN ANYTHING like the inside of that Rivet Joint aircraft. And she never would have, either, had she not maintained her top secret clearance. The jet sat connected to external power on the military ramp at Manas. The Rivet Joint's interior consisted of a long row of crew stations: seats where linguists and other operators could listen on headsets and monitor banks of computers and electronic equipment. A maze of wiring connected all the components. Interphone cords and oxygen hoses hung like vines in an electrical jungle. The air-conditioning system and cooling fans gave off an industrial hum, and the whole place smelled like a new television.

Someone had left a flight jacket draped over the back of a crew seat. A sleeve patch displayed the shield of the 55th Wing, with its motto: *Videmus Omnia.* Gold knew the Latin. *We See All.*

Irena showed Gold the work stations, along with the bunk and galley at the back of the aircraft. Not nearly as roomy as Parson's C-5 Galaxy, Gold noted, but comfortable enough for long missions. She felt a little strange wearing civilian jeans inside a sophisticated spy plane. Irena, with her flight line badge clipped to her flight suit, had escorted Gold to the aircraft.

"My goodness," Gold said, "I could have joined the Air Force and spent the war sitting in one of these things, drinking coffee with you."

"Never too late," Irena said.

As much as the airborne linguist job intrigued Gold, she would not have traded places with Irena. True, she could have served in relative comfort, listening through those ubiquitous David Clark headsets the Air Force issued. A clean uniform every day, a clean lavatory just steps from her seat. Plenty of sandwiches from the fridge. Long hours, no doubt, but above the fray. That assignment would have spared Gold a lot of toil and misery, and a tremendous amount of pain.

But she never would have known Afghanistan as she knew it now. She never would have come to love some of its people as she did now. And she never would have met Parson.

The clomping of boots coming up the crew entrance interrupted her thoughts. Parson appeared at the front of the line of work stations. Webster, Cunningham, and one of the Rivet Joint pilots climbed up behind him.

"Damn," Parson said, "look at all this." Gold supposed he, too, had never seen the inside of this type of aircraft.

"Good morning, sirs," Irena said.

Irena and the pilot explained the layout of the plane in more detail. In addition to stations for linguists, other crew stations seated electronic warfare officers and in-flight maintenance technicians.

"They'll fly a sortie this afternoon," Webster said.

"Wish I could go with them," Parson said.

"Me, too," Webster said.

The pilot appeared to think for a moment. "I could ask," he said. "It would be out of the ordinary, but so is this mission. Do you have TS clearances?"

"Yep," Webster said.

"Oh, yes," Parson said. He pointed to Gold. "Sophia, too."

"Is she a civilian?" the pilot asked.

"Not entirely," Parson said. He described her Army background and her reserve status.

"I can't promise," the pilot said, "but I'll call the ops desk at Offutt and ask."

To Gold's surprise, the request got approved. The pilot must have emphasized the role of Webster and his team in the investigation, to establish their need to know whatever intel the Rivet Joint picked up. True enough. Webster knew how to use evidence, and Parson understood the logistics of shipping things by air, especially from Afghanistan. And the whole thing had started with an accident on their turf. Perhaps it made sense to keep them in the loop. Gold got included as their ad hoc aide.

After lunch, Gold strapped herself into an unused work station beside Irena and put on a headset. Webster sat at Irena's other side, and Parson took a jump seat in the Rivet Joint's cockpit. Gold had eaten only a salad; she anticipated a little queasiness in the windowless cabin, especially if the air turned rough. But after the jet powered through turbulence near the ground, it climbed into smooth levels of the atmosphere. With no way for Gold to see outside, only the rush of the slipstream gave any hint of movement.

Irena opened some sort of checklist, adjusted volume settings on her comm box and on Gold's. Parson, naturally, wanted to follow the pilot stuff on the flight deck. But to Gold, the real action took place back here with the language specialists. Webster apparently thought so, too. He leaned to watch Irena's fingers tapping a keyboard, adjusting knobs on receivers.

The plane seemed to level off. Gold saw nothing that indicated altitude, but the engines quieted as if the pilots had eased the throttles back to a cruise setting. Then one of the officers, presumably a mission commander seated somewhere forward of Irena, called, "Oxygen check."

Irena pulled a quick-don mask over her head, adjusted the mask. Her crewmates took turns checking in on interphone. Eventually, Irena pressed her talk switch and said, "Markovich up on oxygen."

"Good check," the commander called. "Discontinue."

Irena removed the mask, then adjusted the boom mike of her headset. A drill for the primary crew members, Gold realized. In the event of a rapid decompression, they wanted to make sure everybody's oxygen and comm systems worked.

"You guys got here quicker than I expected," Webster said. "Did you come all the way from Nebraska?"

"No, sir," Irena said. "We were in Europe, supporting KFOR."

Gold remembered that acronym: Kosovo Force, NATO's peacekeeping contingent in Kosovo. Serbia had never recognized Kosovo's secession, and the UN administered Kosovo as an autonomous region. Border skirmishes had broken out on occasion between Kosovo and Serbia, and tensions there remained high while most of the world focused on Afghanistan and Iraq.

"Yeah," Webster said, "I imagine Kosovo's still a sore subject for a lot of people."

"Yes, sir," Irena said. Then she pressed her talk switch and said, "Markovich going off headset for a minute."

Another crew member said, "Copy that, Irena. We'll listen for you."

Irena took off her headset and went to the galley. She came back with cups of coffee for Webster and Gold.

"Thanks," Gold said. She took the foam cup, sipped. Not as good as Green Beans, but it would do.

Irena donned her headset, buckled back into her seat, and said, "Markovich back up."

"Rog, Irena," came the answer. "Nobody wants to talk to us so far."

Static crackled on the channel as Gold listened in. She heard snatches of what she assumed was Kyrgyz, along with some Russian. Clicks, pops, then a hiss at a higher tone. The Rivet Joint crew was apparently adjusting receivers, scanning circuits—a vastly different world from the life Gold had known as an Army linguist. She caught a conversation in Pashto. Someone said, "I will return in three days. I must take my goats to market." Gold liked the sound of that. Somebody was having a peaceful afternoon, attending to matters of commerce. The rest of the conversation got cut off as the receiver switched to something else. Goats did not interest the Rivet Joint crew today.

Another language came through the static. Like Russian, but somewhat different. The syllables rose and faded as the signal strength wavered. Gold understood none of it, but Irena sat up straight, harness straps tight across her shoulders. She stared down at her keyboard, and it became clear she was listening closely. With her right hand, a pen angled between her fingers, she pressed two buttons on her console. When the voice stopped, she said to Gold and Webster, "That's Serbo-Croatian."

"What did he say?" Gold asked.

Irena smiled. " 'The food here is awful,' " she said. "He's just chitchatting, but we'll try to locate the call anyway."

"You can do that?"

"Sometimes."

"Man," Webster said, "this whole week is turning into a blast from my past."

"How's that, sir?" Gold asked.

"Last time I heard that language, I was in The Hague. Part of my work on the civilian side."

"What did you do there?" Gold asked.

"I helped prosecute Slobodan Milošević. But before the trial could end, he entered a plea of dead."

Irena looked at her console as if she were staring at something far beyond the airplane. She sat silently for several minutes, jotted on a notepad, tweaked a volume knob. Finally she said, "He didn't speak for all Serbs. Never did."

"I'm sure he didn't," Webster said.

Irena's eyes narrowed. She appeared to wrestle with emotions she could hardly express.

Gold could imagine Irena's mixed feelings on the subject. To come from a proud and rich heritage, and to have that culture associated in the media with war criminals. To hear your parents tell of losing their home in a war they didn't start. And to know that those who did start the war, in large measure, were politicians with the same ancestors as yours.

Bosnia and Kosovo were not part of Gold's area of expertise. But she'd read enough to know a bit of the history and how that history informed the present. This aircrew had just come from monitoring communications over Kosovo, a place of powerful symbolism for Serbs. In 1389, an Ottoman army defeated a Serb prince in Kosovo at the Field of Blackbirds, opening the way for centuries of Muslim domination. Gold pondered about how something that had happened more than six hundred years ago helped drive events today, helped determine the makeup of the crew of this surveillance jet. The thought reminded her of William Faulkner and his line about how the past is not even past.

"What was Milošević like?" Gold asked.

"Arrogant," Webster said. "He said he didn't recognize the court's authority, and he kept refusing to enter a plea."

"He died in his cell, didn't he?" Gold asked.

"Yes," Webster said. "That was—let me think—2006. Milošević wouldn't even talk to his lawyers. He was defending himself at trial. You know the old saying about that, Airman Markovich?"

"No, sir," Irena said.

"If you represent yourself, you have a fool for a client."

Irena smiled politely, but Gold could tell the Serbian-American linguist didn't consider any of this history a laughing matter. The receivers and interphone fell silent, and for a time Gold heard only the baritone of the engines. The aircraft banked slightly, then rolled out of the turn.

Irena made adjustments on her console, jotted figures onto a form on a clipboard. New voices wafted through the circuits. Gold heard what sounded like a radio broadcast in Russian, and more cell phone conversations in Kyrgyz. Then the Serbo-Croatian voice came back. Irena turned up the volume, pressed a button.

"Is that the same phone?" she asked on interphone.

"I think so," a crewmate answered. "I know it's coming off the same cell tower."

Irena scribbled on her notepad as she listened. Gold could not read the notes; her young colleague wrote in Cyrillic. The phone call went on for several minutes. One voice sounded commanding, the other supplicating.

"You got a position?" Irena asked a crewmate.

"Affirmative."

When the call ended, Irena pressed another button, reviewed her notes.

"Did you guys pick up something good?" Webster asked.

"Maybe," Irena said. "I never heard a name or a location, but they were definitely talking about supplies of something."

"What did they say?"

"The boss wants more. The other guy doesn't know if he can do it." Irena ran her finger down the notepad. "Boss says, 'You better find a way.' Other guy says, 'We're having trouble replacing the drivers we just lost.'"

"Whoa. Did you record it?" Webster asked.

"Yes, sir."

"Did they sound like they were Serbian military?"

"The guy called his boss 'Lieutenant,' but the boss said he wasn't a lieutenant anymore."

"And did I hear you guys say you had a position marked?"

"We do," Irena said.

"Where?"

"I'll ask." Irena spoke on interphone with her crewmates and wrote down a set of coordinates. Webster leaned in to look at the numbers.

"Hmm," he said. "I think that's kind of familiar. Airman Markovich, good work. Can you put me on interphone with the front-enders?"

"Yes, sir." Irena flipped a switch on Webster's comm box, and on hers and Gold's. "You're on with the pilots, Colonel."

Webster listened for a moment, then pressed his talk switch and said, "Hey, Parson. You up on headset?"

"Sure am," Parson answered. "That you, Terry?"

"Yeah. You got an extra set of approach plates up there?"

"Lemme check." Parson's voice went off line for a few seconds, and when he came back he said, "Got 'em right here. What do you need?"

"Can you bring me the plates for Manas?"

"Yes, sir. I'll be right there."

Irena pulled her boom mike away from her lips, leaned toward Gold, and whispered off interphone, "Does he always call full-bird colonels by their first names?"

Gold smiled, whispered, "Sometimes. Don't pick up his bad habits."

After a few minutes, Parson made his way aft to Webster's seat. He carried a booklet of navigational charts; aviators used so many different formats and sizes of charts that Gold couldn't keep track of them. Parson leafed through the booklet, stopped on a page, and handed the booklet to Webster. The two men conferred off headset, and Webster cross-referenced with Irena's notes. He raised his eyebrows and gave a thumbs-up to Parson, who took back the charts and returned to the flight deck. Webster pressed his interphone switch and said, "That call came from Manas."

So the trafficking operation still went on, Gold concluded. And Belgrade wasn't just a transshipment point. Apparently, that's where the orders came from. Gold watched Irena continue to work, monitoring circuits and tweaking knobs. Irena wasn't smiling, but she looked content. Gold remembered that feeling: I got this. I know what I'm doing. She saw a lot of her younger self in Irena.

"Do you think you'll make a career of this?" Gold asked.

"If they'll let me, ma'am."

"Oh, I'm sure they'll let you. Even if they stop needing Serbo-Croatian, they can send you to school for another language."

"That would be cool," Irena said. She turned to look at Gold when she spoke. Gold took that as a sign of genuine excitement at the prospect of learning something new. A valuable trait for anyone in the military, Gold considered, but especially for a linguist. Sure, you had to stay fit and tough for a career in the service. But in this job, you needed intellectual curiosity just as much. Your education never ended.

"So, if you could pick another language to learn, what would it be?" Gold asked.

"Ooh, I don't know. Russian seems logical. But maybe I'd take something completely different, like Chinese or Arabic."

"The military will always need all of those languages." To Gold, Irena seemed so professional—so squared away, as they said in the Army—she could practically write her own orders for her future in the military.

With more of her career behind her than in front of her, Gold took satisfaction in seeing the next generation come along. She had spent decades as a warrior, though one who used her mind more than her weapons. Irena would do the same. The long line continued.

12

FROM MILES AWAY, Dušić could see a column of smoke rising above the hills along the Drina River. The wail of sirens split the morning. With Stefan in the passenger seat, Dušić steered his Lamborghini on a recon mission. Thus far, he liked what he'd seen, what he'd read in the newspapers, and what he'd heard on broadcast reports.

His *razvodnik*s had torched three Orthodox churches in eastern Bosnia. After that, two mosques burned to the ground. Then another church burned. Best of all, Dušić's men had nothing to do with the last three cases of arson. His strategic communications plan had succeeded beyond his hopes. New tensions between Serbs and Muslims were escalating into a cycle of violence and reprisals, and the trouble began to feed on itself without further action from Dušić's team. The situation made him think of those American-made "fire-and-forget" self-guiding missiles. Just launch the thing and watch it go.

As he neared the town of Zvornik, not far from Tuzla, Dušić found a full-scale riot in progress. In a square close to the fire—Dušić could not yet see what was burning—officers in helmets, bearing shields and swinging batons, battled with young men. From a road about a hundred meters uphill from the fight, Dušić braked to watch. Lettering across the backs of the officers' uniforms read POLICIJA.

One of the police raised the barrel of a launcher, fired a canister into the crowd of at least two hundred people. White smoke billowed, and when the wind caught it, Dušić felt the sting of tear gas through the open windows of his car. His eyes watered so much that for a moment he could not see to drive. He closed the windows, turned on the air-conditioning, and drove onto a side street. The gas hurt, but he smiled as he reached for a handkerchief, blew his nose, and wiped his eyes.

"You must be the first man in history happy to get tear gassed," Stefan said, dabbing at his own eyes.

"I expected our plan to work," Dušić said, "but I did not think things would spread so quickly."

"The tinder remained dry," Stefan said.

"Speaking of tinder, I want to see what is burning up there."

"We might as well move," Stefan said. "We sparked that riot, but we do not need to get caught up in it."

Dušić wiped his eyes once more, pulled out of the side street. When he rounded a curve, the fire came into view, and Dušić found it a beautiful sight. A mosque burned like fury. A single fire truck shot an arc of water into the flames, but it was too late. The whole structure looked a total loss. Flames encircled a minaret, and in Dušić's professional estimation someone must have poured some type of accelerant down the top of the spire.

"Look at that," Stefan said.

"That must have been a new mosque."

During the war, Dušić recalled, all the mosques in this town had been burned or dynamited. The paramilitaries—the Yellow Wasps, the White Eagles, and Arkan's Tigers—had done some of their best work here. They killed four thousand Turks and drove the rest away. For a few shining years, this land became pure. But then a few Turks trickled back in, unfortunately. At least enough to build a damned mosque. Well, they needn't have troubled themselves.

Dušić had conducted no operations in Zvornik back in the 1990s, but he remembered well another mission not far from here. The Bosnian Serb Army had forced United Nations observers to surrender and leave the area, and most Muslim resistance in that sector had been crushed. Trucks and buses began carrying away Turk women and small children. Some of the younger women got sent to special interrogation centers, often at abandoned hotels, and Serb troops visited those centers for entertainment. The Muslim women did not wear hijabs or burkas like their Arab kin; they dressed in blouses, slacks, and skirts like other Europeans. But that did not fool Dušić; he knew they all bowed toward Mecca, and that was where they belonged.

The Muslim men presented another problem. If allowed to go free, they could take up arms. Orders about how to solve that problem had come down to Dušić and other junior officers. The job would require decisiveness, firmness of mind: qualities lacking in Western Europe and America, those self-indulgent cultures with no sense of blood and history. Dušić directed his men to gather some of the male Turk prisoners in a bullet-scarred house where General Mladić was expected to visit.

When the general arrived, Dušić stood straight as the great man entered the room. At that moment, Dušić thought of Mladić's inspiring orders to his officers when the siege of Sarajevo began: "Shell them into madness." The general wore camouflage fatigues. He removed his commander's cap with the gold braid across the bill.

Perhaps thirty Muslims sat on the floor. They ranged in age from about twelve to seventy, all men and boys. All wore soiled shirts and wrinkled slacks, probably not changed in days. Just like the women Dušić had seen earlier, these males dressed like any Yugoslavs of their class—no dishdashas or turbans like their towel-head cousins—but again, Dušić wasn't fooled. Mladić addressed the prisoners.

"Hello, neighbors," Mladić said. "Do you know who I am?"

Some of the Turks said yes, some nodded, and some remained silent. Dušić found it infuriating that these filth could address this man without bolting to attention, without starting each sentence with "sir." Mladić unwrapped two morsels of chocolate, handed them to the youngest two prisoners. Dušić liked that bit with the candy. Let them hold on to a shred of hope.

"If you did not know me before," the general continued, "now you see me. And now you see what your illicit government has done to you: abandoned you. The United Nations cannot protect you. NATO can do nothing. We are not afraid of anyone."

The Turks fell silent. The odor of their sweat filled the room, and the smell disgusted Dušić. He found it hard not to smirk as Mladić spoke truth to these traitors. Dušić admired the man even more when he considered how the general continued serving his people after such an awful personal loss. The year before, Mladić's daughter had been found dead of a gunshot wound. Western propaganda mills reported that she had taken her own life after reading foreign news reports of how her father savaged Sarajevo. But Dušić had no doubt the beautiful young woman had been murdered by Muslims. Some called Mladić crazy with grief. But Dušić felt grief merely focused Mladić, made him stronger.

The general turned to Dušić and said, "Carry on." Then he strode from the house, boots clomping. Dušić took his mentor's actions as a great compliment: no further instructions, no guidance, no admonitions. Mladić trusted him to complete his own small part in the orders of the day.

At nightfall, Dušić rounded up a few of his young *razvodnik*s. He ordered them to tie the prisoners' hands and march the Turks onto a waiting bus. Stefan and the other sergeants would have handled this task better than the *razvodnik*s. Dušić had even recommended Stefan for a battlefield commission. But Stefan and the rest of the NCOs were supervising similar tasks at nearby sites. Officers and sergeants were spread thin that night because so much had to get done, and quickly. That left Dušić with his newest, dumbest troops. No matter. The *razvodnik*s would not need to use their minds, only their trigger fingers.

As the bound prisoners filed onto the bus, some of them began to murmur questions and protests. This insolence would not do. Dušić drew his CZ 99. Pointed the pistol at arm's length. Fired over the heads of the Turks. They flinched at the blast.

"Silence!" Dušić shouted. "All your questions will find answers soon enough."

On the bus, the three *razvodnik*s guarded the prisoners. The privates held their Zastava rifles, seemed unsure what to do next. Dušić pointed to one of them.

"You," he said, "drive the bus. Follow my truck."

"Yes, Lieutenant," the boy said.

Dušić stomped from the bus, took his seat on the passenger side of the army truck. His driver waited behind the wheel.

"To the field," Dušić ordered.

After the truck rolled through a few miles of dark turns and twists, bright lights shone up ahead. As the truck drew nearer, Dušić saw the lights were the lamps of a backhoe. The backhoe idled at the end of a twenty-meter ditch.

Dušić opened his door, swung himself down from the truck as the bus pulled up behind it. Fresh mud clogged the treads of his boots. He walked around to the back of the truck and retrieved a cardboard box filled with rags. He dropped the box in front of the bus. When the door of the bus levered open, he called to the three soldiers inside.

"Line them up," Dušić said. "Blindfold them."

The *razvodnik*s peered outside the bus windows, looked at each other as if they did not understand. Dušić had not briefed them on tonight's operation for fear of a security breach. But now their task should have become obvious.

Morons. Minds filled with teenage mush, the products of idle hours spent listening to Madonna or, God forbid, those American Negro rappers.

"Now!" Dušić shouted.

The soldiers hefted their weapons, issued instructions in tones that sounded more like requests than orders. Still, the Turks rose, shuffled down the steps and onto the wet ground. When they saw the blindfolds and the ditch, some began to moan and cry out.

One of them turned to Dušić and said, "What wrong have we done to you?"

Who did this impudent Muslim think he was? In a flash of anger, Dušić pulled his handgun. Swung it like throwing a round-house punch. Smacked the barrel against the Turk's face. In the glare of headlamps, the man dropped.

"Get up," Dušić said. Dušić kicked the man until he staggered to his feet, blood streaming from his nose.

In a few minutes, all the Turks stood blindfolded at the edge of the ditch. All remained silent. Dušić gave another order to the *razvodnik*s.

"Are you waiting for Saint Sava's Day?" Dušić said. "Fire!"

A trembling private stared as if he didn't understand Serbo-Croatian. "Sir," he said, voice quavering, "is this proper?" The other troops looked at Dušić and the private. Blank expressions all around.

Weaklings. Sentimental fools. When Stefan and I were laying waste to Sarajevo, Dušić thought, these pups were playing computer games and watching television. Had their parents not taught them what Muslims were like?

Dušić snatched the Zastava from the boy's hands. Snapped the fire selector to *J*, for *jedinacna*. Single rounds, semiautomatic. Pointed it one-handed at the back of the first Turk's head. Squeezed the trigger.

Booming report of the rifle. Glimmer of tumbling brass. Spray of blood and bone. The Muslim collapsed into the ditch. Burned gunpowder salted the air.

Dušić shoved the rifle back into the *razvodnik*'s arms with enough force to push the soldier back two steps.

"You fire this weapon," Dušić hissed through gritted teeth, "or I will put you in the line with them."

The privates raised their Zastavas. Flame spat from the muzzles. Bodies tumbled into the ditch like sacks of laundry. Echoes of the shots reverberated through the night. In the stark glare and shadows thrown by headlights, a few limbs wriggled in the mud. Rifle smoke drifted across the enclave of Srebrenica.

PARSON FIGURED THE INVESTIGATION could go in one of two ways. Agents could trace the opium supply backward and target corrupt Afghan military personnel. Or agents could trace deliveries forward to Belgrade and find out who was selling the narcotics in Europe. When higher-ups chose the latter, Parson felt disappointed at first. He'd invested a lot of himself in creating the new Afghan Air Force, and he wanted nothing more than to get his hands around the neck of anyone who betrayed the oath of enlistment by smuggling that garbage. But he had to admit it made sense to go after bigger fish. Irena and her crewmates had picked up intel that established pretty firmly that the boss operated from Belgrade—or at least someplace where people spoke Serbo-Croatian.

The surprise came when Webster asked if Parson and Gold could help in the probe, wherever it led. At a meeting in the base commander's office, Webster presented the idea as an extension of Parson's duties as safety officer. Gold and Cunningham sat with Parson as Webster described what he wanted.

"Your crash analysis opened this whole can of worms," Webster said. "Cunningham can use someone who knows air logistics. And if the bad guys are talking to people in Afghanistan, I can probably use a Pashto speaker, too, if Ms. Gold is up for it."

Why the hell not? Parson thought. Might as well see this thing through to the end. If another serious accident happened at Manas, God forbid, he could always go back and deal with it. But more than likely, nothing would happen on his watch any more important than the problem before him now.

"Well," Parson said, "I could sit around here telling people not to run with scissors, or I could go help catch this son of a bitch screwing around with the air force I helped build."

"I hoped you'd see it that way," Webster said.

"What about you, Sophia?" Parson asked. He hoped she'd agree to stay with the investigation; he wanted to spend more time with her.

"I'll help if I can," Gold said. "But my civilian status might limit what I can do."

"Ah, I took the liberty of making some calls," Webster said. "If you'd like—and it's entirely up to you—the Army will put you on orders as an individual augmentee for as long as you want."

Gold raised her eyebrows. Then she said, "All right; I'll do it. But I don't have any uniforms with me."

"You won't need them," Cunningham said. "Civilian clothes for this op."

For Parson, that was unusual but not unheard-of. He'd once flown a C-130 into Bangkok on a peacetime relief mission. In a concession to Thai sensitivities, the crew was ordered to wear civvies—not just when on the ground, but while *flying*. One of Parson's weirdest memories involved operating a military aircraft while wearing jeans and tennis shoes. He didn't know who they'd fooled, though. The airplane still had U.S. AIR FORCE painted on the side in three-foot letters. But perhaps wearing civvies made the diplomats happy.

"So where are we going?" Parson asked.

"Sarajevo," Cunningham said.

"Some folks way above my pay grade have been talking to the Serbian government," Webster said. "The Serbs plan to help, but they don't want the Rivet Joint landing in Belgrade."

Probably had something to do with NATO planes bombing targets in Belgrade several years ago, Parson thought. Didn't matter. The surveillance jet could take off from Sarajevo, in Bosnia, and listen to comms all over the Balkans.

After the meeting broke up, Webster motioned for Parson to stay. The commander closed his office door.

"There's another reason I want you and Gold to go with Cunningham to Europe," Webster said.

"What's that?" Parson asked.

"Some of the folks at OSI want to hand this off to Interpol and be done with it. In a lot of ways that makes sense. But given the part of the world this is coming from, I'd like us to stay with it, especially if it involves a bunch of ex-military types."

"The good old FRY," Parson said. "Former Republic of Yugoslavia."

"Nothing in that place is ever simple. This could turn into a lot more than dope peddling. So I want you and Gold to make Cunningham understand why this is important. If he stays on task, maybe OSI will stay on task. You know what happened in Bosnia and Kosovo; you flew there. But Cunningham's not old enough to remember."

Parson knew all too well the things that had happened there, and he wished he *didn't* remember some of it. But how to get Cunningham to understand? He'd have to think on that one.

On their last night at Manas, Parson and Gold had dinner together in the chow hall. Gold teased him that he should call the dining facility by its more correct term: DFAC, pronounced "dee-fak."

"The military's getting way too PC for me," Parson said.

"Yet you're still hanging in there."

She had a point. The Air Force had been Parson's life. He'd devoted himself single-mindedly to his career for two decades. He had enough years to retire and move on to something else, but he could not picture himself as a civilian.

"Yeah," Parson said, "sometimes I think my glory days are behind me. I just don't know what should come next. Looks like you have a pretty good plan, though."

"We'll see if I do. On some days I miss that sense of purpose I had in the Army. I need to spend more time in the new job before I get it all figured out."

"And here I've just roped you into coming back on active duty for a little while. I thought this would give you only a short break. I hope it's not causing too much trouble to leave the civilian job for this long."

"Well, there's never a good time to leave it. And I hate to leave my friends in Afghanistan, but I know I'll have to leave them sooner or later. We're drawing down."

"You do what you can, where you can, when you can. Then you gotta let go."

Peering over her paper cup of iced tea, Gold rolled her eyes at him. He knew what she meant. Both of them had trouble letting go. Both had an instinct to try to fix the world in their different ways. And, Parson thought, both of us should know better by now.

Yet here we are, on the wrong side of the globe from home, because we have the stones to think we can make a difference.

"You know," Gold said, "when you're young and you want to do good, somebody will tell you what to do. Go learn a language. Go learn to fly. But when you get older, you have to find your own path with a lot less help."

"Ain't that the truth," Parson said. Not for the first time, Sophia had found the words to express what he was thinking. He didn't know what should come next in his life. But he wanted to do something helpful. And he wanted her to be part of it.

The next day, Parson sat again in the jump seat of the Rivet Joint as the aircraft thundered off the runway at Manas. The mountains dropped away and dissolved into the haze below. Gold and Cunningham rode in the back with Irena. Up front, Parson sipped coffee and watched the pilots and navigator work, and he monitored their chatter on interphone and radios. He felt like a crew dog again, and he could almost imagine himself waiting to take his turn at the control yoke or the nav console. For the most part, however, those days were behind him. This wasn't his jet, and he didn't know its systems and procedures.

But he did know the sucker had plenty of power. He could see that from the healthy climb rate registered on the vertical speed indicators. After several minutes, the Rivet Joint leveled at thirty-four thousand feet, and the pilots throttled back to a silken cruise.

The aircraft commander put the plane on autopilot and opened his flight manual. The man studied for about half an hour, frequently glancing up at instruments and making sure the copilot had things under control. Eventually he said, "Okay, I'm bored. Nav, can you find us some news on HF?"

"Coming up," the navigator answered. A few seconds later he said, "BBC on HF1."

Parson turned a volume knob on the jump seater's comm box.

A female newscaster spoke in crisp tones, with just a hint of an
Indian accent:

> *"In other news, tensions between Serbs and Muslims are on the*
> *rise across Bosnia and Serbia following a chain of church and*
> *mosque burnings. Officials say three people died in continued*
> *rioting today in the Bosnian town of Zvornik, a scene of wide-*
> *scale atrocities during the 1990s. The leaders of Bosnia and*
> *Serbia have appealed for calm. In Belgrade, the president's*
> *office issued a statement saying Serbs have no desire to return to*
> *the dark days of ethnic warfare."*

"Oh, great," the copilot said. "Why is there always trouble
wherever we go?"

"Because we're in the military, dumbass," the navigator said.

"Seriously, though, I thought that place had quieted down."

"It had," Parson said. "I don't know why this shit's flaring up
again."

Parson thought back to some of the earliest missions in his
career, when he'd been a young lieutenant not long out of ROTC
and nav school. He remembered one night in particular when he'd
sat at the navigator's station in the lead aircraft of a three-ship formation of C-130s. The formation had droned through the darkness, heading for the initial point on a run to drop bundles of food
and medical supplies.

On his scope, he saw the blips of the left wingman and right
wingman. All three C-130s used SKE, or station-keeping equipment, to maintain formation position on instruments in the murk
that shrouded Bosnia. The weather made things tough that night.
Clouds obscured the drop zone.

Parson had to "shack" this drop—put it exactly on target. If he
missed, intelligence officers had warned, the bundles would fall

outside the safe zone. The relief supplies might lure the IDPs—internally displaced persons—to their deaths at the hands of the Bosnian Serb Army, or Arkan's Tigers, a freelance death squad.

The pilots and engineer wore night-vision goggles, but Parson kept his own NVGs turned off. He couldn't drop visually in this soup, so he relied on the adverse weather aerial delivery system's computer to help him. He checked his scope again. Almost time.

"Thirty seconds to slowdown," Parson said.

He watched the numbers count down on his instruments, bathed in the green glow of NVG-compatible lighting.

"Five seconds to slowdown," Parson called. Please don't let me screw this up, he thought. Four Mississippi, three Mississippi, two, one. "Slow down, slow down now."

The pilot knuckled back the throttles, and the flight engineer began reading the checklist.

"Flaps."

"Fifty percent."

"Aux pump."

"On."

Parson's eyes darted between his checklist and his scope and instruments. No room for error now. He breathed through his oxygen mask in the depressurized airplane. The pure oxygen felt cool as it filled his lungs, and it helped settle his nerves.

"Ramp and door."

"Clear to open."

A swirl of cold air entered the flight deck as the back end of the aircraft yawned open. Parson could not see the cargo and the open ramp; the flight deck bulkhead blocked his view. But he could imagine the two helmeted loadmasters back there, standing by for his one-minute call. The engineer and the pilots finished configuring the C-130 for the drop.

"CDS flaps."

"Reset, nine percent."

"Slowdown checklist complete."

"Crew," Parson called, "one-minute advisory."

"Acknowledged," said one of the loadmasters.

Parson rechecked his scope, his instruments, his calculations. Felt his heart thumping underneath his flak jacket. The minute ticked away quickly.

"Five seconds," he called.

Parson exhaled, counted backward again—this time to the release point. The copilot put a gloved hand to a switch on the side console.

"Green light," Parson called.

"On," the copilot said.

The switch triggered an electric retriever that pulled a blade against a restraining strap. Parson knew the strap had parted when he heard the CDS bundles rumble along the rollers in the cargo compartment.

"Load clear," the loadmaster called.

The blips on Parson's SKE scope held steady—the electronic signatures of the two other aircraft in the formation. If all had gone well, their loads were also parachuting to earth now, floating down to precalculated multiple points of impact within the safe zone.

Please let them fall on target, Parson thought. But he'd never know. If this were a training drop, a guy from aerial port would walk over to the practice bundles after they hit the ground, step off the distance to the desired impact point, and radio the results. The navigator who missed by the widest margin would buy the beer that night for all the crews.

The scores for this drop carried higher stakes—whether people would eat or starve, live or die. But no drop zone control officer waited down there to tell Parson how he'd done.

Parson's crew cleaned up the completion-of-drop checklist, and the formation accelerated away into the escape route. As the aircraft climbed and turned, the clouds broke apart enough to reveal glimpses of the dark hills below, snapshots interrupted by mist. The pilot looked down through his windows and said, "Damn, look at that."

"What?" Parson asked.

"Some kind of firefight."

Parson lowered the night-vision goggles on his flight helmet, switched them on. Stepped around the flight engineer's seat to peer out the left windows. At first he saw only rushing stratus so laden with moisture that it sprayed the glass. But when the mist opened up again, Parson noticed the tracers. Ground-to-ground, nothing aimed up at the sky. And as firefights went, a strange one. From the air, night infantry battles usually appeared as random spears of light. The burning magnesium of tracer rounds illuminated scattered angles and vectors in a tangled display of war's hellish geometry. But all these shots came along a single line, and they all flashed in the same direction.

"I don't think that's a firefight," Parson said.

"What is it, then?" the pilot asked.

Parson stumbled over helmet bags to get back to his seat. He pressed a line select key on his nav computer to store the present coordinates.

"I don't know," Parson said. "Not quite sure what to make of it." Now that he had the position marked, he could report what they'd seen to intel.

He gave the pilots a heading to take the C-130 out of the combat zone and back to the normal air routes of peacetime Europe. Parson's unit staged at Ramstein Air Base, Germany, as part of the Delta Squadron formed to fly these relief missions. Delta operated out of an old alert facility hidden among the trees in a remote section of the base. Where fighter-bombers had once poised to launch nuclear strikes against the Soviet Union, transport aircraft now departed on missions of mercy. Or, as Parson saw it, missions of paralysis and indecision. We'll feed refugees when and where the Serbs will allow, he thought, until ethnic cleansing wipes out Bosnian Muslims altogether. A patch on the sleeve of his flight suit bore the effort's name: Operation Provide Promise.

Parson was no historian, but he did see the irony in Delta Squadron basing itself in a disused Cold War alert shack. He planned his routes on a rusting table beside a disconnected rotary telephone. The office boasted a steel door two feet thick, originally intended to keep out Russian nerve gas and radiation. Now the door stayed propped open with a cinder block. An old electric signal board above the scheduler's desk might once have heralded Armageddon, with panels indicating alert status and weapons codes. Some wit had pasted over the panels with other kinds of messages: "Release the Hounds." "Pizza's Here." "Whenever I Sober Up, There's All These Dials and Gauges in Front of Me."

From the alert shack's decay alone, an observer could have surmised that the Cold War had ended. But the breakup of the USSR and its client states had led to other kinds of trouble. Ethnic tensions had brought a bloodbath in the Balkans.

The international community had hit upon an ingenious solution to wide-scale massacre: just let it run its course, and eventually it would stop. That tactic had worked pretty well the year before in Rwanda. Eight hundred thousand dead in a hundred days, while the world stood by.

Aboard the C-130, Parson realized he'd let several seconds pass without watching his scope, scanning his instruments. Do your damned job, he told himself. Keep your mind and your eyes on what you're doing. He checked his charts again, saw that the aircraft was nearing the combat exit point.

When the aircraft passed the next waypoint, Parson called for combat exit procedures, and the engineer read the checklist: External lights on. Night-vision goggles off. Cabin repressurized. Fuel system back to crossfeed. Survival equipment stowed.

Parson popped the clasps on his flak jacket, shrugged out of the heavy armor. Underneath it, his flight suit had dampened with sweat.

With his body armor off, Parson could reach all his flight suit pockets again. He unzipped a chest pocket and fished out a little notebook. Tapped keys on his nav computer to call up the position he'd stored, and wrote down the coordinates.

Then he considered how to describe to intel what he'd witnessed at that location. He could say with certainty only that he'd seen rifle fire from a position along a line, more or less all at once. But given the reports coming out of Bosnia—mass killings, walking skeletons found behind razor wire—he needed little imagination to guess what that rifle fire could mean.

IN THE JUMP SEAT of the Rivet Joint nearly two decades later, Parson remembered that night with profound sadness. He'd known exactly what was happening on the ground below him. A type of crime supposedly relegated to the past. After you knew of such things, he thought, you couldn't withdraw deep enough into yourself not to know them anymore.

14

GOLD HAD HEARD AND READ much about the storied city of Sarajevo: the Jerusalem of Europe, host of the 1984 Winter Olympics. A beautiful multicultural town that endured one of the worst sieges of modern warfare from 1992 to 1995. During the siege, attacking Serb forces tried to make that part of Bosnia all their own. As the Rivet Joint descended for landing, Gold viewed the lights of nighttime Sarajevo from behind Parson's jump seat. He and the pilots had said she could come forward to look at the city, as long as she went aft and strapped in before landing.

From Gold's perspective, the sight gave no hint of the horrors that had once taken place there. Sarajevo's cluster of tall buildings stood sentinel over the Miljacka River, the water painted bronze by glare. A sprawl of homes illuminated the hillsides, and the undulating sparkle made it appear the lights rode waves on a dark ocean.

When the landing gear came down, Gold returned to her seat beside Irena and buckled in. The aircraft thudded onto the runway and, after what seemed like a long taxi, shut down on a military ramp several hundred yards from the main terminal. Parson and the Rivet Joint crew changed from flight suits into civilian clothes, and the American embassy sent a bus to take them to their hotel.

On the bus, Parson slumped into a seat beside Gold and said, "Last time I was here, we got mortared." He seemed a little distracted, like he was reliving that moment. Sometimes it helped to recall those things, Gold realized. But sometimes it just sent you into a spiral. She decided to try to keep him talking.

"Looks peaceful enough now," she said. A Lufthansa Airbus taxied up to the terminal. The scene could have taken place on a slow Saturday night at any civilian airport in the world.

"Hope it stays that way," Parson said. "We heard on the news a while ago that they're burning churches and mosques again."

"Oh, no. Why?"

"Beats the hell out of me. You'd think they'd have had enough of that."

Here, Gold knew, a church or a mosque could have stood for centuries. What a horrible shame to destroy something of such historic, artistic, and spiritual value. She felt glad when Parson changed the subject, and glad that he still felt chatty.

"Back during the siege," he said, "they dug a tunnel underneath this airport. It connected Sarajevo with an area controlled by the UN. The tunnel was about the only way for people in the city to get food to stay alive and weapons to defend themselves."

"Some of the tunnel is still open," Irena said. "It's part of a museum now."

"I didn't know that," Parson said. "Sounds like you've been here before."

"Yes, sir," Irena said. "A few times with my parents."

"So what are we doing tomorrow?" another crew member asked.

"I don't think you guys are flying," Cunningham said. "I gotta meet with some people."

Gold could imagine the coordination required for an operation like this. More than likely, an alphabet soup of agencies from the U.S. State Department to the NSA were talking to counterparts in Sarajevo and Belgrade. Sovereignty issues, as well as nerves still raw from the '90s, would require careful diplomacy. Most of these maneuvers remained invisible to the troops and cops at the tip of the spear. They got an order and carried it out based on decisions made far above their pay grades.

When the bus began to roll, the Rivet Joint commander made a call on his satellite phone. After a conversation of several minutes, he switched off the phone and said, "All right, guys. Agent Cunningham is correct; we're off tomorrow. You know the drill. Sleep in or see the sights. Just don't do something stupid and make me bail you out of jail."

During the ride to the hotel, Gold tried to look for any scars from the war—bullet holes in walls, buildings left unrepaired— but she saw none of that. The bus pulled up in front of a cube-like yellow structure, the Holiday Inn. Beyond it gleamed a pair of silver office towers. Gold thought of her many nights in tents or even on the open ground. If this was how Air Force linguists lived, a job like Irena's might have tempted her when she was that age.

"My dad said this was one of the worst areas for snipers during the war," Irena said. "Reporters used to get trapped in this hotel."

"Looks pretty good now," Parson said.

"You'd never believe those silver towers got burned up, either," Irena said. After a pause, she added, "My parents cry every time they come back."

"I can understand that," Gold said. Well, she thought she could, anyway. She didn't presume to know how people from this land would think. But she'd spent years in Afghanistan, where people also carried a strong sense of place.

"Home is everything," Irena said. "Some Americans don't get that because they move around all the time." But here, Irena explained, home wasn't just property you could buy and sell. Home implied a connection with your ancestors, your blood, your history, and your honor.

Irena said nothing about not wanting to share the land with Muslims, and she'd made clear enough her horror over the war crimes of the past. However, her sentiments helped Gold comprehend the power of the bonds here between the people and their country.

The fliers hoisted their bags and filed off the bus. They lined up to check in at the hotel desk, blue U.S. government travel cards held between their fingers. Irena chatted amiably in Serbo-Croatian with the desk clerk. During the wait, Parson disappeared. He came back from exploring the hotel and said, "Restaurant's still open for a late dinner."

"I need to get a shower after that long flight," Gold said. "See you back down here in twenty minutes."

After her shower, Gold felt a little refreshed but still tired and hungry. At least her old wounds did not hurt much now; on most days she still felt the soreness. Healing, in all its forms, could take time. She found Irena, Parson, and Cunningham at a table in the restaurant. Parson had already downed half a glass of beer. A full glass of red wine waited at an empty seat.

"Thank you," Gold said as she sat and took the glass. Very kind of Parson to remember what she drank. She supposed he had some of his own healing to do yet, physical and otherwise. On some days she still noticed his limp.

Parson nodded at her, sipped his beer, picked up a menu, and asked, "Irena, what's good here?"

"Everything, sir."

Gold had tried food in many parts of the world but never here. She ordered *pljeskavica*, a spicy grilled ground beef. The *pljeskavica* turned out to be better than any hamburger meat she'd ever tasted, though the seasoning made her thirsty. She drained her water glass just as Cunningham asked, "So for you guys lucky enough to have tomorrow off, what are you doing?"

"I'm going to church, sir," Irena said.

"Guess your aircraft commander doesn't worry about you getting drunk and raising hell," Parson said.

"I attend an Orthodox church back home, but I don't often get to hear a service in Serbian."

"You work too hard," Parson said, "like somebody else I know." Gold half smiled, took a sip of wine, said nothing.

"Oh, it's not work," Irena said. "Anybody want to go with me?"

Gold had planned to take advantage of the rare luxury of sleeping late, but here came an opportunity even rarer. Her job had led her deep into many cultures and religions. And now she could experience something new with a native guide. She felt glad to have another woman along on this mission. Gold loved working with Parson, but she'd spent most of her professional life surrounded by men.

"I'll go," she said.

"Terrific," Irena said. "Anyone else?"

"What the hell," Parson said. "I'll go, too."

"They say women are a civilizing influence," Cunningham said, "but I never thought I'd live to see this. I'm out on a Saturday night with a bunch of GIs, and they're talking about going to church."

Parson laughed. "If you tell any of my old squadron buddies," he said, "I'll deny it."

After dinner, Gold sat up and read from her edition of John Locke before turning out her light. She pondered what she would witness the next day, how she'd feel about it. Through her long work among Muslims in Afghanistan, she had plenty of experience navigating the complexities of a great religion that some had misused for their own aims. Tomorrow, she would come across another example.

She remembered seeing a news photo of Radovan Karadžić and Ratko Mladić standing behind an Orthodox priest—two indicted war criminals with a cleric. Hard to fathom, but Gold was sitting in a hotel once shot up by snipers who had fired in the name of religion.

The next day Irena hailed a cab in front of the Holiday Inn. Gold wore slacks; she had no clothing really suited for church, and neither did Parson, who wore a collared shirt and wrinkled khaki trousers. She'd never seen him in a civilian coat and tie, and she guessed she never would. Only Irena dressed appropriately, in a conservative blue dress.

At the Serb Orthodox cathedral, four small domes topped by a crucifix surrounded a large central dome. Irena explained that the nineteenth-century cathedral's formal name was the Cathedral Church of the Nativity of the Theotokos, and that Theotokos was the Greek title for Mary, or the Mother of God. Gold found the copper-colored exterior gorgeous, but when she walked inside, the basilica's interior took her breath away.

Chandeliers lit the arches and columns. The scent of incense filled the nave. As congregants entered, they crossed themselves, kissed an icon, and greeted one another. Gold studied the iconostasis, a partition at the front of the cathedral, covered with icons of Christ, the saints, and the prophets. Priests entered the nave through doors in the iconostasis, and they began the ceremony of the Divine Liturgy.

Gold understood little during the two-hour service, though she knew the moments when the priests chanted scripture, with an inflection nearer to singing than speaking. And then the real music began. Gold needed no translation of the Slavonic hymns. The words almost didn't matter during what was probably the most beautiful sacred music she had ever heard.

What she did not hear was a sermon—at least, not one in the lecture format familiar to most American Protestants. Nearly all the service consisted of formal ceremony, clearly with deep meanings for the congregants. Gold had seen people approach their Creator in many ways: through fasting, through singing, through the deprivations of an ascetic life, even through the exertions of a whirling dervish. Now she had seen one more, and for her, the music alone was worth the experience.

When the service ended, Irena led Gold and Parson through the narthex and out into the street. Several men wearing dark suits, sunglasses, and earpieces moved among the churchgoers. Security, Gold supposed, given the recent news.

"Let's go for a walk," Irena said. Gold took her meaning immediately: Things are a little tense; no sense hanging around and having to explain who we are.

When they had walked a couple of blocks from the cathedral, Parson asked, "Did you see those big dudes in shade glasses?"

"I certainly did, sir," Irena said.

"Did anybody say anything about what's been happening?" Gold asked.

"Oh, yes," Irena said. "They don't know what to make of it. They're scared there's going to be more trouble."

"So they're not ready to lock and load yet?" Parson asked. Gold shot him a look, and he shrugged, but Irena did not seem offended.

"I didn't hear anything like that," Irena said. "You can find hotheads anywhere, but you know how it is. Most people just want to cook their dinner and feed the kids and walk the dog and mind their own business."

Traffic remained light as they strolled through the city. A quiet Sunday morning, Gold thought, just like a Sunday back home. Apart from the security men at the cathedral, nothing gave any hint of new threats of violence. Crossing a street, she noticed what looked like abstract art painted on the pavement. Red resin filled gouges chipped out of the asphalt in a design that looked vaguely like a flower, three or four feet in diameter.

"What's that?" Gold asked.

"A Sarajevo rose," Irena said.

"A what?" Parson asked.

"A Sarajevo rose. Places where mortars hit the streets, filled with red in memory of those who died."

From the sidewalk, Gold examined the rose. Pretty in a way, if you didn't know its origin. Just shallow indentations spattered in a rough circle. Hollywood's version of mortars dug big craters, but Gold knew real mortars left only little pockmarks like this. However, they threw hot, sharp shrapnel in every direction. She wondered about the suffering that must have happened in this very spot.

Parson seemed especially moved by the sight. He said nothing, but he kept looking at the battle damage turned artwork. Gold had seldom heard him speak of Bosnia, but he seemed to have strong feelings on the subject, and he usually kept his feelings to himself. She wondered what he thought now, especially in light of the new spate of arson and riots. Perhaps he pondered how you always had to remain vigilant. Maybe sometimes you had to refight battles you thought you'd won.

After Parson turned away from the rose, Irena led on. Eventually they came to a sidewalk café. Plate glass windows stood in frames reminiscent of Moorish arches. From the windows stretched an awning that covered four small tables. An aproned waiter opened the door and beckoned, and when he did, the aroma of sweetened coffee rolled into the street.

Irena spoke in Serbo-Croatian with the man, then asked in English, "Does anybody want lunch?"

"I could eat," Parson said.

"Me, too," Gold said. She had not enjoyed a day this leisurely since she'd gotten out of the hospital, and she felt grateful to Parson and Irena for making it happen.

"Inside or out?" Irena asked.

"Let's sit outside," Gold said.

They took seats under the awning, and Gold surveyed her surroundings. From the architecture of the windows, she supposed Muslims owned the café. Irena ordered three cups of Bosnian coffee. When the coffee came and Gold tasted it, the flavor reminded her of the coffees she'd tried in countries farther to the east: very strong and very sweet.

Parson looked pensive. He rested his chin on the crook of his thumb and forefinger, and he ignored his coffee.

"What's on your mind?" Gold asked.

Parson took his hand away from his chin, crossed his legs. "Webster wanted us to make Cunningham really understand what happened here. He hopes OSI will stay on this and see it through. Got any ideas?"

Gold thought for a second. "Maybe bring him here and show him a Sarajevo rose."

"Maybe."

Irena glanced up from her coffee. The contentment had drained from her face, and now she looked even more subdued than Parson.

"I just thought of something else we can show him," Irena said. She explained her idea. It involved a visit to the town of Bratunac. "If Sergeant Major Gold has her United Nations ID card, that might get us on the site."

"That's not something I want to see," Parson said, "but if it doesn't make Cunningham feel for this place, nothing will."

No one spoke for a long while. Eventually, Gold tried to change the mood.

"Let's order some food," she said.

From far down the street, the growl of motorcycle engines rose. Gold opened her menu and paid the traffic no mind. She thought to ask Irena for a recommendation, but the bikes roared louder now. When she glanced up from the menu, she saw two motorcycles, each with a driver and a rider.

The bikers came on fast, one machine a few yards in front of the other. Each driver gripped the handlebars and throttle; each rider held an object in his right hand. Before Gold could react, before she could even gauge the riders' intent, they hurled their objects toward the café. Over the noise of the cycles, the bikers shouted something in Serbo-Croatian.

One of the objects spun toward Gold's head. She felt the object flick strands of her hair before crashing through one of the café windows. The other object struck the table, broke Irena's cup and saucer, bounced into another window.

"Grenade!" Parson shouted. With broken glass and ceramic still in motion, he leaped from his seat. Arms outstretched, he hit Gold and Irena like a linebacker. His shoulder thudded into Gold's rib cage, and the force of the blow knocked her backward in her chair.

The three of them tumbled to the ground amid shards and spilled coffee. Gold landed on her back and rolled away from the overturned chair. Irena fell onto her side two feet away. Parson grabbed Irena's arm and yanked her close. He crouched over both of them, in a position as if he were starting a push-up.

In that instant, Gold understood what he meant to do: shield them from the blast with his own body. The alpha wolf again, protecting his pack.

Nothing happened. What was the hang time of a grenade?

Usually about five seconds, Gold recalled. She took a breath, let it out. That much time had passed.

"Stones," Irena said. "They're just stones."

No one moved. Gold's chest hurt like hell from the old gunshot wound and the impact of Parson's shoulder. But as she thought about what he'd done, she put her hand on the side of his neck, met his eyes. Then she moved her hand down to his arm and asked, "Are you all right?"

"Yeah," he said. "Sorry. I guess I kind of overreacted." He picked himself up, brushed at the coffee stains on his shirt.

"No you didn't," Gold said. "They could have been grenades." She sat up, winced with pain. The back of her hand stung, too. Blood trickled from a cut with a sliver of glass still embedded. Gold picked out the glass, let it drop to the sidewalk. She pulled a handkerchief from her pocket and wrapped the cloth around her hand.

"Does that need stitches?" Parson asked.

"No, it's not deep."

"How about you, Irena?" Parson said.

"I'm okay," Irena said. "Can't say the same for my dress." Parson had torn the sleeve in his attempt to shield her, and coffee had spilled down the front. The espresso aroma floated stronger in the air, but now it brought no pleasure.

A flush of anxiety came over Gold. Sweat popped out all over her skin. She took a deep breath and closed her eyes. You can help beat it just by identifying it, she told herself. PTSD. Not everyone who experienced combat trauma suffered debilitating effects. Gold felt she had nearly overcome her injuries, both physical and psychic. She recalled taking the Automated Neuropsychological Assessment Metrics right before leaving active duty. The computerized test included activities such as memorizing symbols associated with numbers, recognizing patterns, and gauging reaction time by clicking the mouse every time an asterisk appeared. Her ANAM results showed no loss of function.

Gold stood, extended her good hand to Irena, pulled her to her feet. Excited voices came from inside the café.

"Oh, they're pissed," Irena said.

"I would be, too, if some asshole trashed my coffee shop," Parson said. "What did those bastards yell when they drove by?"

"Fucking towel heads," Irena said.

"That's just great."

The waiter came back outside, waving his arms and talking fast. Irena spoke with him for several minutes. The man went back inside, and through the shattered windows Gold saw him pick up the telephone.

"He wanted to make sure we're all right," Irena said. "I told him we're fine. He also wants to know if we'll stay to tell the cops what we saw."

"Hell, yeah, I'll make a police report," Parson said. "I'd like to strangle those sons of bitches."

When the police arrived, both officers spoke English well enough to take statements from Parson and Gold without translation. One of the cops went to the trunk of his squad car and brought back a first-aid kit. He wiped the cut on Gold's hand with an alcohol pad, which burned a little. The officer agreed that she did not need sutures, and he placed an adhesive bandage over the cut.

Irena addressed the police in Serbo-Croatian. After she'd spoken with them, she said, "They're offering us a ride back to the hotel."

"That's good," Parson said. "I've had enough playing tourist."

The officers talked to the waiter and manager, took some notes, and opened the back doors of the squad car, a VW Polo. Gold squeezed into the middle between Parson and Irena. During the drive back to the hotel, the police chatted with Irena. The car stopped in front of the Holiday Inn, and Gold, Parson, and Irena got out, waved thanks to the police officers.

In the lobby, Parson asked, "What did you guys have so much to talk about?"

"They were real curious about what we're doing," Irena said. "I just told them we were on vacation."

"Smart."

"I don't know if they bought it. They also said this is about the third time in a week they've had low-grade violence. Nobody's been killed like in that riot at Zvornik, but this stuff seems to be spreading."

Parson shook his head but he said nothing. Irena went upstairs to change out of her ruined dress. Gold accompanied Parson to the hotel restaurant.

"I need a beer," Parson said. "You want a glass of wine?"

"Too early for me," Gold said. But she did not begrudge Parson his beer. Though he showed no signs of emotion, his feelings had to have taken a wild ride. He'd made a split-second decision to save others with a move that could have cost him his own life. That the grenades turned out to be rocks made Parson's impulse no less impressive to Gold. And after someone had acted to sacrifice himself, you could hardly expect him just to forget about it and go have lunch.

When the waitress brought Parson his lager, he took a long pull, then set the glass onto a napkin. He looked like his nerves had settled a bit, so Gold decided to see if he felt like talking.

"This place gets to you, doesn't it?" she asked.

"Well, it's kind of hard to ignore flying rocks and busting windows."

"I mean even before that."

Parson took another drink, put the glass back down. With his index finger, he traced a line in the condensation sweating on the outside of the glass. After a few moments he said, "Yeah, I guess you could say this is where I got my education."

He told her about that night mission long ago when he'd seen the ground fire from his C-130. Through intel briefings and news reports, he'd come to realize he'd watched part of the Srebrenica massacre as it unfolded.

"I was pretty young back then," Parson said. "I guess I just couldn't reconcile a world where those things could still happen." He went on to say he'd seen awful things in Iraq and Afghanistan, too. But he was older and more jaded then. Bosnia had first taught him that cruelty persisted in human nature like a dominant gene. "I don't know the things you know," he added. "I don't know about philosophy and history and religion; I just fly airplanes. But it seems the more I learn about what we're capable of, the worse it gets. I don't see how you stand it."

Gold liked it that he'd said "what *we're* capable of." Not this group or that group. He might feel older and more jaded, but he was also older and wiser.

"I can stand it," Gold said, "because I never lose hope." She never lost hope, she told him, because in addition to the horrors she'd witnessed, she'd also seen great kindnesses. And sometimes great courage to enable the kindnesses. "Remember how you came after me when the insurgents captured me in Afghanistan? You had almost no support at all—just determination and a rifle."

"Seemed like the thing to do."

"That's my point. I don't believe you gave it much thought. You just did it. You went with your gut. Pure instinct. All to help somebody you didn't even know at the time."

"I'm nothing special."

Gold put her hand over his. She looked at one of his fingers, the tip nipped off by frostbite when he'd rescued her.

"That's right," she said. "You're nothing special. Well, no. Yes, you are. I hope you don't mind me saying that. But I mean there are a lot of brave, kind people out there like you. That's why I have hope."

Parson stared into his beer. "You're killing me," he said. Gave a slight smile, shook his head. "But I suppose that's something to think about. I know some pretty high-speed folks, myself." He looked straight at Gold when he said that.

She released his hand. Something to think about, indeed, she thought. You could dwell on darkness or focus on light.

Gold thought she detected a hint of relief in Parson's eyes; she hoped so, anyway. He didn't say anything for a few minutes, and she just let him sip his beer and come down from the adrenaline high of the day's events. Or was he coming back up from a low?

Either way, Parson maintained his usual stoic demeanor. Gold had seen it in worse situations. When Cunningham entered the restaurant, Parson nodded to him as if nothing had happened.

"What have you guys been into today?" Cunningham asked.

Gold told him about the cathedral visit and the vandalism at the café. She left out how Parson had tried to shield her and Irena because she knew he wouldn't feel like talking about it.

"That rock-throwing thing sucks," Cunningham said.

"Yeah, it does," Parson said.

"Well, we all have a big day tomorrow," Cunningham told Parson. "The Rivet Joint will go up, and they want Sergeant Major Gold to go up with them. You and I are taking a road trip."

"Where to?"

"Belgrade."

15

NO MAJOR TRAFFIC ARTERY CONNECTED Sarajevo
directly to Belgrade, so Parson enjoyed the scenery of Bosnia and
Serbia as Cunningham drove the rental car along winding two-
lane roads. The green hills and lush forests looked like great territory for hunting and trout fishing. Parson wondered how such a
beautiful place could have become the scene of the awful things
that had happened here. But he'd asked himself the same questions
in the countryside of Germany, on the old World War I battlefields
of France, and, for that matter, among the fields at Antietam and
Gettysburg. The problem lay not in the terrain but in people's
hearts.

He remained angry about the café incident yesterday and puzzled over why those kinds of things were happening now. Anybody
here over the age of thirty should have a good idea of where it all
could lead. When he tried to put himself in the place of the rock
throwers, to imagine what they must have been thinking, his mind

could not plumb the depth. The effort made him think of a radar altimeter out of its range, whose beam could not find the ground. So its indicator just went blank. At a mental dead end, he turned his thoughts back to the mission.

"So tell me more about this op," Parson said.

"I met with Bosnian and Serbian police yesterday," Cunningham said. "They have a hangar under surveillance at the Belgrade airport. That's where the opium has been going. I think they're going to take it down this afternoon."

"Sounds like somebody's going to have a bad day."

"Yeah, I suppose you'll see some traffickers with their faces in the tarmac."

"Cool. So what do we do?"

"Just observe, I hope. The Rivet Joint will talk to me on Fox Mike if they hear anything."

Parson had never witnessed a drug bust, and he looked forward to seeing a little justice in action. At the airport, Cunningham made a cell phone call, then met an unmarked white van in a parking lot near the cargo terminal. The driver, a dark-haired man of about thirty, introduced himself only by his first name. He spoke English with just a trace of a Slavic accent, and he wore civilian clothes: a golf shirt with blue tactical pants, and those black shoes favored by cops all over the world—enough leather almost to pass as low quarters, but with soles fit for running down a criminal.

"I'm Dragan," he said. "Ministry of Internal Affairs police."

"Thanks again for your help," Cunningham said.

"We'll do this just like we briefed yesterday," Dragan said. "My uniformed guys are already in position."

"Where did you learn such good English?" Parson asked.

"University of Chicago. And I have American relatives."

"Want to do a radio check?" Cunningham asked.

"Sure," Dragan said.

Cunningham plugged a cord into his VHF-FM radio, inserted an earpiece into his ear. Dragan donned a headset with a lightweight boom mike. The Serbian officer walked several steps away. Cunningham pressed a switch and said, "Radio check." Lacking an earpiece, Parson did not hear the answer, but he did hear Cunningham when he responded, "Good. Got you five by five." Cunningham's pronunciation of "five" sounded like "foiv."

Dragan came back over to the rental car, and the two lawmen worked out last-minute details. "The flight's due in about an hour," Dragan said, "but let's set up now in case the plane's early."

"Yeah, we better," Cunningham said. "Where do you want us?"

"There's a few parking spots along the fence near the freight warehouse, and you can see the ramp from there." Dragan pointed as he spoke. "Just stay in your car unless something crazy happens."

"Stay in your car." "Watch what happens." Parson didn't like phrases like those. They sounded too much like the world's initial reaction when the ethnic cleansing began back in the 1990s.

"All right," Cunningham said. "Holler if you need us."

Dragan nodded, sat down in his van, started the engine, and drove away. Cunningham steered toward the warehouse, nosed into a parking spot, and shut down the car. He turned up his radio volume and transmitted to the Rivet Joint somewhere overhead, "Motown, this is Dragnet on secure voice. How copy?" He seemed to listen to something in his earpiece, and then he added, "Got you loud and clear."

All the parts of the operation had come together well, Parson thought. If the bust went down shortly, Cunningham could wrap up the whole mission. Parson almost felt sorry the op would end so soon. Webster wanted him to keep Cunningham on task, but what if the task finished now? Then tomorrow Parson would probably have to head back to Manas. He hated to think that his time with

Gold would end so soon. And he supposed he'd spend the rest of the year giving safety briefings on how not to kill yourself doing something stupid: Don't conduct maintenance on top of an airplane without a safety harness. If you work on an electrical component with power applied to the aircraft, pull the component's circuit breakers and hang warning tags on the breakers and switches. Don't earn the Darwin Award by walking too close to a jet intake.

"Want some coffee?" Cunningham asked. He reached down to the floorboard and came up with a Thermos. "We'd be all mommucked if we had to do a stakeout without coffee."

Parson wondered at Cunningham's slang. Probably the lingo of his coastal North Carolina home. "Sure, thanks," Parson said. "Now I feel like a real cop."

Cunningham unscrewed the Thermos, poured the steaming liquid into a paper cup, handed the cup to Parson. Cunningham poured another for himself. Parson took a sip. It tasted nothing like fancy Bosnian coffee. Just black, bitter, and hot: Air Force coffee. Cunningham must have made it himself in his hotel room. Parson blew across the coffee's surface, scanned the surroundings outside.

"I don't see any SWAT dudes anywhere," Parson said.

"There's one on the roof of the warehouse," Cunningham said. "Left side. Don't point if you see him, but he's up there with some kind of assault rifle."

Parson squinted, saw nothing at first. But then he caught a glimpse of a rifle barrel.

"All right," Parson said, "I see him."

"I think Dragan said there were eight in all. I don't see the others, though."

"I'd hate to have all of them come out of nowhere and jump on me."

"It might get interesting when they make the arrests," Cunningham said. "Laws and procedures vary from country to country. But you probably won't see these guys read them their Miranda rights and give them a cookie."

"I get the feeling you don't think that's a bad thing," Parson said.

"Where I'm from," Cunningham said, "we believed in what my granddad called tidewater justice. Some of those North Carolina islands were pretty isolated back in the day. If somebody was harassing your daughter or breaking in your house, help might be a long ways away. So we knew how to take care of business ourselves."

Parson could respect that. Cunningham's ancestors seemed to have lived by an old code of justice, just as they spoke with remnants of an old English. The OSI man had a way of coming out with words unfamiliar to Parson. But in their context, the old words made sense, and so did the old justice.

Several minutes passed in silence. The two men watched the warehouse and ramp, but nothing moved and no one appeared. Finally Cunningham said, "So Webster tells me you did some flying in these parts."

"A little bit." Parson described offloading relief supplies in Sarajevo with the airfield under attack, gunners walking mortar fire toward the airplane.

"That must have sucked," Cunningham said.

"Pretty much," Parson said. "We used to take off from Ramstein at oh-dark-thirty so we could get in and out of Sarajevo before the afternoon. By one or two o'clock, the snipers would wake up and start drinking, and those fuckers would shoot at anything."

Parson didn't say any more on the subject, but he thought back to that time. He'd always wondered what sort of drunkenness the snipers entered. Parson had known giggling drunks, sobbing drunks, and belligerent drunks. But what combination of slivovitz and hatred would lead you to center your crosshairs on just any-body who presented himself? The thought reminded him of what could be at stake here, given the history of this place.

Every few minutes, arriving aircraft appeared over the roofline of the warehouse—winged specks vectored onto final approach. Eventually one appeared that loomed larger than the rest. The air-craft lumbered through its turn from base leg to final like a flying whale, and it reminded Parson of his own C-5 Galaxy. But the tail looked different: a conventional empennage rather than the Lock-heed T-tail. An Antonov An-124. The same type of plane they'd seen picking up cargo at Manas.

"Here comes the guest of honor," Parson said.

The An-124 disappeared behind the warehouse as it descended the glide slope. Cunningham looked down at his radio, pressed the transmit button, and said, "Roger that. We see it." When the air-craft reappeared in Parson's field of view, to the right of the ware-house, it floated just yards above the runway. Now the jet looked even bigger, and its size made it appear to fly with impossible slow-ness. The An-124 touched down first on its main gear, and then the nose wheels lowered to the pavement. Cunningham made another radio call. "Motown, Dragnet," he transmitted, "Target's on the ground."

Parson waited a moment to make sure Cunningham wasn't still listening to the radio. When the OSI agent shifted his gaze to out-side the car, Parson asked, "Is the Rivet Joint hearing anything?"

"Not that they mentioned," Cunningham said.

Several minutes later, the whine of the Ivchenko-Progress engines rose as the aircraft taxied toward the ramp. Exhaust gases shimmered from the tailpipes, and grass alongside the taxiway whipped and danced in the jet blast. The noise grew louder as the pilot nudged the power on the number four engine to help with the turn. The Antonov swung ninety degrees to the left and rolled into the freight ramp. A ground crewman stood by the corner of the warehouse, held his thumb in the air to indicate good wingtip clearance. The plane eased forward several feet, stopped. Its engines quieted to idle.

Cunningham turned the volume control on his radio and transmitted, "Dragnet copies." He turned to Parson and said, "The pilot's already on the phone to someone."

Parson wondered what that meant. Maybe the pilot was just checking in with a wife or girlfriend. But Irena probably wouldn't bother to mention something that routine. Didn't really matter, though. Dragan and his boys would probably roll up everybody, ground crew and flight crew, and sort the innocent from the guilty later.

A ground crewman connected an external power cart to the jet, and the four engines shut down. A sprinkle of raw fuel fell from each nacelle as the combustion flames were extinguished and the drain valves closed. The fuel droplets left dark stains on the pavement underneath the wings. Parson watched with professional interest, and he wondered if this crew would ever fly again. Screw 'em if they carried drugs knowingly.

"So what now?" Parson asked.

"This might take a while," Cunningham said. "I think Dragan wants to wait and see if they offload cargo and then put it right back on the plane. That'll be a good indication they're pulling something out of the packing material."

The Antonov crew opened the aft ramp and the pilots went inside, but half an hour went by before any cargo came off. The loadmasters eventually began using the jet's internal crane to lift the pallets. Parson had never seen such a device; no American military cargo plane had one. He decided the crane was pretty novel, but in the end no more efficient than sliding cargo over the omnidirectional rollers on the floor of a C-5. As the third pallet got lowered onto a forklift, Cunningham pressed his transmit switch and said, "Dragnet copies." Then he told Parson, "The pilot's talking to somebody who sounds like a boss. Irena says they never used the word 'opium,' but the conversation seems suspicious."

"Anything a prosecutor could use?" Parson asked.

"Probably not. The evidence that really matters is the dope itself. We'll probably know about that in just a little while."

The forklift disappeared into the shadows inside the warehouse. For about twenty minutes, Parson saw no activity on the ramp. He began to wonder if the ground crew had quit for the day. But then the forklift rattled its way out of the warehouse and back to the Antonov, carrying a pallet of assorted boxes just like the ones the workers had offloaded.

"Uh-oh," Cunningham said. "I think that's what Dragan was looking for."

The forklift driver wore a light blue work shirt, untucked. A cigarette dangled from his lips, half an inch of ash sagging from the cigarette's tip. The ash fell onto the man's lap, and he looked down and brushed at his clothing. He did not see the two policemen sprinting toward him.

Both officers wore black balaclavas, black tactical vests, black cargo trousers. One carried a Zastava M21 assault rifle. The other ran with a pistol in one hand. Pistol Guy grabbed the forklift driver by the shirt, yanked him off the forklift, yelled something in Serbo-Croatian. The driver struggled, and the officer jerked him into a choke hold and wrestled him to the pavement.

"Damn," Cunningham said. "Getting all tidewater on him."

The officer with the rifle reached up to the forklift, apparently shutting off its engine. Then he pointed the rifle at the driver while the other officer took out a set of flex-cuffs. When the driver resisted being rolled onto his stomach, the cop slugged him, pushed him over, cuffed him. Two other policemen charged into the aircraft.

Shouts came from within the warehouse. But to Parson's relief, he heard no gunfire. A man screamed; Parson imagined some dumbass had made the mistake of fighting back and wound up with a boot on his face. As Parson tried to follow the action, he noticed Cunningham furrow his brow. The OSI agent pressed his transmit button again and said, "Dragnet copies. But it's too late."

"Too late for what?" Parson asked.

Cunningham held up his hand for silence as he listened to his earpiece. He nodded, then responded to whatever he'd heard by saying, "Negative. Dragnet out." He removed his earpiece and said to Parson, "Now, that's weird."

"What?" Parson asked.

"Right about the time our boy there got a mouthful of the tarmac, the mission commander in the Rivet Joint recommended an abort."

"Why?"

"Irena heard something. The Antonov pilot was on the phone again, and his boss said something about an op that had nothing to do with drugs and nothing to do with flying cargo."

"Still, why would the cops abort?"

"So they could wait and find out whatever those jackasses were talking about. It's a moot point now, though."

Parson wondered what that other operation could be. Had they blown a chance to make even bigger arrests?

Several minutes ticked by with no apparent activity. Eventually, Dragan emerged from the warehouse, pistol in hand. He walked casually; the stakeout had ended with success. However, he wore a puzzled expression. Evidently he'd heard the call from the Rivet Joint and, like Cunningham, didn't know what to make of it. With a practiced motion, he put his handgun's safety on and slipped the weapon into a concealment holster. As Dragan approached the car, Cunningham rolled down the window.

"You find opium?" Cunningham asked.

"Yeah, a shitload."

"Your guys okay?" Parson said.

"Yeah, nobody's hurt on my team. One of the suspects has a broken nose, but he brought it on himself."

Cunningham laughed out loud. "So his face is all whopper-jawed now," Cunningham said. "Serves him right. Can we see the haul?"

"Yeah, come on in and take a look. The bus will get here soon and take these losers downtown."

Inside the dimly lit warehouse, Parson needed a few minutes for his eyes to adjust. The black-clad policemen were taking photos and placing evidence in cartons. That evidence consisted mainly of cellophane packages wrapped in clear plastic bags.

Nine men sat on the floor, hands cuffed behind them. Five wore the blue flight suits of some Russian freight airline, and one suffered a black bruise that spread from his swollen nose all the way across both cheekbones. Blood streamed from his nostrils. All the suspects stared silently at the concrete floor. One of the police officers barked something in Serbo-Croatian, apparently an order to stand up, and he marched the men outside.

"Normally I'd feel like spiking the football after a raid like this," Dragan said. "You don't get a bust this big every day."

"I guess you wonder why they wanted you to hold off," Parson said.

"Yeah. I talked to your Airman Markovich on secure voice after we got everything settled down."

"So what did she hear?" Cunningham asked.

"Something about the narcotics being just a sideshow, and now it's time to focus on the main event."

"Who was the pilot talking to?" Parson asked.

"No idea," Dragan said. "Not yet, anyway."

Parson wondered if whoever was on the other end of that phone call knew his little side business had just been shut down for good. If he didn't know now, Parson realized, he'd know very shortly. The next time he tried to call his minions, he'd get no answer because their cell phones would be sitting in evidence boxes.

And if the drug trafficking was just a sideshow, what was the main event? Webster would sure as hell want to know. So the mission hadn't ended. Parson knew his part of that mission: help motivate Cunningham to think outside his island.

Dragan ran his fingers through his hair and sighed, looked at the scene around him. "I don't know what we have here," he said, "but I really don't like it."

"Whatever it is, I think OSI's part might be wrapped up now," Cunningham said.

"Not necessarily," Parson said.

"What do you mean?"

"Webster is real interested in what's going on here, and he wants you to be, too. You took me on a road trip today. I'm taking you on one tomorrow."

16

GOLD READ THE MAP while Parson drove the rental car
through the Bosnian town of Bratunac. Irena and Cunningham
rode in the back. They took several wrong turns as they searched.
As a last resort, Gold knew, they could have Irena ask for directions. But they didn't want to put Irena in that position. How could
Irena just walk up to a local resident and ask about a place like that?

The GPS proved useless; they weren't looking for a location
with an address, a spot meant to be found. But Parson spared
Irena an awkward task when he said, "How about this right turn?"
Just outside Bratunac, he steered the car onto an unpaved path
too narrow for two vehicles to meet. Gravel crunched underneath
the tires. A lone European beech tree stood sentry at the corner
where the path met the road. Gold considered all the things that
tree might have witnessed, here where grief pooled in the valleys
like floodwater.

The path led uphill alongside fields, some planted anew and

some thick with last year's stubble. The land leveled, then pitched down again. In a meadow against a stand of trees, Gold saw what they'd come to find.

Workers in white suits stepped around in a muddy patch that had been opened in the grass. Some of the workers held trowels in hands covered by blue latex gloves. Forensic specialists, Gold knew. Here and there through the mud, red marker flags fluttered in a light breeze.

If Gold had not known where she was, she might have thought this an archaeological dig, or perhaps a group of agricultural scientists taking soil samples. But just outside the mud, in the grass where the ground remained unbroken, about a dozen transfer cases sat lined in a row, each case covered with green fabric. Here was a Bosnian mass grave.

Parson stopped the car. Gold got out feeling as if she had arrived late to a funeral. An older man approached her immediately. He wore the same white trousers as the other workers, but he had removed his white overcoat to reveal a flannel collared shirt. The man carried a clipboard and a satellite phone. Someone in charge, Gold presumed, and used to shooing away curiosity seekers.

Gold took out her United Nations ID and her passport—not the blue civilian passport but the burgundy one. The one that read *The bearer is abroad on an official assignment for the United States government.* She introduced herself by name but not by rank, and she passed the man her documents.

"Sir, I cannot give you details, but my team is investigating something that may or may not have a connection to events like"— Gold gestured toward the open pit—"like this."

"If you are looking for evidence, you will find much here," the man said, "though not much to tie this massacre to a particular perpetrator."

British accent. The man did not bother to give his name or title, but Gold assumed he was a colleague from the UN. He inspected her ID and passport and handed them back.

"We have come not so much for evidence as for—" Gold paused, unsure how to explain.

"Perspective?"

"That's a good way to put it. May we visit the site?"

"You may. Do not touch anything."

"Yes, sir."

Gold made a beckoning motion toward the car. Parson, Cunningham, and Irena got out and joined her.

"Are we sure we're not trespassing?" Cunningham asked.

"It's all right," Gold said.

"Webster wanted us to understand just how bad things can get around here," Parson said. "Nothing will do that like a visit to a spot like this."

A half-truth, Gold knew. Parson needed no convincing. But there was no reason for Cunningham to feel like he was getting some kind of remedial schooling. And Gold believed she, too, had things to learn here. She would leave Bratunac a little wiser and much, much sadder.

They walked through the grass to the edge of the grave site. Gold expected to pick up whiffs of the stench of death, but then she realized far too much time had passed for that. The place smelled only of churned soil; the flesh that had covered these bones had become soil itself.

On a black tarpaulin, the workers had placed a number of objects from inside the grave. Gold saw a mud-caked watch with a metal band, hands long stilled at 3:12. Had that been the time of death two decades ago? Probably not. She imagined the watch strapped to a decaying wrist underneath the ground, running on battery power perhaps for a few years in a hopeless effort to track eternity.

Next to the watch lay a wedding ring and a wallet. The wallet looked as if it had been dropped in the dirt yesterday. The owner might wipe it off and return it to his pocket. But the owner resided in that pit somewhere, represented by a red flag.

Gold found it odd that these valuables remained. She'd seen horrific scenes of mass murder in Afghanistan, and the killers usually took everything useful from the bodies. These victims had been slaughtered and buried by people in a hurry.

Irena bowed her head as if in prayer. Parson stood with his hands clasped in front of him, as near to reverent as Gold had ever seen him. Cunningham just shook his head, turned away and looked into the woods, turned again and faced the grave.

"God, this is horrible," he said. "Hard to believe these things went on."

"They went on because the world didn't care enough," Irena said.

Gold thought of words from John Donne. "'No man is an island, entire of itself,'" she said, "'every man is a piece of the continent . . .'"

Cunningham looked at her, nodded. He went over to the edge of the pit and kneeled. His eyes wandered across the grave site and seemed to stop where a forensic specialist dug at a skeleton only partially visible. Beside one of the red flags, accompanied by a placard with the number 15 on it, there was a human skull. The specialist used a trowel to work at the other bones. Roots curled around a clavicle as if the land resisted giving up its secrets.

As Gold looked more closely, other skulls became visible in the grave. She had to observe with care; the bones were not bleached white but had taken on stains the same color as the earth around them. Some of the skulls bore bullet holes in the back. A few of the skulls appeared too small to be those of adults.

Nearer to Gold, a specialist dug where no skeleton was apparent. The worker shoveled soil onto the screen of a sift box and began to shake the box. The wet earth did not sift well, but eventually enough dirt fell away to expose the delicate metacarpal bones of a hand, detached like puzzle pieces. The next bite of the shovel brought up what at first looked like a primitive bracelet. Gold recognized it as the circles of wire that had bound the hands.

"Who does things like this?" Cunningham asked.

"I don't know," Parson said, "but I think Webster's point is that some of the people who do these things are still around."

Another shovel full of dirt went into the sift box. This time the soil filtered away to leave a single shell casing. Not the short casing of a pistol cartridge but the longer, necked-down brass of high-powered rifle ammunition.

Gold imagined the scene that had taken place here. She could see the trucks trundling up the narrow path, the victims herded into a swale near the woods. If the atrocity had happened at night, headlights of vehicles would have thrown stark beams and shadows.

What last words had these victims spoken? Had they screamed or cried, pleaded for their lives? Had they said anything at all? And what thoughts could have gone through the minds of the shooters?

Another shovel of earth went into the sift box. The sifting yielded two more empty rifle cartridges. The forensic worker placed them next to the first casing, lined up in a row on a strip of plastic sheeting. Gold could almost hear the explosions of gunfire, the rifle reports rolling in waves, the dead dropping in ranks.

Now the dead who remained in the pit waited their turn to be placed into a transfer case. Perhaps they would make one final journey to a proper cemetery to rest with their ancestors.

Cunningham stood up, stepped away from the pit. "You guys

up in the airplane heard something about a sideshow and the main event," he said. "Is this what somebody could mean about the main event? More of this?" He swept his hand toward the mass grave.

"There's no telling," Parson said. "But I think we want to hang in with this mission until we find out."

Cunningham looked into the grave, then off into the woods. "Yeah," he said. "Yeah, we do."

17

AT HIS DESK, dušić seethed. He fought the urge to hurl his telephone through the office window. No answer from the pilot, Dmitri, since yesterday. No answer at the warehouse. For security reasons, Dušić never left voice mail messages, but if any underlings ever missed his call, they'd dial back right away. So far, nothing. He could not escape the obvious conclusion: Those fools had gotten themselves arrested. Thank God he'd not been at the warehouse himself.

"Milica," he called to his secretary in the next room, "has anyone phoned on the landline this afternoon?"

"No, sir. It is nearly six, Mr. Dušić. Do you have further need of me?"

Dušić ground his teeth, but he saw no reason to take out his anger on Milica. She was his youngest employee and the only woman on his payroll, and he saw her as the future of Serbia. The chaste daughter he never had, the counterpoint to those Muslim whores who bred like rabbits. He had never once raised his voice to her, and he often counseled her to find some promising Serb officer and start a family. Do not let the Turks outnumber us, he joked with her.

"You may go, my dear," he said. "Business may take me out of town for a few days. Sort the mail and tell any callers I can be reached on my mobile. If they do not already have the number, do not give it out."

"Yes, sir."

Dušić listened to her gather her things and leave. When the outer door clicked shut, he closed his eyes and tried to settle his mind. Unlike the recent plane crash in Kyrgyzstan, this disruption was no mere setback but a genuine combat loss. However, a commander must handle these things. What would General Mladić do in this situation? He would adapt.

Now Dušić needed to act quickly: withdraw some funds, procure some weapons, go to ground. He hoped those idiots who got arrested wouldn't talk; surely they could imagine the consequences of betraying him. But even if the underlings kept their mouths shut, the authorities might still pick up the trail.

He would have to complete his mission under less-than-ideal circumstances, but that was war. No plan survived contact with the enemy.

Dušić removed his jacket and tie, rolled up his sleeves. He slid open the bottom drawer of his desk and lifted his CZ 99 and shoulder holster. Slipped on the holster, drew the weapon, and pulled back the slide just enough to see the gleam of the brass cartridge. Satisfied that the gun was loaded, he released the slide, holstered the pistol, and donned his jacket over the shoulder rig.

At a safe mounted in his office wall, Dušić tapped a combination into the keypad: 15-6-1389. The date of the battle at the Field of Blackbirds. A moment in time that transcended time, a portal through which vengeance flowed forever.

The lock's bolt retracted, and Dušić opened the safe. He removed a manila envelope filled with euros, American currency, and Serbian dinars—in all, just over one hundred thousand dollars.

By the time he pulled out of the parking garage in his Aventador, a charcoal dusk had turned Belgrade to shades of black and white, highlighted only by the colors of traffic lights. Pigeons flapped into the cornices of buildings, settling into their roosts. Dušić considered the problem of communication. Were his phone calls being monitored? He decided his throwaway cell phone was safer than his landline. His office location was public knowledge, and if the authorities decided to investigate him, they'd probably start by tapping his office numbers. As he drove, he used the cell phone to ring Stefan.

"Can you meet me tonight at the storage facility?" Dušić asked.

"I can," Stefan said. "But I am home in Sarajevo. I will need some time to make the drive."

"Very well. Just make sure you get here. Bring your utility van. A problem has arisen."

"Are you calling off the operation at the Patriarchate?"

"Security, my friend," Dušić said. Though he doubted this number would ever be monitored, he did not want any carelessness. "I will answer your questions when you arrive," he added.

At an automatic teller machine, Dušić withdrew additional cash. He knew how events could overtake even the best commanders, and he wanted to have plenty of emergency money on hand. If police closed in, he might not be able to risk making an appearance at a bank or using his credit cards. His latest withdrawal left an electronic signature that placed him in Belgrade, but so what? That's where he lived. But if he needed to start moving around, the cash would allow him to do so without leaving more clues.

His safest move, he knew, would be simply to disappear. He could go to Russia, where kindred spirits and expatriate veterans would give him shelter. Mladić and Karadžić had hid out for years right here at home; in Russia or perhaps Ukraine, Dušić could vanish forever. But a life in hiding held no appeal. And if his plan succeeded, Serbs would hail him as a hero, and there would be no more need to hide.

Dušić felt he had pushed off from a shore to which he could never return. He had started across the Rubicon, and he would lead his people to the glory they deserved.

Full darkness had fallen by the time he reached his storage facility in Novi Beograd—New Belgrade, just across the Sava from the old part of the city. A chain-link fence with an automated gate surrounded rows of corrugated metal sheds, most of them available to the public for rent. But Dušić had bought one set of the storage units, wired them for electricity, installed climate control, and enclosed them with his own locked inner fence. He stopped his Aventador at the outer fence, reached through his open window, waved his security card at a card reader. The reader box beeped once, and its indicator light changed from red to green. An electric motor began to hum, and the gate inched open.

Dušić took his foot off the brake and rolled forward a few meters through the gate. He stopped to wait for the gate to close behind him. When the gate lurched shut again, he drove forward and turned left onto a concrete driveway that ran between the rows of storage units.

He kept his own fence locked with low technology: a padlock and chain. Dušić shut down his car and keyed open the padlock. More sophisticated gear protected the roll-up doors to his storage sheds. At one of them he entered a code for an electronic lock, and when it released, he raised the door and turned on the lights.

Man had always channeled much of his ingenuity into inventing ways to kill, and Dušić prided himself in trading on that ingenuity. The fluorescent tubes buzzing overhead illuminated the best of his stock in small arms, optics, night-vision devices, and other infantry gear. He bought and sold equipment up to and including Sukhoi jets, but hardware a man could carry represented Dušić's bread and butter. He always kept supplies on hand for small orders, and from that cache he would outfit himself and his team.

AK-47 assault rifles hung from racks along one wall. Dušić hoped Stefan had recruited more *razvodnik*s, and he selected five AKs for the attack on the Patriarchate. For his own use he preferred other firearms, but Kalashnikovs were usually the weapon of choice for Muslim terrorists, probably because the rifles were durable as earth itself and could be operated by any fool. The whole point of his upcoming operation was to make it look like a towel-head strike on an Orthodox holy place.

But Stefan, Dušić knew, had the talent for instruments of more precision. For his friend, he reserved an American M24 sniper rifle. Though Dušić had no use for Americans, his judgment in weapons knew no politics, and he cared only about quality. And the Americans, he admitted, made some of the finest weapons in the world. In the right hands, this thing could deliver death from afar like bolts of lightning, guided by a telescopic sight with fine adjustments marked in increments that looked like the scales of a micrometer. In keeping with Stefan's preference, the rifle was a bolt-action. Dušić had long since quit trying to talk his friend into using automatics; Stefan had demonstrated well enough what he could do with one bullet at a time.

Dušić set the weapons by the door, the equipment protected by foam-padded cases. Then he collected cans of 7.62-millimeter ammunition, batteries, handheld radios, and other accessories that might come in handy over the next few days. He even picked up body armor and a few fragmentation grenades for good measure. The Holy Assembly of Bishops would take place in the following week. If all went according to plan, the clerics would become martyrs by Dušić's hand, and their deaths would serve a more sacred cause than their lives ever had. Those clerics who must die had been called by God to the service of the church. Dušić had been called to the service of his people. Surely fate had intended this convergence.

Small chores kept him occupied while he waited for Stefan. Dušić conducted function checks on his radios and optics. He made sure everything turned on and tested good, and that things adjusted, focused, zoomed, and tracked. When he completed all of those tasks, he sharpened tactical knives and charged up nickel-cadmium batteries. After what felt like an eternity, the glare of headlights and the crunch of gravel announced the arrival of a vehicle. Dušić walked to the main entrance. When he recognized Stefan's van, he opened the gate. Stefan waved as he drove through. Neither man smiled. Stefan stopped and lowered his window.

"Drive down to small-arms storage," Dušić said. "I will brief you there."

Inside the shed, Stefan surveyed the gear Dušić had collected. "This feels like the old days," Stefan said, "when we visited the quartermaster before an operation."

"I had the same thought," Dušić said, "but we have no time for reminiscing." Dušić told Stefan about the arrests.

"A sad turn of events," Stefan said.

"If they talk, they die."

"To be sure."

Dušić outlined his plan for the days remaining before the Assembly of Bishops: lie low, brief the *razvodnik*s on their final instructions, and watch for any hint of betrayal by the fools now in custody.

"The car bomb is ready," Stefan said. "I wired together three shells, as we discussed. I need only to install the battery and drive the car into place."

"Excellent," Dušić said. He considered the yield of such a

weapon. The explosion would amount to three simultaneous direct hits by large-caliber artillery. It would rip the Patriarchate right off its foundations. And the act would rip away the inhibitions and caution of the Serbian people, stir them to finish what they had started in Dušić's youth.

"I obtained the vehicle as well. Everything is set."

"Were the funds I gave you sufficient?" Dušić asked. He had wired Stefan nearly two million Serbian dinars to purchase a car for the operation.

"Actually, I can return all the funds to you. I hot-wired some Turk's Citroën. If any identifying marks remain on the engine block, the police will trace it to a Muslim who says his car was stolen."

Dušić laughed, clapped his friend on the back. "Brilliant, absolutely brilliant," he said. "At least something has gone well. And I have a gift for you. Open that long case."

Stefan gave a puzzled look, kneeled, and popped the fasteners on the case. He opened it to reveal the M24.

"A Stradivarius for the maestro," Dušić said.

"Very fine," Stefan said. He lifted the rifle, clicked open the scope's spring-loaded lens caps. Shouldered the weapon and sighted through the scope. Then he placed the rifle across his knees and unscrewed the thread protector at the end of the barrel. The effort revealed the threads that could accept a noise suppressor. Stefan found the suppressor inside the rifle's case, and he twisted the device onto the barrel. Hefted the rifle and looked through the scope again. "Very fine," he repeated. "I thank you."

"If you do not need such a rifle in our opening phase," Dušić said, "you will surely need it later."

Stefan examined the markings on the Leupold scope. "Telescopic sights keep getting better and better," he said. "With this reticle, one can estimate range very accurately."

The two men loaded the gear into Stefan's van. Prudence dictated that Dušić leave Belgrade until the day of the bombing, and that he travel in something less eye-catching than the Aventador. He removed his briefcase and laptop computer from the car and placed the items in the van.

"I will leave the Lamborghini here," Dušić said, "if I may ride with you."

"Of course."

"I have kept the car in my enclosure here before, so the people who rent storage units should not think it strange. But I believe we should get out of the city for now."

"Where shall we go?" Stefan asked.

"Tuzla. That is a fairly central location for the *razvodnik*s to meet us when the time comes."

"It is. And I have found three more, all veterans of volunteer units."

"You have no doubts about their commitment?" Dušić did not want to have to shoot another weak-minded, untrainable moron.

"None. I interviewed them extensively."

"Good. Then let us be on our way."

Dušić turned off the lights in his small-arms room, rolled down the door, and activated the electronic lock. He chained and padlocked his fence, scanned his surroundings for any witnesses. He saw no one, heard only the distant barks of a dog and the rush of traffic on the two-lane highway that ran past the storage units.

"What shall we do in Tuzla?" Stefan asked.

"Little, I hope. I will pay for our rooms with cash, and we will register under assumed names. Barring something unforeseen, all we have left to do is give the shooters their final instructions."

After the bombing, naturally, there would be much to do. But Dušić's moves during that dynamic phase would depend on unpredictable factors. Would the Belgrade government begin an offensive against the Turks immediately? Or would politicians follow public opinion rather than lead it? Volunteer militias might have to make the first strikes. In that case, Dušić could find himself leading bands of ruffians in tactical operations rather than commanding entire armies from a post within the Ministry of Defense. No matter. He could lead wherever necessary.

On the passenger side of Stefan's van, Dušić buckled into his seat. He said nothing while his friend pulled away from the storage units and headed down the blacktop into the night. Dušić felt gratified that Stefan had found more triggermen to rake any survivors of the blast. The question of personnel had worried him. Did he have enough men to do this thing properly? As the glow of the city's lights receded behind him, Dušić considered his resources. He decided they were sufficient. After all, that American lunatic Timothy McVeigh had destroyed a larger building than the Patriarchate, and he'd done it with fewer support personnel and less expertise. McVeigh had also faced trial, conviction, and execution for the 1995 bombing of the Oklahoma City federal building.

With proper fieldcraft Dušić could avoid the fate of an ignorant extremist. Instead, he would take his proper place as a leader in the war to come.

18

AT DAYBREAK, the rivet joint lifted off the runway at Sarajevo and climbed into Bosnian skies. Sunrise lit the horizon as if the gods had ignited a signal flare. In the cockpit jump seat, Parson squinted, unzipped the left breast pocket of his flight suit, and reached for his aviator's glasses. On the ground below, the misting waters of the Miljacka meandered in cursive lines.

"Motown Six-Four, Sarajevo Tower," a voice called on VHF. Slavic accent but confident English. "Left turn heading zero-eight-zero, contact departure. Safe flight."

To Parson, it still felt strange to take off from Sarajevo under reasonably peaceful circumstances, equipped only with a headset, his flight suit sleeves casually rolled up. A couple decades ago he wore a flak jacket and survival vest with a Beretta on his side, the hums and squeaks of the radar warning receiver sounding in his flight helmet. And as a last resort, parachutes hanging in the cargo compartment, straps pre-fitted for each crew member.

He'd flown with such gear pretty recently in Afghanistan. Would he ever lift off from Afghanistan in a time of peace? And here in the Balkans, how fragile was this peace?

When the Rivet Joint leveled off at altitude, Parson unbuckled and headed aft. In the back, Gold sat next to Irena. Both wore headsets. On the console before her, Irena placed an open checklist and a notepad. Thus far she'd written nothing on the notepad; her pen rested on a clean sheet of paper. Parson took a crew seat at an unused station beside Irena and plugged his headset into an interphone cord.

"Can I get you anything?" Parson asked. Not a question lieutenant colonels often asked junior enlisted personnel, but as an observer, Parson had little to do. Irena, by contrast, had important tasks right now.

"No, thanks," Irena said. "Just waiting to see if anybody wants to talk to me."

"Anything yet?"

"No, sir. Not a peep, or at least not one that we care about."

Parson didn't understand all of this crew's procedures, but he did know that, in a way, they were not just listening but hunting. If the Rivet Joint crew wanted you badly enough, they could find you, listen to you, and get information about you to other people on the ground. The machine's information processing capability, Parson mused to himself, represented the ultimate revenge of the nerds.

He sat silently as he watched Irena do her job. She chatted with crewmates, usually about technical matters he could not follow. Occasionally she tapped a button on her console. Parson heard several conversations in Serbo-Croatian, none of which seemed to interest Irena. At least an hour passed with nothing happening, and Parson almost dozed off, slouched in the crew seat with his harness adjusted loosely.

Irena's body language brought him wide awake. She sat bolt

upright, glanced at her watch, and wrote the Zulu time on her notepad. The young linguist froze, listening hard, her pen poised in the air. Her manner put Parson in mind of a bird dog trotting easily along a row of corn stubble until it stopped—locked up on point, with whiffs of prey in its nostrils.

He longed to ask her *What you got?* but he knew to leave her alone for the moment. Gold noticed, too. She watched her colleague, glanced at Parson, looked back at Irena. After a few minutes, Irena spoke on interphone.

"That's the same voice," she said. "The boss."

"The same guy the Antonov pilot was talking to?" Parson asked.

"Yes, sir."

"How did you zero in on him?"

"One number leads to another," Irena said. "I think they took a lot of numbers from the cell phones they picked up in the arrests."

"Where is he?" Gold asked.

"Not Belgrade. They're tracking." Irena tilted her head toward the crew members closer to the front of fuselage.

"What did he say?" Parson asked.

"He told somebody to suspend the shipments for now."

"Sounds like he knows he has a problem," Gold said.

"Stand by," Irena said. Some tech talk followed; Parson wasn't sure what she and her crewmates were saying. Then Irena flipped a switch and said, "All right, I'm on that channel, too."

Now Parson heard other languages as well as Serbo-Croatian. Some of it sounded like Pashto. When Gold leaned forward and turned up the volume on her comm box, Parson was sure. Irena slid her notebook over to Gold, and Gold began to write. Somewhere within this aircraft's equipment racks and miles of wires, digital recorders saved everything. But Parson imagined notes could come in handy, too. Idly, he wondered if whatever the linguists jotted down became a classified document.

Gold lifted her pen from the page, listened for a moment, then resumed scribbling. Parson could see that she wrote in English, so he unfastened his harness and stood to peer over Irena's head. In Gold's handwriting, so elegant it bordered on calligraphy, the note-pad read *We may need more of your product in the future, but we can take no more now.* Above that line, Irena had made other notes, mostly in Cyrillic. She also wielded her pen neatly, but with more sweeping lines. Funny how you could always tell women's hand-writing from men's. Whenever Parson needed to fill out a hard-copy flight plan, he had to remind himself to print clearly enough so that someone could actually read it.

He could tell Gold enjoyed this new way to put her skills to use. She looked up at him, gave that rare half smile of hers, glanced back to her notes and the console.

The Rivet Joint, Parson judged, had reeled in some pretty damning evidence about the drug trafficking. Cunningham would be pleased. Parson supposed the OSI and all kinds of other agen-cies had worked with legal beagles for approval of the cell phone monitoring. Maybe the Serbian and Afghan cops could move in and make more arrests. Parson presumed a lot of the data sucked up by this aircraft got beamed back home to the NSA, and perhaps to similar agencies in friendly countries.

He worried, though. The recent riots and burnings made him nervous. By his recollection, things could go very badly very quickly in this part of the world. Parson remembered when the Soviet bloc starting falling apart, and in his historical ignorance, he'd assumed the end of Communist dominance would bring an era of prosperity to Eastern Europe. Democracy and dollar signs, rainbows and puppy dogs. Some countries fared pretty well, but the former Yugo-slavia took a different path. He'd seen a reminder of that yesterday that would leave images in his mind forever. He hoped the grave had also moved Cunningham.

The knowledge that such things could happen had always troubled Parson, and he doubted he'd ever reconcile it. Gold, with her knowledge of faith and philosophy, seemed to understand these things better; at least she could find words to help her accept the world as it was. He'd once heard her talk about Calvinist theory and the depravity of man. Parson took that as a fancy way of saying some people were just assholes. He did not consider himself a righteous person, but he knew right from wrong. That at least gave his life a kind of directional stability, the way the lands and grooves inside a rifle barrel impart a spin to the bullet and send it true on its course.

The morning wore on. Irena continued monitoring her circuits, but she never mentioned hearing anything worthwhile. At midday, Parson got up and went to the galley. He opened the refrigerator and gathered the food and soft drinks they had brought for lunch. Gold had picked up a turkey panini and a bottle of green tea. Irena brought a gyro with shavings of beef covered in tzatziki, and vitamin water to drink. For Parson, a ham sandwich, chips, and a Coke. He placed the food on the console table beside Irena's keypad.

"Thanks, sir," Irena said.

"You should eat healthier," Gold said.

Parson rolled his eyes, patted Gold's shoulder, sat in his seat, and unwrapped his sandwich. The radios and interphone remained quiet. Between bites, Parson asked Irena, "So what made you choose the Air Force?"

Irena took a swallow of her pink vitamin water, thought for a moment, and said, "I guess it was my dad's great-uncle."

"He was an Air Force man?"

"No, sir. But he helped rescue some American fliers in the Second World War."

"Oh, yeah? Wow."

"Recruiters from all the services wanted to sign me up, but I picked Air Force because of that."

Irena went on to tell a story that rang true to Parson because he'd heard the first half of it. The second half he'd never known.

On August 1, 1943, nearly 180 B-24 Liberators took off from Benghazi, Libya, to bomb German-held oil refineries around Ploesti, Romania. During the flight to the target, cascading navigational errors turned the mission into what fliers of Parson's day called a goat fuck. Some of the aircraft droned right into a fire-storm of German antiaircraft guns and got blown out of the sky. More than fifty planes went down, with a loss of several hundred men. However, enough of the formations hit their targets to ignite the refineries into cauldrons of fire. Columns of smoke dark as ink boiled into the air. The day came to be known as Black Sunday.

Some of the airmen bailed out over occupied Serbia and Bosnia. Those lucky enough to parachute into friendly hands found themselves under the protection of Serb guerrillas, then working with the Allies.

For months, hundreds of American fliers hid out in peasant homes, while teams led by guerrilla leader Draža Mihailović built improvised airstrips. The Serbs did it the hard way, with hand tools and ox carts, mainly by night. Work crews cut down trees, dug out stumps, carried away rocks, and leveled ground so that C-47 transports could land. With little more than signal fires to guide them, the C-47 pilots touched down on dirt and gravel runways in an operation coordinated with help from intelligence agents dropped by parachute. The effort, code-named Operation Halyard, rescued more than five hundred U.S. aviators from imminent capture by the Germans.

"My great-great-uncle helped build the runways," Irena said.

"So you might say he was an Air Force civil engineer," Parson said.

"Yes, sir," Irena said. "Unofficially."

The story about Irena's Serbian elders reminded Parson that no group was always on the wrong side. You could find great deeds and awful crimes in the history of just about every culture, a truth he had learned from Gold.

By the middle of the afternoon, the Rivet Joint fliers began to wrap up their sortie. One of the officers announced on interphone, "Front-end crew says we're almost bingo fuel, guys. Everybody ready to pack it in?"

Parson was getting hungry, and he looked forward to dinner back at the hotel with Gold, and maybe Irena and Cunningham. So he was glad to hear several crew members answer with "Yes, sir" or "Affirmative." But Irena did not speak. She furrowed her brow, turned up a volume knob. A conversation in Serbo-Croatian flowed over the circuits, and when the chatter paused, Irena said, "Stand by, sir. Please tell them not to descend yet." She held up her hand as if to keep the plane at altitude by force of will.

Amid the clicks, hums, and cross-talk, Parson heard the officer say, "Give us just a minute. Markovich is onto something."

Irena's mouth curved into a hint of a smile. Parson noticed the rose-colored lip gloss, the only thing about her that wasn't all business. He stared at her and her console, dying to know what she was hearing. She gave no hint. Parson could only wait. His eyes focused on Irena's console as he tried to guess what news it had brought. Off interphone, Irena whispered to Gold, "I got a name." She wrote on her notepad: *Viktor Dušić.*

GOLD EXPECTED COLONEL WEBSTER to show interest
when Parson phoned him with the name. But she did not expect
him to drop everything, leave Manas in the hands of his vice commander, and fly commercial to Sarajevo. In a rented Ford, Parson
and Gold met him at the airport and drove him to the Holiday Inn.

Webster wanted to meet with everyone in private, so they
ordered room service for dinner and had the food sent to Cunningham's room. Gold and Parson crowded into the small room. Webster, in khaki trousers and a button-down shirt, took the reclining
chair, and Parson introduced Webster and the Serbian police officer, Dragan, to each other. Dragan sat on the desk chair, and he
offered up bottles of Tuzlanski pilsner.

Parson took one of the bottles, and he and Gold leaned against
the wall. Cunningham sat cross-legged on the bed, his Beretta and
shoulder rig beside him on the bedspread. Next to the weapon,
an open manila folder revealed photos of Viktor Dušić at various

ages. Some showed a young man in uniform. Others depicted a middle-aged businessman, usually in an expensive-looking suit and tie.

"Witnesses place him at Srebrenica back in 1995," Webster said. The colonel reminded everyone that more than eight thousand Muslims died there in probably the worst single incident of mass murder in Europe since World War II.

"Why hasn't he been arrested?" Parson asked.

"We've always had bigger fish to fry," Webster said. "Slobodan Milošević, Radovan Karadžić, Ratko Mladić, and other people at the top. This guy was just a lieutenant. But it's always bothered me that more people haven't paid for that crime."

To get the top commanders took years, Webster explained, let alone the trigger pullers. But Webster wanted the smaller fish, too. Especially if one of them was screwing with his airfield at Manas now, and maybe up to something worse.

Gold wondered just how deeply Webster had been involved with the prosecution of war criminals. Deeply enough, she gathered, to know people with enough horsepower to cut him loose from his post in Kyrgyzstan at a moment's notice. This country lawyer seemed to wield more authority in civilian clothes than in uniform.

"The Russian pilots we busted confirmed they'd been smuggling for Dušić, so we went to his office today to arrest him," Dragan said. "He wasn't there. His secretary said she didn't know where he was, and he wasn't at his home, either. I'm afraid he's gone underground."

"How did you get the pilots to talk?" Webster asked.

"They were looking at a long prison sentence, but they really didn't want to give us anything. I think they're real scared of Dušić. We had to offer complete immunity to get them to sing."

"Maybe we need to talk to that secretary again," Cunningham said. Dragan nodded.

If Cunningham had been reluctant to pursue this case to the end, Gold noted, he seemed to have a fire under him now. Gold felt almost guilty about the visit to the mass grave at Bratunac, but perhaps that day had made an impact on the young OSI agent.

Gold watched Parson sip his beer. How he must feel about Srebrenica and all that had happened in Bosnia, she could well imagine. She wouldn't call him a deep thinker, but Parson possessed a basic decency that could propel him to action swift and fierce. Webster seemed cut from similar cloth. However, Gold gathered that the colonel preferred to channel his outrage into the workings of the law. A legal mind of that caliber could have earned millions as a corporate attorney, but Webster apparently spent much of his time making far less in the pursuit of justice. Gold appreciated people who put personal gain aside for better callings. She wished she could articulate a theory about why people chose certain paths, what steered hearts toward good or evil. But she knew the wisdom of sages across the millennia had never answered those questions.

The next morning, Gold rode with Parson and the others to Belgrade. Cunningham and Dragan wanted to question a woman named Milica Vasović. Gold and Parson had no law enforcement authority, so they could take no role in the interrogation. But Dragan told them they could watch through a one-way window, with no audio feed, as he interviewed the secretary. Cunningham and Webster were allowed to sit in the room with Dragan, deep inside the Ministry of Internal Affairs headquarters.

Dragan ushered Milica to a chair. She was not handcuffed. Given Dragan's courtesy and the lack of restraints, Gold supposed the police considered Milica a witness rather than a suspect. Understandably, the young woman looked scared. Gold wondered if her face always stayed so pale and drawn. She wore her auburn hair at shoulder length, and she had dressed in a gray business outfit with the skirt cut at the knee.

Gold could hear nothing as Dragan began to speak. She didn't know Serbo-Croatian anyway, but now she lacked even the subtle cues of voice tone. Gold had nothing to monitor but body language.

The Serb officer gestured with open hands, fingers spread. He pursed his lips, nodded grimly as if delivering bad news to a friend. Gold detected nothing threatening in his manner, but Milica still seemed ill at ease. Dragan spoke for several minutes. When Milica finally spoke, she did so only briefly. Dragan appeared to ask a question. She spoke again, just for a few seconds. He offered her a cigarette and she took it. Dragan lit it for her, and the smoke curled toward the ceiling.

"So," Parson said, "do you think she's lying?"

"No. She doesn't look like she's hiding anything."

"How's that?"

"Gestures. She's facing him, not shifted to the side. She's making eye contact."

"So?"

"I've seen a lot of interrogations," Gold said. "You learn what lying looks like."

Parson at least had the grace not to ask her for details. But Gold had interpreted the words of many suspects under questioning, nearly all of them guilty. Some cursed and spewed threats. Some spat. Some refused to talk at all. Some broke down and sobbed. At one point or another, most attempted to lie. When they did so, they looked away. They looked at the floor. They folded their arms, clenched their fists. Only the most expert operatives could fake the gestures of honesty. That feat required both knowledge and presence of mind. It was almost as hard as defeating a lie detector.

Milica began to weep. She placed her cigarette in an ash tray. She opened her purse, found a tissue, and dabbed at her eyes. Gold wondered how much Dragan was telling her. At a minimum, she supposed, he was telling Milica about the narcotics trafficking. But if he wanted her cooperation, he might also talk about her boss's history.

That would amount to a gamble, though. What if the woman was a hard-line Serb nationalist? What if that's why Dušić hired her in the first place? Not likely, Gold considered. Women could hate just as well as men, but an educated European woman of the professional class didn't fit the usual profile of a bigot.

Dragan opened a manila envelope. From the envelope, he drew a handful of black-and-white prints. Gold saw that he had taken the gamble. One photograph showed a pile of skulls, some still wearing blindfolds. Fresh dirt surrounded the skulls, as if they had just been dug from the ground. The terrain did not look like Bratunac; the picture showed a different mass grave somewhere else. Another photo depicted Sarajevo in flames, smoke billowing from an office tower. Yet another showed a victim of shelling. A man in civilian clothing sat up on a stretcher, holding his right leg. The foot was gone; the ankle ended in a tangle of lacerated muscle tissue. Shrapnel did not cut cleanly but ripped and tore.

Milica turned away from the photos. She cried for a few minutes. Dragan placed his hand on her shoulder. Then she seemed to pull herself together. With a fresh tissue, she wiped her eyes again. She blew her nose. She picked up the cigarette, tapped the ash into the ash tray, and took a long drag.

Come on girl, Gold thought. Find your courage. Do the right thing.

The secretary exhaled a plume of smoke. Took another drag, held it. Gold had never smoked, but she'd observed that smoking brought its own particular syntax to body language. As Milica kept the nicotine inside her lungs to calm her nerves, she was thinking. When oxygen debt finally got the better of her, she let out the smoke and put down her cigarette. She opened her purse, took out her cell phone. Scrolled through stored contacts. Now and then she stopped and read off a number. Dragan jotted the numbers onto a writing pad.

"That looks like progress," Parson said.

"It does," Gold said. "But can't the Rivet Joint crew pick up the phone communications anyway?"

"They can. But I think if they have numbers, they can narrow things down a lot quicker. They have Dušić's cell, but they might not have all his contacts."

Gold looked forward to flying again, to seeing what else Irena might learn armed with new intelligence. Parson would want to get back into the air as well. Strange to see him on duty wearing blue jeans instead of a flight suit.

The interview ended, and everyone filed out of the interrogation room. Gold and Parson waited for about half an hour in the observation room. Maybe the police were briefing Milica on the steps they'd take to protect her now that she'd cooperated, Gold thought. Gold wished she could meet the young woman, offer some assurance that she'd made a good decision. But by the time Dragan came into the observation room, Milica had gone home.

"Did you get anything useful?" Parson asked.

"We did," Dragan said. "Seems our friend Dušić has a right-hand man named Stefan, and she gave us his phone number."

"She looked pretty rattled," Gold said.

"She was. I tried not to frighten her. She's a nice girl, and I don't believe she had any idea her boss was up to no good."

"Arms dealers aren't usually the salt of the earth," Parson said.

"Yeah, but everything Dušić did in the daylight was legal, and I think that's all Milica knew about."

When Gold and the others left the Ministry of Internal Affairs, it was nearly seven in the evening. Dragan led the group to a local pub for dinner. During the walk, he stopped at a newsstand for a paper. The police officer tucked under his arm a copy of *Večernje Novosti*.

The pub appeared to be a watering hole for workmen. Patrons crowded around the bar. Blue smoke hung in the air. Pulsing electronic dance music blared from speakers, though the pub had no dance floor. The music and the chatter and babble of the crowd made conversation difficult, so Dragan suggested a table outside.

Cunningham and Dragan, Gold noted, sat with their backs to the wall so they could observe everyone coming and going. Police instinct, she supposed. Gold sat next to Webster, across from Parson. The waitress came to their table, and she looked no more than nineteen. The woman had dyed streaks of red and purple into her black hair, and she wore a ring through her lower lip. Loose white T-shirt with no bra, black leather pants. Dragan said in English, "Beers?" Parson and Webster said yes. Dragan spoke in his native language, and the waitress nodded and disappeared.

Peals of drunken laughter emanated from the bar. Another workday done for plumbers and electricians, postmen and truck drivers, looking forward to the weekend, Gold imagined. Dragan opened his newspaper and scanned the top fold. He sighed and tossed the paper onto the tabletop without reading further.

"What does it say?" Gold asked.

"More trouble," Dragan said. "Another riot. Cars torched."

"What the hell?" Parson said.

"I was just thinking that," Dragan said. "Why now, after all we've been through? I worry that it won't take much to set off something very bad."

Without further comment, Dragan watched bar customers come and go. The waitress returned with a tray of beers. She set down each glass with a dull thunk, and she sloshed suds down the side of Parson's glass. He wiped away the spill with his own handkerchief.

"I wonder if the service here is always this good," Parson said. Dragan shrugged, and he eyed the waitress as she disappeared back inside.

Several minutes later, two men came out. Both looked drunk; Gold gathered they were the source of some of the laughter and roars she'd heard from inside. One of them stopped and stared at Parson. The man swayed on his feet. He looked like he weighed more than two hundred and fifty pounds, most of it muscle. Beard stubble and a dirty sweatshirt. The other guy was thinner, and both were probably in their thirties. Gold took them for coworkers in some city public works department, or maybe an auto body shop. The big one muttered in Serbo-Croatian, and Dragan looked straight at him. Then the big one spoke in English.

"You Americans," he said to Parson. Gold couldn't tell if it was a question or a statement.

By way of greeting, Parson raised his beer glass. Probably as good a response as any, Gold figured. Courtesy with as few words as possible was the best way to get rid of a drunk.

"You bomb my country and give it to Turks," the big guy said. He leaned over Cunningham to glare at Parson.

Dragan spoke in Serbo-Croatian, and the drunk answered with what sounded to Gold like epithets. The smaller guy pulled on the drunk's arm, and the drunk pushed his friend away.

"Come on, dude," Cunningham said. "We don't want any trouble."

"You, too, American," the drunk said.

Once more, Dragan said something in his own language. The drunk spat a response that made Dragan reach for an object under his jacket. His badge or ID, Gold hoped, instead of his gun.

"Policija," Dragan said. He flipped open an ID folder, but the drunk didn't see it. The man lunged at Cunningham and Parson,

grabbed Cunningham by the shirt collar. Tried to push over Cunningham's chair.

Cunningham did not push back. With what seemed an effortless motion, he took the drunk by the head with both hands and pivoted out of the chair. Using the drunk's own momentum, Cunningham shoved the man's head against the wall. Gold heard a nasty thud when the drunk's skull contacted wood, but the blow did not put him out. He scrabbled to his feet, snatched up a bottle, and raised it like a club.

Against whatever skills Cunningham possessed, the big drunk's size and strength seemed only to work against him. When the drunk swung down with the bottle, Cunningham stepped inside the arc of the swing. He took the man's wrist in what could have been a dancer's move. Sidestepped behind the drunk, folded the bottle arm against the man's back. Bent the man's hand.

Gold heard the wrist crack. The bottle dropped and shattered. The drunk screamed. Cunningham kicked his feet out from under him and dropped him to the ground. Dragan pulled his handgun, pointed it at the man, and shouted, *"Policija!"* Then he smiled slightly and added in English, "Police, you stupid son of a bitch."

Cunningham turned toward the drunk's friend. The man raised his hands and said, "Soh-ree, soh-ree."

"Cover this genius for me while I make a phone call," Dragan said to Cunningham. Cunningham drew his own service weapon. Dragan dialed his mobile phone. "I'll get a car down here to take this guy to jail," he said.

"Why the fuck did they pick on us?" Parson asked.

"He got drunk in there talking about how much he hated Muslims," Dragan said. "Wait—hang on." The Serb officer began speaking on the phone in his native language.

Webster picked up the thought. "He got all drunked up, and

then he came out here and heard us speaking English. Maybe he noticed your blue jeans."

"Oh, shit," Parson said. "My bad."

Gold could understand Parson's mistake. Every U.S. military member knew you didn't advertise your nationality in certain places. You wouldn't put on a cowboy hat to walk through a mall in Saudi Arabia. But blue jeans shouldn't have been enough to cause trouble in the former Yugoslavia. The atmospherics here were changing, and not for the better.

Dragan ended his mobile call, and he spoke in Serbo-Croatian to the drunk's friend. The man responded with what sounded like gratitude and apology, and he turned and walked away.

"Damn," Parson said to Cunningham, "you just about made that guy kick his own ass."

"They teach you all kinds of good stuff in OSI," Cunningham said. "He shouldn't have made me get all tidewater on him."

"Guess not."

Dragan pulled the injured drunk to his feet, sat him in a chair, and handcuffed him. The man moaned when the cuff went around his right hand.

"Quit crying," Dragan said. "You did it to yourself." Then Dragan switched to Serbo-Croatian and spoke for two full minutes. A lecture.

A police car pulled up in front of the pub. Its lights flashed, but the officers did not use the siren. When two uniformed police officers got out of the vehicle, Dragan motioned them over and briefed them. Then he said in English, "You know why I despise people like our Nobel Peace Prize winner here? If they could, they would drag us straight back to hell."

DUŠIĆ TURNED ON his laptop computer in his hotel room in Tuzla. Ever since the arrests at the airport, he had worried whether any of the fliers or ground crew would talk. He'd awakened this morning with a brilliant idea: check the flight schedule for the Russian freight airline he'd been using. The police would surely have impounded the aircraft. If they released it, and if the same flight crew flew it out, that would be a good indication those fools had cooperated with the authorities.

The airline's website came up quickly; Dušić had listed the address under "Favorites." Only the company's best customers got passwords to view the flight schedules and crew rosters. Dušić typed ZASTAVA#1, then pressed ENTER. He gazed out the window while he waited for the schedule to pop up. Outside, the early morning fog drifted like smoke from a firefight.

The flight schedule appeared on his screen, with origin and destination cities listed in alphabetical order. He chose cities of origin and began scrolling down: Adana, Ankara, Aviano Air Base, Bali. Dušić stopped when he found the Slavic spelling for Belgrade: *Beograd*.

And there it was. Same tail number, same crew. Departing this evening.

Dmitri had betrayed him.

Dušić felt anger rise within him. The emotion came in hard lines and sharp points, like a bucket full of nails. He could not tolerate security breaches such as this. By now, all his underlings should have understood the price of failing him, but he could see they needed a reminder. He phoned Stefan in the next room.

"Change of plans," Dušić said. "Pack your things."

"What is wrong?" Stefan asked.

"Get in here and I will tell you."

Stefan sat on the bed while Dušić briefed him. He nodded gravely, opened his mouth to speak. But he held his silence until Dušić finished outlining his plan.

"Are you sure this is a good idea?" Stefan asked finally. "It could jeopardize the main operation. And the damage is already done."

"I intend to see no more damage is done."

"But we are so close to zero hour, Viktor. We have only to drive the bomb to the Patriarchate and get the *razvodnik*s in place with their weapons."

"Who is to say more people will not talk?" Dušić said. "What if the *razvodnik*s lose their nerve? I find a little retribution tends to keep mouths closed."

"It is risky to return to Belgrade now."

Dušić closed his eyes and sighed. He mustered patience he could find for no one but Stefan. The man had proved his courage and loyalty, and he deserved a little forbearance. "My friend," Dušić said, "if you wanted safety, you would not have chosen the path of the warrior."

That ended the argument. Whenever Stefan needed persuading, Dušić found he could appeal to his war comrade's soldier ethic or Serb pride. Either worked pretty well.

They checked out of the hotel, and Dušić paid with cash. Stefan drove the van. He scanned the terrain as the vehicle rolled by villages, forests, and fields. The fog was lifting now, and sunlight dappled the wet road.

"Has that M24 ever been fired?" Stefan asked.

"No," Dušić said. "It is brand-new."

"If we're going to do this, I will need to sight it in, at least roughly."

"Very well. Find a good place and do what you need to do."

With the sound suppressor, Stefan could sight in the rifle without drawing too much attention. The device would eliminate much of the rifle's report, though not all. Dušić thanked his stars and his own good judgment that he'd purchased the full M24 sniper system, silencer included. Cutting corners never paid off. When it came to weaponry, he believed in eliminating every technical disadvantage. You still needed the right men behind those weapons, but you owed your troops proper equipment.

Stefan slowed as he approached an open meadow, but then he accelerated, evidently rejecting the spot as too exposed. He repeated the process at two other fields. But at a bend in the road where the forest grew so near that spruce limbs overhung the pavement, Stefan coasted to a stop. He examined the woods, and he pulled the van onto a farm path.

"This spot will do," Stefan said. "If we are discovered, we can just say we were poaching game."

Dušić hoped it wouldn't come to that, but they had to take the risk. Without fine-tuning the rifle's optic, Stefan's bullet might fly wild and render this entire side mission pointless. Stefan shut off the engine, unbuckled his seat belt, got out, and opened the back doors of the van. He lifted the M24 from its case. Paused and looked around.

"I have no paper targets," Stefan said.

On the floor of the van, Dušić saw a yellowed copy of *Politika Ekspres*, a defunct nationalist tabloid. He tore off the front page and folded it in half. "Use this," he said.

Stefan took the paper, turned, and stalked into the forest. The crackle of his footsteps over twigs and spruce needles remained audible even after he disappeared from view. When he returned, he gathered up a box of 7.62-millimeter cartridges. For ammunition, Dušić had also selected the best: hollow-point, match-grade bullets, 175-grain. Expensive little bastards, nearly a hundred dinars every time you pulled the trigger. Stefan pressed four of them into the rifle's magazine and closed the bolt on a chambered round. He carried the weapon, the box of ammunition, and a pair of binoculars to the edge of the woods. The nearest house was about a kilometer away.

Dušić followed him and watched as he extended the legs of the rifle's bipod, opened the lens caps on the scope, and settled into a prone position. Stefan sighted through the scope along an avenue among the woods; these trees had not grown naturally but had been planted in rows. On a branch perhaps a hundred meters away, Stefan had spiked the page of newsprint. He let out a chestful of air, held his breath, and fired.

The bullet made a crack as it pierced the sound barrier, but without the usual booming slam of a high-powered rifle. Bark flew from the tree trunk beside the newsprint. The paper appeared untouched.

"Hmm," Stefan said. "Would you call that six inches off?" Western measurements for an American scope. He racked the bolt, ejected the expended brass, and chambered a fresh round.

"At least," Dušić said. He picked up the fired cartridge and placed it in his pocket. No sense leaving evidence.

Stefan turned the rifle on its side, looked at the windage knob. "Half minute of angle," he muttered to himself. "Twelve clicks left." He turned the knob, counting aloud to twelve.

The maestro tunes his Stradivarius, Dušić thought. Stefan rested the M24 on the legs of the bipod, sighted, fired again.

The newsprint barely trembled as the bullet cut through it. Dušić squinted, could not see where the round had hit. Stefan raised his cheek from the rifle stock and looked through the binoculars.

"Centered pretty well, but a little high," he said.

"Maybe crank the elevation down a click or two," Dušić suggested.

"No, I like it a little high at this range. From the environment you describe, I'm anticipating a target perhaps two hundred meters out."

"That sounds reasonable." Dušić deferred to Stefan on the technical details of marksmanship. A good officer should not micromanage.

Stefan fired two more rounds, reloaded, and fired four more, just to confirm the zero point. When Dušić borrowed the binoculars, he saw that all of the bullets had grouped within a centimeter of one another. He gave the binoculars back to Stefan and picked up the rest of the empty brass. The fired cartridges clanked in his pocket like spare change. He stepped through the woods to retrieve Stefan's makeshift target, and he observed the neat, round holes drilled through the paper. The searing passage of the bullets had left blackened edges around each hole. Two of the rounds had struck in nearly the same spot; their holes overlapped as if two half-moons had linked.

The whole effort took less than twenty minutes. No curious passersby or farmers angry over trespass ever appeared. Dušić felt gratified as Stefan steered the van back out onto the road. The success of a mission could depend on attention to details, and the two men had just taken care of an important one. Ideally, Dušić would have seen the weapon sighted in well ahead of time, but he'd not expected to need it so soon. The drug bust had forced him to move fast, and he had adapted and recovered. This was war, and war was chaos.

And now he would send a message: Those who let him down would pay dearly.

Dmitri should have known better. But what disappointed Dušić even more than the betrayal was Dmitri's lack of vision. Russians, close cousins to the Serbs, also knew what it meant to struggle for their land and their people. Well, most of them did, but apparently not Dmitri and the rest of that crew. The Russian pilot should have held his tongue and accepted his prison sentence as a matter of Slavic unity.

As the van crossed from Bosnia into Serbia—the border Dušić hoped to erase someday—he considered operational details for the rest of this side mission. More than likely, no one at the airport knew Stefan's van. He and Stefan could probably drive around the freight terminal and scout a good firing position, as long as they weren't too obvious. They didn't need to enter any secured zone of the airport; Stefan could fire over or through the chain-link fence. The van itself could serve as a hide. As urban sniping environments went, this one seemed quite favorable. And Stefan had plenty of experience in urban sniping.

A few hours later, in Belgrade, Dušić felt a bit like a fugitive as the airport came into view. Just days ago he'd visited this place openly as an important businessman, a captain of commerce. Now he needed to stay as unobtrusive as possible. Dušić could imagine how President Karadžić and General Mladić must have felt, once-powerful men forced to live this way for years until they were captured.

Plenty of time remained for scouting. As the van rolled along the airport's perimeter road, Dušić could see the big tail of the

Antonov looming among the warehouse and hangars. When the van moved farther along the road and closer to the aircraft, he spotted a ground power cart's cable plugged into a receptacle on the side of the Antonov. The cargo doors yawned open. So the schedule had been correct. The ground crew was loading cargo for a departure this evening.

"There is your target area," Dušić said. "The pilot will be a thin man with gray and black hair, and he is often unshaven. I will help you identify him. Get him first, and if you can hit other crew members, so much the better."

Stefan said nothing. He lowered his sunglasses and peered over the lenses. The gesture made Dušić think of a musician examining a score, or perhaps a civil engineer sizing up the river where he must build a bridge. Professional analysis.

Dušić envied his friend's cool detachment. Killing unemotionally came with so much more precision and elegance. Many times when Dušić had killed, he'd done so in fury. Righteous anger had its place, but so did cold blood.

Stefan drove past the Antonov, and he began to circle the airport. A Qatar Airways jet lifted off, its vertical fin bearing the company's logo. The logo, painted in burgundy, depicted the antlered head of an Arabian oryx. Dušić noted that if circumstances allowed, Stefan could try to time his shot with the roar of a takeoff and mask what little sound escaped the rifle's suppressor.

In the flow of traffic, Stefan followed the lanes to a parking deck marked AERODROM NIKOLA TESLA. Stefan grunted in dismissal. The parking deck was no good. No clear shot, and with other vehicles and people too close. This environment called for a bit of blending in, but not too much. The vehicle needed to remain far enough from passersby so that no one could look inside. But a van simply parked on the shoulder of the highway would draw the immediate attention of police.

After a right turn down another access road, Stefan slowed to survey other possibilities. Across the access road from the freight terminal, an office building bore a sign that read JAT TEHNIKA, an aviation engineering company. The company's maintenance hangars probably operated in shifts around the clock, but Dušić supposed these office workers would all go home soon.

"What do you think?" Dušić asked.

Stefan craned his neck to look back toward the freight ramp and the Antonov. He pulled into the Jat Tehnika parking area and nosed into one of several open spaces.

"If the car park does not fill up," Stefan said, "I can make this work. But it is a longer shot than I anticipated."

Dušić did not worry about the distance. He had seen Stefan kill at much greater ranges.

A balding man wearing a loosened tie, his paunch bulging beneath a white dress shirt, emerged from the office building. Two of his coworkers followed. The balding man carried car keys in his right hand. He pressed a button on a key fob to unlock his gray sedan, then sat in the car and drove away. His colleagues followed him.

"I think this car park will empty out rather than grow more crowded," Dušić said. He checked his watch. "We have more than an hour before the aircraft takes off. Drive around for a bit and then come back."

"Very well."

The two men cruised the airport grounds for a time, avoiding passing the same area more than once or twice. They threaded among the taxis waiting at Arrivals, coursed through the traffic dropping off people at Departures. When they returned to Jat Tehnika, sunset shot the sky scarlet.

"Will you have glare in your eyes?" Dušić asked.

"I am more concerned about the firing angle," Stefan said. He stopped with the van diagonally across two empty parking spaces. Shut off the engine and set the parking brake.

"Do not park carelessly," Dušić said. "It could draw the attention of traffic police."

"I'm afraid I have to," Stefan said. "Watch."

Stefan walked around the side of the van and opened the back doors. He climbed in and shut one of the doors. In a duffel bag he found a bungee cord, and he hooked one end of the cord to the bottom of the open door. Working on his knees, he attached the other end to the bumper in such a way that the door hung slightly ajar. Stefan crouched and peered through the resulting crack. He took the M24 from its case, rested his back against the inside wall of the van, and looped the sling around his arm. At an oblique angle, he sighted through the opening. With the van parked askew, that opening allowed him to aim toward the freight ramp. Now he had a natural line of fire toward the Antonov.

"Ah," Dušić said, "the perfect urban sniper's hide."

"Not perfect," Stefan said, "but it will do."

Dušić moved to the van's driver seat and adjusted the side mirror to give him a view of the Antonov. The reflection would at least let him see when figures moved toward the aircraft. He'd have to turn in his seat or even get out of the vehicle to positively identify Dmitri.

Fifteen minutes went by with no sign of the crew. The whine of an auxiliary power unit rose from the jet. Dušić cursed under his breath. Apparently a flight engineer was already in the cockpit, powering up systems. What if the whole crew was on board?

"Stay alert," Dušić said. "I do not know if we have missed our chance."

Stefan turned the zoom adjustment on the rifle's scope, steadied the weapon across his knees. He looked ready. Dušić had studied the fine art of killing, and he knew taking life came more easily with distance from the target. Stefan had a few hundred yards of spatial distance, which made the act a little more antiseptic than a point-blank shot. But psychic distance helped, too. That distance happened naturally when shooting Muslims—inferior people in every way, to Dušić's mind. Less simple to shoot Russians, tied to Serbs by faith and culture. Dušić hoped Stefan could find psychic distance through Dmitri's sin of betrayal, a moral flaw. Stefan would probably need such moral separation. That was one of the few drawbacks to soldiers like Stefan, who killed with premeditation but without rage. They had too much time to think.

At the edge of the mirror, Dušić noticed movement. He twisted to get a better look, and he saw two figures walking toward the Antonov. Both held those large briefcases pilots used to carry their manuals and charts. So it wasn't too late. Thank God.

"You have a target," Dušić said. "The taller one is Dmitri."

"I see them," Stefan said. He shifted his shoulders against the wall of the van, thumbed the rifle's safety.

Dmitri put down his briefcase at the foot of the Antonov's crew ladder. He turned and appeared to speak with his copilot. Stefan raised his head from the stock, looked around.

"What are you waiting for?" Dušić asked.

Stefan aimed, placed the first joint of his index finger on the trigger. Dmitri began climbing the ladder, holding the rail with his right hand and carrying his briefcase in his left. Stefan still did not fire, and now Dušić was worried.

"You had better—" Dušić began, but the rumble of a takeoff drowned out his sentence. He saw recoil jolt Stefan's shoulder, but he heard no report from the rifle at all.

Dmitri slumped on the ladder, clung to the rail with the crook of his arm. He dropped the briefcase, which thudded down the steps and struck the copilot square in the chest. The briefcase bounced to the pavement and broke open, spilling books and papers.

Stefan racked the bolt and chambered a fresh round. He closed one eye, watched through the scope. Dušić saw blood drip from somewhere on Dmitri's body and spill onto the steps below him. As the pilot bled, his arm let go and his body rolled and tumbled down the ladder until he struck the tarmac headfirst. Stains darkened Dmitri's flight suit, but Dušić could not tell exactly where the bullet had struck.

The copilot, most likely still dumbfounded by what was happening, kneeled beside Dmitri. Incomprehension was probably the last emotion he felt. His head jerked, and Dušić saw a burst of vapor: the red mist of the bullet strike. The copilot collapsed across the body of his crewmate.

"Excellent," Dušić said.

Stefan did not reply. He ejected the empty brass and put down the M24. With one swift motion, he released the bungee cord and closed the rear door. Dušić moved to get out of the driver seat, but Stefan said, "No. You drive." Stefan came forward, stepped over the console, and lowered himself into the passenger seat. Dušić started the engine.

"That was fine work, my friend," Dušić said. He stepped on the accelerator and drove out of the parking area.

Stefan reached under the seat and produced a bottle of slivovitz. The image on the label appeared festive: a cluster of ripe plums. He twisted the cap, broke the seal. Took a long swallow, closed his eyes hard, wiped his mouth with the back of his hand. Stefan stared out the window. He did not offer a drink to Dušić.

21

ALOFT IN THE RIVET JOINT, Gold sat in what had become her accustomed seat next to Irena. A night flight this time, but night and day hardly existed in the back end of the surveillance jet. No windows, just computers and monitoring gear. Gold imagined Parson found a much better view up front in the cockpit jump seat. The plane had taken off into a clear Balkan night with a glittering canopy of stars. Cunningham sat in the back with Gold and Irena. All three wore headsets for monitoring the Rivet Joint's channels.

Thanks to information given up by Dušić's secretary, Milica, they now monitored another specific cell phone. The mission reminded Gold of a jigsaw puzzle with tiny pieces. If you found where one piece fit, the picture took shape a bit more, and offered further clues to solve the rest of the puzzle.

But so far tonight, nothing. Irena doodled on her notepad. Her console's utility light cast a pale glow on the paper. She drew a picture of a seagull in flight, wings outstretched in a glide. She wrote characters in Cyrillic, which Gold could not decipher. She went back to the seagull and drew a little set of headphones on it.

"So you're putting him to work, too," Gold said.

"Might as well," Irena said.

"This makes me think of my granddad's stories," Cunningham said.

"How's that?" Irena asked.

"He'd fly these long patrols off the Outer Banks, looking for submarines. Hours and hours of droning, and then all of a sudden things would get exciting."

The OSI agent described his grandfather's flights in a Stinson 10A, a little yellow single-engine plane that looked nothing like a threat to the Third Reich. The Stinson skimmed just a few hundred feet above the ocean. The elder Cunningham had talked about how he learned to recognize the difference between heavily loaded freighters riding low in the water, and empty vessels riding high. From time to time, he would catch a glimpse of a dark form beneath the waves. Sometimes he discerned only the shadow of a cloud. But sometimes the dark form held a consistent shape and course, and turned out to be a member of Admiral Doenitz's wolf pack.

"My granddad hunted with his eyes," Cunningham said, "and you guys hunt with your ears. Except your plane cost a few dollars more."

"Just a few," Irena said.

Parson came into the aft section of the airplane. He held a slip of thermal paper in his hand. Gold wondered about the serious look in his eyes. Parson seemed to enjoy flying with this crew, learning about a corner of the Air Force he hadn't experienced before. At altitude in the Rivet Joint, he'd appeared as relaxed as Gold had ever seen him while on duty. But now he wore his mission face.

Standing behind Irena, he plugged his headset into a spare

interphone cord, pressed his talk switch, and said, "Just got this satcom message." He dropped the paper on the table in front of Cunningham. The message read

TWO RUSSIAN PILOTS WHO TURNED EVIDENCE AGAINST DUSIC WERE SHOT DEAD TODAY. SNIPER FIRE AS THEY PREPARED TO BOARD AIRCRAFT. NO ONE SAW ANYTHING. INTERNAL AFFAIRS MINISTRY POLICE INVESTIGATING.

WEBSTER.

"Oh, my God," Irena said. "What does all this mean?"

"It means Dušić is one dangerous son of a bitch," Cunningham said. "He's an arms dealer, so we know he has resources. But this is damned crazy, so it means he's unpredictable. No telling how he'll use those resources."

A good point, Gold thought, and a frightening one. Money and irrationality made a bad combination. And irrationality had to play a role. Why else would you commit murder to protect a drug ring that's already been exposed?

"Well, sir, I sure hope we can find something useful," Irena said. She turned a volume control as if that somehow could extract more information from the earth below.

"Can you get a fix on his location?" Parson asked.

"The guys up there will try," Irena said, pointing to crew members in seats farther forward. "It'll help if he makes a call."

For Gold, the latest turn of events brought forth an old sadness. She struggled to reconcile the things that had happened in this part of Europe during the 1990s. Someday she would step back from the action and take the rest of her life to reflect and study. Gold looked forward to an academic career, spending her days among students, surrounded by marble, mahogany, and great thoughts. But for now she would ride this expensive piece of machinery and help Parson see this thing through to the end. Parson seemed to have carried a free-floating grudge ever since the Bosnian War, a resentment that such things could happen in his lifetime. And now he could affix that grudge to a face and a name: Viktor Dušić.

"Do your drug cases always get this weird?" Parson asked Cunningham.

"Not usually," the OSI agent said. "Most of the time it's some dumb airman selling pot out of his car. The crime rate in the military is actually lower than in the general population, but we still get a few losers."

Cunningham explained how he'd spent more of his career protecting service members than arresting them. On one of his first deployments, the Air Force gave him a tough task: help stop the rocket and grenade attacks launched every night against one of the forward bases in Afghanistan. The QRF teams, the quick reaction force, had killed a few insurgents; one trio of bad guys had gotten vaporized when an Apache gunship caught them on infrared. But the rockets kept coming. An RPG-7 round exploded just outside Cunningham's hooch one night. He clutched his mattress, rolled it off the bed frame, and took cover under it on the floor, wondering if a Posturepedic would stop shrapnel. At that moment he realized he needed to get creative. The coalition couldn't just shoot its way out of this problem.

He noted that every Wednesday and Sunday local merchants set up a market outside the base, selling rugs and junk souvenirs to GIs. Cunningham suspected some of the merchants were scoping out the base for targets. But even if they weren't actively helping the bad guys, they probably knew the bad guys. Or they knew somebody who knew the bad guys.

Cunningham made a suggestion to the commander: Tell those merchants no more market days until they give us some names, or at least until those rocket attacks stop. On the days they sold to Americans, the merchants probably made more money than they could earn otherwise in a year. He got the idea from the old watermen back home. Their livelihoods depended on the market for the seafood they caught. No market, no money.

Money talked. The merchants fingered some Haqqani Network bastards, and a night raid by American and Afghan special ops troops netted twenty terrorists. Twelve captured, eight dead. Half of them came from Pakistan.

"But even that," Cunningham said, "seems like simple stuff compared to this."

"Webster wants this guy real bad," Parson said.

"I do, too," Cunningham said.

"I see why," Irena said. "It's hard to believe I've been listening to the voice responsible for that." She pointed to the satcom message.

"He's responsible for a lot more than that," Gold said.

"Damned straight," Parson said. "Hey, we might have a long night ahead of us. Who wants coffee?"

"I do, sir," Irena said.

"Make it two," Cunningham said.

"Three," Gold said.

Parson made two trips to the galley. Each time he came back with two foam cups of bitter black coffee. He kept the fourth cup for himself, and did not return to the cockpit. With no more open crew stations available, he stood behind Gold's seat, sipped from his cup and watched the linguists work. Gold calculated that, at the moment, he cared more about catching bad guys than flying airplanes.

Irena removed her shoulder straps but kept her lap belt fastened. She slid her seat back a bit, clearly trying to get comfortable and concentrate better. Voices in Serbo-Croatian, Italian, and German flowed through the circuits. Irena showed interest in none of it. But after another hour of flying, suddenly her back stiffened. She turned a volume knob, wrote down the time.

Gold glanced at Parson, who had also noticed Irena's posture. Parson smiled. He had told her these airborne linguists were like English setters: You could tell from their body language when they were onto something. She'd thought it a crude comparison, but he was right.

"I got Dušić on two-alpha," Irena said on interphone. Then she held up her hand for silence. For several minutes she monitored the call and took notes in Cyrillic. The elegant lettering on her writing pad looked almost like written music.

But all at once, something broke the spell for Irena. She slapped her pen down onto the pad. She whispered in English, off interphone, "Give me a fucking break." The skin on her nose wrinkled as if something smelled bad. A sign of disgust, Gold supposed. First time Gold had ever heard Irena swear.

Irena pressed her interphone switch and said, "All right, he hung up. I'll let you know if I hear anything else."

"Copy that, Irena," one of her crewmates said. "We'll geolocate that signal."

"Is he in Belgrade?" Cunningham asked.

"Negative," the crewman said, "and I think he's moving."

"What did he say?" Gold asked.

"He was talking about some kind of operation," Irena said, "but I couldn't tell much about it."

"You heard something that pissed you off," Parson said.

"Yes, sir. He started talking about poetry. And he quoted from *The Mountain Wreath*."

Irena told them *The Mountain Wreath* was a classic Serbian epic from the 1800s. She also said present-day hard-line nationalists read it as a celebration of ethnic cleansing. Dušić had quoted some favorite lines:

May God strike you, loathsome degenerates,
why do we need the Turk's faith among us?

"But the poet was writing about a tribal way of life that doesn't exist anymore," Irena said. "That story is an artifact, not a manual for anything we need to do now."

"Sounds like the way the Confederate flag gets misused," Cunningham said. "The Stars and Bars should just stand for a bygone era, but dumbasses use it as a symbol of modern hate."

"Exactly, sir," Irena said. "I never made that connection before, but you're right."

Gold could see that Irena took pride in the Serbian language and Serbian literature, and took offense when that literature got used for a twisted purpose. But Irena didn't take more time to talk about old poems. The young linguist spent several minutes conversing on interphone with some of her crewmates. Gold had learned that the people who sat in forward crew stations were not language specialists but electronic warfare officers called Ravens. Irena spoke with the Ravens about where those cell phone signals originated.

"Sir, did you say he was not in Belgrade?" Irena asked.

"That's right, Irena," the Raven answered. "And here's something else: That new phone number, the Stefan guy, is coming up in the same location."

"They're riding together?"

"I think so."

"Damn, you guys are scary," Parson said.

"If I ever have a girlfriend who flies on one of these planes," Cunningham said, "I sure won't cheat on her."

Irena smiled, but she never took her eyes off her console and notepad. "All right," she said, "if they call anybody else, we'll have even more clues."

The buzz on the interphone and monitoring circuits settled down for a while. Parson went for more coffee. The brewed stuff had run out; this time he came back with cups of hot water and packets of Nescafé. The packets bore a company website with a dot-UK address. At some point this crew must have stocked up supplies at a British base.

Gold ripped open the packet, poured the instant coffee into the hot water. As she stirred with a plastic straw, she noticed Irena sit up straight.

"She's on point again," Parson whispered.

"I got another call," Irena said on interphone. She wrote down the time, adjusted a volume control.

"It's that Stefan number," the Raven said.

"Roger that," Irena said. She made more notes in Serbo-Croatian. She stopped writing and leaned back in her seat. Whatever she'd heard drained the color from her face. The lividity of Irena's skin reminded Gold of expressions she'd seen in Afghanistan. People looked that way when frightened.

She picked up her pen again, and now she wrote in English: HOLY ASSEMBLY OF BISHOPS. PATRIARCHATE. A few lines down she added another phrase: CAR BOMB.

22

PARSON SAT IN WHEN IRENA briefed Dragan and other Serbian and Bosnian law officers about the call she'd intercepted. The group converged at the Sarajevo Holiday Inn. Cunningham and Webster also joined the meeting. As Irena and the lawmen spoke, a lot of things that hadn't made sense to Parson suddenly fit a deadly pattern. Dušić probably had a connection with the church burnings and resulting riots. The fires had reopened wounds only just starting to heal. With small-time arson, the arms dealer had effectively piled up kegs of gunpowder for a big-time explosion. The attack on the Holy Assembly of Bishops would light the match.

"Dušić is pretty cagey," Dragan said. "How did you get all this?"

"Not from Dušić himself," Irena said. "Most of it came from a conversation Stefan had with one of the worker bees. *Razvodnik*s, as Dušić calls them."

"Privates," Dragan said. "Yeah, sounds like something an old Serb officer might say."

"Stefan sounded drunk. Maybe that's why he got sloppy with OPSEC."

"Thank God he did."

"So why don't you just ask the bishops to postpone their get-together until you catch these bastards?" Parson asked.

"We did," Dragan said. "They say they won't give in to terrorism. And the assembly convenes in three days."

So now some war criminal wanted to blow up people of his own faith to relive his glory days, to start a new conflict. Parson lacked Gold's knowledge of history and religion, but he figured nobody's religion locked down divine truth. At best, you could just get a far sighting of truth, like a fleeting echo on a radar scope set to max range. Some people, like Gold, found wisdom in their faith. And some found excuses to spill a hell of a lot of blood.

"Now it comes down to old-school police work," Webster said. "They just have to find Dušić before the assembly starts."

"They have to get him in time," Irena said.

"Every cop in Bosnia and Serbia carries a description of Dušić, and of the vehicles registered in his name and in Stefan's name," Dragan said. "We'll need some luck, but maybe that fancy plane of yours can make us some luck."

"We'll do all we can, sir," Irena said.

"If they find Dušić," Cunningham said, "they'll have murder charges to hang on him now. Even if they can't prove war crimes, they can put him away for a long time."

"I'll take what I can get," Webster said.

"I hope they just shoot his ass," Cunningham said.

"I don't want that. I hope we get him alive. I want him on trial."

The cop and the prosecutor, Parson thought. Both wanted wrongs made right, but in different ways. Cunningham preferred to deal with Dušić the way Cunningham's forebears might have dealt with a boat thief or rapist: slit his throat and feed him to the sharks. Webster wanted a teachable moment for the whole world to see. Either one worked for Parson.

After the meeting, Parson found Gold in the lobby with the rest of the Rivet Joint crew. They were waiting for Irena. Time to fly.

Webster looked pleased to see the fliers getting ready to go up on another mission. He folded his arms and smiled. *"Fiat justitia, ruat caelum,"* he said. Gold raised her eyebrows and nodded; evidently she understood the Latin.

"Okay," Parson said, "is that some funky legal term?"

"A legal maxim, really," Webster said.

Gold told Parson the literal meaning: *Though the heavens fall, let justice be done.*

AT A COLLECTION OF ABANDONED stone farm buildings near Kotorsko, off the E73 motorway in the Serb sector of Bosnia, Dušić and Stefan met their triggermen. Andrei and Nikolas were joined by three other recruits. The three new shooters had served with the White Eagles during the war. One had a missing front tooth. The second wore a full beard. Dušić liked that; the man looked like a damned Muslim. The third had a shaved head shaped like a pistol bullet. None of them officer material, Dušić guessed, but probably up to their task.

"Gentlemen," Dušić said, "I trust Stefan has briefed you on your mission."

All nodded. "Yes, sir," Andrei said. Dušić smiled at him.

"Then you know the most important thing is for you to be heard shouting *'Allah-hu akbar!'*" Dušić said. "I scarcely care if you hit anything. Just spray a lot of bullets and make your voices loud. If you kill a few extra, so much the better. But do leave witnesses."

"Yes, sir," Nikolas said.

"Your escape from the target area is your responsibility. If you survive and get away, you will do so richer than when you arrived."

Dušić reached into his coat pocket and withdrew a checkbook. The gap-toothed man grinned. The others watched intently. Dušić wrote out five checks; Stefan reminded him of the men's full names. For this transaction Dušić did not worry about secrecy; these checks were drawn on a Swiss bank known for its discretion. He planned to pay the *razvodnik*s not in dinars but in EU currency. He held up the checks for the men to see. Each check paid thirty thousand euros. Gap-tooth stepped forward, hand outstretched, still wearing that stupid grin.

"Ah-ah," Dušić said, wagging his finger. He tore the checks in half. Gap-tooth looked crestfallen. Dušić handed out half checks. "If you complete your mission to my satisfaction," he said, "you will receive the other half. Do not worry about cashing torn checks. This bank has seen taped checks from me before."

Stefan opened the back of the van. He passed out the new AK-47s to the *razvodnik*s, along with magazines and boxes of ammunition.

"Do any of you need instruction on this particular firearm?" Stefan asked. Ever the good NCO.

"I have used an AK many times, but it has been a while," Bullet Head said.

"You will recall that the weapon is very simple," Stefan said. "First, pull back the bolt and check that the chamber is empty." The men followed Stefan's direction; their weapons made shucking and clacking sounds as they opened the chambers.

"Let the bolt slide forward," Stefan said. Five bolts snapped closed. "Take your magazine in your left hand and place the upper corner against the opening of the magazine well." Stefan reached to Bullet Head's gun, repositioned the magazine. "Like this," Stefan continued. "Now rock it into place."

The men rotated the magazines into position. Dušić heard five nearly simultaneous clicks.

"That's it," Stefan said. "We call this 'rock-and-lock.' Do it that way every time, and you will find you can reload quickly even in the dark. So now you must chamber a round. Point your rifles in harmless directions and take them off SAFE."

The men stepped apart from one another and trained the barrels at ground or sky. Each found the safety without instruction.

"Now pull the bolt all the way back, then let the spring return it forward."

Dušić watched the men charge their weapons. No one shot himself in the foot, he observed, so perhaps these idiots would do. Maybe two or three might even live to cash their checks. If they survived, he would use them again in bigger operations.

Stefan briefed the *razvodnik*s on last-minute details of the operation. He showed them a photo of the Patriarchate and pointed out the main entrance, where he hoped to place the car bomb.

"But remember that circumstances may require me to park elsewhere," he warned. "Just stay well away from a black Citroën."

"Yes, sir," Nikolas said, "a black Citroën." The others nodded.

As Stefan gave the final orders, Dušić gazed out over the countryside. A green meadow stretched before him, and beyond that a forested hillside defined the horizon. A lone hawk wheeled above the trees, circling and hunting for prey. Such a beautiful land. Perhaps that's what had drawn the ancient Ottomans here: They'd wanted more fertile ground than the dusty hellholes where they belonged. Soon enough, no more mosques would defile this country. As always, getting out into the field reminded Dušić of younger days, with a platoon to lead and a job to do.

On the road that wound along the foot of the hill, he saw something that brought him out of his reverie. Two police cars sped along without lights or sirens. They slowed and turned onto the farm path.

"Get to cover!" Dušić shouted. "Stefan, grab your rifle." Dušić pulled his CZ 99 from his waistband.

The *razvodnik*s hesitated. "Is this some kind of test?" Gap-tooth asked.

"No, it's not a test, you bloody fool," Dušić said. "If those police take you now, you will spend the rest of your life in prison. I do not know how they found us."

Stefan snatched up his M24 from the back of the van. He directed the men inside a stone barn. They took up firing positions at windows long since robbed of glass.

"You're going to earn some of that money right now," Stefan said.

The two police cruisers eased up to the farm path. They stopped perhaps a hundred meters from Stefan's van. Each car carried two men.

"When do we fire?" Andrei asked.

"As soon as they get out and you have a clear shot," Dušić said. "We have no choice."

Inside the barn, Dušić took stock of his tactical situation. His team benefited from the defilade of stone walls. The police had no cover but their vehicles, and bullets could penetrate the doors. Dušić's broad strategic situation was somewhat worse. How in God's name had they known his location? He would worry about that later.

The barn smelled of straw and dried manure. A light breeze caressed the grass outside. Dušić analyzed each moment, a field commander once again. He drew binoculars from his pocket and surveyed the scene.

The driver's door on one of the cruisers opened. The officer began to step out, but then he crouched behind the door.

"They see us," Dušić said. "Hold your fire, but stay ready."

The officer behind the car door reached for something. Dušić assumed it was a weapon, but it turned out to be a hand microphone for the cruiser's public-address system.

"You there in the barn," the officer called. "Identify yourselves."

The *razvodnik*s looked at Dušić and Stefan.

"No one speak," Dušić said.

Stefan stepped back from his window and looked around. He propped his rifle against the wall. An ancient scythe lay among decaying straw. The tool bore not only a blade but a cradle—four wooden tines parallel to the blade, to catch the cut wheat or barley. Stefan upended the scythe so that it rested on the end of its handle and on the tips of its blade and cradle. He placed it about three meters back from his window, kneeled, and rested his rifle across the scythe. A stable platform for an accurate shot. Stefan could still see well through the window, but the enemy outside would have difficulty seeing him. Another poetic move, Dušić thought. The reaper and his scythe.

"You there," the police officer repeated, "place your weapons on the ground and walk out slowly. You will not be harmed."

In the other car, an officer appeared to make a radio call. Sending for backup, presumably. For now, Dušić and his team faced four policemen. Good odds. Those odds would worsen dramatically when backup arrived. Cover and terrain worked in Dušić's favor. Time did not.

"Stefan," Dušić called, "give the man an answer."

Stefan adjusted the elevation knob on his telescopic sight. He placed his cheek to the stock and clicked off the safety. The M24 coughed.

The bullet slammed through the door of the first police car. The officer who had demanded surrender fell and dropped his assault rifle. Weeds and the door obstructed view of his body. After a moment, the man cursed and crawled behind the car with his weapon.

"Body armor, Stefan," Dušić said.

"I see that."

Not just any body armor but probably Level III gear, since it had withstood a high-powered rifle bullet. Dušić imagined the door had absorbed some of the energy, too. This operation would require true precision.

"We do not have all day, Stefan," Dušić said.

Stefan racked his bolt, chambered a new cartridge. Adjusted the parallax on the scope. Settled his cheek back on the weapon for another shot.

At the second police car, an officer crouched by the vehicle. The open passenger door and the dashboard concealed his head and torso, but his legs remained visible underneath the door. Stefan adjusted his aim, tilted the barrel downward just a few degrees.

The M24 spoke again. Through the lenses of the binoculars, Dušić actually saw the bullet's trace; the projectile displaced air ahead of it so forcefully that it made a visible shimmer—right under the car door and into the policeman's leg. Dušić thought he even heard the slap of impact. He knew he heard the cry of agony.

"I'm shot!" the man shouted. And probably down for good, Dušić figured. A strike from a 7.62 round nearly anywhere on the body would incapacitate.

"Do not move," one of his colleagues said.

"Help me," the wounded man called. "I'm bleeding."

The *razvodnik*s gripped their weapons, looked at Dušić as if they needed guidance.

"What now?" Nikolas asked.

Dušić thought for a moment. "Draw the others out," he said. "Shoot him again. But do not kill him yet."

Nikolas gaped with his mouth half open, as if he couldn't

understand simple instructions. Might as well get some use out of this one while I can, Dušić thought. He's too stupid to last long.

"Yes, *you*, imbecile," Dušić said. "And do not waste ammunition."

Nikolas pointed the AK through a window. His hands shook as he fired from an offhand position with no support, and of course the idiot missed.

"Again," Dušić ordered. "Try aiming this time."

Nikolas kneeled, rested the AK on the stone sill. He popped off two shots on semiauto, and the second round connected. Another hit the same leg, and the wounded officer screamed again.

"Help me, for God's sake!" he shouted. "I'm bleeding out."

The wounded man's partner, who had taken cover behind the open driver's door of the same car, lunged across the front seats and pulled him inside. One of the injured officer's boots remained visible. Blood trickled off the heel and onto the grass.

His partner's head and shoulders bobbed in and out of view behind the windshield. Presumably the partner was trying to render first aid, perhaps apply a tourniquet.

Stefan shifted his aim, waited. Pressed the trigger.

Gases spewed from the end of the noise suppressor. Straw stirred on the floor beneath the rifle barrel. The bullet punched a white-rimmed hole through the windshield. Something spattered inside the police car. The policeman who'd tried to help his wounded partner collapsed and did not rise again.

Unintelligible cries emanated from the police car, probably the wounded man crying out over his partner, now dead, who had likely fallen on top of him. After a few seconds the cries grew weaker. That did not surprise Dušić. Back during the war, his platoon medic told him that if a bullet severed a major artery, a man could bleed to death faster than he could suffocate.

From the other car, Dušić heard voices. Not panicked wailing but focused conversation. These are trained lawmen, not amateurs, he reminded himself. Do not get careless just because you have the upper hand. Dušić asked himself what he would do in their situation.

"Men," Dušić called to his team, "the other two will try something, maybe launch tear gas. If they come from behind cover, I want you to pour fire on them. If they get off a tear gas round, hold your breath and hold your position."

Dušić didn't know if his *razvodnik*s could manage that kind of discipline, and he hoped he wouldn't find out. One of the officers appeared to grab something from inside the car. Stefan followed the movement through his scope and even put his finger to the trigger, but he did not fire. The policeman had not exposed himself long enough for Stefan to get a shot.

When the officer appeared again, he came up from behind the car, holding some kind of launcher. He rested his elbows across the trunk lid and fired. Stefan fired, too.

The bullet knocked the officer backward, and the tear gas canister flew wild. It bounced off the barn's stone wall and ricocheted into the grass. Most of the white chemical blew harmlessly with the breeze, but enough of it drifted into the barn to burn and sting. Dušić's eyes streamed, and the *razvodnik*s hacked and cursed.

"Hold your breaths, idiots," Dušić ordered. "It will clear in a moment."

Rifle fire chattered from outside. Dušić heard the policemen's bullets slam against the stone wall. He ducked beneath the window, held his pistol with both hands. The air, still tainted with tear gas, felt like barbed wire going down his trachea. It hurt, but he knew if he broke and ran from the cover of the barn, the bullets would hurt more. He cleared his throat, spat phlegm into the straw.

"Stay put," Dušić ordered. "If you run now, they will kill you."

Andrei placed the barrel of his weapon across a sill. Without aiming, head down and exposing only his hand, he unleashed a burst on full auto. Dušić started to yell at him for wasting ammunition, but he saw how the fusillade made the policemen stay down. That gave him an idea.

"Stefan," Dušić said, "if they give you covering fire, can you make some hits?"

"Absolutely." Stefan took two extra rounds from his jacket pocket and held them between the fingers of his left hand for quick reloading.

"*Razvodniks*," Dušić called, "do what Andrei just did. On my command, open up on them and keep them pinned down." More bullets from the policemen's weapons tore into the barn. Several rounds zinged through the windows and impacted the opposite wall. Flying chips of stone peppered Dušić's cheek.

Stefan kneeled once again with his rifle across the scythe. "We will have only a few seconds for this to work," he said. "Our men have just one magazine apiece."

"I know it," Dušić said. He thought for a moment and altered his plan slightly. "Nikolas," he said, "trade weapons with me."

"Yes, sir."

Dušić handed his CZ 99 to Nikolas and took the AK-47. He pulled back the bolt enough to confirm that a round was chambered, smacked the magazine to make sure it seated. He took a position by the barn's open side door. From there he saw the police car where the two uninjured officers were firing. One of them ejected an empty magazine and slammed home a full replacement.

"Stefan, are you ready?" Dušić asked.

"Ready." Stefan sighted through the scope. The two extra cartridges between his fingers looked like the brass spikes of some ghastly medieval weapon.

"Fire!" Dušić shouted.

The *razvodniks* spewed a hail of bullets from their AKs. Nikolas pumped shot after shot from Dušić's handgun. Recoil jolted Stefan's shoulder. He racked his bolt to fire again.

Dušić charged from the barn. As he sprinted, he angled away from the line of fire. But he ran in a direction that brought the rear of the police cars into view. His vantage point also brought him within good distance to hit the two policemen still standing. He lifted the AK to his shoulder and held down the trigger.

Dušić's bullets stitched across the nearest officer. Rounds struck the man's hip, his armor-protected torso, and his neck. He never saw Dušić until he lay dying.

A round fired from the barn, probably by Stefan, struck the other officer in the arm. The man fell backward from his crouched stance, dropped his assault rifle. He twisted to place his right hand over the wound in his upper left arm. And he looked right into the muzzle of Dušić's rifle.

"Cease firing!" Dušić shouted. He kept the AK leveled at the officer's head.

"Please," the officer said. "Please." Blood streamed across his fingers and dripped into the dirt.

Dušić held his fire.

23

AT THE SARAJEVO HOLIDAY INN, Parson paced the lobby. Cunningham drummed his fingers on the armrest of a leather chair. Dragan kept checking his watch and looking at his mobile phone. The day had begun well: Gold and the Rivet Joint crew left to go fly. Almost as soon as they got the landing gear up, they received a solid hit on Dušić's phone. That luck reminded Parson of wading a stream and catching a salmon on the first cast. Police had been dispatched from a station somewhere up in northern Bosnia. They must have found something; they'd called for backup. But after that, nothing.

"Did they ever get any help?" Cunningham asked.

"I don't know," Dragan said. "I want to get my guys up there, but it's out of my jurisdiction."

"Can you get somebody to give you clearance?" Parson asked.

"Yeah, that's what I'm waiting for. My boss needs to get a green light from their boss."

Their boss better get off his ass, Parson thought. When you lost contact with a unit, it usually meant very bad things. Just like when you lost contact with an airplane.

Finally, Dragan's cell phone chimed. He spoke for a few seconds in Serbo-Croatian. Then he closed the phone and said, "Let's move."

Parson and Cunningham climbed into one of the two vans that carried Dragan's de facto SWAT team. They had come for a meeting, not an op, so Parson guessed they didn't have all their usual gear. But he watched with interest as they set up what equipment they did have. Parson compared their effort to stop some crazy son of a bitch from reigniting a war to aviators working to prevent an accident: If you took out one error, one link in the chain that led to disaster, then the disaster would not happen. In this case, the error that needed taking out was named Viktor Dušić.

Dragan sat in the back of the van across from Parson. He barked an order in his native language, and the driver pulled out of the parking lot. Four other Serbian police officers rode in the van. Two of them nodded to Parson and Cunningham, said "Hello" in thick Slavic accents. Parson supposed they knew few other words in English. He regretted that he'd not asked Irena how to offer thanks and greetings in Serbo-Croatian.

A hardside case rested on the floor at Dragan's feet. Dragan opened it to reveal a stripped-down sniper rifle. Parson had never seen a weapon quite like it. The rifle looked vaguely like a Dragunov: similar shape, with a PSO-1 scope. But a much bigger barrel than a Dragunov, an AK-47, or an SKS. The magazine seemed large, built for big cartridges. If anything, the gun appeared even meaner than a Dragunov.

"What the hell is that?" Parson asked the police commander.

"It's a Vintorez rifle," Dragan said as he began to assemble the weapon. "The Russians make it."

"What does it fire?"

"It shoots these." Dragan slid an ammo box from under his seat and opened it. The rounds inside were nearly as thick as a man's finger. The brass had been necked out to accommodate a good-size bullet, and the cartridges reminded Parson of the large-caliber black-powder ammunition used by the old buffalo hunters. Parson pulled out one of the cartridges. It felt substantial in his hand. He turned it over and examined the head stamp. The stamp read 9X39MM.

"Nine millimeter," Parson noted. Not nearly the biggest bullet made, but large for a police or military rifle. And this ammunition differed from the nine-mil pistol bullets he knew well. These cartridges were longer and heavier, designed to penetrate body armor.

"It's a subsonic round," Dragan said, "so you don't get that supersonic crack."

That made sense to Parson. He saw that the Vintorez's noise suppressor didn't just screw into the muzzle; it was integrated with the entire barrel. Very quiet and very deadly.

"You're loaded for bear, that's for damned sure."

"I got this on special order," Dragan said. "Just about had to pound my fist on the quartermaster's desk, because the police don't normally issue these. But we're going against an arms dealer. No telling what that nut job keeps up his sleeve."

To Parson, it still sounded strange to hear a Serbian police commander speak such flawless English and even use American idioms. But then he remembered Dragan had gone to school in the United States. The 1990s upheaval in the former Yugoslavia scattered a lot of people. Parson considered it his own country's good fortune that Irena had come to stay. And Serbia benefited because Dragan had left and come back. Parson liked this well-traveled, well-educated cop.

Maybe there was hope for this place after all. It just depended on who won out—the haters like Dušić and that idiot who'd gotten a beat-down from Cunningham, or the folks like Irena and Dragan who wanted a better future.

Parson could understand the roots of bigotry. After his C-130 had been shot down in Afghanistan and all his crewmates killed, he'd wanted to blow away every Muslim in the world. He'd probably still think like that, he conceded, if Sophia had not helped him work through his rage. She'd also acknowledged the evils of militant Islam, and she'd helped him put away one militant Islamist for a long, long time.

What he could not understand was how hate persisted down through generations. Bigotry with such longevity put him in mind of the great rafts of trash that floated across the oceans. He had flown over such collections of garbage: things thrown out and discarded, yet coalescing in the eddy of a far-flung current to create a new eyesore or worse.

Dragan's driver accelerated down an on-ramp to the E73. The outskirts of Sarajevo gave way to rural hills. Parson hoped local backup had arrived for the police who'd gone after Dušić; by the time Dragan's team could get there, it might be too late.

DUŠIĆ SLUNG THE AK-47 over his shoulder and looked down at the wounded police officer. The man breathed heavily, as if he might hyperventilate. Eyes wide with fear, he stared up at Dušić while holding his hand over the bullet hole in his left arm. Blood slicked his fingers as he kept pressure on the wound. Sweat beaded on his forehead. The injury bled heavily enough to soak the officer's sleeve, but Dušić judged that the bullet had not broken the bone.

"What are you going to do with me?" the officer asked.

Dušić ignored the question. *"Razvodniks,"* he called, "check the other policemen. We have a prisoner." He kicked away the prisoner's assault rifle, and he reached down and took the man's sidearm. The officer did not resist. Dušić checked the pistol's safety and stuck the weapon in his waistband.

Andrei, Nikolas, and the other men ran from the barn. Stefan remained in place behind his M24, maintaining overwatch. Dušić appreciated the proper procedure; police backup might arrive any moment. He needed to get his team out of the area, but first he needed some information. And he did not want to take the prisoner. Dušić would have to leave bodies and evidence here; he could not avoid it. But he did not wish to leave another body and more evidence somewhere else.

The *razvodnik*s examined the policemen. Andrei leaned into the police car farthest from Dušić. The result of Stefan's head shot must have sickened Andrei; he placed the back of his hand over his mouth for a moment. These men were supposed to be veterans, Dušić thought, but perhaps they had grown unused to the gore of battle. They would see much more if they lived long enough.

Andrei seemed to regain his composure. "All dead, sir," he said.

"Good," Dušić said. "Help me get this prisoner into the barn."

"Yes, sir."

Andrei took the wounded man by his good arm. Dušić held the officer by the fasteners on his body armor, and they pulled him to his feet. The man groaned in pain. "My friends," he said. "You have murdered my friends."

"Can you walk?" Dušić asked.

"Yes. What do you want with me?"

"I am asking the questions here. Get into the barn."

Blood must have pooled inside the man's sleeve, perhaps contained by the tight weave of tactical fabric. Gouts of it flowed from underneath his cuff and spattered over his hand. The officer staggered as he walked, and he leaned on Andrei. He'd apparently suffered more blood loss than Dušić had expected.

Inside the barn, Dušić found an old milk stool lying on its side. He set it upright in the middle of the floor.

"Sit," he commanded.

Andrei eased the officer down onto the milk stool. The wounded man looked around at his captors.

"Just leave me alone," he said. "You can get away if you leave now."

"Let me worry about that," Dušić said.

"He is bleeding, sir," Nikolas said. "Shall we bandage his wound?"

Dušić considered the suggestion. Not a bad idea, really. He didn't want the prisoner to pass out from blood loss before interrogation. "Yes," Dušić said. "Go ahead."

"There is a kit in the back of the vehicle," Stefan said.

Nikolas went outside, and Dušić regarded the prisoner. The man wore the emblem of the ministry of internal affairs of the Serbian entity of Bosnia and Herzegovina. Dušić did not particularly like harming an officer wearing a Republika Srpska patch on his uniform, but duty sometimes required unpleasant tasks. Besides, this policeman represented a pale version of Republika Srpska, not the Greater Serbia that Dušić envisioned. Under Dušić's leadership, Republika Srpska would be born again.

Nikolas came back with the medical kit. Evidently, Stefan had bought it only recently; it was still wrapped in a shopping bag from a Sarajevo pharmacy. Nikolas removed the kit from the bag. Inside the kit he found a small pair of scissors. He cut away the prisoner's sleeve to reveal torn muscle tissue still oozing blood. The kit contained tubes and vials of ointments and antiseptics. Nikolas began fumbling through them.

"Just put a tight bandage on him so he stops bleeding," Dušić said.

"Yes, sir," Nikolas said.

The prisoner watched as Nikolas wrapped the wound in gauze.

Blood soaked through the cloth even as Nikolas added layers. When he finished, he tied the loose ends together in a square knot. A blotch of burgundy spread through the bandage from the inside, creeping through the gauze strand by strand. The wounded man would interpret the medical help as mercy, Dušić knew. Good.

"So tell me," Dušić said, "how did you know where to find us?"

The man looked up at Dušić. "I cannot tell you that," he said.

"You will tell me that, and you will do so quickly."

The prisoner made no response. He simply gazed out a window, no doubt hoping to see his deliverance arrive. Dušić slapped him. The palm of Dušić's hand stung, and Dušić liked that. Surely the man's face stung worse.

"Look at me, fool," Dušić said. "Answer my question."

The man ran his tongue across the inside of his lower lip. He spat a mixture of blood and saliva. "You know I cannot do that."

Dušić pulled the pistol from his waistband, clicked off the safety. "I will kill you if you do not."

"Viktor," Stefan said, "he is a Serb police officer."

"So are the other officers we just shot. What is wrong with you? This man has information I need."

Stefan looked stricken, and that worried Dušić. This was no time for Stefan or anyone else on the team to go soft. True, killing Serbs brought no pleasure. But this one and several more at the Patriarchate must die for Greater Serbia. Then the real battles could begin. When the war against the Turks resumed, Muslims would die in numbers that would make the 1990s war look like a skirmish.

Dušić knew he didn't have much time. He needed to make a tactical retreat out of here, but not before he learned how the police had located him. Maybe this officer did not fear a bullet to the head. The man was a Serb, after all, and even if he served a weak government, the courage of his ancestors flowed through his veins. A fine thing, really. Dušić would just have to give him something else to fear. He pointed to the pharmacist's plastic bag, now lying discarded amid the straw.

"Give me that," he ordered. Nikolas handed him the bag.

With one hand, Dušić snapped the bag open. He still held the pistol in the other hand. He placed the bag over the prisoner's head and squeezed it tight around the man's neck.

The prisoner gasped, and the bag collapsed around his head. Plastic took the form of his nose and open mouth. He used his good arm to claw at the bag, and he tried to stand. Dušić forced him back down onto the milk stool. The prisoner struggled and kicked as he began to suffocate, but his injury and blood loss had left him too weak to offer real resistance.

Dušić snatched the bag off the man's head. The prisoner drew a ragged breath that trailed into a spasm of coughing. Sweat dripped from his nose and hair.

"We will take you with us and continue this all day," Dušić said. He had no intention of taking the man anywhere, but the statement would serve its purpose.

The prisoner shook his head, kept his eyes to the ground. "I cannot," he said. "I cannot."

Dušić placed the bag over the policeman's head. "No!" the man shouted. The plastic muffled his cry. Once again, Dušić squeezed the bag closed around his victim's neck.

The man writhed, convulsed. Dušić kept his fist tight on the bag for several more seconds. When he released his grip and removed the bag, the prisoner's lips had turned blue from cyanosis. The man sucked in air, filled his chest. As he exhaled, he hacked and spat.

"Son," Dušić said, "you are a police officer, not an intelligence agent. You have no state secrets; you could not harm your country if you wanted to. All I want to know is a little about your police procedures."

The man shook his head. Dušić spread open the bag.

"No," the officer said. "Please, no."

"Your friends would not have you suffer to protect such mundane information. Just tell me how you found me."

The man took another deep breath of air. "Your mobile phones," he said.

Dušić's stomach knotted. He'd been careful about what he'd said, especially over his landlines but even on his cell. Had the *razvodnik*s blabbed carelessly? Even if they had, how could the authorities locate him like this?

"How do you track us?" Dušić asked.

"They have an airplane."

"An airplane? What do you mean? Who is 'they'?"

"I do not know, exactly, I swear. But I think they are NATO. Or perhaps the UN or the Americans."

Dušić roared, kicked over the milk stool. The prisoner tumbled into the straw and cried out in pain. God curse those damnable Americans, Dušić thought. Once again interfering in matters not of their concern.

Nikolas righted the stool and helped the prisoner sit back on it.

"I thank you for your service to Serbia," Dušić said. He pointed the pistol he'd taken from the officer, pressed the muzzle to the man's temple. Pulled the trigger.

The man collapsed from the stool and fell onto his side. His eyes, already lifeless, stared straight ahead as if he did not want to look at Dušić. A fountain of red jetted from the entrance wound until the blood pressure died away, and then the dead man stopped bleeding.

"Turn off your phones and give them to me," Dušić said. He collected mobile phones from all the men. *"Razvodnik*s," he added, "make sure you meet me at Pionirski Park in Belgrade at the appointed time. You will receive no further communication. Now get out of here and lie low until zero hour."

Riding in the van with Stefan a few minutes later, Dušić pondered his situation. Did the authorities know he was behind a plot to bomb the Assembly of Bishops? The whole plan depended on the false-flag nature of the operation. People must think it a Muslim attack. The authorities would not have a recording of his voice mentioning the Patriarchate on the phone; of that he was certain. Even if an idiot *razvodnik* made a slip of the tongue, the police would record no evidence any Serb would believe. The Serbian public would just consider it a Muslim ruse. Given the burnings and riots of late, people would readily accuse the Turks of all manner of perfidy. The tinder remained plentiful and dry, just waiting for the match.

In the worst case, narcotics allegations might bar him from high office in the Ministry of Defense. No matter. He could lead a militia of his own funding; he'd planned on doing that in the beginning, anyway. Once the war resumed, no Serbian court would convict him on petty trafficking. And he'd come too far to stop now. The mission was still on.

Stefan drove in silence for several minutes. "Where are we going?" he asked finally. "A different hotel, I presume."

"Not yet," Dušić said. He thought for a moment. "Find me a public phone, if you can. A landline."

"What do you have in mind?"

"A telephone call, obviously."

Dušić seldom spoke curtly to Stefan, but he was still angry. Those Americans and their damned aircraft. They had helped relieve the siege of Sarajevo, dropping their bundles of rat food to keep the Turk rats from starving. And later, in Kosovo, their bombers had rained hell on Serb troops battling for their cultural heartland.

Americans dared not face Serb men toe-to-toe. They preferred to push buttons from thirty thousand feet. Dušić remembered graffiti spray-painted on the wall of a bombed-out bunker by a frustrated Serbian soldier: COME DOWN FROM THE SKY AND FIGHT.

The spy plane that monitored his team's phones might have come from anywhere. Given the Americans' aerial refueling capabilities, the aircraft could have taken off in fucking Nebraska.

Or not. What if the plane landed somewhere closer?

Even though Stefan drove, he reached under the seat and took out a new bottle of slivovitz. He cracked the cap, spun it off the bottle, and took a long drink.

"I need you focused," Dušić said.

"I *am* focused."

"Do you need to settle your nerves now when you kill?"

Stefan did not answer. He only stared straight ahead and drove. When he spoke, he changed the subject.

"So who are you going to call?"

"I am going to try to find out where that airplane is based. I do business at all the airports in Serbia, Croatia, Macedonia, and Bosnia, and I know people."

"It could be based anywhere in the world." Stefan took another drink from the bottle.

"I know that. But if it is close, we might do something about it."

"Like what?"

Dušić turned in his seat to look back at all the gear he'd brought with him. Some of it he'd gathered only as an afterthought. Like the fragmentation grenades.

24

FROM A MILE AWAY, Parson could see backup had arrived too late. Blue lights flashed from police cars and ambulances. No civilian vehicles, though the first cops on the scene had reported finding a van and SUVs. Dušić and his band of scumbags must have outgunned the police and escaped. The emergency vehicles sat parked near an ancient stone barn in the middle of the Bosnian countryside. Parson wondered about the police officers who had encountered Dušić here. If they'd died, what had been their last thoughts? After bullets tore your flesh and bone, what went through your mind as you looked out over such a pastoral setting?

"Damn it," Dragan said. "Damn it, damn it, damn it." Then he spoke in Serbo-Croatian, and the vehicle turned onto the farm path.

Guys like Dragan, Cunningham, and me should be coming to a place like this to hunt and smoke cigars, Parson thought, not to sort through a firefight's aftermath. We should carry shotguns for partridges instead of high-powered rifles for men.

The two vehicles carrying Dragan's team stopped alongside the path, well away from the police cars and ambulances. Even before Parson left the van, he could surmise what had happened. Bullet holes pocked two of the cars; blood smeared one of the open doors. Two bodies lay across the front seat of the nearest car. A third policeman had died at the other shot-up vehicle. One of the dead officers still gripped the receiver of an assault rifle. Shell casings littered the ground; these men had gone down fighting.

They must have taken fire from the barn, Parson concluded. The angle of bullet strikes on the cars told him, much the way gouges on the ground might tell him the angle of a crashed plane. These poor guys never had a chance. Their enemies had opened up on them from behind the impenetrable cover of stone walls, while the officers' only protection had been their cars. Most high-powered rifle ammunition could pierce anything on a car except the engine block unless the car was armored. These cars clearly were not.

"I see they tried the only thing that might have worked," Dragan said.

"What's that?" Cunningham asked.

Dragan pointed to a tear gas launcher in the grass next to the cars. "They'd have had to put tear gas through one of the windows," he said, "but the bad guys probably had them too pinned down to get off an accurate shot."

Parson ached for the dead policemen. All three looked too young to have played any role in the Bosnian War. In those days, Serbian police committed atrocities, but he hoped these guys were different. Maybe they'd thought like Dragan, working for a better future instead of nursing grudges from the past.

Like many war veterans, Parson often thought about returning to places where he'd fought, and Bosnia was his first combat zone.

But he'd wanted to see Bosnia in a secure peace, not under threat of a new war. To visit an old battle site gone quiet might bring tranquillity to a warrior, reassure the warrior that despite all the horrors of the world, life's broad currents tended toward the good. But for Parson, a war that wouldn't ever quite go away brought the opposite effect.

Dragan and the other officers examined the scene, taking photographs and writing notes. Investigators wearing latex gloves picked through the evidence. One of them inserted a pencil into the open end of an expended cartridge, lifted the empty brass, and dropped it into a plastic bag.

Inside the barn, Parson found more investigators looking over a fourth body. The dead man had been shot in the arm and in the side of the head. Flies buzzed around the corpse and landed in the blood congealing on straw that covered the floor.

Cunningham came into the barn with Dragan, and Dragan spoke with the other officers in their native language. They conversed in the hushed tones one might use at a funeral.

"Looks like they executed that guy after he got wounded," Cunningham said.

"I was thinking the same thing," Parson said. "So what are these police doing now?"

"They'll gather all the evidence they can. Pictures, fingerprints, blood samples. We can look around right here and see pretty well what happened. But if their system is anything like ours, a prosecutor will have to reconstruct the scene in a courtroom."

"If there's ever a trial," Parson said.

"Yeah," Cunningham said, "these sons of bitches seem like the type to go out shooting and take as many cops with them as they can."

"That would disappoint Webster. I think he really wants Dušić tried for war crimes."

"I wish somebody would just blow his ass away."

You gotta like a tough cop, Parson thought, as long as he's tough only on people who deserve it. Cunningham's attitude seemed about right for a coastal country boy from a place called Dare County.

Dragan continued his conversation with the local Bosnian Serb officers. Now they spoke in more animated tones, as if they were debating some point. Parson wondered how much Dragan had told them about Dušić's intentions to embroil them all in a new war, and to spark that war by murdering their own clergy. Parson also wondered how these Serb cops felt about the recent past. Did they want truth commissions and war crimes trials to sweep away all the denial? Or did they take comfort in denial, in dismissing genocide as the collateral damage to be expected in any war? Judging by their rapid-fire words and hand gestures, they had differing opinions on whatever they were discussing.

Eventually, Dragan broke away from the conversation. He kneeled by the policeman's body, looked into the dead man's face. Parson noticed the equipment on Dragan's belt: the magazine cases made of ballistic nylon, the mini-flashlight holder, the clip of the folding knife. Though Dragan worked in civilian clothes, he and the uniformed officer fallen before him wore similar tools of the trade. Parson could imagine the bond Dragan must feel with this officer. Cops hated nothing worse than cop killers. If you wanted policemen to give up their vacations, to come in on overtime, to devote all their resources and put aside all their differences in an effort to take you down, just kill one of their fellow officers. The principle held true all over the world.

DUŠIĆ AND STEFAN STOPPED at three service stations before they found one with a working public telephone. Little need of public phones anymore, since everyone carried a cell. But now that Dušić knew cell phones betrayed his location, he and his team would not use cells until the day of the bombing. Stefan had rigged the explosives with a cell phone detonator, and Dušić did not want to make him reconfigure the bomb at this late stage. Stefan would turn on the phone only after he'd driven the bomb into place, and the meddling Americans probably would not have enough time to pinpoint the signal. With some luck, Dušić might tilt the odds in his favor. Especially if he could take care of that damned airplane.

He paid cash for a phone card in the service station, then stood in the phone booth with the receiver cradled on his shoulder. He made calls to airports all over the region, but no one among his contacts with air freight companies had seen a suspicious aircraft. Dušić didn't know exactly what the plane would look like, though he guessed a large multiengine jet, either unmarked or with U.S. Air Force identification. More than likely the plane carried an unusual number of antennas.

Dušić, about to give up, decided to place one more call. He did not trust the freight companies in Sarajevo; they hired too many Muslims and Croats. But many years ago, when he'd first started his business, he'd sold a rifle to a loyal Serb who drove a jet fuel truck in Sarajevo. They had traded war stories and lamented the war's outcome. The man hated Muslims as much as Dušić, and he hated Americans even more. That womanizing bumpkin Bill Clinton, he'd said, had robbed the Serbs of sure victory. What was that patriot's name?

Bratislav. Of course. A name that meant "brother of glory." Bratislav would be years older now. Did he still work for the same aviation services company? Only one way to find out.

Dušić dialed information and jotted down the number for Aero Drina. He thought for a moment, considered his tactics. He would ask for Bratislav by name, and he'd talk to no one else. If the man wasn't there, Dušić would drop this idea. But it was worth at least one more try.

On the third ring, a woman answered. "Aero Drina. How may I help you?"

"May I speak to Bratislav?" Dušić asked. "I am an old friend."

"He is in the break room. I must put you on hold. May I tell him who is calling?"

Dušić smiled. Nothing like steady employment. "I am Darko," he lied.

"One moment, please."

After what felt like a long wait, Dušić heard a click on the other end, and a voice said, "This is Bratislav Stekić. But I do not remember any Darko."

"Perhaps the receptionist misunderstood," Dušić said. "My name is Viktor. You may not recall, but I sold you a Mauser many years ago. We talked of the war."

Bratislav paused. "Hmm, yes. I still have that rifle. Yes, I do remember you, Viktor. I have taken many red stag with that weapon."

"Very good, my friend. I hope my product has served you well."

"Indeed, it has."

"I am glad. But that is not why I called. May I ask you a question in the strictest confidence? As one old warrior to another."

"Certainly."

"Have you seen an American military aircraft at Sarajevo?"

"I have. A large Boeing has been here for a few days. One with many antennas. It takes off for a while and it comes right back here. I have no idea what it does."

"It does what Americans have always done, Bratislav. It helps to keep from our people the glory they have earned."

Bratislav said nothing. Dušić let silence hover for a moment, to see if the man would hang up or become frightened. Many years had passed since Bratislav's days as a fighter. Did he still have the spirit?

"I am listening, Viktor," Bratislav said finally. "Are you serving our people in some higher capacity now?"

"Yes, but not the way you are thinking. Would you like to punish the Americans for what they took from us?"

"Very much, Viktor. But how?"

"I understand. You need to know more before you commit. Can we meet today?"

"My shift ends at five. I can see you then."

"Tell me where."

Bratislav gave Dušić the address of a pub near the airport. They agreed to meet in the parking area, away from the ears of the patrons inside. When Dušić returned to the van, Stefan asked, "Did you have any luck?"

"Possibly. I never forget a customer, and I found one who might help us give those Americans a bad day."

Dušić told Stefan about Bratislav, and he gave him the address. A few hours later Stefan parked outside a pub called Knez Lazar. Music pulsed from the place, some pop tune too modern for Dušić to recognize. The smell of cooked meat, along with garlic and onions, wafted from the kitchen vents. *Ćevapčići*, Dušić guessed. Sausages without casings, grilled over a fire. The pub seemed a hangout for airport workers. Men and women, some still in the duty clothing of baggage handlers, mechanics, and ramp coordinators, entered the building. Without knowing their names, Dušić could not tell which were Muslim, Croat, or Serb. He wondered how much intermingling went on. The thought made him want to vomit. He felt he was about to give a great gift to the Serbs among them. The rest could go to hell.

Bratislav had said he drove an old Zastava Koral. Perhaps the years since he bought his rifle had not turned out prosperous for him. Unfortunate, but something Dušić could turn to advantage. Thirty thousand euros might mean a lot to a man who could not afford a decent car. Maybe enough to bolster his courage, if need be.

Right on time, a battered Koral sputtered into the parking lot. One of the fenders had rusted through, and the tailpipe hung by strands of wire. The car belched blue smoke until its driver shut it down.

Just as Dušić never forgot customers, he never forgot faces. But when Bratislav emerged from his rattletrap, Dušić barely recognized him. The man's jowls had swollen with weight gain; his mustache and hair had grown bushier and gone gray. His paunch drooped over his belt. He pulled himself up from the car as if the effort hurt. Maybe Bratislav had once scaled mountains in pursuit of stag, but not recently. No matter. The task to which Dušić would set him required a bit of cunning, but not strength.

Dušić stepped out of the van and waved. His old customer smiled, met him in the middle of the parking area. A handshake showed Bratislav's grip still firm.

"So, what have you done all this time, Viktor?" Bratislav asked. "Still selling guns?"

"To different kinds of buyers now. But yes, I remain in the weapons business."

"How may I serve you?"

Dušić liked this sort of talk. Respectful and to the point. Perhaps somewhere under the rolls of fat and the sagging skin, remnants of a professional soldier still existed.

"I command a mission that could avenge all the wrongs done to our people in the 1990s," Dušić said. "For your own protection, I will tell you no more than that. But Americans stand in my way now as they stood in our way back then."

"My nephew was killed by a NATO bomb," Bratislav said. "They did so much worse than merely stand in my way."

"Then you need no convincing of the need to punish their continued interference."

"None."

"And I will make it worth your while. Let me show you something."

The more Dušić talked with Bratislav, the more he liked him. Money or fear could motivate the weak. Bratislav, apparently, responded to higher callings. Yet Dušić would gladly pay him if he succeeded.

In the back of the van, Bratislav gaped at the store of weapons. Dušić opened a plastic case and revealed a pair of fragmentation grenades.

"Do you remember these?" Dušić asked.

"I have used one or two."

"These are yours, if you choose to help me. I need you to take care of that damned American jet."

"Not really the weapon for that, Viktor."

"True enough. But my options are temporarily limited."

Dušić explained that he would love to blow that Yankee airplane out of the sky and kill every meddler aboard. But he would settle for merely disabling the plane. Bratislav could use a technique employed by low-budget terrorists all over the world. The method involved pulling the retaining pin on the grenade, then either wrapping the lever with thin tape or placing the grenade inside a foam or plastic cup. In time, the lever would force its way through the tape or cup, and the grenade would detonate. A poor man's delayed-fuse bomb.

"Very imprecise, Viktor. Without experimentation, we cannot know when the grenades will explode."

"An inelegant solution, I admit. But for this, we do not need precision. I do not even care if the grenades explode on the ground or in the air. If you bring down the plane, so much the better. But even if you only rupture tires, it will ground the Americans, delay them."

"You wish me to plant these aboard the jet?"

"Yes. Whenever you can, but preferably three days from now. Will you help me?"

Bratislav stared into the distance for several seconds. "I will," he said. Dušić noted that he did not ask how much he would get paid.

"It is a pleasure to know you, Bratislav. But now to details. Can you get these grenades through security? I assume you must pass through some sort of checkpoint on your way to work."

"Yes, but the security agents are accustomed to seeing me. They have X-ray, but my toolbox is always filled with metal objects. Some agents hardly look at the screen."

"Very good, very good." Dušić slapped his old customer on the back. "You need a new car, my friend. If you succeed, you can get that and more." Dušić wrote out a check, tore it in half, and explained his method of payment. Bratislav gasped when he saw the amount, and he did not complain about having to wait for the other half.

ABOARD THE RIVET JOINT, the day that had begun so promisingly turned frustrating. Gold had noticed the crew's excitement when they picked up Dušić's trail while the aircraft was still climbing. Irena and her crewmates relayed Dušić's position, somewhere in northern Bosnia. But then the contact went cold. The eavesdropping electronics sensed no signal from any number associated with Dušić or his helpers. Gold followed the crew's speculation as they chatted on interphone: Maybe the cell tower went dark. Maybe we have a malfunction; everybody check circuit breakers. Or maybe Dušić's team got wise.

To pass the time, Gold and Irena talked shop. Gold had read there were more than seven thousand languages spoken around the world.

"I had no idea there were so many," Irena said. "How is that even possible?"

"Micro-languages exist in pockets isolated by geography. You still have remote tribes deep in jungles, that sort of thing. And the sad part: One of those languages goes extinct about every two weeks."

"That's a shame. I hope somebody's recording the last speakers. Have you ever visited any of those tribes?"

"One," Gold said. "In Afghanistan, the Korengal Valley people have a language all their own."

"Do you speak it?"

"Not a word. Lucky for me, a lot of the Korengalis speak Pashto, too."

During lulls in the conversation, Gold heard only the surf of the slipstream and the unbroken hiss of circuitry. After a few unproductive hours, the mission commander spoke up on interphone.

"Crew," he said, "I just got some bad news from the ground. Agent Cunningham says they didn't find Dušić, but they found where he'd been. He left behind some dead police officers."

Irena leaned back in her seat, stared straight ahead at her console. Gold could see the disappointment in her eyes, not just for the immediate mission, but for the turn of events in her native land.

"What's going on down there?" Irena asked. She didn't press her interphone switch when she spoke. A rhetorical question, Gold realized, that Irena probably meant in the larger sense. What was happening with her people and her country? Would a handful of hotheads succeed in bringing back one of the darkest chapters of the late twentieth century?

Gold had seen evil in many forms, but she found something especially disturbing about hate that could lie dormant for decades, then explode in a paroxysm of violence like a forgotten land mine. That's what had happened in the former Yugoslavia during the 1990s, and now there were people who wanted it to happen again. What was the half-life of hate? Generations, apparently.

The Rivet Joint continued its mission and never picked up another hit. After the front-end crew called back to say they'd reached bingo fuel, the jet turned for its temporary home. The aircraft landed at Sarajevo after dark. On the parking apron, the engines whined down, leaving only the buzz of avionics sounding through the aircraft. The lights inside the plane blinked, an occurrence that no longer concerned Gold. She'd spent enough time around Parson to know the electrical interruption happened as the crew switched from the onboard auxiliary power unit to an external generator cart.

Irena unplugged her headset and stuffed it into her helmet bag a little more roughly than necessary. The gesture made Gold think of an athlete putting away sports gear after a losing game. The young Serbian-American linguist said nothing, and she looked dejected. Gold could imagine how she felt. Irena probably wondered if she could have done more to save those police officers, even though that made no sense. She cared too much. Gold wished she could tell Irena of an antidote, but none existed. Gold cared too much as well, and she probably always would.

Outside, a pleasant Balkan breeze swept across the airfield. Gold looked forward to a shower, a quick dinner, and maybe some reading in bed. An announcement from the Rivet Joint's aircraft commander interrupted her thoughts of relaxation. The commander spoke as he closed his cell phone.

"Sorry, guys," he said, "but we're stuck out here for a little bit. They can't send a crew bus to get us until the ramp freeze ends."

"Why the ramp freeze, sir?" a crewman asked.

"I don't know," the commander said, "but I bet it has something to do with that." He pointed to activity taking place farther down the parking apron.

Airport police vehicles, blue lights flashing, surrounded an aircraft. The plane looked like a private charter; it bore no airline livery. Gold didn't know the model, but it was a two-engine jet that looked like it might carry thirty people or more.

As she looked closer, Gold saw the police had their weapons out. Not just pistols, either, but shotguns and assault rifles. She heard no shots. Several men lay prone on the tarmac. Officers trained their guns on the men as other officers handcuffed them. Indistinct shouts mingled with the sounds of truck engines and idling jet turbines.

"Can you hear what they're saying?" Gold asked Irena.

"Not much," Irena said. "Stuff like 'Don't move. You're under arrest.'"

"A drug bust?"

"Maybe."

Eventually, the police yanked the prisoners to their feet. Officers herded them into trucks and vans. Gold counted fourteen men under arrest. The police vehicles sped away. A few minutes later the ramp freeze lifted and the crew bus came.

The bus let the American fliers off at the main terminal. During the wait for the embassy vehicle to take them to the hotel, Irena struck up a conversation with a policeman standing watch at the exit for ground transportation. The man wore full tactical gear—flak vest, kneepads, earpiece—and he carried a rifle with a high-capacity magazine. He spoke amiably enough in Serbo-Croatian, probably charmed by Irena's good looks. But Irena did not smile. Her eyes widened, and she looked worried. She shook her head, said something that sounded like "Thank you," and rejoined her crew.

"What did he say?" Gold asked.

"He probably told me more than he should have. That charter came in from Bahrain, and it carried Muslim fighters drawn here because of the mosque burnings."

"Oh, no."

"He said some were Chechens, some were Kuwaiti, and some came from Saudi Arabia."

"That's all we need."

"I'm worried, Sergeant Major," Irena said. "This place is ready to blow up all over again."

THE NEXT MORNING FOUND DRAGAN, Parson, and Cunningham in Belgrade. Two days remained before the start of the Holy Assembly of Bishops, and Dušić seemed to have vanished. Webster stayed back in Sarajevo, saying only that he needed to make some phone calls. He wouldn't give details, but Parson guessed most of those calls went to The Hague. The Rivet Joint bored holes in the sky and reported nothing. The Serbian police had little choice but to go into full defensive mode.

Parson and Cunningham rode with Dragan in his personal car, a BMW. Dragan wanted to inspect the preparations at the Patriarchate. "I really hoped to take the fight to Dušić," Dragan said, "but it looks like he'll take it to us."

"Unless he gets cold feet," Cunningham said.

"I don't think that will happen," Dragan said. "Dušić has crossed the river, and he can't go back. He could have sat in his office for twenty more years, selling weapons and getting richer. But if he knows we're onto his drug trafficking, he also knows his business is gone. I'm thinking the only future he sees for himself is that of a warlord. And for that, he needs a war."

Dragan stopped his car in front of the Patriarchate. Parson admired the mosaic above the entrance, an image of some religious figure. Gold would know who. But the police activity interested him more.

Officers were building vehicle checkpoints on Kralja Petra and

every other approach to the Patriarchate. They were not yet stopping cars, but Parson could see they planned on leaving nothing to
chance. A sandbagged machine-gun pit overlooked the checkpoints. While Dragan spoke in Serbo-Croatian with his fellow officers, Parson and Cunningham examined the gun pit.

"They know what they're doing," Cunningham said.

"How's that?" Parson asked.

"See how they built two rows of sandbags with some space in
between? That's good. A rocket-propelled grenade will blow right
through one wall. But this way, it'll hit the first wall and detonate.
The second wall protects guys from unpleasantness happening at
the first wall."

"Sounds like somebody's thinking." Based on what Parson had
seen at other highly protected venues, he figured the cops would
stop each vehicle and inspect the underside with an angled mirror.
They'd probably put a spiked chain across the street, and they'd
remove the chain only after a bomb dog had sniffed the car. Then
the chain would go back into place, and the process would start all
over again. A tedious process. Traffic would back up and people
would bitch. But, with some luck, the checkpoint might prevent
disaster.

Parson's thoughts turned to the sky. As another way of prevent-
ing disaster, the Rivet Joint would take to the air again as the Holy
Assembly of Bishops began. He tried to think of some way he could
help. Parson wasn't a lawman; he could not carry a weapon on the
ground here. But he could talk with the jet.

"When game day arrives," Parson said, "how about if I come
with you and handle comms with the Rivet Joint? That will free
you up to watch the crowd and the cars."

"Works for me," Cunningham said.

Up on the roof of the Patriarchate, two policemen in tactical
gear pointed and conferred. Defensive marksmen, Parson guessed.

Snipers getting the range and angle of all their likely shots. Men who looked like they knew their jobs; Parson certainly hoped they did. But he dared not make predictions about how this would all go down. Dušić knew his job, too, that son of a bitch. Everybody involved on both sides here brought experience. Everybody was a warrior.

FOR DUŠIĆ, CONDITIONS COULD NOT get much worse. In Belgrade with one day to go, he conducted surveillance at the Patriarchate. The central dome, topped by a cross, overlooked the grounds and the street below, where officers busied themselves stringing razor wire. The columns and arched windows conveyed a stateliness not diminished even by coils of concertina and flashing lights of squad cars.

The Holy Assembly of Bishops had never seen such a high level of security. Police had also built a sandbagged gun emplacement that covered Kralja Petra. If they had gone that far, no doubt they planned other measures as well. Dogs, snipers, explosives detectors. God only knew what else. Maybe the Americans had heard something in that damnable airplane of theirs. Or maybe Dušić's efforts at stirring up trouble in advance had worked too well, and the Turks had made some kind of threat of their own. Either way, he knew he must alter his tactics.

In Stefan's van, now bearing stolen plates, Dušić told Stefan to make no more passes along the block where Kralja Petra began. Circling would invite suspicion. Dušić had seen enough, anyway.

"What do you think?" Stefan asked. At least he was sober this morning.

"The mission will require some precision," Dušić said.

"How so?"

"I will drive the Citroën. I need your skills for something else."

"Viktor, driving the bomb is the most dangerous task."

"I have faced danger before. And you can see for yourself what we are up against. The tactical environment has changed."

Dušić suspected American eavesdropping had more to do with this than Muslim terrorists. Americans had hit him, quite literally, with setbacks before. In 1995, after the ethnic cleansing of Srebrenica and much of the rest of Bosnia, his unit took up positions in the town of Lisina, near Banja Luka. The mission: guard the air defense control sites that directed Serb antiaircraft missiles. Those missiles had scored a great victory earlier in the year when they'd shot down U.S. fighter pilot Scott O'Grady. That American bastard had eluded capture after ejecting from his F-16, but presumably he'd learned a lesson about trifling with Serbs.

When Dušić's platoon began protecting a radio relay tower at Lisina, they expected little resistance. Those pathetic blue helmets of the United Nations would not dare try to take the relay tower by force; they could barely protect themselves. And according to intelligence, no Muslim forces operating in that region possessed the strength to attempt such an operation. If enemy forces made such an effort, Dušić's platoon would rip them apart. Dušić had ringed the tower with a series of gun pits. The position of the automatic weapons created interlocking fields of fire; Dušić's men could have held off a force three times their number. He took pride in the impregnable defense that he and his NCOs had created. Dušić could still smell the freshly dug earth, the well-oiled weapons. It was in September; the coolness at night offered the first hint of fall.

But on one evening, with no warning, no approach by any visible enemy, the world exploded. As Dušić and Stefan rode in a truck between the relay tower and a nearby radar warning site, thunder pealed from a cloudless sky. Fire and smoke erupted from the earth with volcanic force.

"Air strike!" Dušić shouted. Those NATO meddlers again and

their damned endless supply of aircraft. Dušić, Stefan, and the truck driver leaped from the vehicle to take cover in a ditch. The ground rolled and shuddered with one more explosion. A scent of explosives filled Dušić's nostrils, but he had difficulty placing the odor. Not like gunpowder, and certainly not like old-fashioned cordite.

What was more strange, Dušić heard no jets. Usually the whistling of turbines accompanied any air attack. Even jets dropping bombs from high altitude left at least a faint noise signature. But instead, a deathly quiet descended on the hills.

"What in the name of holiness is that?" Stefan asked.

"Fucking Americans," Dušić said, "and maybe the British. I do not know how but I know who."

"Our men," Stefan cried.

"Back in the truck—now," Dušić ordered. "Get me back to the radio tower."

They scrambled back into the vehicle, and the driver made a three-point turnaround. When the truck topped the rise, the scene made Dušić sweat and shake.

The relay tower lay toppled. So did most of the trees around it. The low buildings at the tower base had been reduced to chunks of concrete. Flames flickered across churned and blackened soil.

Dušić's platoon seemed to have vanished. Some strange weapon had visited such destruction on the site that Dušić could not even recognize where the gun pits had been dug. He called names, but no one answered. He saw no intact bodies, only limbs and viscera in the dim light as darkness closed in. He realized that's all that would have been left of him and Stefan had they remained at the site for five more minutes. Silence reigned until one man, and only one man, began to scream. He yelled no words, simply howled an unintelligible animal sound. Fear and pain had taken him to a primal place.

Dušić and Stefan ran toward the cries. They found a young *razvodnik* with both legs and one arm ripped off. Blood and soil covered him so that he appeared like some shrieking ghoul that had crawled up from the grave. But he did not shriek for long. The shrieks turned to gurgles, and the boy died clutching Stefan's hand.

Later, Dušić learned what had rained down such hell. Not an airplane but a naval vessel. The USS *Normandy*, a Ticonderoga-class guided missile cruiser, had fouled the beautiful Adriatic with its presence. The warship had launched Tomahawk cruise missiles against air defense sites in Bosnia. The crushing blows helped force Serb leaders to sign that document of shame, the Dayton Accords.

The Americans had bested Dušić on that day. He would not let it happen again.

26

ON THE OPENING DAY of the Holy Assembly of Bishops, the Rivet Joint powered through a cloud layer and leveled above a pearl undercast. Gold glanced outside through the cockpit windows when she got up to stretch her legs. The mist spanned from horizon to horizon; it appeared to wrap the entire earth in a peaceful embrace. Gold felt a twinge of irony as she gazed out from behind her sunglasses, knowing what lay beneath the clouds. She returned to her seat beside Irena, took off her shades, put on her headset, and began listening.

Now that authorities knew Muslim fighters were trickling into Bosnia, attracted by the new tensions, Gold owned a bigger piece of the mission. The Rivet Joint flew mainly to zero in on Dušić and his men, and that remained Irena's focus. But Gold tuned to a broadband setting, listening to a wide spectrum of channels to pick up on signs of more triggermen arriving from abroad. Whatever she heard might not help capture Dušić, but it might measure how dangerous the atmosphere had become. With her fluent Pashto and smattering of Arabic, she was glad to help. She just wished the circumstances were different.

Gold adjusted a volume setting, clicked her ballpoint pen. She tapped the pen on the top page of a fresh notepad. The effort left a pattern of little black dots.

"Nervous?" Irena asked.

"More like worried," Gold said. "I hope Lieutenant Colonel Parson and the other guys don't run into trouble today."

"Me, too. Have you heard anything interesting?"

"Negative. You?"

"Snake eyes. It's like Dušić has dropped off the grid."

Gold did not like the sound of that. You could call a man like Dušić a lot of things, but not stupid. He had figured a way to exploit religious and ethnic hatreds so deftly that he might just start a new war almost by himself. What a tragic human failing that people so often killed over what they found most holy. After years of reflection, Gold thought she had finally begun to understand why. God was eternal and unchanging. But religion—how man approached God—was a human institution. So of course religion could be as flawed and misused as any other human institution.

The airplane banked into the initial turn of a holding pattern. Gold heard one of the officers up front check in with Parson on the ground in Belgrade.

"Dragnet," the crewman called, "this is Motown on station. How copy?"

"Dragnet has you five by five," Parson said. "Got anything for me?"

"Negative. We'll advise. Everything normal down there?"

"Pretty much. Just a lot of people who don't like to have to wait."

That relieved Gold a little. Parson seemed safe enough for now with Cunningham and Dragan close by. So far so good, but the day had only begun.

Irena loosened her shoulder straps and leaned back in her seat. Fiddled with the controls on her console.

"Still nothing," she said.

Gold listened to her own channels. Eventually she picked up a conversation in Pashto. Pakistani accent.

"I have made it to Bihac, my brother," the voice said. Gold tried to bring up a map of the Balkans in her head. She did not have a photographic memory, but like most experienced soldiers she possessed a fair knowledge of geography. Where was Bihac? Oh, yeah. Northern Bosnia.

"What mood did you find?" An older voice in Pashto. Maybe some organizer or middleman.

"The faithful are tense, but things remain quiet at the moment. The crusaders burned a mosque a few days ago."

"If they try to wipe out our people again, we will take revenge."

"Indeed. The supplies have arrived in good order."

Supplies? Probably weapons and ammunition. With the cycle of mosque and church burnings, Dušić had created the perfect backdrop for what he wanted to do, and it continued to feed on itself.

"Are we recording this?" Gold asked on interphone.

"Always," a crewman answered. "What do you have, Sergeant Major?"

"Foreign fighters coming into Bosnia, I think."

"Lovely."

AT THE SPECIFIED TIME, Dušić met Stefan and the *razvodniks* at Pionirski Park. Dušić drove Stefan's van. Stefan arrived in the Citroën, now heavy, wired, and deadly. Nikolas, Andrei, and the other men came in two Land Rovers. Mist drizzled from an overcast sky. In the distance, a church bell tower tolled a *trezvon* while Dušić addressed his team. Though Dušić still held to the agnosticism taught by his earliest Communist teachers, he took the triple rings of soprano, alto, and bass bells as an auspicious sign. As a commander on the verge of his signature mission, he wanted his words to inspire.

"History teaches that any war left unfinished must be fought again," Dušić said. "And so we shall. I know you may find today's operation distasteful. I share your feelings. But today we only set the priming charge. The real explosion comes later. A few of the good must die so that we may eliminate the evil, the Turks who have infested this land long enough. Go with courage. If you survive, I will reward you and offer you further missions. If I should fall, press on without me. Stefan will know how to see that you get the other half of your checks."

Dušić explained how the tactical situation had changed, and he outlined his plans for addressing that problem. The *razvodnik*s would no longer fire indiscriminately, at least not at first. They were to aim for police officers and any defensive snipers on the rooftops. Stefan had his own specific targets: the machine gunner and anyone else who looked particularly dangerous. Further, Dušić himself would drive the car bomb. When he finished speaking, he slipped his arms into his body armor, hefted the armor into place, and began snapping the fasteners closed. He held out his hand for the key to the Citroën.

"Are you sure about this, Viktor?" Stefan asked.

"I am. I need you for your marksmanship now. Any fool can drive a car."

Stefan smiled faintly, handed over the key. "And you have the number to call to detonate the weapon?"

"I do." Dušić patted an outer pocket attached to his body armor, which contained his mobile phone. "But if something happens to me, you know what to do."

"I have the number as well. Do not forget that you must turn on the trigger phone and your own cell."

"Then all is in readiness," Dušić said. "Gentlemen, execute the mission."

Stefan pumped his fist into the air and sat down in the van. The *razvodnik*s climbed into their SUVs. At the wheel of the Citroën, Dušić inserted the key into the ignition. As he started the engine, he eyed the trigger phone duct-taped to the console. Two wires led from the phone. The wires ran under the seat and back toward the trunk.

INSIDE A MOBILE COMMAND POST on Kralja Petra, Parson listened on VHF through a lightweight headset. He still felt a little strange performing official duties in civilian clothing. Performing those duties surrounded by Serbian policemen made it all even weirder. At one time, these guys might have been his enemies; he even wondered if any of them had ever manned anti-aircraft guns. But today they nodded to him politely enough. Maybe they'd gotten word he and Cunningham were friends of Dragan.

Through a window, Parson could see Dragan and Cunningham working outside, making the rounds of the checkpoints and the machine-gun pit. To give them any news from the Rivet Joint, Parson had only to change frequencies. But so far he had nothing to report. Dragan walked with his Vintorez rifle at the ready. Traffic had backed up behind the nearest checkpoint, which was positioned to keep uncleared vehicles well away from the Patriarchate. Officers patrolled the line of cars. A few of the men held the leashes of bomb dogs; Parson recognized a Labrador, a Belgian Malinois, and two German shepherds. The drizzle dampened the Labrador's fur enough that the animal stopped, shook itself, then resumed sniffing fenders and wheel wells.

Bishops and priests gathered at the Patriarchate's entrance. To Parson, they all looked like ancient men of wisdom with their black vestments and long beards. He wondered if any of them had been wise enough to speak out against ethnic cleansing back during the war. That would have required both wisdom and guts.

At the checkpoint, Dragan and Cunningham conferred about something. Dragan pointed to one of the dog handlers and appeared to give some kind of order. Parson switched to their frequency.

"Anything the matter?" Parson asked.

"I noticed a car in line that's riding low like an overloaded boat," Cunningham said. "Maybe just bad shocks, but—"

Cunningham stopped talking. He turned around as if he sensed something wrong.

At the machine-gun pit, the gunner's face exploded in a spray of red.

27

ABOARD THE RIVET JOINT, Gold stood at the galley and poured cups of coffee for Irena and herself. As she made her way back to her seat, she heard a thump. Very strange. The noise came from somewhere underneath her feet. Felt like driving a car over a shallow pothole. Hot coffee sloshed over Gold's fingers.

She put down the cups by Irena's console, wiped her hands with a handkerchief. From the murmurs and furrowed brows, she could tell the crew was puzzled by the noise.

A louder bang shook the jet. The airplane began to vibrate. Gold strapped into her seat, glanced over at Irena. Irena yanked her shoulder straps tight. She met Gold's eyes with an expression that said, *I have no idea what's going on.*

Gold's ears popped. She swallowed hard and they popped again. She put on her headset and listened to the crew on interphone and the radios.

"What the hell was that?" a crew member asked.

"I don't know, but we're depressurizing."

"Everybody on oxygen."

Gold donned her sweep-on mask. The first whiff of pure oxygen flooded her lungs with coolness. Irena donned her own mask, gave Gold a thumbs-up. The blinkers on their oxygen regulators flipped from black to white with each breath. Gold felt light in her seat. She heard the crew sort through the emergency in clipped voices.

"Control, Motown Eight-Six is in an emergency descent to flight level two-five-oh. Rapid decompression."

"Motown Eight-Six, we copy your emergency. Report level at two-five-zero."

"Can you give us vectors for Sarajevo?"

"Affirmative. Turn left heading one-seven-zero."

"Crew, check in."

"Markovich up on oxygen," Irena said.

Gold fumbled for her talk switch. "Gold up on oxygen," she called.

The rest of the linguists and aviators checked in—nearly thirty people—and the aircraft commander addressed his crew.

"I have no idea what just happened," he said, "It sounded like something near the landing gear, so we'll see if all the wheels come down. Whatever it was obviously opened a hole in the pressure hull. We've lost some hydraulics, too. Just stay on oxygen for now. We'll get on the ground in a few—"

The aircraft rolled hard to the right. Gold felt the g-forces press her into her seat. Someone cried out off interphone, clearly startled by the wounded airplane's spasm. Unlike airlift crews used to low-level banking and yanking, these linguists usually cruised in more tranquil flight. Now the Rivet Joint pitched down. Irena grabbed her armrests. For this jet to pitch and roll like a C-130 zipping through mountain passes, something had to be *wrong*.

The plane leveled for a moment, yawed left. As the pilots fought for control, something else seemed to draw Irena's attention. She tapped at her keyboard. What the heck was she doing? Gold realized Irena was still monitoring her channels even as the aircraft staggered on the edge of controlled flight in an emergency descent. The hole in the plane be damned, she still had a job to do.

"Two-alpha again," Irena said. "Lock it up."

"We're on it," a crewmate called. "What you got?"

"Signal but no voice. Dušić just turned on a phone. Where is he?"

"Right where we thought he'd be."

THE MACHINE GUNNER at the checkpoint lay sprawled against sandbags, most of his head blown away. Parson was trying to see where the shot came from when the call came.

"Dragnet," the Rivet Joint crewman said, "we have a signal lock at your position."

Strange tone of voice. The man sounded scared, with a lot of ambient slipstream noise behind him. What was wrong up there? Parson wanted to ask but had no time.

"Copy that," Parson said. He switched frequencies and transmitted to Cunningham and Dragan, "Motown advises they have a lock."

"Copy that," Dragan radioed.

The murdered gunner proved Dušić was here, and now Dušić had turned on a cell phone. So where was the son of a bitch? Parson did not have to wonder long.

A black Citroën nosed out of the backed-up traffic and jumped the curb. Policemen shouted orders in Serbo-Croatian. The car charged toward the Patriarchate's entrance.

Oh, God, this is it, Parson thought. Just as in his worst dreams, he could not make his mind or his body work fast enough to do any good. Nothing seemed to move quickly but the Citroën. Must be the car bomb. In an instant, the theoretical worst case became reality.

Rooftop snipers opened up on the Citroën. The booms of their heavy-barreled rifles echoed through the falling drizzle. Rounds punched into the car's hood and windshield, but the vehicle kept coming. Rifle fire chattered from points all around the Patriarchate. Who was firing? In front of the mobile command post, Dragan kneeled, brought up his Vintorez. Before he could fire, something knocked him sideways as if he had been kicked.

Now Parson understood. Dušić had sent an assault team to take out the checkpoint, to clear the way for a vehicle-borne IED. The front of the Patriarchate had become a kill zone. Next, it would become ground zero.

Parson tore off his headset and ran outside. A bullet scorched past his face and slammed into the side of the command post. These bastards had their own sniper.

Men with AK-47s came from somewhere within the traffic. They sprayed on full auto, firing at policemen. One officer fell; others took cover behind police vehicles and returned fire. Shots from the rooftop dropped one of the gunmen, then another.

Parson grabbed Dragan by the arms and pulled him behind the command post. The Serbian officer groaned.

"I'm all right," Dragan said. Saved by his body armor.

Rounds peppered the Citroën as it lurched to the Patriarchate's facade. Parson expected flame and steel to swallow him at any moment. But a strange thing happened. The driver's door opened and a man got out and ran. Not a suicide attack, then.

The sound of automatic fire lifted in a crescendo. One sniper atop the Patriarchate slumped over the edge of the roof. His weapon plummeted to the concrete below. Someone shouted *"Allah-hu akbar!"* The man who'd leaped from the Citroën stumbled, fell, regained his footing, and ran toward a side street.

A SEARING PAIN from a bullet wound burned Dušić's left calf. The round had hit him just after he'd exited the car. Run, he told himself. Just run. Covering fire has got you this far.

Bullets cracked in front and behind. He could not tell if they came from his team or the policemen trying to kill him. Spray-and-pray from the *razvodnik*s seemed at least to force the officers behind cover. And the odds improved every time Stefan pressed the trigger of that M24.

He saw the van on the street perpendicular to Kralja Petra, Stefan barely visible behind it, aiming over the hood. The vehicle's rear door stood open, waiting. His deliverance. Victory so near. Had Prince Lazar felt like this as he fought his way to death and glory across the Field of Blackbirds?

Dušić dived into the back of the van. Stefan racked the bolt of the M24, fired once more. He threw the rifle into the van and swung himself into the driver's seat. Slammed the door shut, put the vehicle into gear, and stomped the accelerator. Dušić closed the rear door as the van sped away. He heard the impact of rounds hitting the engine compartment. Blood all over the floor now. He paid it no mind. Dušić dug for his cell phone.

28

DRAGAN AND PARSON CROUCHED behind the mobile command post, watched the van escape. One of the police marksmen on the rooftop fired at the vehicle, but Parson could not tell if the bullets connected.

"We gotta evac this place now," Dragan said. He barked an order in Serbo-Croatian into his radio, then shouted, *"Svi napolje!"*

Parson needed no translation to know that meant *Get everybody the hell out of here!* Clerics and laymen poured from the entrance of the Patriarchate, apparently alerted by officers inside who'd heard Dragan's radio call. People fled across the street and down the sidewalk in an effort to put as much distance between themselves and the building as possible.

An elderly man in black vestments stumbled down the entranceway. The man lost his footing and went down amid the rush of the crowd. Parson pushed his way toward the old priest. He found him at the base of the steps, clothing dirty and trampled. Parson leaned down, lifted the priest by the armpits. He swung the priest's arm around his neck, bent low, and put the man across his back in a fireman's carry. The burden felt light; the old cleric must have weighed barely a hundred pounds. Parson ran across Kralja Petra as the priest moaned something unintelligible. Rifle fire popped to Parson's left and right. He could not see the shooters. Dragan sprinted the other way and charged into the Patriarchate.

Other police joined Dragan's effort to clear the area. *"Svi napolje!"* the officers yelled.

At what Parson hoped was a safe distance, he stopped and lowered the priest to the sidewalk. From there, Parson could still see people running from the Patriarchate's entrance. The old man sat on the concrete and yammered in his own language. Parson had no idea what the man was saying, but he did not seem seriously hurt.

A flock of buntings swished overhead, startled by the rush of humanity into the street. Even the birds knew something was wrong.

A thundercloud of black and orange boiled up from the Patriarchate. The boom registered so loudly that Parson's eardrums transmitted not sound but shock. A flash of heat burned his cheeks. The blast wave took his breath, flung stinging objects into his face. The fire did not dance like normal flames but twisted through itself, curled around rolls of smoke.

Debris shot from the fireball, trailed plumes of smoke and flame. A gnarled chunk of steel clanged to the sidewalk near Parson. Dust and smoke rolled down the street, enveloped Parson and the priest in a blinding, choking netherworld. When Parson tried to breathe, his lungs seemed to fill with sand. For an endless instant, all physical matter seemed intent on burning, cutting, and suffocating.

"FINE WORK," DUŠIĆ SAID as he turned off his cell phone. Stefan's car bomb had performed flawlessly. Dušić looked

behind him to see the pillar of smoke rising above the Patriarchate, receding into the distance. His limbs felt damp with sweat
and blood. He took a moment to catch his breath. Finally he said,
"For a second there, I thought they had me."

His lower leg throbbed, but he felt flush with success and victory. Dušić could not tell how many casualties the bomb had
inflicted, but it almost didn't matter. Serbs would view this strike
as a Muslim act of war, and history's wheels would turn as they
should. He wanted to savor the moment, but immediate problems
needed attention.

For one, a pair of bullets had slammed into the van. The first
had only popped through the windows, left white holes to the left
and right. The second had entered the engine compartment. Dušić
had thought his getaway nearly perfect, but now the engine rattled,
and a temperature light displayed on the dashboard. He could not
afford a breakdown now, especially not here—surrounded by Belgrade traffic and never far from police.

"We will not get much farther," Stefan said.

"Can you reach the storage facility?" Dušić asked, still breathing heavily. "We can take my Lamborghini." His car lay just a few
kilometers away, across the river in Novi Beograd.

"Very conspicuous," Stefan said.

"Yes, but it is fast, and we have few options. Damn, this leg
hurts."

The other problem was his wound. Dušić raised his trouser cuff
as Stefan coaxed the overheating van to struggle on. A bullet had
ripped through Dušić's calf. Fortunately, it had missed the bone.
But the slug's passage had not left clean entrance and exit wounds.
Instead, the bullet had torn away a chunk of flesh and left a ragged
gash that would not stop bleeding. He reached for the medical kit.

"How is that injury?" Stefan asked.

Dušić regarded his leg, clamped his fingers above the wound to stanch the bleeding. With a more narrow laceration, he would have had Stefan sew it with thread. The kit lacked any anesthesia, but Dušić could have borne a little pain for his people. However, this gash gaped too wide for inexpert sutures, and some of the shredded muscle probably needed debridement. Dušić had seen such wounds in the field before.

His sock sagged with blood. Some had splashed over his boot, but the sock now acted as a wick and drew blood down inside the boot. Dušić felt his own blood squishing between his toes.

"I must get to a doctor eventually," he said.

Dušić tore open a gauze dressing and placed it over the wound. Blood soaked into the fibers.

The sound of sirens rose across the city. Stefan turned a corner, headed out of the old section of Belgrade. Smoke began to curl from under the hood.

"Did the *razvodnik*s survive?" Dušić asked.

"I saw two go down. I do not know about the others."

"I hope they made their escape. They conducted themselves well. As did you."

Stefan did not react to the praise. Perhaps he needed time to process what he'd done. Of course, he would take no pride in killing Christian clergy. But from this point on, operations would focus on the true enemy, the Turks. Serbs deserved their land and their glory, but Dušić did not believe in predestiny. They would have to take what was theirs, and now he had opened the way.

Fingers sticky with blood, Dušić unrolled a bandage and wrapped the fabric over the dressing. He tied it off with care, hoping to stop the bleeding without cutting off circulation. The bleeding seemed to slow down.

"Will you be able to walk?" Stefan asked.

"Not well, but I am mobile."

A helicopter thudded overhead. More medical and police response to the bombing. Dušić's own medical needs would have to wait. He knew of an old army surgeon who might help him, even shelter him, but right now he just wanted to get out of Belgrade.

More smoke boiled from under the hood. The van left a wisping trail as it crossed the Gazela Bridge.

"We must not become stranded," Dušić said.

"It now comes down to luck," Stefan said.

He had a point. The van would make it to the storage facility or not, simple as that. The vehicle sputtered into the streets of Novi Beograd, smelling of burned oil and overheated radiator fluid. Traffic flowed lighter now, and no one seemed to pay any attention to the smoking engine.

Stefan turned one more corner, and Dušić saw the storage buildings ahead. Relief flooded Dušić's whole being. His luck continued to hold; he saw no cars but his own at the storage center. Good; no witnesses. If people showed up, Dušić would have to make a quick decision about whether to let them live. He opened his wallet, found his security card, and handed it up to Stefan.

"Wave this at the card reader to open the gate," Dušić said. He unsnapped his body armor and removed it. The weight off of his shoulders and chest came as a mercy.

Stefan lowered his window, stopped at the entrance, waved the card. The gate began inching open.

When Stefan drove through, Dušić felt a strong urge for them just to get into the car and flee. But a commander had to think clearly amid the fluid nature of battle. And there was nothing more suspicious than an abandoned, bloody van with bullet holes in it.

"Stop by my car," Dušić ordered. "Open the inner fence and move the weapons from the van into the front boot of the car."

Dušić gave Stefan the key to the inner fence's padlock. Ahead he saw his prized Lamborghini, a little dusty but still mission ready.

Stefan stopped, got out, unlocked the padlock. He let the chain rattle to the ground. He swung open the gate, returned to the van, drove through. Stopped beside the Aventador.

"Let me help you," Stefan said.

"No. I think I can move. Just transfer the weapons. You may have to unscrew the suppressor from your rifle to fit it into the boot. Take some AKs, too, and plenty of ammunition."

Dušić also told Stefan to drive the van to the back of the storage buildings, hose away the blood, and knock out the windows punctured by bullets. Drape a floor mat to cover the bullet hole in the engine compartment. Make the vehicle look like a derelict smashed by vandals instead of something recently used in a crime. Leave it in the back.

Under normal circumstances, that might not fool the police for long. But Dušić hoped war would overtake all other concerns for the police and everyone else very soon.

More helicopters pounded across the city skyline. All headed to the Patriarchate, no doubt. And if witnesses had seen the van, Dušić needed to get himself and Stefan as far away as possible, regardless of how Stefan changed the vehicle's appearance.

"We should move," Dušić said. He opened his door, stepped out of the van by himself.

When he put weight on the injured leg, pain stabbed harder than he'd expected. Dušić hissed through clenched teeth. But he remained on his feet.

"Viktor," Stefan said, "let me—"

"Just put the equipment in the car," Dušić said, "then do what I said with the van. Hurry."

Dušić limped to his car, leaned against the driver's door. Closed his eyes and fought the pain. He unlocked the Aventador so Stefan could open the boot. Then he hobbled to his small-arms shed and keyed in the lock code.

Inside, he looked for something he could use as a cane or crutch. Found nothing more satisfactory than an old Mauser. He opened the bolt, placed the muzzle to the floor, and held on to the grip. The weapon wasn't long enough for use as a proper crutch, but better than no support at all.

They still had the storage center to themselves. Dušić thanked his stars it wasn't a weekend, when storage renters would be more likely to show up. Bangs and crashes sounded from out back— Stefan taking care of the van's windows. Good. Dušić scrounged for anything else that might prove useful in the coming days. He chose an RPG-7 grenade launcher. Old technology, but highly effective. Recalling the tear gas police had used earlier, he also took a pair of gas masks.

Dušić waited for Stefan to finish the job on the van. The vehicle had made awful noises as it lurched away; perhaps its life had ended by the time Stefan got it behind the storage units. When Stefan came back, Dušić gave him the RPG-7 and some rounds for it. Stefan also loaded more pistol and rifle ammunition into the car. The Aventador's small cargo space could not accommodate all the gear, so Dušić sat in the passenger seat with the RPG-7 resting on the floorboard. Stefan locked up the small-arms shed, sat behind the wheel.

"Where to?"

"A place outside Novi Sad," Dušić said. "I know a doctor there." About seventy kilometers away.

Stefan started the engine. Dušić talked him through the use of the paddle shifters, and Stefan steered out to the street. Dušić cautioned him not to speed through the city; the Lamborghini drew enough attention standing still. But once the avenues of Belgrade gave way to the E75, Dušić let his friend drive the Aventador as its designers intended. The car accelerated to 150 kilometers per hour. The V12 ran smoothly, more like the hum of an electric motor than the controlled explosions of internal combustion.

Dušić watched the trees blur past. Finally, he allowed himself a moment of satisfaction. History did not flow in straight lines and constant speeds the way his Lamborghini now rocketed along this highway. History turned on certain events, swung on pivot points engineered by great men. Like him.

THE RIVET JOINT SHUDDERED through its descent. Gold gathered that the pilots had recovered control of the aircraft; she felt no more steep banks or rapid dives.

"We're below ten thousand," the aircraft commander announced on interphone. "You can come off oxygen."

Gold pulled off her oxygen mask. The nape strap felt damp; she hadn't realized she'd sweated that much. Irena untangled herself from the mask and hose and adjusted her headset.

"What do you think happened?" Gold asked.

"Beats me," Irena said. "I don't know as much as the fly guys up front, but airplanes don't just go bang and start swerving all over the sky. I've heard of engines disintegrating by themselves, but nothing like this."

Had the jet been sabotaged? Quite a coincidence to suffer a failure nobody could explain just as the bishops began their session. What was happening down there, anyway? Dušić had shown up and turned on a cell phone. That could mean nothing but bad things.

"Any report from the ground?" Gold asked, off interphone.

"I'll check," Irena said. She keyed her talk switch and asked, "Collins, anything from Dragnet?"

"They don't answer."

Gold's anxiety rose. Parson would never have abandoned his post at the radio unless something forced him. Dear God, had Dušić pulled it off? Every indication—even the plane's unnatural tenor—suggested he had. Gold wondered if the altered tones of air rushing over the jet resulted from parts sticking out where they weren't supposed to be. She wondered whether Parson and the others were dead or hurt, whether Irena and her crewmates would get out of this aircraft safely. Chatter on the interphone and radios confirmed the most immediate dangers.

"Motown Eight-Six, Sarajevo Tower. You are cleared to land. Crash response standing by."

"Motown copies cleared to land."

"We better get configured."

"You're right. Gear down. Before-landing checklist."

"Gear down."

Groans and hisses sounded from underneath the airplane. Not the usual soft clunks of landing gear locking into place.

"Left gear's stuck in transit."

"Try emergency extending it."

As the pilots spoke, a warning horn blared in the background. Probably proclaiming the obvious, Gold thought. Unsafe landing gear.

"Silence that horn, will you?"

"Yes, sir."

The blaring stopped. What seemed like an eternity passed with no more talk from the cockpit. Gold imagined they were consulting an emergency checklist, flipping switches or pulling levers to get the landing gear to work.

"No joy," someone said.

"Did it move at all?"

"Negative."

"All right, we got the nose gear down, the right gear down, and the left gear jacked all to hell."

"That'll pull us off the runway."

"I know it."

"Book says it's better to land on the belly."

Silence for a few seconds. Then a click on the interphone, a heavy sigh, and terse orders.

"All right. We'll bring all the landing gear back up and then we'll emergency extend the nose gear. At least we got that much going for us."

"Yes, sir."

"Gear up."

More groans and clangs. The noise put Gold in mind of cogs and gears fouled with sand.

"Up and locked. Okay, let's get the nose gear back down."

"All right. I got the emergency extend handle."

Long silence, then clanks from beneath the jet. But at least these noises sounded like something that was supposed to be happening.

"Nose gear down. Both main gear up."

"Okay, tell Sarajevo Tower we're about to fuck up their runway. And tell everybody in the back to stand by for a crash landing and emergency egress."

"Yes, sir."

Briefings and instructions followed. The crew would brace for impact, prepare to evacuate the aircraft, pop the slide if necessary.

In the back of Gold's mind, behind the sick worry about Parson and the others, she wondered if she was witnessing the opening of a new Balkan war. To Gold, Dušić's plan had sounded audacious, but he clearly had resources and contacts. And wars had been started by less than the bombing of a holy site. As the Rivet Joint slowed for a crash landing at Sarajevo, Gold remembered that a mere pistol shot in the city below had ignited World War I.

"We're on final," someone announced. "Touchdown in about one minute."

Gold watched the linguists and technicians finish stowing loose equipment. Checklists and clipboards went into flight cases and helmet bags. No sense having loose objects flying around on impact. Gold pocketed her pens and notepads.

The engines hushed as the pilots throttled back.

"We're in the flare," one of the pilots said. "Hold on."

A metallic scraping came from underneath the jet. The noise sounded awful, but Gold sensed no violent jarring. She'd expected a hard impact, perhaps even the fuselage breaking open. But only some heavy vibration made this landing feel different from any other touchdown.

When the nose came down, the vibration actually eased a bit. Gold remembered the nose gear had extended, so at least that part of the aircraft had rubber rolling under it.

"Good job," the aircraft commander said. "You're right on centerline."

Gold felt the plane slow down, and the scraping ended.

"Ground egress," someone said.

Crew members unbuckled their harnesses, came out of their seats. The engine noise whined down to nothing, and the lights blinked out. Hatches and doors came open. Rays of sunlight beamed into the Rivet Joint's shadowed interior.

Gold followed Irena down an escape slide. She slid down the inflated fabric on her buttocks. When her heels contacted the pavement, her own momentum forced her upright into a running stride. She jogged away from the escape slide to make room for crew members coming behind her.

Firefighters sprayed foam along the underside of the aircraft and over the engines. Their effort amounted to a precaution; Gold saw no fire, not even smoke. Irena hugged two of her crewmates, then embraced Gold.

"That's a first for me," Irena said.

Gold said nothing. This wasn't her first crash landing, and it wasn't anywhere near her worst. Crew members backslapped and celebrated their escape from injury. She could not share in their mirth. She knew that in Belgrade civilians might have just been burned and torn apart by someone who thought the world had not seen enough war.

29

AFTER THE BOOM came a beat of silence. The blast had hit Parson like a kick to both sides of his head, and it left his ears stunned and deadened. Yet in the quiet he could sense the siss of grit settling to the pavement, the world falling back into place.

Then the screams began. Not words but formless cries of agony. People in mind-bending pain. People finding mangled tissue where arms and legs used to be. People who could see their own bones or internal organs.

The priest Parson had carried away from the Patriarchate put his hands together and began to pray, sitting on the ground in torn vestments. The old cleric seemed reasonably safe. Parson ran toward what was left of the Patriarchate.

He found a scene that brought his worst memories to reality, only magnified. Corpses and pieces of corpses lay coated in dust. The wounded crawled and writhed. A priest young enough to have no gray in his beard sat armless amid the rubble. He rocked back and forth slightly, made a keening sound through his clenched jaw. Blood poured from both stumps.

Parson fought the urge to panic, forced himself to think. Where were the medical kits? In the mobile command post, maybe. He ran to the CP, yanked open the door. No police officers inside. Good. Maybe they'd escaped injury and were now searching for survivors, treating wounded. Apparently the cops had already called for help; down the street, a helicopter was landing, dust swirling under its rotors.

In the CP, Parson found a first-aid kit. He could not read the lettering but recognized the red cross on the cover. He sprinted back to the injured priest and ripped open the first-aid kit.

He could see the kit was meant for minor injuries. It contained small adhesive bandages, a tube of ointment. One little roll of gauze. Nearly useless. Parson unrolled the gauze and wrapped it around the priest's left stump, the one bleeding the most profusely.

Blood soaked the gauze and poured right through it, smeared Parson's hands. The priest stared straight ahead and never made eye contact. Parson tried to find a pressure point under what remained of the upper arm. He squeezed hard over the stump; blood sponged through his fingers. The priest's eyelids fluttered, and the man fell backward. Bleeding out, Parson knew. He lost his grip on the stump, shifted around on his knees, groped for the pressure point again. Now blood and dirt coated his hands in a wine-colored slurry. A life was flowing away between his fingers; lives were flowing away all around him.

"Dragan!" Parson shouted. "Cunningham!"

No one answered. Parson had last seen Dragan running into the Patriarchate. The building now sat ripped open and smoking, its facade and front walls torn away. He held little hope that Dragan remained alive, and he had no idea about Cunningham.

From the helicopter that had touched down on the street, a

crewman ran toward Parson. A medic, apparently. The man carried a pack of gear, and in a pouch on his uniform he wore a pair of medical shears. He never took off his flight helmet.

The medic kneeled beside Parson, shouted in Serbo-Croatian. Parson let go of the priest's wound and allowed the medic to do his job.

Smoke and dust still drifted from the ruined Patriarchate, though the flames had gone out. A fire truck blared onto Kralja Petra. Fire-fighters descended from their rig and ran into what remained of the building. Survivors began to mill through the broken masonry. Some appeared uninjured, others bloody and burned. Parson stood up and started looking for Dragan and Cunningham.

He felt a deep personal failure. He had known when and where this would happen. Serbian and American agencies had known when and where this would happen. And yet they couldn't prevent it. Parson wondered what was wrong with him, what was wrong with his country and his world. They couldn't stop one nut job bent on war even when they knew his plans?

He felt that same sense of futility he'd known back in the 1990s. The same frustration when he'd land in Germany after a Bosnia mission and, still in a sweat-damp flight suit, slump behind the wheel of his Mustang at Ramstein. With the top down he'd tear along the autobahn at ninety miles an hour, blasting the Gin Blossoms on his CD player as if guitar riffs and speed could clear his mind of the horrors that lay just a few hours of flying time behind him.

Now the horrors lay all around him.

A burst of gunfire spat from somewhere across the street. Parson turned toward the sound. He saw Cunningham running down Kralja Petra, pistol drawn. The OSI agent raced toward a car where a gunman had taken cover. The gunman popped up from behind the vehicle and fired another burst from his AK. The bullets missed

Cunningham, who ducked behind another car. Serbian police officers also converged on the gunman.

Parson had thought the attack was over, but here was a strag-
gler, still deadly. Cunningham and the other officers now faced a
cornered shooter armed with an automatic weapon.

Parson dropped flat to the ground. Without a firearm, he could
do little but make himself a difficult target.

Behind a concrete barrier placed near what had been the Patriarchate entrance, a policeman ejected a spent magazine from his
rifle. Slammed in another. When he raised himself to fire at the
gunman, the officer caught rounds in the upper body. He slumped
behind the barrier, bleeding.

Parson could see Cunningham bobbing and weaving behind a
car. The OSI agent appeared to be sizing up the situation while
making the best use of cover. And the situation looked like a stale-
mate. The gunman had a commanding view of the scene. He might
pick off several more people before running out of ammunition.
Parson feared casualties would mount until the police could get
heavier weaponry into place.

Cunningham did not wait for that. Holding his Beretta with
both hands, he charged from behind the car. The gunman swung
his rifle to fire. But before the man could shoot, Cunningham
dived for the street. He hit the ground on his right shoulder and
slid, gun pointed. With his eyes now at ground level, Cunningham
must have had a good view of the shooter's feet and ankles. The
OSI agent began to fire.

The move impressed the hell out of Parson. If you couldn't
shoot to kill, shoot to wound.

The gunman screamed and fell to the pavement. But he held on
to his weapon with one hand as he writhed on the ground. Bullets
sprayed under cars and up into the air.

A Serbian officer broke from cover and ran toward the gunman.

Parson saw the policeman stand over the attacker and pump several rounds into him with a handgun. The man's body jerked with each shot. The AK fell silent.

Thinking to congratulate Cunningham on his bold move, Parson got up. The OSI agent still lay on the ground.

Blood pooled around him.

Fingers of ice clawed at Parson's guts. He ran toward Cunningham. Kneeled beside him. The flight medic from the helicopter caught up.

Cunningham's eyes were open but did not register recognition when they turned to Parson. The agent held one hand to a bullet wound through the neck. Blood slicked his fingers. Blood ran across the pavement. His handgun lay on the ground beside him, still cocked and ready to fire again.

The medic moved Cunningham's hand out of the way and placed a compress to the wound. The agent's leg jerked spasmodically.

Cunningham moved his lips as if trying to speak, but no sound came out. He sighed; Parson heard the outbreath. No inbreath.

The medic felt for a pulse, began chest compressions. Felt for a pulse again. Placed the heels of his hands back onto Cunningham's chest, resumed the compressions. After a few minutes it became clear the medic was just going through the motions.

Parson leaned down and clicked the safety on Cunningham's weapon so the gun wouldn't fire. Then he pressed his thumb and forefinger to the bridge of his nose, squeezed his eyes shut. "Son of a bitch, man, I'm sorry," he said. "I am so fucking sorry." He hadn't known the OSI agent well, but he'd grown fond of the guy. Parson had helped teach Cunningham to care about this part of the world. Now that had gotten him killed.

That feeling of impotence came back full force. The bombing, the deaths and injuries around him, seemed to mock him, to mark defeat. If the war here wasn't finished, if some people wanted so much to resume the killing, who was he to think he could stop it? In an Air Force officer's course, he'd once read that in more than three thousand years of recorded history, fewer than three hundred years had passed without war anywhere. Peace now seemed like a distant valley on the back side of a ridge you could see through your scope, but you knew it was too far to walk.

Around him, the noises of destruction assaulted his ears. Sirens and screams. Dragan emerged from the shattered building, helping a policeman carry a wounded cleric. At least Dragan had survived.

Someone turned off the siren. The screams trailed off as the injured grew weaker, passed out, or died. The helicopter lifted off, taking wounded to a hospital.

A funereal quiet took hold. Mist drifted from an overcast sky. The trees along Kralja Petra stood silent until a breeze gave them voice.

DUŠIĆ HAD STEFAN STOP the Aventador at a home on the edge of a village outside Novi Sad. The house looked like the dwelling of a country gentleman. Manicured shrubbery high-lighted the front garden. The outbuilding behind the house could have served as a stable for horses, though no animals grazed in the adjoining paddock.

"Who lives here?" Stefan asked.

"Do you remember Captain Bradić, the field surgeon?" Dušić said.

"Vaguely."

"He patched up many of our men. Bradić has gone into private practice, and he seems to have done well for himself. Go knock on his door. Tell him as little as possible."

Dušić's leg hurt worse now; the injury had stiffened. Apart from bringing medical kits, he had not arranged for treating wounds in this operation. To recruit a doctor or medic might have been a good idea, but Dušić had opted for maximum security. The more people who knew his plans, the greater the risk of a security breach.

A good judgment, he decided. The operation had succeeded. He longed to turn on a news broadcast, to hear reports of the explosion. More importantly, he wanted to hear reactions to it. Would Serbs see it as a Muslim act of war? Would they mobilize? Would the old paramilitary units form up again? He would find out soon enough.

Bradić came to the door. Dušić watched him conversing with Stefan. The doctor looked troubled. How much had Stefan told him, and had Stefan explained it in the proper way? No matter. Dušić remembered the old field surgeon as a patriot; the doctor knew all too well the bloody results of Muslim perfidy.

Stefan and Bradić came down to the car. "Viktor, you old warrior," Bradić said. "Let me help you into the house. What have the Turks done to you?"

The Turks? Very good; let him think that. Operational security.

"I have a leg wound," Dušić said. "I need a hospital, but in my line of work, I try to stay off the radar."

"Very wise, Lieutenant. I only wish President Karadžić and General Mladić could have remained off the radar."

"Indeed."

"I have no general anesthetic in the house, but I can deaden your leg locally and fix you up if the damage is not severe."

Dušić levered himself out of the car, using the old Mauser as a crutch. The doctor frowned when he saw the rifle and the RPG launcher but he said nothing. Dušić put his arms around Bradić and Stefan, and the two men helped him up the steps and into the house.

Bradić had set up one room with an examination table and medicine cabinets. Perhaps there he ministered to family members and villagers, apart from his work at the hospital in Novi Sad. The doctor put on surgical gloves and unwrapped the bandages over Dušić's calf. Dušić winced as the dressing, sticky with drying blood, came off his leg. Bradić adjusted his glasses and looked at the wound.

"You are lucky," Bradić said. "The bullet could have hit bone." Bradić uncapped two hypodermic needles. "I am going to give you an antibiotic and an anesthetic."

"Before you begin," Dušić said, "may we park the car behind your house?"

"Ah, yes," Bradić said, "in the barn."

"Stefan, if you please. And bring the gear inside."

Stefan went out the front door. While he was gone, the doctor gave Dušić two injections.

"Do you have family, Bradić?" Dušić asked.

"My daughter is away at school. My wife died in the war."

"I am very sorry. When?"

"In 1999, when the bombs hit Novi Sad."

Dušić remembered the time well. When the Muslims in Kosovo—by all rights a Serbian province—dared to declare a separate state, Serbs moved with vengeance. The Americans interfered again, bombing targets in Belgrade, Novi Sad, and other locations to stop the righteous ethnic cleansing. The West divided its record of meddling into what it called the Bosnian War, the Kosovo War, the Croatian War, and so on. But to Dušić, it was all one long conflict. An unfinished conflict.

Stefan came back inside. "You may not wish to watch this procedure," Bradić said. "There is tea in my kitchen. You may make yourself at home."

"Thank you, sir. Ah, do you have anything stronger?"

"Scotch whisky in the far left cabinet."

"Thank you, sir."

Dušić shook his head, but Stefan did not see the gesture. Perhaps Stefan wished to drink to celebrate success, though the look on his face did not seem celebratory. The act was done now; Dušić hoped his friend could keep his mind on the big picture.

The doctor began to scrape at the wound with a scalpel. Dušić felt no pain; his leg seemed a slab of cold meat. But he sensed the abrading and pulling.

"So tell me how you suffered this gunshot wound," Bradić said. "Your friend was unclear."

"It is better that you do not know the details. But our struggle against the Turks continues, and it will reach new heights. In fact, we will need a man of your skills once more."

"I have seen enough of war, Viktor."

The doctor put down his scalpel, threaded suture material through the end of a curved needle. Dušić saw his own blood on Bradić's gloved fingers, and it made him proud. He was bleeding for his people. Bradić's comment disappointed him, though. But perhaps it was just the sentiment of a tired middle-aged man suddenly asked to treat a kind of injury he had not seen in a long time.

Bradić sewed up the wound, gave Dušić another injection, placed fresh dressings over the injury. "You will limp for a time," the doctor said, "but you will walk again. Now you need to rest."

Stefan and the doctor helped Dušić to a bedroom. They removed his shirt and trousers, stained with blood and sweat. Dušić sat up in the bed, exhausted but too excited for sleep. For a light dinner, Bradić brought him tea, black bread, and sausage. Eventually Dušić fell asleep to the sound of a news broadcast from a television in another room.

WHEN PARSON LEARNED what had happened to the Rivet Joint, he could think only of how Sophia and Irena might have died in a smoking hole in the ground. Dead like Cunningham and the twenty-four other people killed at the Patriarchate. Gone like the people represented by numbers and red flags in that pit at Bratunac. And now the whole region seemed poised to go back to the days of the killing fields.

In Parson's room at the hotel in Sarajevo, he and Webster watched CNN International. A female reporter wearing a khaki correspondent's jacket stood in front of the remains of the Patriarchate. The building's entire front had been ripped away. An interior stairway stood exposed to the outdoors. The reporter spoke from where the main dome with the crucifix had once been, but that was gone, too.

> *"The Serbian government has called for calm following this morning's terrorist attack on the Holy Assembly of Bishops. The president says Serbs should draw no conclusions until authorities complete an investigation. However, some nationalist politicians call the blast a Muslim act of war. In fact, witnesses report hearing gunmen shout 'Allah-hu akbar' while spraying survivors with gunfire. A few firebrand leaders are already calling for the reconstitution of Serbian paramilitary units. Bosnian Muslim officials have, in turn, placed their own police and defense forces on high alert, raising the specter of another all-out war in the former Yugoslavia."*

Parson switched off the television. "Well, there you have it," he said.

"This place is gonna burn itself down again if the police don't catch Dušić," Webster said. "The best that could happen now would be to get him alive and put him on trial. Officially, this isn't our fight. But for me this is personal, especially after what happened to Cunningham. I know it is for you, too."

Hell, yeah, it's personal, Parson thought. Because of Cunningham. Because of what could have happened to Sophia and Irena. Because of all the things that had happened here in the past that Parson and the rest of the world failed to prevent.

"USAFE, U.S. Air Forces in Europe, has been talking to Central Command," Webster continued. "They want us to stay here and stand by. The most valuable things we have now are the recordings the Rivet Joint guys picked up."

Parson could follow the logic. Maybe, just maybe, if they got Dušić, the recordings would prove what he'd done. And then, just maybe, people would follow the trial and chill out instead of going for one another's throats. But the whole thing depended on hope and goodwill, two commodities in short supply here.

He thought about Cunningham and all the years the young agent should have had ahead of him. Other losses came to mind: Parson's C-130 crew in Afghanistan, and Afghan fliers he'd known during his tour as an adviser. Losses made him angry. Made him want to take some kind of action: start engines, call in air strikes, pull triggers. Merely observing and witnessing didn't square with his nature.

That's why the Bosnian hills had become so soaked with blood twenty years ago. Too much witnessing and not enough ass-kicking.

VIKTOR DUŠIĆ AWOKE in the morning refreshed from ten hours of uninterrupted sleep. For just a second the unfamiliar surroundings of Bradić's guest bedroom left him confused. Then he remembered all that had brought him here. He closed his eyes for a moment, relished the sense of accomplishment.

During the night, Dušić had dreamed of final victory. In a mountain village, Serbs gathered to celebrate the death of the last Muslim in the Balkans. The war had raged for years, but the Americans and the British and NATO had stayed away this time, weakened by recession and riven by political infighting.

To honor the architect of final victory, the villagers danced a kolo in Dušić's honor. The women wore traditional dresses of red and white. The men wore white shirts and red vests. The dancers joined hands and formed concentric rings around Dušić, spun and twirled to the music of *tamburica*s and *frula*s.

Dušić stood in the center of the dancers, and he held high the old Mauser he'd used as a crutch. Each time he raised the weapon above his head, the townspeople cheered. They did not know the details of how he had engineered the last stage of their struggle, and they did not care. The villagers knew only that their land was theirs, all theirs, now and forever.

The dream left a glow inside Dušić's heart, but he knew such a moment of completion lay far in the future. Much work remained. The most immediate tasks concerned eluding capture by the current Serbian authorities, those lapdogs of the West.

His wound felt stiff and sore, but not unbearable. He sat up and examined the dressing. The bandages remained all white, not pinked by bleeding. Bradić had done a good job.

At the foot of the bed, the doctor had left a change of clothes. Bradić had not kept himself as well conditioned as Dušić, so Dušić imagined the dress shirt and black cotton trousers would hang a bit loose on him. Too large would have to do. Dušić put on the clothing, found it ill fitting but adequate. His Mauser stood in a corner. To replace it, Bradić had brought a proper set of crutches. Dušić lifted the crutches from a trunk beside the bed, tested his weight on his good leg. He curled his fingers around the rubber padding of the grips and raised himself to a standing position. He did not call for help; he despised the role of an invalid. Unaided, he hobbled down the hall. What he found disgusted him.

Stefan lay on a couch, still fully dressed. His left arm lolled onto the floor, knuckles against the hardwood. An empty bottle rested beside his hand.

"Get up, you drunkard," Dušić said. "It is well to celebrate success, but we must remain alert. What if the police showed up right now?"

Stefan stirred, opened his eyes. They were shot with red. He rubbed his hand over his mouth and groaned as he sat up. Put his elbows on his knees, his head in his hands.

"Saint Sava, forgive us," he said.

Dušić kneeled beside Stefan. The effort sent a stab of pain through Dušić's leg. He let go of the crutches and grabbed his old comrade by the shoulders.

"You stop this!" Dušić shouted. Looked around, lowered his voice to a hiss. "You know the grand strategy. You know we've only set a priming charge. Do not become weak like that lily-livered *razvodnik* I had to shoot."

Stefan looked up, perhaps wounded by the implicit threat. He opened his mouth to speak. Before any words came out, Dušić punched his shoulder almost playfully.

"Change is hard, Stefan," Dušić said. "It requires strong men. Serbian children will sing of us a hundred years from now if we hold fast and see this thing through."

Stefan raised his head, looked at Dušić. His eyes did not show resolve, but at least his words conveyed purpose.

"Then we shall," Stefan said.

"Very well. Now check your weapons and make ready for anything. I believe we are as safe here as anywhere, but you must not let down your guard like this again."

Dušić noticed movement in the corner of his eye. He turned to see Bradić standing in a doorway. Had the doctor heard the conversation? Bradić held two steaming cups.

"Good morning, gentlemen," the doctor said. "Is something wrong?"

"No," Dušić said. "Not at all."

Bradić came into his living room and set down the cups on a table beside Stefan's M24 rifle.

"The news reports since last evening are troubling," Bradić said. "What do you know about that explosion in Belgrade?"

Dušić cut his eyes at Stefan, thought for a moment. He knew Bradić had no use for Muslims. But could the doctor understand the broad context of the events now unfolding? Bradić had received his commission because of his medical training. He'd functioned primarily as a healer, not truly a combat officer. How much steel did he carry in his spine? Better not to have to find out.

"We know only that the Turks have committed an act of war," Dušić said, "and a war they shall have."

OUTSIDE THE SARAJEVO HOLIDAY INN, Gold saw what she considered the saddest sight on earth: preparations for battle. No war had been declared, and top leaders still called for reason. But arson and riots had broken out all over Bosnia, Serbia, and Croatia.

The hotel manager remembered what had happened in his neighborhood before, and he'd started stacking sandbags behind all the windows. Razor wire stretched around the hotel grounds. Police and army patrols rumbled past, driving what Gold's Army colleagues unofficially called BFTWGs, pronounced "biftwigs," for "big fucking trucks with guns." The gloom of low-hanging clouds made it all seem even more dire.

Dragan arrived at the hotel with a contingent of Serbian police. In a conference room, they met with their Bosnian counterparts, along with Parson, Webster, Gold, and the Rivet Joint crew. Dragan wore black tactical clothing, pistol and magazines on his belt, Vintorez rifle on a sling over his shoulder. He spoke in Serbo-Croatian for a couple of minutes, then he addressed the Americans.

"I just told my Bosnian Muslim friends we have a common goal now," Dragan said. "This isn't 1995. You guys have a role, too. We'll take all the help we can get."

"What can we do now that the jet's grounded?" Parson asked.

"What we need from the jet now is not its wings but its

recordings. I think we've already got enough to prove Dušić is behind this."

"You bet we do," Webster said.

Still the prosecutor, Gold noted.

"Don't ever think your help isn't valuable," Dragan said. "Information from American and British intelligence helped us get Radovan Karadžić back in 2008. I was a rookie officer then, but I took part in Karadžić's arrest. That bastard had lived as a fugitive for more than a decade."

Dragan told them about the long hunt for the former Bosnian Serb president. At one point, authorities thought they'd tracked him to a church compound in Pale. The British SAS raided the compound, but found that Karadžić had slipped through their fingers, perhaps by just seconds. Eventually, the politician who'd whipped his people into a genocidal fury changed his name and appearance.

"He went all granola on us," Dragan said. "Started calling himself 'Dr. Dabić, alternative healer and spiritual explorer.' I'm telling you, you can't make this shit up."

Most of the Americans laughed, and Dragan continued. Serbian police finally caught up with Karadžić as he rode a bus through the Vračar district of Belgrade. As a young police sniper, Dragan watched the arrest through his rifle scope, ready to fire if Karadžić tried to use deadly force.

"I would have loved to put a round through him," Dragan said, "but we took him without firing a shot. He just pushed and shoved a little bit."

"Better that way," Webster said. "He gets to sit and think about what he did."

"You should have seen him," Dragan said. "Long white beard, and he had tied his hair in some kind of topknot like Santa Claus on meth."

More laughter, but Dragan turned serious.

"We have every law enforcement agency in the world looking for Viktor Dušić," he said, "but we don't think he could have gone far. Listen, you got Osama. You got Saddam. We got Karadžić and Mladić. And we will find this son of a bitch."

AFTER THE MEETING, Parson bought three cups of coffee in the bar and sat down with Dragan and Webster. The other bar patrons eyed Dragan's clothing and weapons but did not seem surprised. Perhaps they'd seen it all before.

Parson thought Dragan had given a good briefing, but he still had questions. To begin with, if Dušić hadn't gone far, where might he be? Traveling by air would likely prove impossible for him. Crossing borders by road would, too, if every country had been alerted.

"He may not need to cross borders at all," Dragan said. "He could find plenty of sympathy and shelter among the old hard-line Serbs, sad to say."

"Sounds like he could hide off the grid for a long time," Parson said.

"Unless someone gives us a tip," Dragan said. "Even Serbs who hate Muslims might not tolerate what he's done, if they suspect he did it."

"Have you found any more evidence?" Webster asked.

"We found the van he used as a getaway vehicle. It's registered to a guy who served with Dušić back in the war."

"So if he's not with the van, how's he traveling?" Parson asked.

"Not sure. Dušić has a Lamborghini. Witnesses say it was parked at the storage facility where we found the van, but it's not there now."

"Storage facility?" Parson asked.

"Yeah. Dušić has a whole row of buildings where he keeps weapons. Most of it's legal; he's an arms dealer. No doubt he took some stuff with him, so if—when—we find him, we're probably in for a fight."

A fight that, in a larger sense, Parson had fought before. Sometimes old evils returned, and you had to face enemies you believed had been defeated.

He thought of a hunting trip he'd taken a few years ago. An Air Force buddy brought him to the mountains of east Tennessee to pursue wild boar. The animals were descendants of domesticated hogs escaped and gone feral; in just a few generations they returned to their wild nature in both appearance and spirit. An unaccustomed quarry for Parson, more used to taking deer and elk in the West.

For this hunt, Parson did not carry any of his usual scoped rifles, fine-tuned for long-range accuracy. Instead he used a brush gun, a lever-action .30-30 with open sights. Near the end of the day, the dogs jumped a big male hog with black fur and tusks like scimitars. The boar charged uphill through the woods, well ahead of the pack. But the redbones and blueticks gained on their prey, and they cornered it against a rocky outcropping.

Beyond the outcropping, a sheer rock face dropped five hundred feet to the valley below. With nowhere to run, the boar whirled and fought.

A dog lunged at the boar, bit down on its hindquarters. Parson wanted to fire, but the dogs closed in too near. A redbone snarled and leaped for the boar's throat. That was the dog's last mistake.

In a flash of white tusks, the boar gored the redbone in the ribs. The dog yelped and fell back bleeding. Perhaps energized by the smell of blood, the boar shook free of the dog at his hindquarters and gored that animal in the neck. Now two dogs lay whimpering and writhing among dry leaves spattered with blood.

Sensing an opening, the boar plowed through the other three dogs. With a clear target now, Parson took a snap shot, brought the .30-30 to his shoulder and pressed the trigger. The instinctive aim at a moving target felt more like wing shooting than riflery, but Parson knew he'd scored a good hit. The boar stumbled and rolled, yet it ran on.

Surely he'd dealt the animal a mortal wound; the boar left a blood trail that disappeared into a rhododendron thicket. But the sound of its hoofbeats through the leaves continued for several seconds. The wild hog took the bullet and just kept going.

At this point Parson wished he'd never joined this fight. Not his territory, not his game. But the hunt had exacted an awful toll already, and he felt obligated to finish what he'd started.

Rifle across his chest, Parson waded into the thicket. The sun sank lower, and in the heavy vegetation he had trouble distinguishing solid from shadow. He lost the blood spoor, and he had no idea where the boar had gone.

Parson's buddy stayed back to attend to his two gored dogs, both dying. The other three dogs ranged the mountain, looking for scent. Occasionally one of them bayed, far out of sight, the howl echoing through a forest fast approaching darkness. To Parson, it sounded like a cry of anger and grief.

Just before blackness descended completely, Parson heard an explosion of rustling leaves. At first he could not determine the direction of the sound. Then he saw the boar. Tusks darkened with blood, it charged from behind a dead hickory. The wild hog came straight on, all sinew and spite. Intent on killing again.

Parson shouldered the .30-30 and fired. The bullet sent up a spray of leaves and dirt beside the boar. The animal kept charging. Parson knew if he ran now, the boar would likely catch up with him and slash those tusks through his leg.

With a flick of the wrist, Parson cycled the rifle's lever. The expended brass tumbled to the dirt.

Nearly too dark to aim now, Parson pointed his barrel at the head of the onrushing boar. He pressed the trigger. The muzzle flash brightened the woods for an instant.

The boar kept coming without so much as a flinch. But then its legs buckled and the hog collapsed. It slid forward across the forest floor until it stopped at Parson's feet. Bullet wound in the head, another in its side.

Parson chambered another round. Nudged the boar with the tip of his boot. Stone dead.

A question from Dragan brought Parson back to the present day.

"We're staying," Webster answered. "In fact, if you take Dušić alive, I'm going to come off active-duty orders."

"How's that?"

Webster explained that he was Air National Guard, not regular Air Force. And he wanted to get back to his civilian role and help prosecute Viktor Dušić.

"I'll even do it pro bono if I have to," Webster said.

"Who's going to run Manas Air Base?" Parson asked.

"Are you kidding? There's fourteen colonels lined up behind me who want to get their tickets punched for command of an expeditionary wing. Get that star pinned on."

"What about you? Don't you want to make brigadier general?"

"I don't know, maybe," Webster said. "But right now there's something I want more."

That impressed Parson. Most colonels would give their left kidney for a star. But he gathered that, for Webster, reaching the pinnacle of an officer's career was just an afterthought. Something less important than justice.

Dragan's cell phone rang. He opened it, looked at the screen. "Excuse me, guys," Dragan said. "I gotta take this."

DUŠIĆ HAD THOUGHT HIS INSTINCTS never failed him. He could always judge a man's loyalty, character, and competence. He had seen Bradić in action as a field surgeon during the war, patching up patriots, a patriot himself. But something had happened to the doctor in the intervening years. Dušić realized it too late, on the third day after the bombing. Bradić had gone away in the morning with hardly a word and had never come back. Now Dušić understood why. Two police cars and an armored tactical vehicle rolled down the narrow road to Bradić's village. From inside the village, two other police cars approached.

As he stood at the window, Dušić's heart filled more with disappointment than anger. His nation could become so much more if its people would only see the hard things through. So many lacked vision. Evidently, so did Bradić.

"Stefan," Dušić called from the guest bedroom, "we have been betrayed."

"I see them!" Stefan shouted from the front room.

At the front of the house, glass shattered. Dušić picked up one crutch, leaned against the wall. As he made his way down the hall he saw that Stefan had knocked out a window and now lay with his M24 pointed over the sill.

Dušić tried to think of escape routes. None existed. The police vehicles, slowing to a stop about two hundred meters distant, blocked the road in both directions. He could not get around them. The Aventador was fast, but in the soft soil of the surrounding fields, it would only bog down.

These lapdogs would not take him alive. He had known all along this operation could cost him his life. Dušić had made his

peace with death, as a soldier should. Long ago he had tallied it
better to die for Serbs than live with Turks. The Serbs he had killed
were martyrs, deaths regrettable but necessary. If he must become
a martyr himself, so be it. He tossed aside his crutch, lifted an
AK-47. Dragged himself to the window beside Stefan.

"My friend," Dušić said, "we may not see our work's fruition."
Dušić placed his hand on Stefan's shoulder. "But we will cross the
river together as warriors."

Stefan looked at him, eyes hollow. "The fruit of our work is
right outside," Stefan said, "and in Belgrade."

Stefan's fatalism pained Dušić, but he had no time to ponder it.
Now he had to consider the tactical situation. Bradić's house had
been built with imported brick. Hardly blastproof, but a natural
defilade for rifle fire. Dušić thought he might manage to hold out
for a time, depending on police weaponry. However this ended, he
hoped the traitor Bradić would return to a destroyed home. The
doctor had said he'd seen enough of war. Apparently he had meant
it. Dušić chided himself for not seeing Bradić's weakness.

Breeze through the window stirred the curtains. The air carried
with it a cool mist descended from clouds scudding low overhead.
Already Bradić's house hinted of desperation, the scene of a last
stand. Then let it come, Dušić thought. This is my Kosovo, my
Field of Blackbirds. He had wanted victory. He could settle for
glory.

On the village road, police officers stepped from their vehicles,
took cover in ditches and behind armored doors.

"Fire at will," Dušić said.

He unleashed a burst from the AK on full auto. Aimed generally
at the nearest police car. Chips and white dust flew from the windshield. The glass frosted, crazed, buckled, but never yielded. No
round holes. Bullet resistant, then.

Stefan's M24 whispered through its silencer. A man screamed.

A police officer prone on a ditch bank had exposed only his elbow, and that had been target enough for Stefan. The officer disappeared beneath the lip of the ditch. Moans came from the grassy roadside as the man clutched what had to be an incapacitating wound.

"Good shot," Dušić said. "Stay low and keep your gas mask close."

As Stefan racked the bolt on his M24, the police returned fire. Slugs slammed into the masonry around the window, tore through the remaining glass, stitched holes in the opposite wall. Chalky powder invaded Dušić's lungs, dust from bullets against brick. He fought the churn of fear in the pit of his stomach.

Of course he felt fear; strikes of rounds from high-powered rifles would cause anyone to fear. But that was just part of the combat environment. Dušić accepted his fear, moved through it, fired again. His rounds scored the plating of the police tactical vehicle. He hit none of the officers, but that hardly mattered. Dušić had plenty of ammunition. He needed only to make the officers keep their heads down. Buy time. Give himself time to think, even if it was only to think of last words.

"Stefan," Dušić said, "where is that grenade launcher?"

"In the hall."

Stefan rolled away from the M24, left it standing on its bipod. He scurried across the room, came back with the RPG-7. Crouched low, handed the loaded launcher to Dušić.

"We shall show these lapdogs how to fight like men," Dušić said.

He yanked the safety pin from the round's fuse, pointed the launcher through the broken window. The HEAT round—high-explosive antitank—felt like a heavy lobe at the end of the barrel. Dušić's leg hurt now, but adrenaline carried the pain to someplace where it could not distract. He curled his fingers around the grip of the trigger mechanism. Aimed. Fired.

The weapon bounced on Dušić's shoulder. Backblast scorched

the floor. The grenade traced a white path to the armored vehicle. A few meters from the barrel of the launcher, the round's rocket motor ignited. The rocket held true on a short flight to the target. As the round struck the side door of the tactical vehicle, it detonated.

Flying metal sliced through tires, fenders, fuel tanks. Sparks from propellant and explosive mingled with gasoline vapor. After the boom of the grenade blast came the whoosh of ignition, and flames engulfed the truck and the men around it. Writhing figures of fire danced within fire. Police officers sprayed their burning comrades with fire extinguishers. Black smoke lifted into dark clouds.

31

GOLD HAD FIRST ENTERED her career field by acing the ASVAB—the Armed Services Vocational Aptitude Battery. One needed a particularly high test score to become a linguist. That helped ensure recruits could hack the academic rigors of learning a new language. But no test could gauge whether she possessed the mental toughness to stare into the darkest corners of human nature. As she rode in a police van with Parson, Webster, and Dragan, she knew she'd need that part of her strength when she arrived at their destination.

They sped toward a village near Novi Sad. Dragan had received word of a tip on Viktor Dušić's whereabouts. But when the first police units arrived, things had turned bad in a hurry.

"The son of a bitch has heavy weapons," Dragan said, "and he knows how to use them."

"So why don't they just lob in some tear gas and shoot him when he runs out?" Parson asked.

"We want him alive if at all possible," Dragan said.

"And I want witnesses," Webster said. "That's our main job. Stay well back from the action, but keep your eyes open."

"Yes, sir," Gold said.

Webster explained that if police could take Dušić alive, his trial could serve as something of a truth commission—a way to defuse the new tensions, to show people how they'd been manipulated. Maybe prevent a new war. A dead Dušić would become only a one-day story that people might not believe.

"Do you think Dušić will surrender?" Gold asked.

"I don't know," Dragan said, "but they're sending a negotiator."

Dragan did not sound hopeful, and Gold understood why. For Viktor Dušić to go this far, to restart a war and relive his glory days, he'd have to be a dead-ender. Someone who disliked the present so much he'd die to change the future.

Gold dreaded the things she might be about to see. She knew better than most the pains of extreme violence and its aftermath. That bullet through her chest in Afghanistan had collapsed her lungs and put her in the hospital for months. Her time for healing at Landstuhl had given her plenty of opportunity to ponder man's inhumanity to man.

She had reached this conclusion: Hate happened as a part of human nature, one of its common failure modes. For one group to blame another for its problems came easily, perhaps even naturally. The grammar and syntax of prejudice held a lasting appeal. Only in the next world would hate become a dead language.

DUŠIĆ WATCHED THE AMBULANCES carry away the burn victims. He and Stefan held their fire as the medics worked; the situation bought time. And in that time, Dušić observed that the police had removed their roadblocks so ambulances could get through. Smoke wisped from the wreckage of the police tactical vehicle, but the fire ignited by Dušić's HEAT round had nearly gone out. The remaining policemen gripped their rifles and peered at Bradić's home from behind the cover of their cars.

As Dušić held an AK-47 and pondered his next move, the telephone in the doctor's house began ringing. Perhaps Bradić's daughter was calling home, or perhaps it was that traitor Bradić himself, expecting police to answer. It didn't matter; Dušić had nothing to say to anyone. He let the phone ring.

After maybe twenty rings, the infernal racket stopped. Dušić was getting tired, and every noise annoyed him. When the rings started again, he cursed under his breath and ordered Stefan to answer it.

"I'll guard the windows," Dušić said. "Whoever it is, get rid of them."

Better yet, Dušić thought, yank the cord out of the wall. But before he could speak again, Stefan was on the phone.

"Yes?" Stefan said. "No. Yes, he is here. One moment." Stefan cupped his hand over the receiver and nodded to Dušić.

Dušić felt a flash of anger. He was long past words and wanted only action.

"Man the weapons," Dušić said. "If anyone takes a step toward this house, kill them."

Dušić took the phone, watched Stefan settle in behind his M24 and sight through the scope.

"Who is this and what do you want?" Dušić asked.

"Viktor Dušić," the voice said, "I am Inspector Petrov of the Ministry of Internal Affairs. I am speaking to you from just outside."

"Petrov," Dušić said, "you will withdraw from your position, and you will allow me to pass."

Several seconds passed with only hiss on the phone line. In that time, Dušić took Petrov for a weakling. Indecisive even for talk, let alone for deeds.

"I am afraid you are in no position to make demands," Petrov said finally. "But if you put down your weapons, I promise you will live. My men will treat you professionally."

Professionally? What did this lapdog know of the profession of arms? Dušić fumed, considered whether simply to hang up the phone. No, perhaps he could intimidate this weakling, put this lapdog's tail between his legs.

"Petrov," Dušić said, "are you a Serb?"

"Of course I am a Serb."

"Then you should know the forces at work here. Look around you. The Turks are rising again, and—"

"You are wanted for multiple counts of murder at the Patriarch-ate," Petrov said.

"That was a Muslim act of terrorism!" Dušić shouted.

"Then surrender and let the evidence speak. There is no need for anyone else to die. Everyone here is a Serb."

Now Dušić's temper burned like white phosphorus. He slammed the receiver against the wall as if he could bash Petrov through the phone line. Then he put the receiver back to his ear.

"Don't you dare lecture me on what it means to be a Serb," Dušić said. "Where were you when the bombs fell on Belgrade and Novi Sad? Where were you when NATO cut out our hearts and handed Kosovo over to the Turks?"

"I was in the army."

"And what oath did you take? What people did you serve? We have held back the Muslim hordes for centuries, and look at the thanks we receive."

"Mr. Dušić," Petrov said, "this is not the 1300s."

"I do not need a history lesson from you. I helped forge that history, and I am forging it now. You listen to me, lapdog. On 9/11 the Americans learned what we have known for a thousand years. Yet they still fail to understand. And you do their bidding like an errand boy."

"My orders come from Belgrade, Mr. Dušić. Nowhere else."

"Your orders come from traitors."

More silence on the line. This was a waste of time and breath. Petrov proved it with his next statement.

"Mr. Dušić, we can end this peacefully. There is no need for further violence."

Yes, there is, Dušić thought. More violence than you can imagine. A crucible of bloodshed that will lead to true peace, with a Greater Serbia for Serbs alone. A lapdog could never understand the mind of a wolf.

"Petrov," Dušić said, "how much combat have you seen?"

"I served in logistics."

Logistics. This pale excuse for a police officer had no idea what he was doing, who he was facing. The police could have staged an assault on the house in the time they'd spent talking. Dušić judged Petrov and his men reluctant and afraid. He ripped the phone cord from the wall.

"Arm that grenade launcher," he told Stefan.

FOR PARSON, the scene at the village near Novi Sad presented a postcard setting with its rows of trees spreading over tiled roofs. Perhaps it could have served as the cover to a children's book of fairy tales. Yet police aimed weapons at one of the houses. Dušić was holed up in there, apparently with plenty of fight left in him. The burned-out hulk of some kind of police truck still popped and smoked.

Horrors in such pastoral locations carried an especially disturbing quality for Parson. He recalled flying an approach into Pristina,

Kosovo, with defensive systems armed against shoulder-fired missiles. But on the ground, in a field beside the runway, he'd watched two boys fork unbaled hay into a wagon drawn by a tractor. The mowed field carried the smell of autumn. The farm setting looked so serene, he wanted to take part in it, to grab a pitchfork and gather wheat straw while wearing a sidearm and survival vest.

Crouching behind Dragan's police van with Gold and Webster, Parson focused on the present. Dragan and the other Serbian police faced an awful tactical problem: They needed to keep alive a suspect willing to die. This battle would end here one way or another, and Parson saw no way it could end well.

Clouds hung low, shrouded the plains of the Danube in the distance. Just beneath the layer of steel-gray mist, a helicopter buzzed toward the village. A police surveillance aircraft, Parson figured. He thought of Cunningham.

"Cunningham should be here," Parson said to Gold.

"I know what you mean," Gold said. "I keep thinking I'll turn around and he'll be there."

For a moment Parson wondered if the departed were that close, just on some other plane. During his trek through the Afghan snows after getting shot down years ago, he thought he felt the nearness of dead crewmates. But that was a subject for another time; right now he had more immediate problems.

Webster had brought binoculars with him. With the optics, he scanned the house. He shook his head.

"What do you see?" Parson asked.

"Rifleman at the window. Dušić has some help in there."

"Do you think the police can pry them out?" Gold asked.

"I don't know," Webster said, "but it doesn't look good."

One of the Serbian police picked up a bullhorn. From the cover of his car, he began to speak. Serbo-Croatian phrases, artificially loud and tinged with the resin of electronics, echoed across the village. Parson wondered what words of persuasion the policeman spoke, whether he appealed to reason, mercy, or fear.

Though Parson could not understand the statement transmitted by the bullhorn, he had no difficulty deciphering the answer. A rifle shot spat from the house, nearly inaudible, fired from something tipped with a noise suppressor. The bullet tore into the car that shielded the officer. The policeman dropped the bullhorn and shouted words that could only be curses.

32

GOLD KEPT HER HEAD DOWN, waited for more gunfire from the house. None came; she heard only the beat and slap of rotors from the police helicopter orbiting the village, and the pop and squelch of radios. The police officer who'd held the bullhorn gazed at the house for a moment, then spoke into a handset. He appeared to be an on-scene commander or at least the head negotiator. The man backed away from his car and, using the cover of the ditch bank, made his way over to Dragan and the Americans.

The officer spoke with Dragan in their own language for several minutes. Then, in English, Dragan introduced him to Gold, Parson, and Webster.

"This is Inspector Petrov," Dragan said. "One of my mentors."

"Pleased to meet you, sir," Gold said.

"Sorry about the circumstances," Webster said.

"So am I," Petrov said. Practiced English, but with a heavy Slavic accent. Graying hair. His rimless glasses made him appear almost academic, and they softened the effect of his web belt and pistol.

"So what happens now?" Parson asked.

"That very much depends upon Viktor Dušić," Petrov said. "My conversation with him achieved nothing. We have breach kits and tear gas at the ready, and we are weighing several options."

"I am very sorry about your men who were burned," Webster said.

"Indeed. My officers would like to kill Dušić and be done with it, but I have explained to them the value of capturing him alive."

"Can't blame them for wanting to take this guy out," Parson said.

"Neither can I," Petrov said. "But if placing him on trial will defuse tensions, vengeance can wait. The situation is deteriorating all around us. Just this morning, in a town not far from here, Muslim youths beat to death an Orthodox priest. And Serbs in Kosovo have torched another mosque."

So the trouble was not just intensifying, Gold noted; it was spreading.

A burst of automatic-weapons fire spat from a window of the house. Slugs impacted the ditch bank, the pavement, and two police cars. Gold saw no one hit, but Petrov removed his glasses and rubbed his right eye. Perhaps flying grit from a bullet strike had sprayed into the side of his face. He scowled, spoke an order into his radio. Police returned fire. Gold noticed that their rounds struck nothing but brick. Maybe Petrov had told his men only to make Dušić and his gunman keep their heads down. She admired the discipline of the police officers who controlled their fire and their emotions.

Petrov and Dragan conferred in Serbo-Croatian again. Then Petrov made a cell phone call, and Dragan spoke into his radio. Answers came back on the radio in single syllables. Officers swapped magazines, checked weapons.

"What's happening?" Gold asked.

"Normally we would wait them out in a situation like this," Dragan said. "Let them get tired and hungry. But we're not going to sit here and wait for the next rocket."

DUŠIĆ FELT THAT CLARITY of mind he had known only in the worst combat situations. Cool reason came when you accepted death as inevitable. Hope only clouded your thinking. If you decided you were already dead, you could function so much better, focus on the mission.

He would go down fighting and die with glory. But in the unlikely event he escaped, he would flee into the mountains and gather support to lead a militia. He could evade the authorities more effectively and longer than Karadžić or Mladić because he was not so well known. An attractive option, better than dying, but how might he get away?

With Dušić's mind purged by the purity of death, ideas came easily. That damned helicopter buzzing and turning overhead could serve his purposes if it came low enough. He needed to think on it a bit more.

Before he could voice his idea to Stefan, one of the officers outside popped up from behind his car. Leaned across the hood with some kind of launcher. Fired.

A large projectile sailed in through the broken window and struck the wall. The canister bounced to the floor, spewing white smoke. Dušić's eyes and throat stung.

"Gas, Stefan!" Dušić shouted.

Dušić reached for his gas mask carrier and ripped out the mask. Placed the mask to his face, sealed the outlet valve with his hand. He exhaled hard to blow out stray fumes around the edges of the mask. Then he covered the air inlet port and tried to breathe in.

The mask collapsed around his face. That told him he had a good seal. He took a tentative half breath.

The air he inhaled came through clean, scrubbed by the filter. But now he could not see, blinded by the mask's hood and head straps stowed in front of the face shield. He pulled the straps over the back of his head and yanked them tight. Tossed the mask's hood over his shoulders.

He didn't really need the hood; it was meant to help keep blister agents off his skin. Not necessary for police tear gas. But now he could not remove the mask to shed its hood. Through the face shield he saw white gas filling the room.

Stefan had not moved so quickly. He struggled with his mask. He had it over his face now, but he coughed and gagged with the chemicals he had drawn into his lungs. Something had dulled the man's reflexes—perhaps drink, perhaps his state of mind.

Dušić took pity and adjusted Stefan's mask for him. Tugged at the temple strap, tightened the cheek strap. Pulled over the hood so Stefan could see. Stefan still coughed, his hacking muted now by the mask, but at least he could breathe.

The canister on the floor continued spewing gas. Dušić grabbed it and threw it outside. Stefan stumbled, coughed again. He staggered in front of the broken window, exposing himself to police fire. Dušić pulled him back behind the cover of the wall.

"Are you all right?" Dušić shouted. The mask muffled his words.

"What?"

"Are you all right?"

Stefan nodded. He lowered himself back to the floor and lay prone beside his rifle. Good, Dušić thought. Stefan remained effective, or at least partially so.

Tear gas drifted in the room. The sight put Dušić in mind of the smoke of Serb villages sacked by Ottoman murderers. Then the chemical cleared enough that Dušić could see outside. The helicopter rattled over the house, turned, came back on a new heading. It flew lower now, probably watching to see if anyone bolted from the house.

Come by a little lower, friend, Dušić thought. I have need of you.

Stefan seemed to have recovered his wits. He crept nearer the window, careful to stay behind cover. After he looked out for a minute, he tried to speak. The mask muffled his words.

"What?" Dušić asked. He leaned closer to the voicemitter of Stefan's mask. The voicemitter made communication possible but not easy.

"They will burn us out!" Stefan shouted. "When they see their gas has not worked, they will set the house afire."

Dušić picked up the grenade launcher. "They will not get the chance," he said.

"What are you doing?"

Dušić looked up at the helicopter. It circled closer now.

"I'm going to give them another problem," Dušić said. "When I do, we will run to my car and slip through them."

Stefan stared. Dušić could see him blinking behind the lenses of his mask.

"Impossible," Stefan said. "They will riddle the car—and us."

Impossible. Dušić disliked that word. Stefan had used it when he first heard Dušić's plan to resume and win the war, to cleanse Greater Serbia of Muslims. History and logic had eventually brought Stefan around. Why was Dušić's vision impossible? What he wanted to do for Greater Serbia had already been done elsewhere in Europe. Centuries ago—in a region that became parts of Spain, Portugal, and France—Muslims had so infested the land that they considered it theirs and called it Al-Andalus. Moorish

Iberia. But brave warriors hurled the Muslims back across the Strait of Gibraltar into the desert wastelands where they belonged.

"We do the impossible, Stefan. We have the strength to achieve what others only imagine."

Stefan looked outside again. He put his hand on his M24, closed his eyes for a moment. Was he praying? A superstitious exercise, Dušić thought, but if it helped Stefan find strength, then let him pray.

"Get ready to go!" Dušić shouted through his voicemitter.

"No, my friend. You get ready to go. Hand me your Kalashnikov."

It took a moment to process the import of Stefan's words. Dušić knew the man had courage, but he hadn't expected this.

"You will need covering fire," Stefan continued. "If we both go out together, we both will die. If I make them keep down, you stand a chance."

Ever the good NCO. Stefan avoided death only because death interfered with the mission. But now his death might further the mission.

Dušić wanted to believe in the integrity of Stefan's motives, that Stefan wanted to die for the cause. But the man had seemed troubled, had taken again to the bottle. Dušić knew of troubled men inducing police to kill them, suicide by proxy. Whether Stefan acted from despair or devotion, Dušić could not tell. No matter. The effect would be the same. Dušić gave Stefan the AK. Using crutches, he could make it to the car alone. He would carry only his pistol.

Stefan placed the automatic weapon on the floor next to his M24. He sighted through the scope of the precision rifle, made a slight adjustment to the parallax knob. Dušić found two fragmentation grenades, the hand-thrown type, in a kit bag. He set the grenades down beside Stefan.

Above, the helicopter turned again. It came straight on, back-dropped by clouds the color of zinc.

TEAR GAS WAFTED ACROSS the village road, over the scene of police vehicles and officers poised with their weapons. Parson caught just a whiff, and even that felt like inhaling tacks. He could see more of the chemical hanging inside the house. Any-one in that room must have been overcome, and Parson began to wonder if this whole thing was over. But then he detected move-ment within the house, and he understood. Gas masks. Of course the bastards wore gas masks; Dušić was a damned arms dealer.

Dragan and the other police officers held clipped conversations by radio. Gold and Webster watched the house and the helicopter circling overhead. Parson imagined the police were setting up to storm the building. He couldn't predict how this day would play out, but it seemed pretty clear that not everyone here would live to see nightfall. Maybe Dušić wanted to die, and he probably wanted to take as many people with him as possible. Parson did not know what to expect from his journey to the hereafter, whenever it came. He liked to imagine spending eternity in an outdoorsman's Val-halla, dwelling in a hall lined with antlers and pelts, surrounded by hills filled with fish and game in an endless crackling autumn. But he didn't want to go today.

The helicopter, a Bell 212, overflew the house and entered a left turn. Parson's aviator's mind noted that the pilots had a solid over-cast above them but good visibility underneath. He wondered how long their fuel load would allow them to remain on station.

As he watched the aircraft, the cackle of automatic-weapons fire erupted from the house. Bullets flayed the police vehicles. The offi-cers hunkered down, held their weapons, waited for orders. The helicopter rolled out of the turn.

A smoke trail rocketed up from the window. At the tip of the smoke, a dark object traced a path straight toward the chopper's main rotor.

The round detonated against the rotor hub. The blades appeared to flex as if made of foam. For an instant Parson thought the Bell had absorbed the blast and might fly on. But one of the blades detached itself from the hub, tumbled away from the aircraft like a discarded plank. The rest of the rotor, now unbalanced, lurched through arcs of smoke and flame. The aircraft pitched down, rolled sideways. Spiraled like a falling leaf. Centrifugal forces flung something from the chopper's cabin, perhaps a checklist binder or a crash ax.

Two helmeted figures struggled behind the windscreen. They grappled with controls that could do nothing for them. One pilot placed outstretched gloved fingers against the coaming of the instrument panel. The helicopter plunged into the garden of the home next door. A fireball erupted on impact, a swell of black and orange. Parson felt the heat flash against his cheek.

Flaming fuel splashed through the garden fence and against the side of the house. The odor of burning kerosene filled the air, and black smoke obscured the burning wreckage. Through the fire and smoke, only a bent tail boom remained recognizable as part of an aircraft.

Parson bolted from behind Dragan's police van. He knew full well the pilots were probably dead, but he wanted to get to a fire extinguisher. Perhaps by some miracle one of the fliers might have survived.

Dragan beat him to it. The Serbian officer unclipped the extinguisher from its mount inside the van. Ignoring gunfire popping from the house, Dragan ran toward the crash site. He sprinted with his Vintorez rifle slung across his back. The weapon bounced against his shoulder blades.

Parson and Gold followed close behind. He worried about leading Gold out from the cover of the van, but they could accomplish nothing while hunkered down and motionless. More police officers ran toward the helicopter, some with extinguishers. Other police returned fire at the house. Bullets peppered the police cars.

DUŠIĆ KNEW he had only seconds. With half the officers trying to save the helicopter crew and half pinned down by Stefan's fire, he saw his chance. Using just one crutch, he stumbled through the house and out the back door. Tore the gas mask from his face and dropped it. Pain seared through his calf. He felt a ripping sensation as he descended the steps and headed for the barn. He'd torn his sutures, and the wound began to bleed anew. Blood darkened the fabric of his trousers as he opened the door of the Lamborghini. He ignored the injury, sat in the driver's seat, punched the starter button. The V12 growled to life.

Stefan, Saint Sava bless him, had backed the Aventador into the barn. By the time Dušić pulled around the side of the house where police could see him, he'd be facing forward and gaining speed. He took his CZ 99 from his waistband, placed the weapon on the seat beside him. Curled his fingers around the padding of the steering wheel, took in a deep breath. Stepped on the accelerator.

33

GOLD TRIED TO PROCESS several things happening at once. Bullets pocked the ground around her. Dragan fell as if tripped; he was shot in the leg. He dropped the fire extinguisher, and it tumbled into the dirt. Blood spurted from the wound in his thigh.

He shouted something in Serbo-Croatian. Another officer grabbed the extinguisher and ran. Gold and Parson kneeled beside Dragan, took hold of his arms, and dragged him to cover behind his van.

In the corner of her eye, she saw someone toss a grenade out the window of the house. The explosion hurled shrapnel against the police vehicles.

A blue sports car, something fast and expensive, charged from behind the house.

From inside the home, a gunman kicked open the front door. He screamed as he trained his rifle on the nearest officers—a guttural, primal cry. The man held down the trigger of an AK-47 and sprayed. Police officers fell—some perhaps from bullets, some from grenade shrapnel, and some as they dived for cover.

The sports car fishtailed as its tires found purchase. Though police vehicles blocked the road in one direction, officers had opened a path for ambulances in the other. The driver aimed for that opening.

"Take my weapon," Dragan told Parson. "Don't let that son of a bitch get away."

Dragan placed the heel of his hand against the ground. Winced in pain. Raised himself so Parson could get the rifle's sling off his shoulder. Parson freed the rifle, checked the fire selector.

The sports car sideswiped a police cruiser and shot the gap in the roadblock. The officers concentrated their rounds on the most immediate threat, the rifleman at the door. No one except Parson tried to aim at the car. He shouldered that strange-looking weapon of Dragan's. Sighted through the scope, swore. Too many police-men between him and his target. No clear shot.

The gunman who'd just come out of the house kept firing, but he began to stagger. As rounds struck him, his body jerked like a poorly manipulated marionette. He fell to his knees, blood stream-ing from wounds. Hands dripping. Lower jaw shot away. His rifle clattered from his fingers. He tumbled forward down the steps, dark smears behind him. The man lay on the flagstones with his head tucked under his shoulders, knees beneath his chest.

"Get Dušić!" Dragan yelled to Gold and Parson. "Chase him down!" Then he shouted something in Serbo-Croatian.

Gold looked at Dragan's wound. Messy, but she had seen inju-ries bleed a lot faster. Maybe the bullet had not cut a major blood vessel.

"I'll be fine," Dragan said. "The keys are in my vehicle. Go, go, go!"

Gold pulled open the driver's door of Dragan's police van.

Parson jumped into the passenger seat. The van had been parked
on the end of the line of police vehicles, facing onto an open road.
But pursuing a fast car that had a head start seemed a hopeless task.

"We'll never catch him in this," Gold said as she started the
engine.

"We don't have to," Parson said. "Just get me close enough, and
I'll catch him with this." He gestured with the weird rifle. "To hell
with observing and witnessing," Parson added.

Maybe he'd given up on taking Dušić alive. But shooting him
dead seemed a better option than letting him escape. Gold put the
transmission into drive and peeled out in pursuit.

DUŠIĆ COULD NOT BELIEVE his luck. No, not luck. Ini-
tiative, enabled by Stefan's self-sacrifice. His friend no doubt was
dead by now. Dušić would mourn later. In days to come, he knew,
he would have much to consider about his brave but troubled war
comrade, addicted to drink and haunted by needless guilt. But
now the mission demanded Dušić's full attention.

The winding road from the farming village denied the Aventador's main advantage—top-end, flat-out speed. But the Lamborghini still took curves better than anything those lapdogs were
driving. In the rearview mirror Dušić could see them coming now
in a police van. He almost laughed; that thing would never catch
him. He braked for a bend in the road, felt the car's suspension
compress and expand. The turn placed a screen of trees between
Dušić and the vehicle giving chase. He steered out of the curve and
saw a tractor on the road in front of him.

The tractor was cresting a rise; Dušić could not see beyond
the hill.

Taking chances had carried him this far and would have to
carry him further. He jerked the wheel, sped around the tractor.

Glimpse of a surprised elderly farmer and the plows bolted to his machine.

The top of the hill revealed an onrushing truck. Dušić steered hard again, swerved back into his lane. Blast of a truck horn.

Short straight stretch ahead before the next curve. Dušić pressed down with his right foot, held his left foot poised. Dismissed the pain from the bullet wound and the torn stitches. He would slip to the nearest highway, make a speed dash, and disappear into back roads again. Surely General Mladić and President Karadžić had endured close calls like this.

When at Bradić's house, Dušić had nearly decided his struggle was over. But now he felt renewed, with great deeds ahead of him. For his cause, he might yet draw a blade, chamber a round.

PARSON SWORE when he lost sight of the Lamborghini. He faced a difficult enough task already: to hit a moving target from a moving platform with an unfamiliar rifle. As a lifelong hunter, he had developed the skills of an experienced marksman. He'd also taken some training; in his wallet he carried a military fire-arms authorization. The gun card said he was qualified on the M9 aircrew pistol, but it said nothing about a Soviet-bloc automatic weapon that fired tungsten-tipped ammunition.

The van careened through a curve in the road. Gold took the bend so fast, Parson feared the vehicle would roll over. A truck speeding in the opposite direction rocked the van with a wave of displaced air. Gold accelerated out of the curve, topped a hill, and hit the brakes for a damned tractor.

"Hold on," Gold said.

She took her foot off the brake, stomped the accelerator, and whipped around the tractor. Rifle in his lap, Parson braced himself against the dash as he rolled down his window. The old man driving the tractor shouted something Parson couldn't understand. Seconds later, the tractor became a speck in the rearview mirror. Parson stuck the barrel of the Vintorez out the window. He knew his only hope was to catch Dušić with a crossing shot on the far side of a curve. If the bastard made it to a long straightaway, he'd be gone.

Ahead, Parson caught a glimpse of the Aventador, snatches of blue flashing behind trees. Dušić had a long lead that was getting longer. Parson surveyed the road ahead.

The pavement vanished into another copse of trees. Beyond the trees, the road curved beside a disked field and rose to a higher hilltop.

"When you get past those trees," Parson said, "I want you to stop."

"Stop?"

"Stop."

Gold pressed harder on the gas, and the van groaned with the higher rpm. Mist collected into droplets on the windshield, and the trees flitted by like an irregular picket fence. When the van cleared the woods, Gold hit the brakes.

The vehicle shuddered to a stop as the antiskid engaged. Up the road and uphill, Dušić's car snapped through the curve and accelerated away.

Parson now had a stable shooting platform, with a target moving left to right above him. A fighter pilot would have called it a deflection shot. Parson sighted through the PSO-1 scope, guesstimated the range. That car had a rear-mounted engine, right? For lead, Parson held on to the passenger compartment. Fired a burst.

The noise-suppressed weapon practically whispered, but Parson heard it when three armor-piercing bullets slammed into the Lamborghini's engine. Sounded like three strikes from a jackhammer.

The car showed no immediate sign of damage. If not for the

sound of bullets impacting, Parson would have thought he missed. The Lamborghini topped the hill and disappeared. Now Dušić would get away clean if he still had a good power plant.

"Okay," Parson said, "follow him."

"Did you hit him?"

"I think I hit the engine. We'll know when we get over that hill." Parson held out hope. He had made long shots before.

Gold hit the accelerator again. Parson felt himself jerked back against his seat. He appreciated the doggedness of Gold's pursuit, but speed didn't matter anymore. He'd taken his one chance; he'd either connected or missed. They'd find out on the other side of the rise. Parson held his finger across the trigger guard of the Vintorez, strained to see the road ahead.

When the van cleared the crest, Parson spotted the Aventador closer than he'd expected. The car trailed gray smoke. Its engine made a popping noise, and the gray smoke turned black.

On that stretch of country road, the shoulder had eroded. Driving too fast and probably distracted by his wounded engine, Dušić skirted the edge of the road. The Aventador rocked when the wheels left the pavement, and Dušić overcorrected. The car swerved to the opposite shoulder, departed the hard surface completely, and veered into a ditch. Rolled side over side into a field. The Lamborghini came to rest upright on its tires, spattered with mud and smoking.

Flames guttered underneath the engine compartment. Something, perhaps a hose, burned as it melted, and fire in liquid form dripped into the grass.

THE PAIN IN DUŠIĆ'S LEG spread as if acid were being poured over it. But the pain did not center on the old gunshot wound. The agony came higher up, where the bone had just broken. Walking had been difficult. Now it was quite impossible.

Where was his weapon? Dear God, that pistol had been on the seat right beside him. He should have known better than to leave it unsecured.

There. On the floorboard. Dušić released his safety belt, leaned forward. The movement magnified his pain so much that he cried out in a growl, but he wrapped his fingers around the grip of the CZ 99.

Heat rose inside the Aventador. Black smoke churned from the engine. Dušić could see no flame, but, damn it to hell, the car had to be burning.

He had come so close. So close. And Stefan had sacrificed all.

But perhaps Dušić had not failed. War seemed imminent all over the former Yugoslavia. He had lit the match, and it yet burned. The burning would continue as long as Serbs never learned the details of his operation.

He knew that if he got captured, his trial would reveal those details day by day, inch by inch, repeated in every news cycle. So he must do one more thing to ensure the success of his mission. Such a shame that he would never get to see that success.

One day, Serbs would dance kolos in his honor, like in his dream. Only they would dance without him.

SMOKE FROM THE BURNING LAMBORGHINI drifted over the police van and stung Parson's nostrils. He'd had Gold stop the van in the middle of the road; there was no place to pull over. Other police vehicles caught up. Out of the corner of his eye, Parson noticed Webster and Petrov emerge from a car.

But Parson kept his gaze focused on Dušić. He could see the man moving inside the car; at least the rollover hadn't killed him. Would he fight or give up now? Parson got out of the van, rested the Vintorez across the hood.

More police officers pulled up. Some got out of their cars, poised with their weapons. One or two held fire extinguishers. Petrov shouted something in his native language, probably "Surrender!" Dušić looked toward Parson and the gathering of police. He said nothing, and he made no effort to get out of the Lamborghini. Parson peered unblinking through the rifle scope. Moved the fire selector off the full-auto setting. And waited.

He had a fleeting thought of Cunningham. If the OSI agent had lived, he'd probably be the one holding this weapon. The last time Cunningham had fired a gun, he was in full forward motion. But Parson remained still. As he watched Dušić, he considered all the things he'd witnessed in this part of the world. For Parson, Dušić personified atrocity. This guy didn't deserve to breathe the air. After all the deaths he's caused, Parson thought, we're supposed to go around our asses to bring him in alive? After he helped cause the death of Cunningham, a young man with such a bright future? Webster had said a trial would settle things down. But wouldn't that just give Dušić a forum for his ideas? With the Vintorez in his hands, Parson faced a choice. Under the circumstances, no one would question his decision.

Flames now wrapped around the entire engine compartment. Parson wondered if Dušić was trapped, or if he'd decided to end it all here.

The answer came as Dušić placed the barrel of his gun into his mouth. In the weird center arrow of the Russian scope's reticle, Parson had a good side view of Dušić's arm, hand, and the semiautomatic pistol. Time for justice.

Dušić would have known well the mess small arms make at point-blank range. Perhaps for that reason he hesitated.

Parson did not.

He touched his finger to the trigger of the Vintorez. A single round slammed through the Lamborghini's side window. Blood spattered the glass.

Through window, now nearly opaque from crazing caused by the bullet, Parson could not see exactly where his round had struck. But he could discern movement; at least he'd not blown off Dušić's head. He had aimed as precisely as he could, minding breath control and trigger squeeze, for Dušić's hand.

WEBSTER AND PETROV RAN toward Dušić's car. Gold caught up with them. Other officers began dousing the engine with fire extinguishers, and the sharp smell of halon mingled with the odor of burning oil, paint, and rubber. Spray from the extinguishers spattered Petrov as he yanked the driver's door.

The open door revealed Dušić with his right hand torn off at the wrist.

Blood covered his shirt, and more blood stained his trousers. Flecks of safety glass tinted red lay in his lap.

Dušić screamed in Serbo-Croatian. Curses and threats, Gold presumed.

Petrov held his pistol on Dušić, but Dušić paid it no mind. With his good hand, he lunged toward the passenger seat where his own weapon had fallen. Webster grabbed him by the arm, and Gold took hold of him by the shirt. Dušić struggled pointlessly. It occurred to Gold that although she'd seen and done much in her career, she'd never put her hands on a war criminal resisting arrest. She pulled with Webster and dragged Dušić out of the car.

Dušić lay on the ground, bleeding from his mangled wrist. He continued spewing curses. Petrov shouted back at him. The inspector gripped his weapon with both hands and kept the muzzle trained on Dušić's head.

"Does he speak English?" Webster asked.

"Some, I think," Petrov said.

"Tell him he's charged with murder, violations of the Law of Armed Conflict, and crimes against humanity."

Petrov began speaking in Serbo-Croatian, but Dušić interrupted him.

"Fuck you," Dušić said.

Webster folded his arms. The gesture had an air of completion about it.

"I'll see your ass in The Hague," Webster said.

PARSON WATCHED A POLICE MEDIC bandage Dušić's wound. The medic had trouble applying the dressings; the bullet had exploded Dušić's hand and left shredded tendons and muscle that dangled and dripped. The injury looked a lot like some of the blast wounds Parson had seen at the Patriarchate.

Rain began to fall from a leaden sky. Big droplets hit the pavement like pistol rounds, stung Parson's face. He leaned on the police van, clicked the safety on the Vintorez's fire selector, and made no move to get out of the weather.

Gold came toward him. She had blood on her arms from manhandling Dušić. Parson said nothing to her, and she said nothing to him. He liked it that way; he had a lot of thoughts and memories to process right now, and chatter would not have helped. But he appreciated her nearness.

She took the Vintorez by the forward hand guard. Parson gave her the weapon, and she placed it on the hood of the van. Gold put a hand on his chest, placed her other arm around his waist. Her touch flooded Parson with relief like an injection of morphine. Finally she spoke, but only two words.

"Nice shot."

He pulled her closer, shivered in the cold rain. In the distance he could see a line of harder rain advancing across the fields and hills. It came down in sheets, fell with such force that a mist formed at ground level. Parson watched how vapor seemed to rise up out of the soil. The mist thickened and shifted, obscured the terrain, and swirled among the fog and shadows and ghosts of this tormented land.

EPILOGUE

(THE HAGUE, NETHERLANDS) — *Serbian war criminal Viktor Dušić has received a life prison sentence from the UN's International Criminal Tribunal for the Former Yugoslavia.*

Dušić was convicted on multiple counts of murder of Bosnian Muslims during the 1990s. Witnesses testified that he took part in the 1995 Srebrenica massacre.

He maintained that the court had no authority over him, and he refused to take the stand or even enter a plea. The trial revealed that Dušić and a small band of supporters bombed the Patriarchate of the Serbian Orthodox Church two years ago in an effort to rekindle the Bosnian War.

Orthodox leaders denounced the defendant during testimony that began soon after Dušić's arrest. Though riots and skirmishes had broken out across Bosnia and Serbia, the trial dampened tensions in the region, and an uneasy peace continues to hold.

American attorney Terrence Webster, a veteran of NATO missions in Bosnia and Kosovo, led the prosecution. He accepted no compensation for his services.

"The world hunted down Nazis until they were in their nineties," Webster said. "We will do the same for those who committed genocide in the Balkans."

Dušić remains under heavy guard, on a twenty-four-hour suicide watch.

THE STORY BEHIND
THE WARRIORS

EVEN NOW, WHEN I HEAR music from the 1990s, it puts me back at Delta Squadron headquarters at Ramstein Air Base, Germany, preparing for a flight into Bosnia or Kosovo. Those Air National Guard missions seemed otherworldly, flying relief supplies to a region where an ethnic group had been targeted for extinction.

This kind of thing wasn't supposed to happen anymore. After the Holocaust, the world had said *Never again*. But it turned out the world didn't really mean it. Marshaling the forces to stop what was taking place in the former Yugoslavia took far too long. While thousands died, politicians vied for political advantage. Whether American congressmen supported or opposed action seemed to depend on party affiliation. Academics split hairs over whether it was *really* genocide. (During that time, I worked as a journalist in civilian life, and the discussion reminded me of a macabre newsroom joke about when to use the word "massacre." Not enough dead? Then here's the lead: *Five people shot to death today narrowly avoided being massacred.*)

While the debate in government halls and academia turned Kafkaesque, the dying on the ground was all too real. Images coming out of the Balkans—civilians shot dead by random sniper fire, prisoners so emaciated their ribs protruded—looked like something from the 1940s, except the pictures came in color, transmitted by satellite.

We flew our C-130s over shelled villages and besieged towns, sometimes delivering food and medicine, sometimes delivering weapons for NATO combat missions. In operations with names like Noble Anvil and Provide Promise, allied military personnel gave their best effort. But that effort came too late for at least a hundred thousand people.

We owe those dead, some of whom rest in mass graves, remembrance. Yet the conflict in the former Yugoslavia has become a forgotten war. Perhaps this novel offers a small reminder.

My villain, Viktor Dušić, is entirely fictitious. I know of no Serbian war criminal who became a wealthy arms dealer. But that would have been less outlandish than other events that *did* happen, such as Radovan Karadžić's transformation into an "alternative healer and spiritual explorer." The real-life Karadžić has published poetry, and the lines attributed to him in *The Warriors* are his own.

The literary masterpiece that Dušić misunderstands, *The Mountain Wreath*, is one of the most important works of the Serbian canon. Published in 1847, it is a play written in folk verse, not a political tract.

My novel's historical references, including the murder of the Bosnian Romeo and Juliet, come right out of the era's headlines. On May 19, 1993, Admira Ismic and Bosko Brkic were shot to death on the Vrbanja Bridge in Sarajevo. According to reports, Ismic and Brkic had dated for years, and they were buried together. She was a

Muslim; he was a Christian. In my novel, the character Stefan pulled the trigger. The real gunman has never been identified.

Dušić's flashback to a cruise missile strike by the USS *Normandy* is also based on an actual event. During the Bosnian War, the *Normandy* launched an attack on an air defense control site. As of this writing, she remains in active service.

Through the characters of Dragan and Irena, I hope I have presented the better angels of Serbian culture. To create those characters, I took inspiration from Serbian-Americans I have known, including a favorite college professor and a pilot with whom I shared many enjoyable hours in the cockpit. I believe Dragan and Irena, and the professor and the pilot, represent the vast majority of that proud and storied people.

The Rivet Joint aircraft described in *The Warriors* is real, though my portrayal of its procedures is speculative. The Rivet Joint's true capabilities and methods are classified, and I have never served with the electronic warfare community.

The novel's depiction of Manas Transit Center in Kyrgyzstan is fairly true to life. The American commanders at Manas, like my character Webster, often come from reserve components of the Air Force. I wrote the description of the base's coffee shop from memory, right down to the cat. Who knows? Maybe the cat's still there, sleeping on the lap of some off-duty aviator, providing a moment of calm and normalcy.

As *The Warriors* goes to press, twentieth anniversaries approach for some of the worst events of the Balkan wars. I hope we will take time to reflect on those events, and to consider the costs of turning a blind eye to things we'd rather not face.

—TOM YOUNG
Alexandria, VA
July 2013

ACKNOWLEDGMENTS

While on an Air National Guard mission a few years ago, my crew stopped at a German pub for dinner. We had some time off before resuming our journey to Southwest Asia, and we looked forward to the luxury of a full meal and a good night's sleep. As we waited for our food to arrive, we discussed our civilian job prospects.

I had just been furloughed from a struggling airline, and I mentioned that I had considered flying for a contractor known for taking on some of the government's more unpleasant missions. But, as I told my crewmates, I dropped the idea after my wife, Kristen, weighed in on the subject.

Kristen's pronouncement: "If you fly for that company and the insurgents don't kill you, I will."

An Army master sergeant and his wife sat at the next table, not taking part in our conversation. But the wife overheard my story, and it must have touched a nerve. She stood up and addressed all the servicemen in the pub.

"That's right!" she said. "You guys listen to your wives. They're why you're still alive."

She probably overstated the case, but I do know this: My wife is why I'm still an author. I'm always astounded by her talent for taking my manuscript and identifying flaws I can't see, finding ways to sharpen the story. Good editing requires a special genius, and I lucked into a marriage with a bonus.

I also lucked into a working relationship with the best in the business: Putnam publisher and editor-in-chief Neil Nyren, Putnam president Ivan Held, and executive editor Thomas Colgan at Berkley. Thanks are also due to Michael Barson, Sara Minnich, Kate Stark, Chris Nelson, and everyone at Penguin Group. My agent, Michael Carlisle, makes it all possible, along with Lyndsey Blessing, who helps bring my novels to readers overseas.

Without the kindness of author and professor John Casey, these stories would probably not have progressed beyond scribblings in my notebooks and files on my computer. My parents, Bob and Harriett Young, provide endless support and encouragement, with a lot of promotional help thrown in as well. And on each manuscript, I have received good advice from author and editor Barbara Esstman.

From two very different worlds I've been blessed with two important friends and mentors, both of whom helped shape this novel. My old broadcast journalism professor Richard Elam remains a constant friend and adviser. Retired squadron mate Joe Myers, as a pilot and aircraft commander, always brought me home safely. Now he helps keep me safe from technical errors in my copy.

Two other squadron mates, Ryan Hawk and Don Magners, provided valuable background on the duties of an Air Force safety officer. I also owe a word of thanks for input from Mike Land, Liz Lee, Jodie Tighe, and Robert Siegfried.